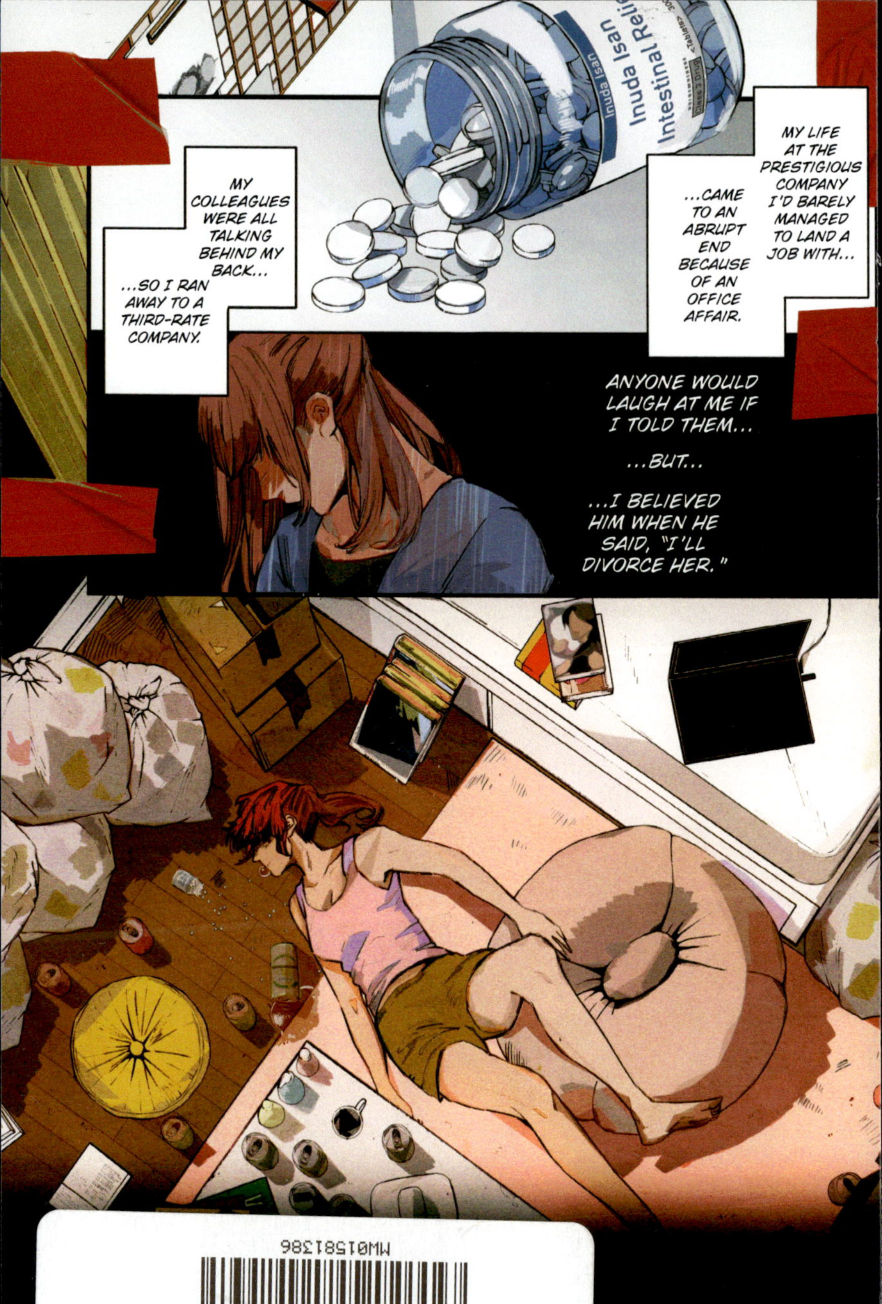

Inuda Isan
Inuda Isan Intestinal Relie
Class 3 Drug
MY LIFE AT THE PRESTIGIOUS COMPANY I'D BARELY MANAGED TO LAND A JOB WITH...
...CAME TO AN ABRUPT END BECAUSE OF AN OFFICE AFFAIR.
MY COLLEAGUES WERE ALL TALKING BEHIND MY BACK...
...SO I RAN AWAY TO A THIRD-RATE COMPANY.
ANYONE WOULD LAUGH AT ME IF I TOLD THEM...
...BUT...
...I BELIEVED HIM WHEN HE SAID, "I'LL DIVORCE HER."

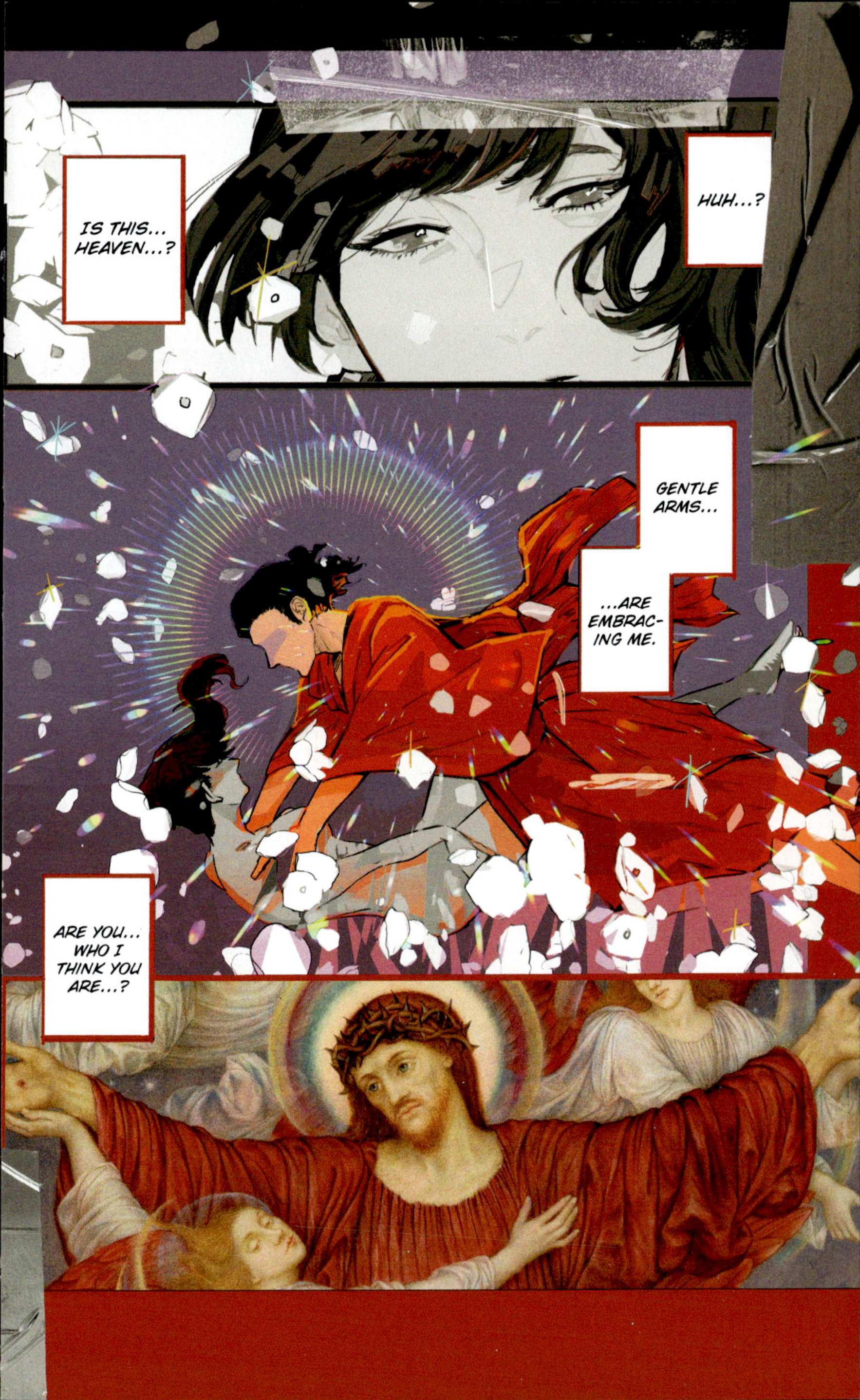
HUH...?
IS THIS... HEAVEN...?
GENTLE ARMS...
...ARE EMBRAC-ING ME.
ARE YOU... WHO I THINK YOU ARE...?

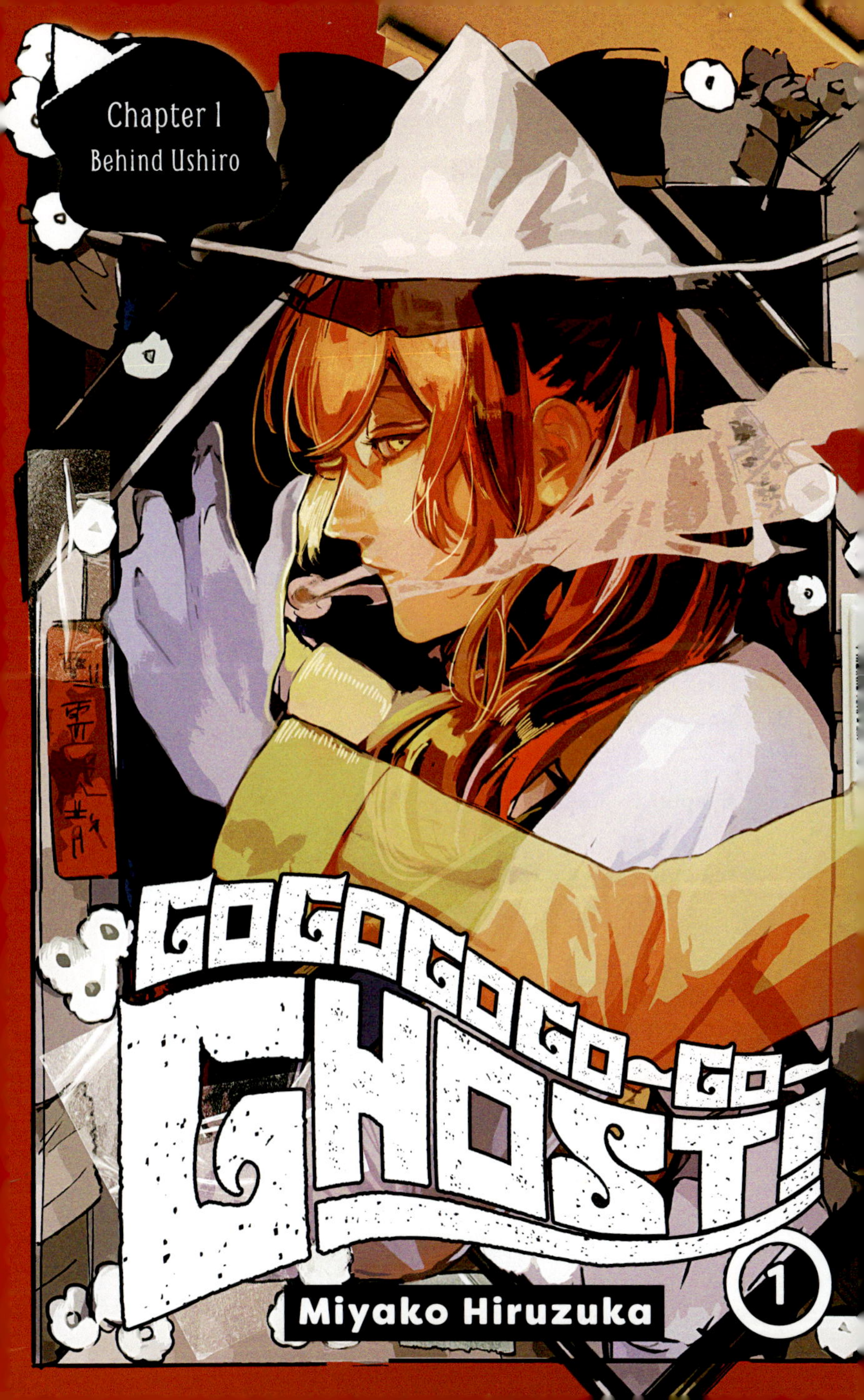

Chapter 1
Behind Ushiro
GOGOGOGO-GO-GHOST!
1
Miyako Hiruzuka

Contents

Chapter 1 Behind Ushiro ——— 001

Chapter 2 My "Love" ——— 023

Chapter 3 The First Revenge ——— 047

Chapter 4 Hardcore Neighbor ——— 073

Chapter 5 Regarding That Faithful Dog ——— 097

Chapter 6 Café 6th ——— 123

Chapter 7 Every Rose Has Its Thorn ——— 147

Bonus: Me and My Guardian Spirit ——— 177

By the time this story ends,
we'll be laughing about
how stupid we were anyway.

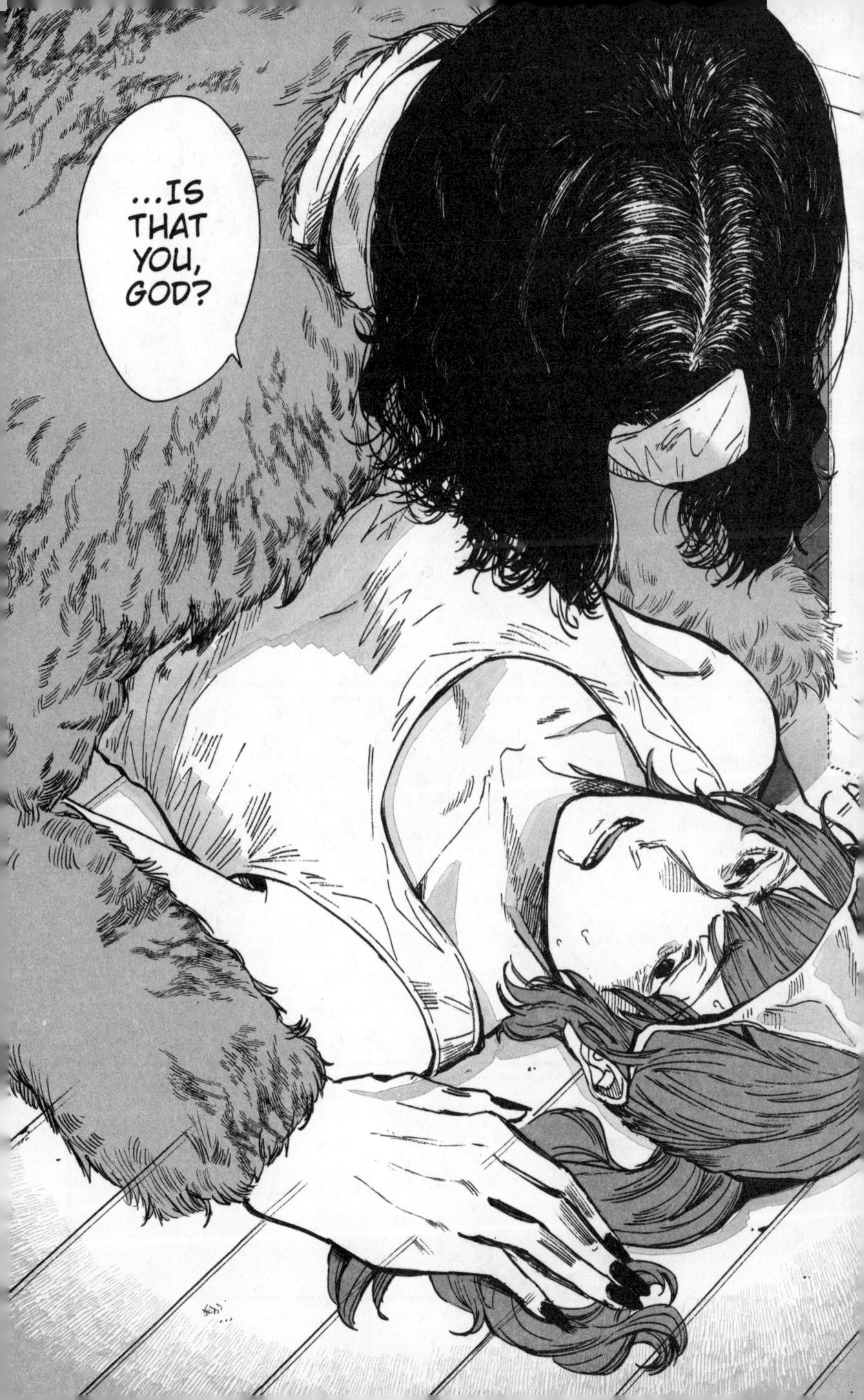
...IS THAT YOU, GOD?

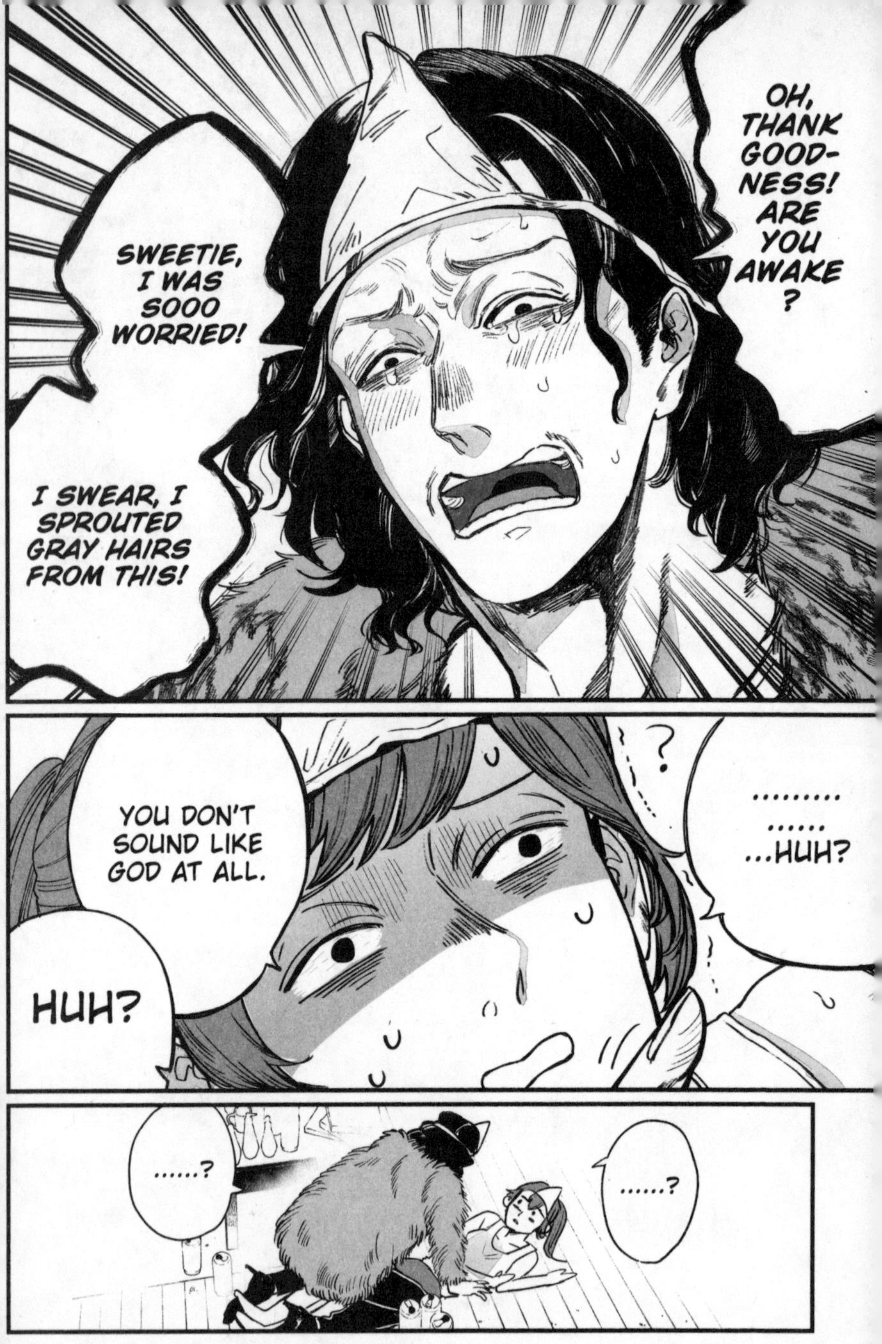
OH, THANK GOOD-NESS! ARE YOU AWAKE?
SWEETIE, I WAS SOOO WORRIED!
I SWEAR, I SPROUTED GRAY HAIRS FROM THIS!
?
....HUH?
YOU DON'T SOUND LIKE GOD AT ALL.
HUH?
......?
......?

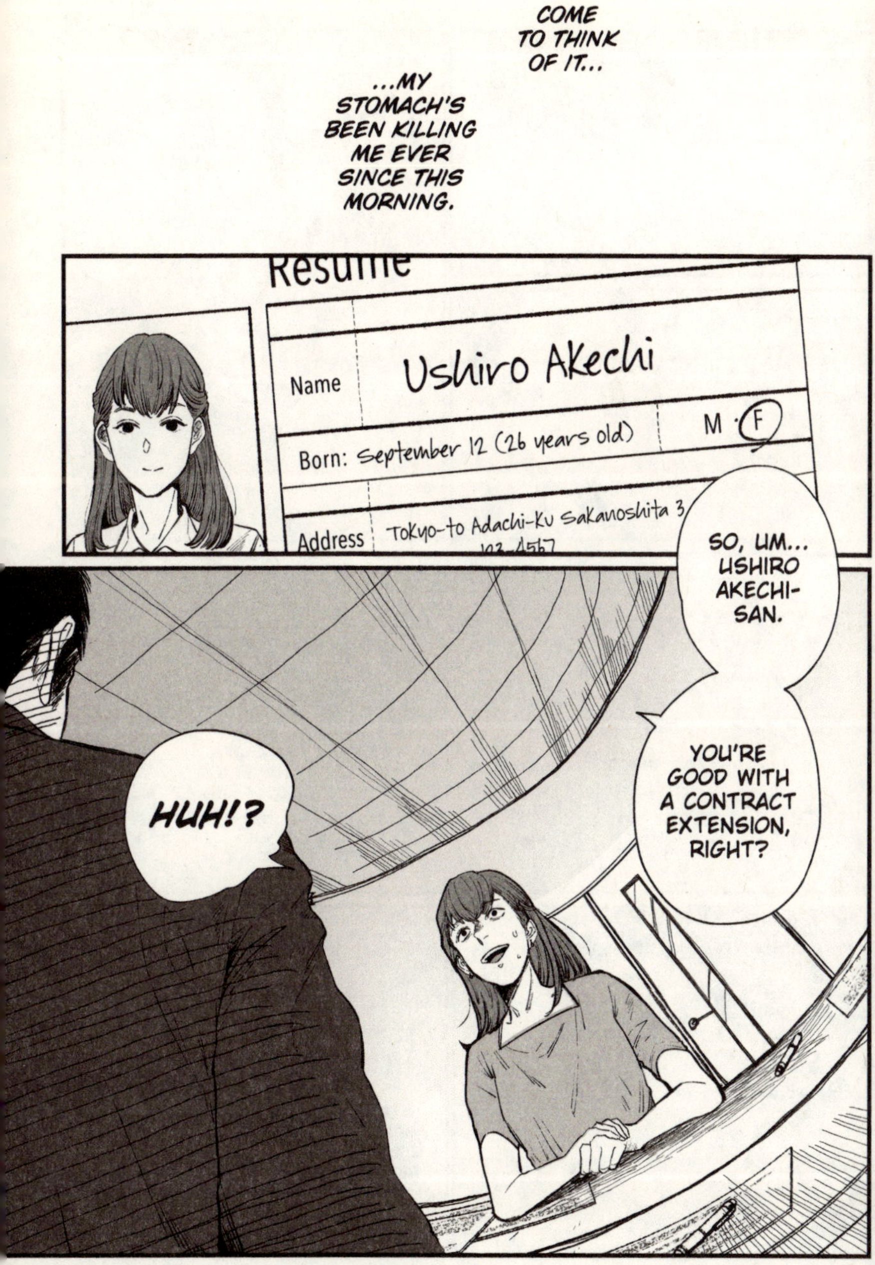
COME TO THINK OF IT...
...MY STOMACH'S BEEN KILLING ME EVER SINCE THIS MORNING.
Resume
Name Ushiro Akechi
Born: September 12 (26 years old)
M · F
Address Tokyo-to Adachi-Ku Sakanoshita 3
SO, UM... USHIRO AKECHI-SAN.
YOU'RE GOOD WITH A CONTRACT EXTENSION, RIGHT?
HUH!?

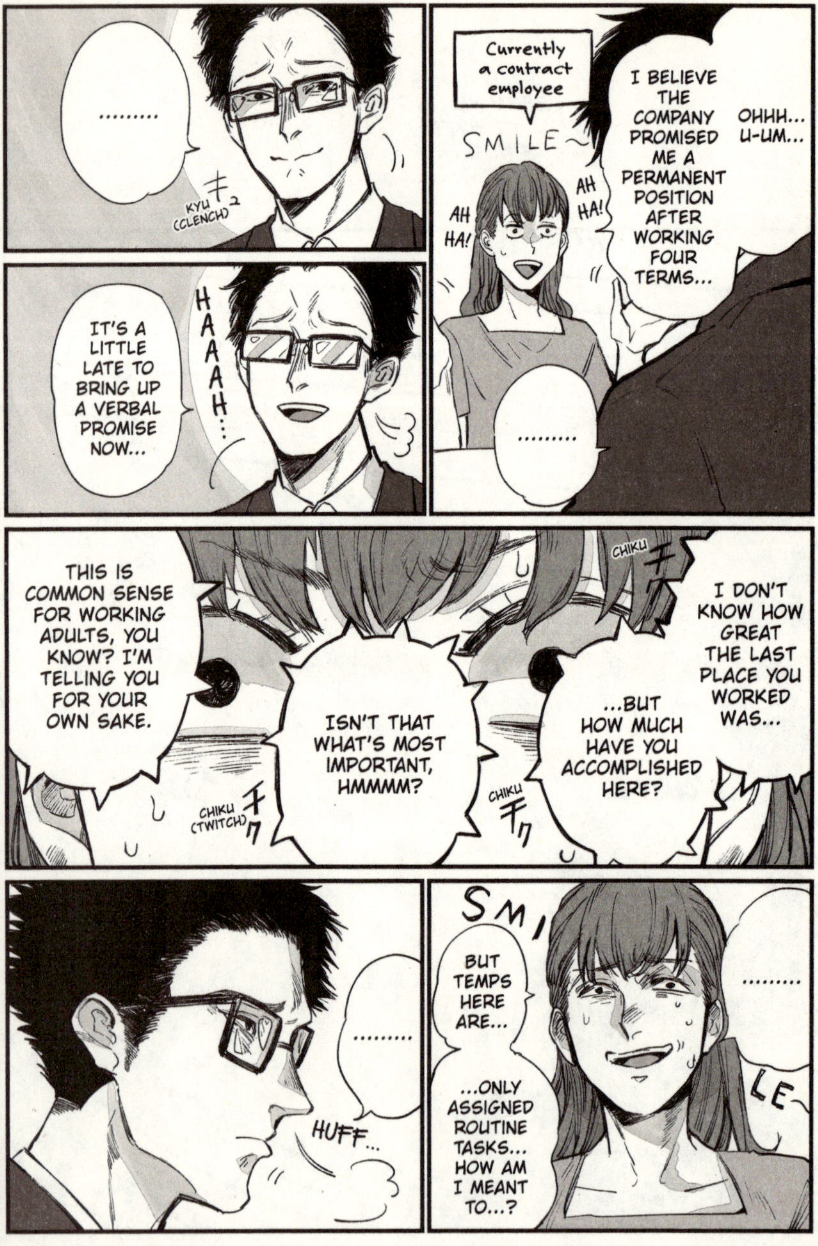
Currently a contract employee
SMILE~
OHHH... U-UM...
I BELIEVE THE COMPANY PROMISED ME A PERMANENT POSITION AFTER WORKING FOUR TERMS...
AH HA!
AH HA!
....
....
KYU (CLENCH)
HAAAH...
IT'S A LITTLE LATE TO BRING UP A VERBAL PROMISE NOW...
CHIKU
I DON'T KNOW HOW GREAT THE LAST PLACE YOU WORKED WAS...
...BUT HOW MUCH HAVE YOU ACCOMPLISHED HERE?
CHIKU
ISN'T THAT WHAT'S MOST IMPORTANT, HMMMM?
CHIKU (TWITCH)
THIS IS COMMON SENSE FOR WORKING ADULTS, YOU KNOW? I'M TELLING YOU FOR YOUR OWN SAKE.
....
SMILE~
BUT TEMPS HERE ARE...
...ONLY ASSIGNED ROUTINE TASKS... HOW AM I MEANT TO...?
....
HUFF...

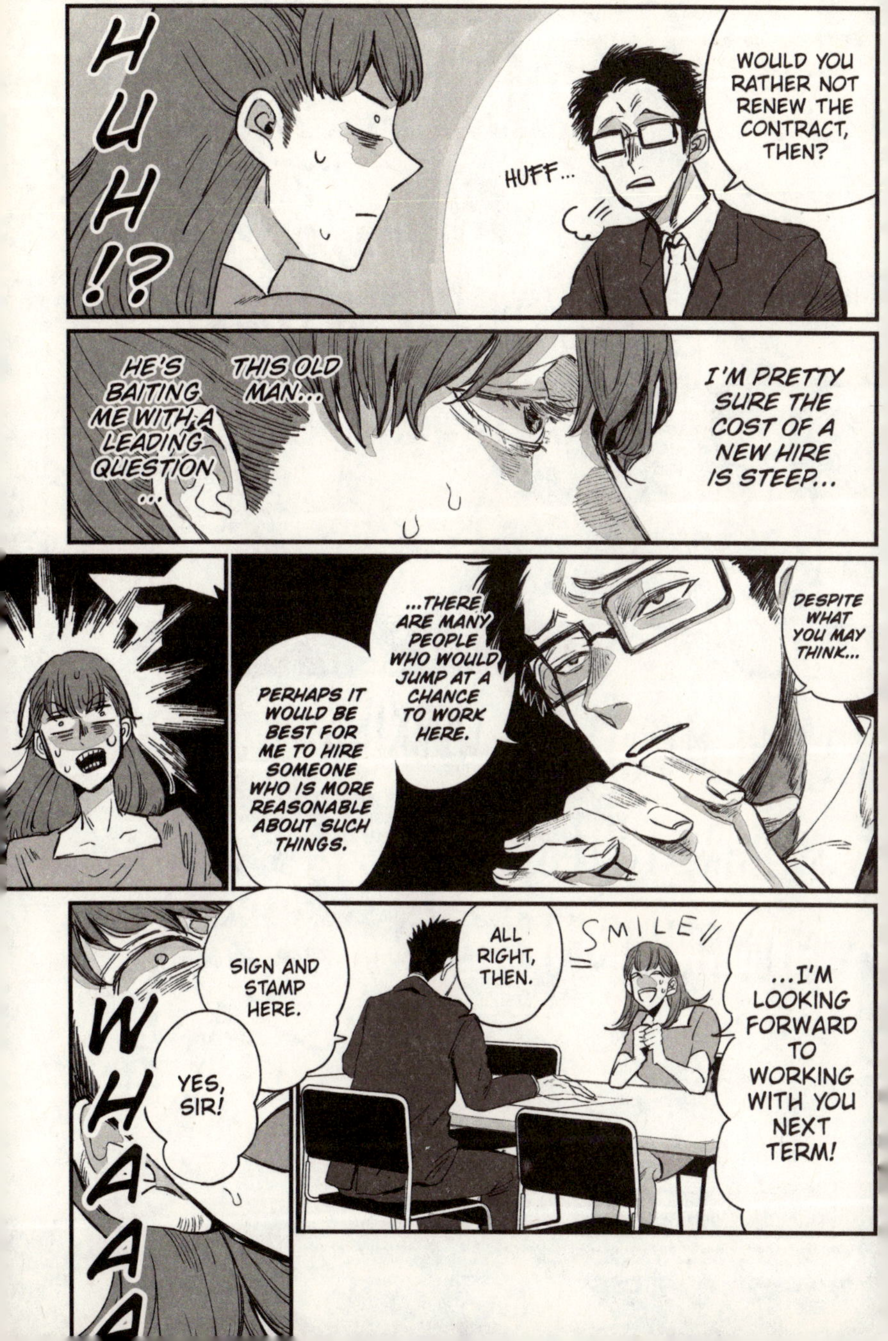
WOULD YOU RATHER NOT RENEW THE CONTRACT, THEN?
HUFF...
HUH!?
I'M PRETTY SURE THE COST OF A NEW HIRE IS STEEP...
THIS OLD MAN...
HE'S BAITING ME WITH A LEADING QUESTION...
DESPITE WHAT YOU MAY THINK...
...THERE ARE MANY PEOPLE WHO WOULD JUMP AT A CHANCE TO WORK HERE.
PERHAPS IT WOULD BE BEST FOR ME TO HIRE SOMEONE WHO IS MORE REASONABLE ABOUT SUCH THINGS.
...I'M LOOKING FORWARD TO WORKING WITH YOU NEXT TERM!
SMILE
ALL RIGHT, THEN.
SIGN AND STAMP HERE.
YES, SIR!
WHAAA

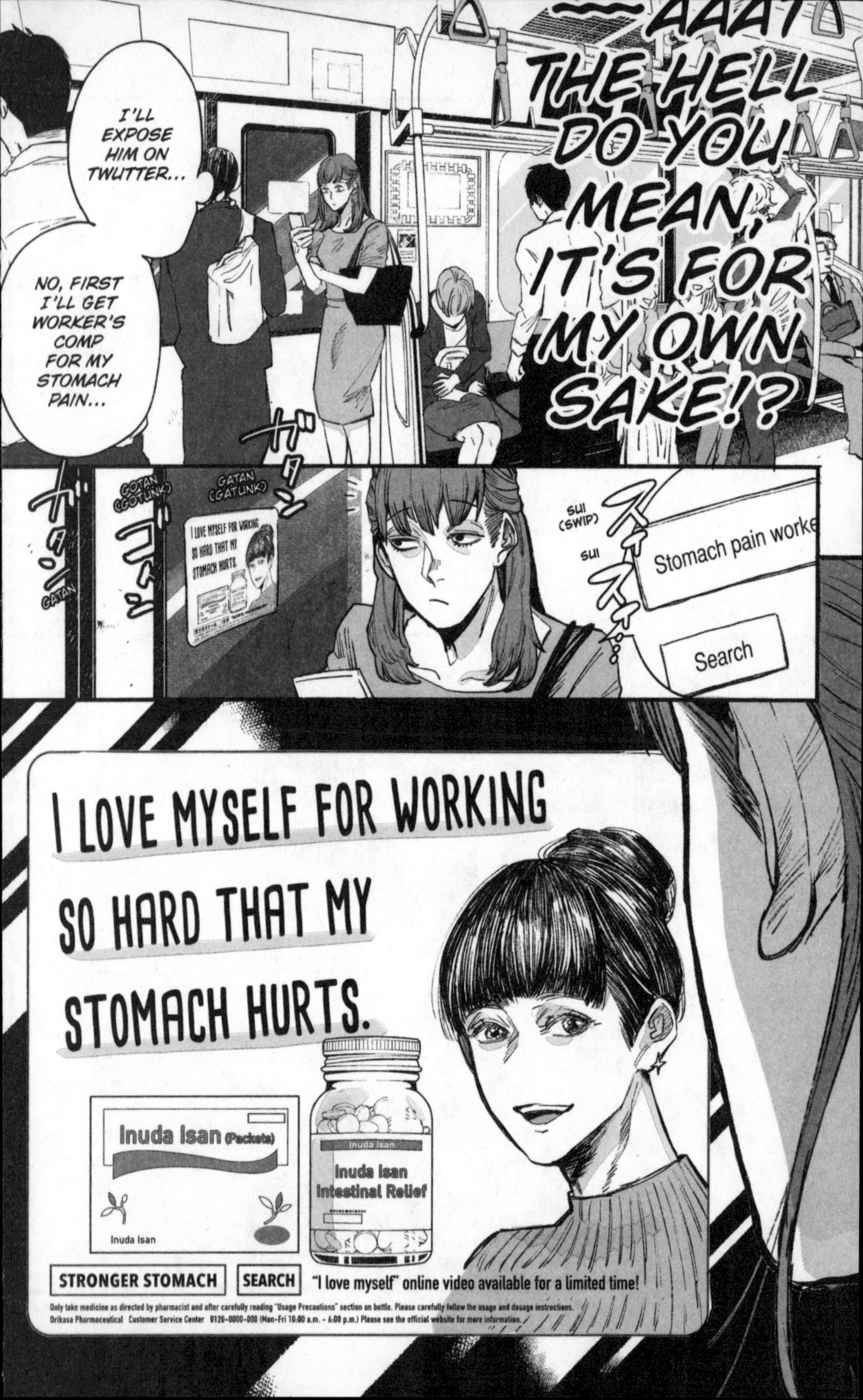
AAA! THE HELL DO YOU MEAN, IT'S FOR MY OWN SAKE!?
I'LL EXPOSE HIM ON TWUTTER...
NO, FIRST I'LL GET WORKER'S COMP FOR MY STOMACH PAIN...
SUI (SWIP)
SUI
Stomach pain worke
Search
GATAN (GATUNK)
GOTAN (GOTUNK)
GATAN
I LOVE MYSELF FOR WORKING SO HARD THAT MY STOMACH HURTS.
I LOVE MYSELF FOR WORKING SO HARD THAT MY STOMACH HURTS.
Inuda Isan (Packets)
Inuda Isan
Inuda Isan
Inuda Isan Intestinal Relief
STRONGER STOMACH
SEARCH
"I love myself" online video available for a limited time!
Only take medicine as directed by pharmacist and after carefully reading "Usage Precautions" section on bottle. Please carefully follow the usage and dosage instructions.
Orikasa Pharmaceutical Customer Service Center 0120-0000-000 (Mon-Fri 10:00 a.m. - 6:00 p.m.) Please see the official website for more information.

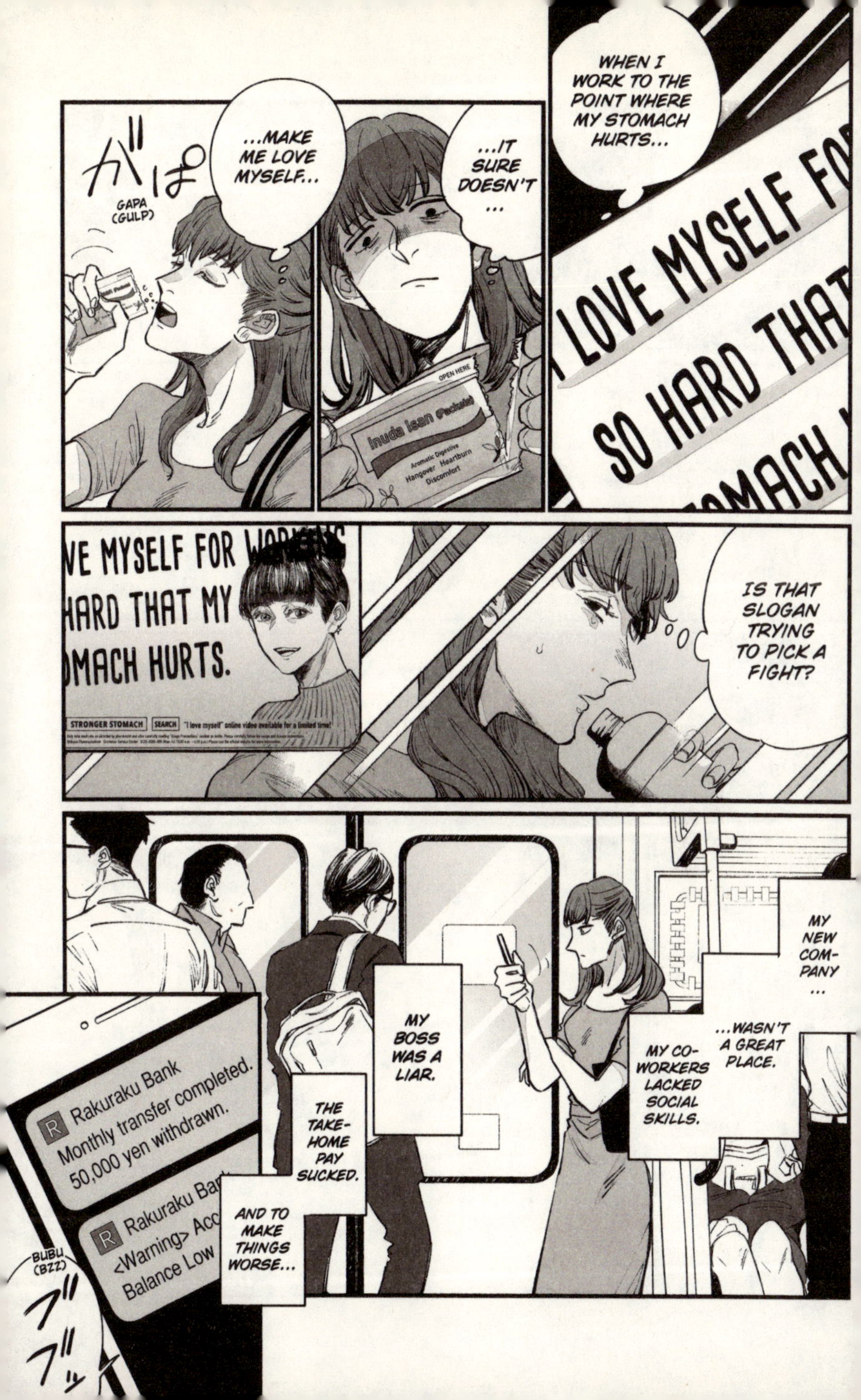
WHEN I WORK TO THE POINT WHERE MY STOMACH HURTS...
LOVE MYSELF
SO HARD THAT
...IT SURE DOESN'T ...
OPEN HERE
Inuda Isan (Packets)
Aromatic Digestive
Hangover Heartburn
Discomfort
...MAKE ME LOVE MYSELF...
ガぱ
GAPA (GULP)
IS THAT SLOGAN TRYING TO PICK A FIGHT?
MYSELF FOR
HARD THAT MY
STRONGER STOMACH
SEARCH
"I love myself" online video available for a limited time!
MY NEW COMPANY...
...WASN'T A GREAT PLACE.
MY CO-WORKERS LACKED SOCIAL SKILLS.
MY BOSS WAS A LIAR.
THE TAKE-HOME PAY SUCKED.
AND TO MAKE THINGS WORSE...
Rakuraku Bank
Monthly transfer completed.
50,000 yen withdrawn.
<Warning>
Balance Low
ブブッ
BUBU (BZZ)

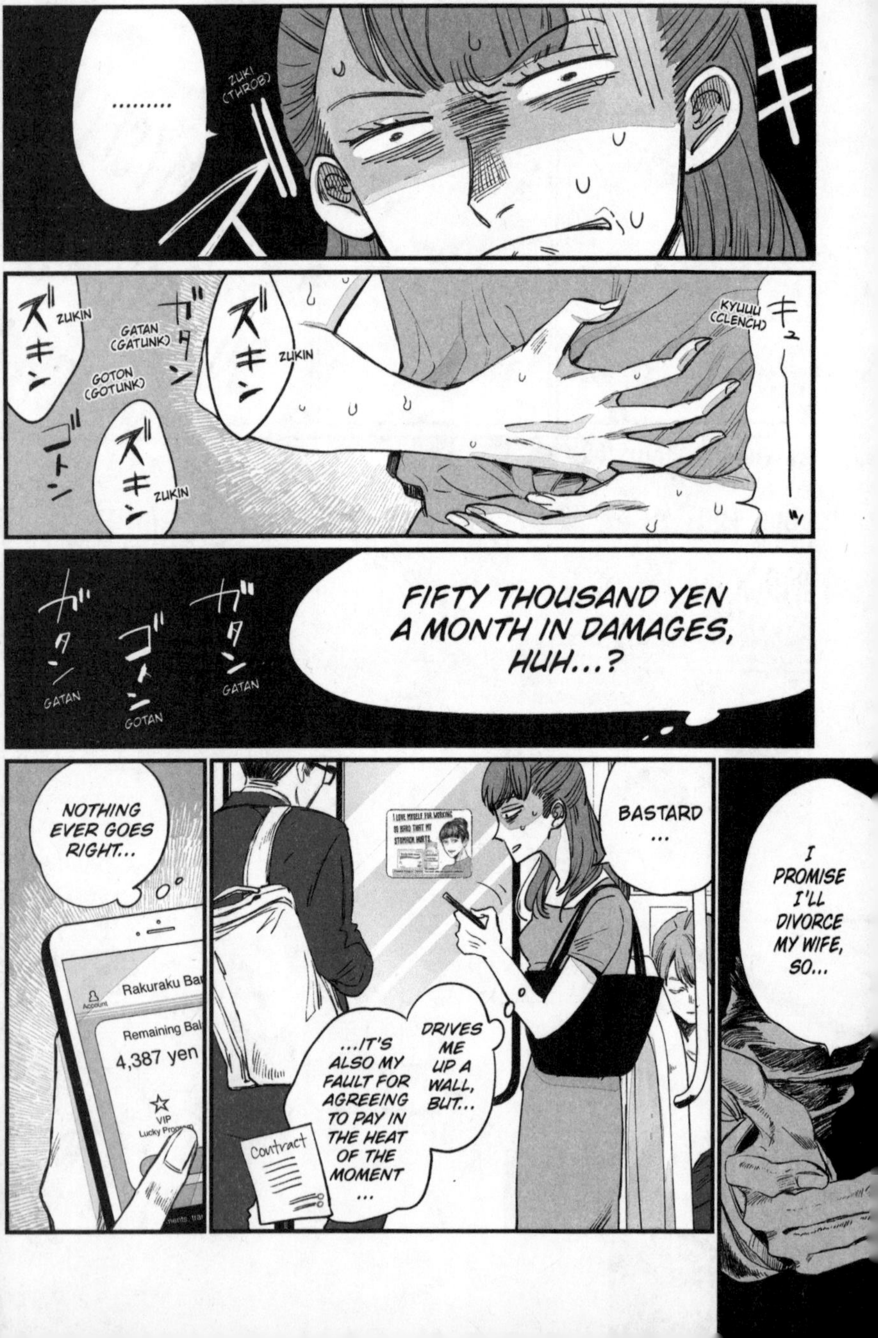
ZUKI (THROB)
....
KYUUU (CLENCH)
ZUKIN
GATAN (GATUNK)
ZUKIN
GOTON (GOTUNK)
ZUKIN
FIFTY THOUSAND YEN A MONTH IN DAMAGES, HUH...?
GATAN
GOTAN
GATAN
I PROMISE I'LL DIVORCE MY WIFE, SO...
BASTARD ...
I LOVE MYSELF FOR WORKING SO HARD THAT MY STOMACH HURTS
DRIVES ME UP A WALL, BUT...
...IT'S ALSO MY FAULT FOR AGREEING TO PAY IN THE HEAT OF THE MOMENT ...
Contract
NOTHING EVER GOES RIGHT...
Rakuraku Ba
Account
Remaining Bal
4,387 yen
VIP
Lucky Program

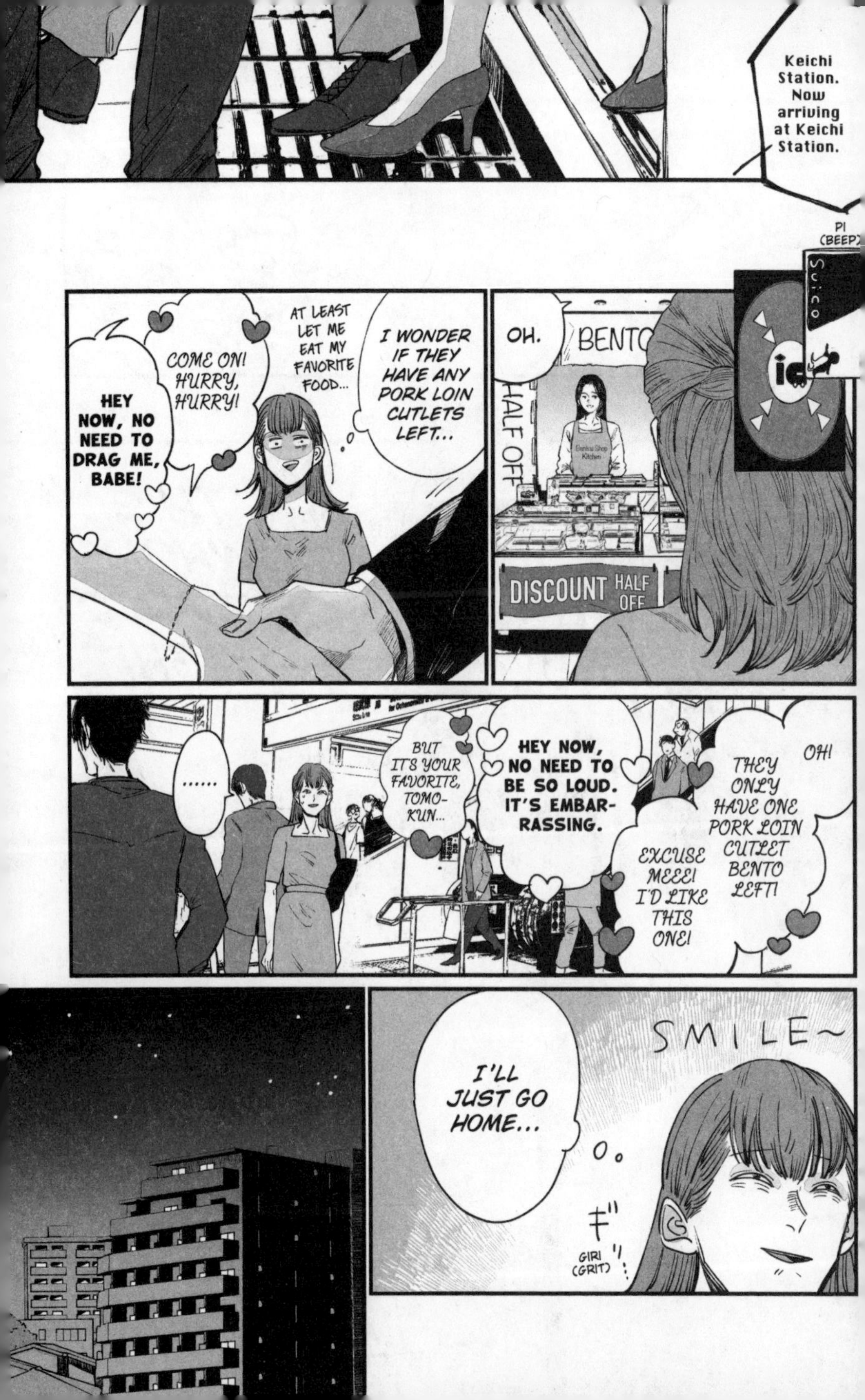

Keichi Station. Now arriving at Keichi Station.
PI (BEEP)
Suica
OH.
BENTO
HALF OFF
DISCOUNT HALF OFF
I WONDER IF THEY HAVE ANY PORK LOIN CUTLETS LEFT...
AT LEAST LET ME EAT MY FAVORITE FOOD...
COME ON! HURRY, HURRY!
HEY NOW, NO NEED TO DRAG ME, BABE!
OH!
THEY ONLY HAVE ONE PORK LOIN CUTLET BENTO LEFT!
EXCUSE MEEE! I'D LIKE THIS ONE!
HEY NOW, NO NEED TO BE SO LOUD. IT'S EMBARRASSING.
BUT IT'S YOUR FAVORITE, TOMO-KUN...
......
SMILE~
I'LL JUST GO HOME...
ギ
GIRI (GRIT)

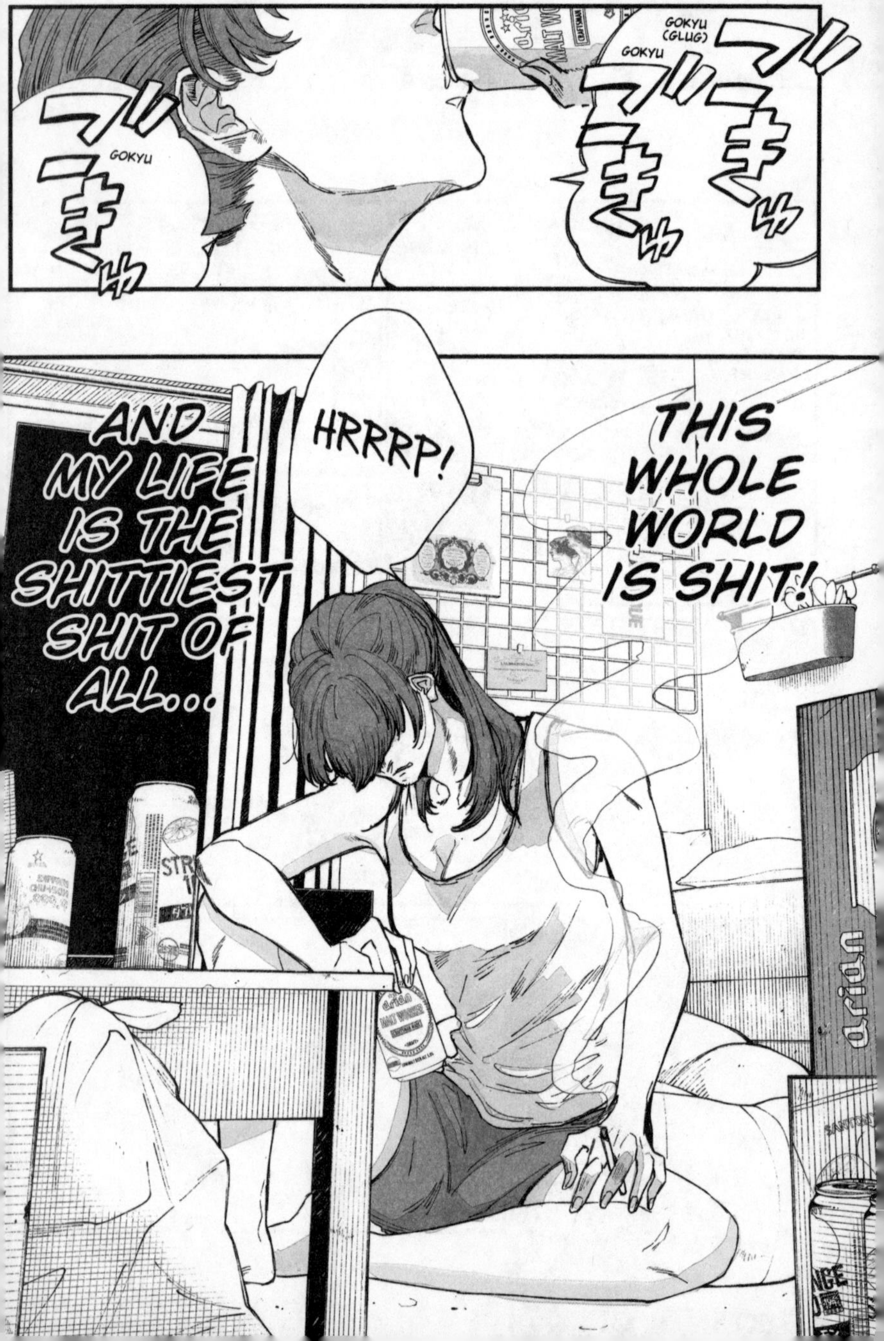
GOKYU (GLUG)
GOKYU
GOKYU
THIS WHOLE WORLD IS SHIT!
HRRRP!
AND MY LIFE IS THE SHITTIEST SHIT OF ALL...

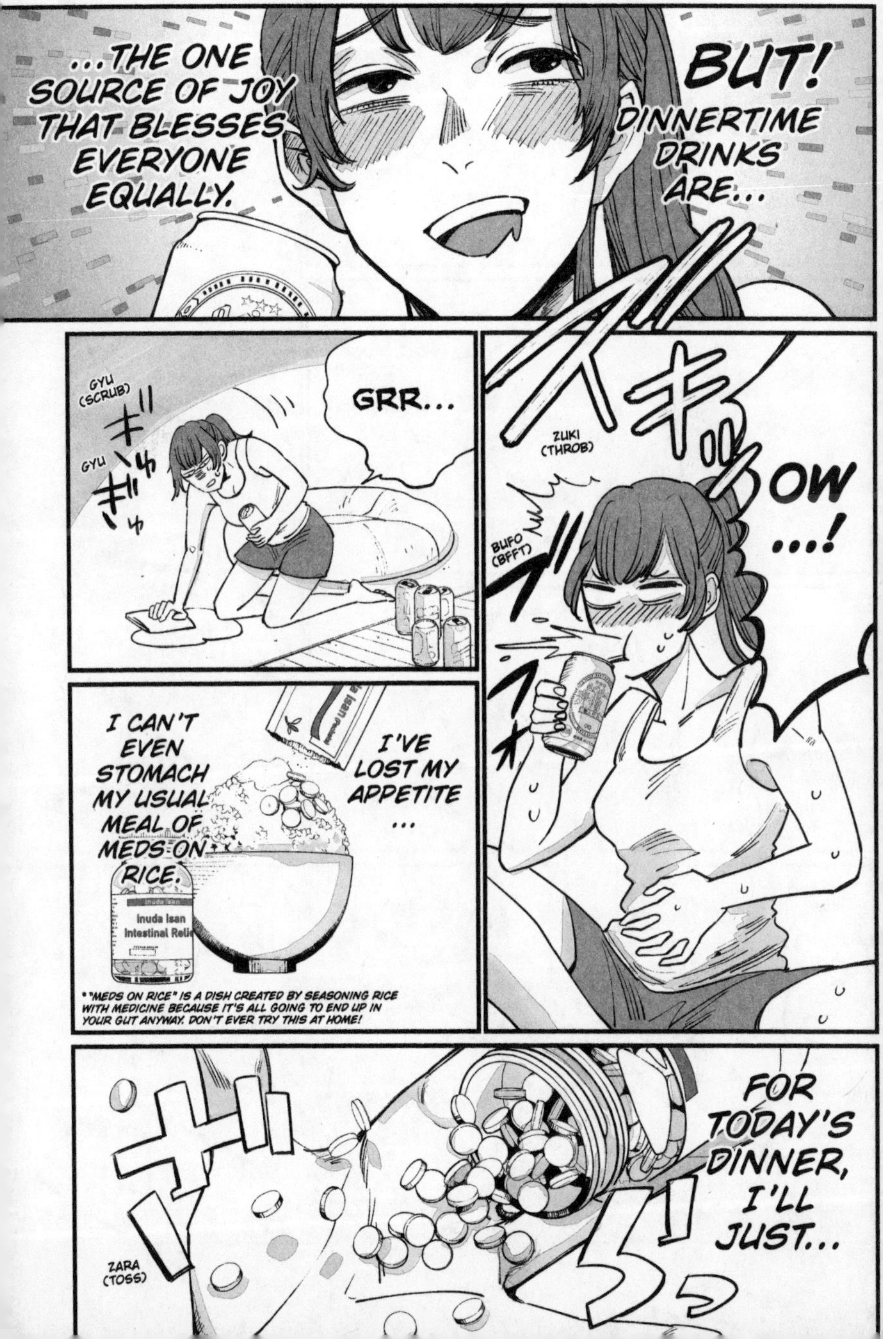
BUT! DINNERTIME DRINKS ARE...
...THE ONE SOURCE OF JOY THAT BLESSES EVERYONE EQUALLY.
ZUKI (THROB)
OW...!
BUFO (BFFT)
GRR...
GYU (SCRUB)
GYU
I'VE LOST MY APPETITE...
I CAN'T EVEN STOMACH MY USUAL MEAL OF MEDS ON RICE.
Inuda Isan
Inuda Isan Intestinal Relie
* "MEDS ON RICE" IS A DISH CREATED BY SEASONING RICE WITH MEDICINE BECAUSE IT'S ALL GOING TO END UP IN YOUR GUT ANYWAY. DON'T EVER TRY THIS AT HOME!
FOR TODAY'S DINNER, I'LL JUST...
ZARA (TOSS)

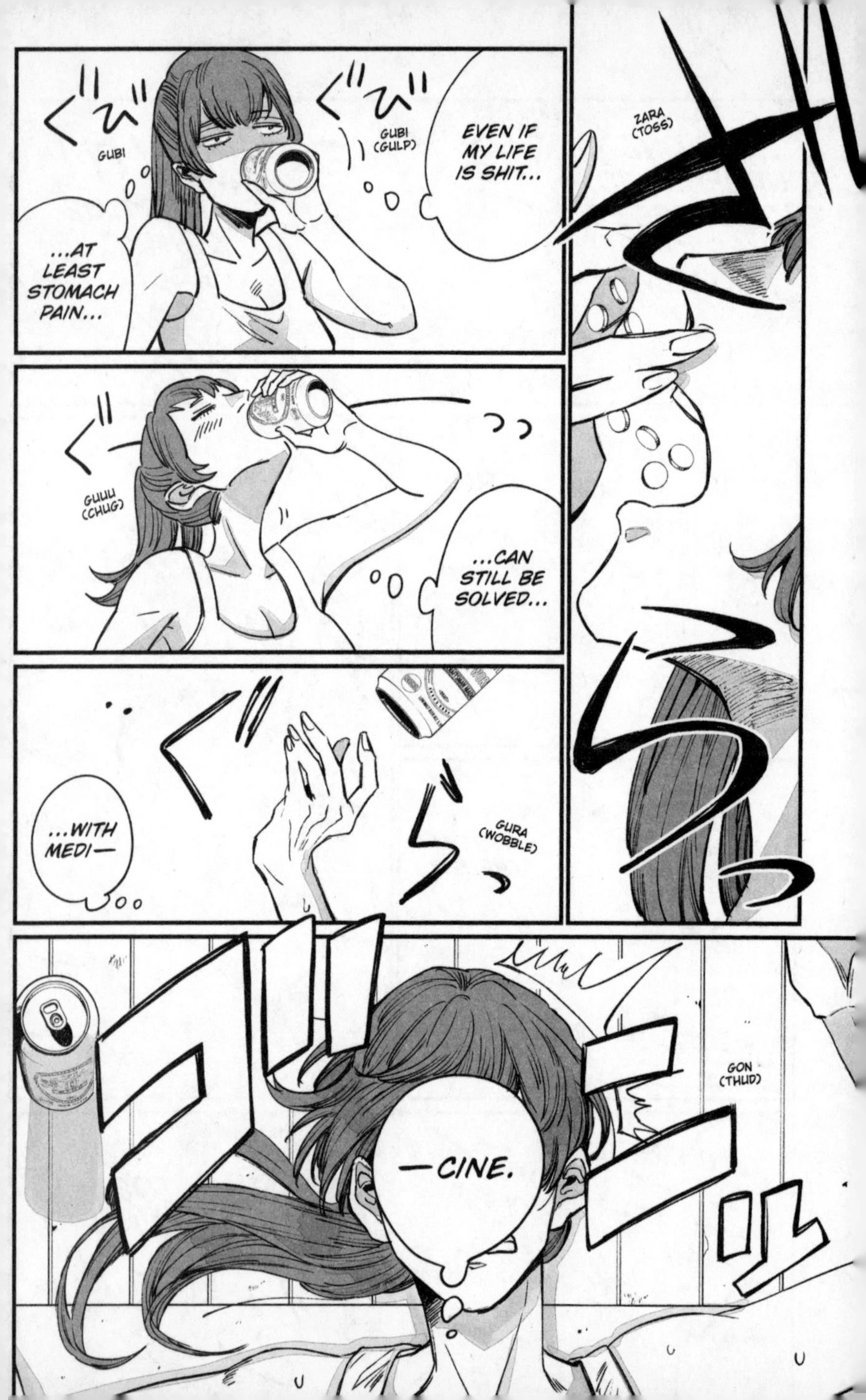
ZARA (TOSS)
EVEN IF MY LIFE IS SHIT...
GUBI (GULP)
GUBI
...AT LEAST STOMACH PAIN...
...CAN STILL BE SOLVED...
GUUU (CHUG)
GURA (WOBBLE)
...WITH MEDI—
GON (THUD)
—CINE.

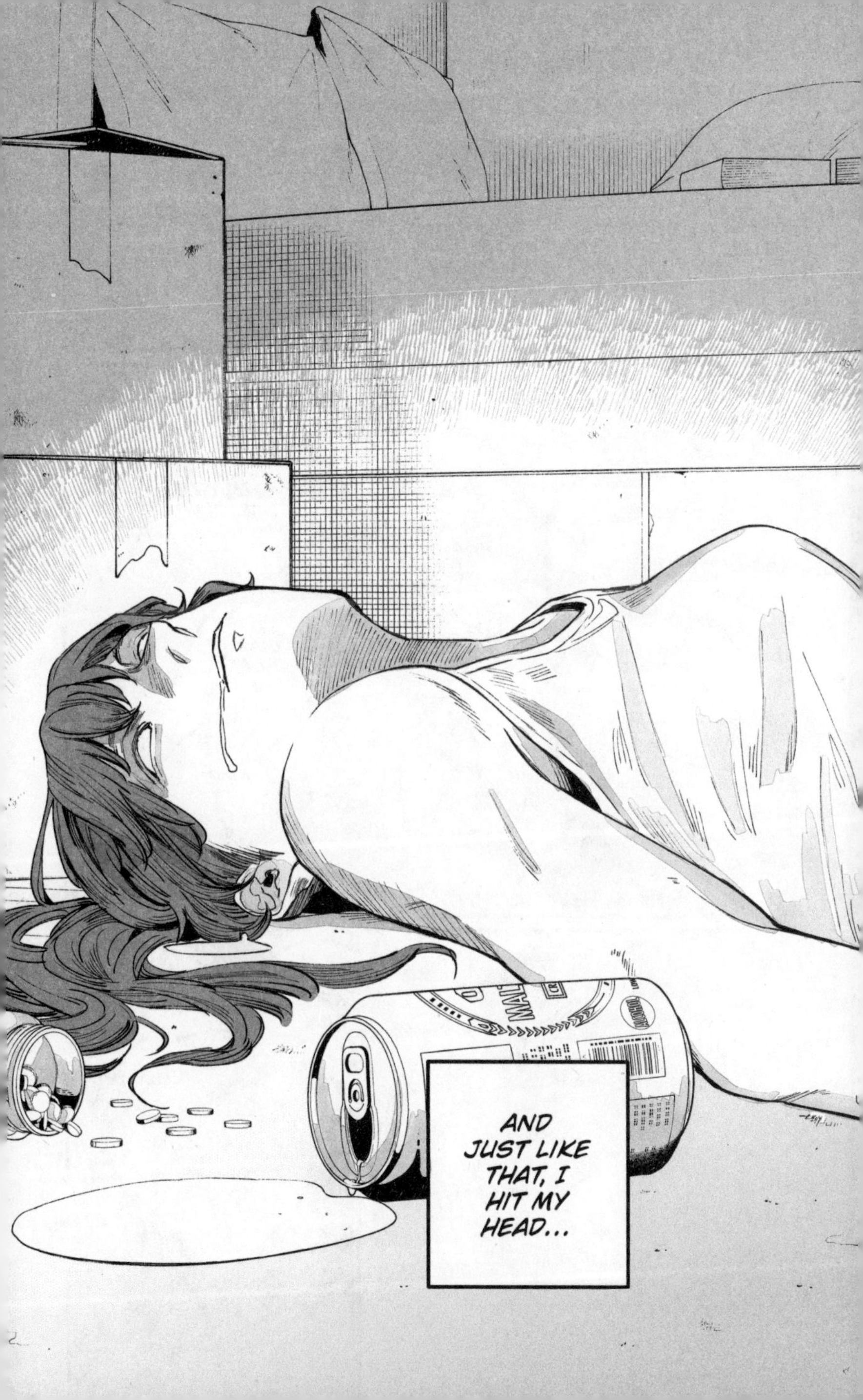
AND JUST LIKE THAT, I HIT MY HEAD...

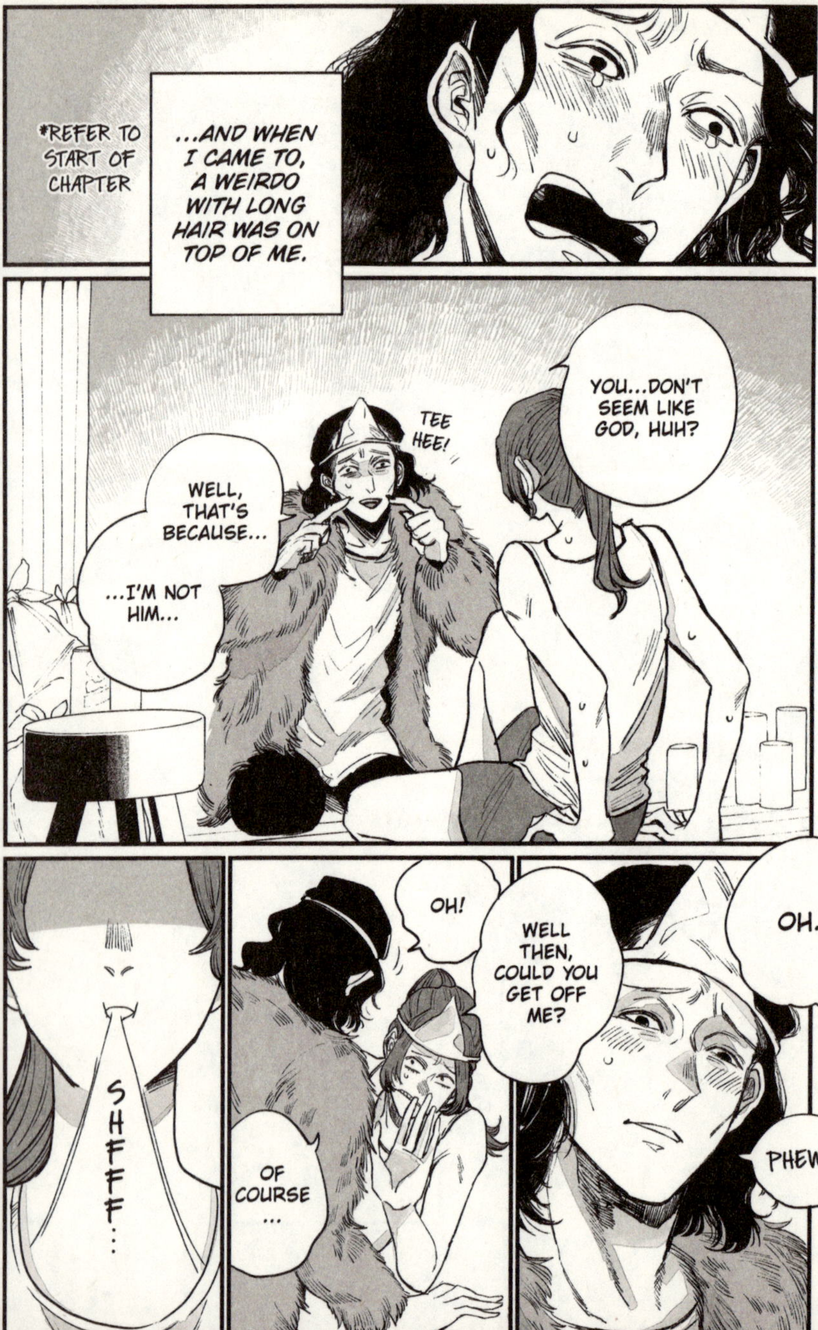
...AND WHEN I CAME TO, A WEIRDO WITH LONG HAIR WAS ON TOP OF ME.
*REFER TO START OF CHAPTER
YOU...DON'T SEEM LIKE GOD, HUH?
TEE HEE!
WELL, THAT'S BECAUSE...
...I'M NOT HIM...
OH.
WELL THEN, COULD YOU GET OFF ME?
PHEW.
OH!
OF COURSE...
SHFFF...

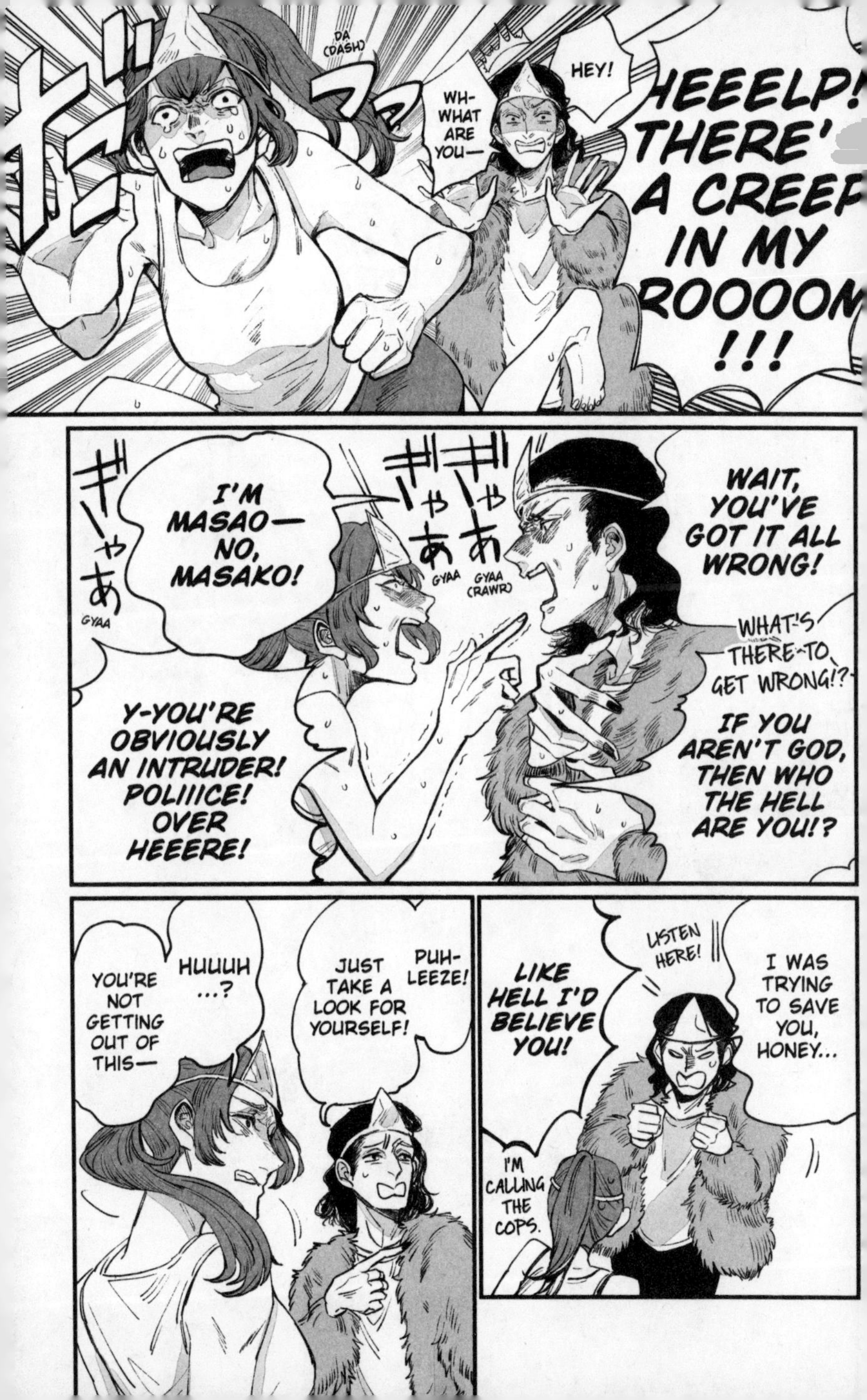
HEEELP! THERE' A CREEP IN MY ROOOOM !!!
HEY!
WH-WHAT ARE YOU—
DA (DASH)
WAIT, YOU'VE GOT IT ALL WRONG!
WHAT'S THERE TO GET WRONG!?
IF YOU AREN'T GOD, THEN WHO THE HELL ARE YOU!?
ぎゃあ GYAA (RAWR)
ぎゃあ GYAA
I'M MASAO— NO, MASAKO!
ぎゃあ GYAA
Y-YOU'RE OBVIOUSLY AN INTRUDER! POLIIICE! OVER HEEERE!
I WAS TRYING TO SAVE YOU, HONEY...
LISTEN HERE!
LIKE HELL I'D BELIEVE YOU!
I'M CALLING THE COPS.
PUH-LEEZE!
JUST TAKE A LOOK FOR YOURSELF!
HUUUH ...?
YOU'RE NOT GETTING OUT OF THIS—

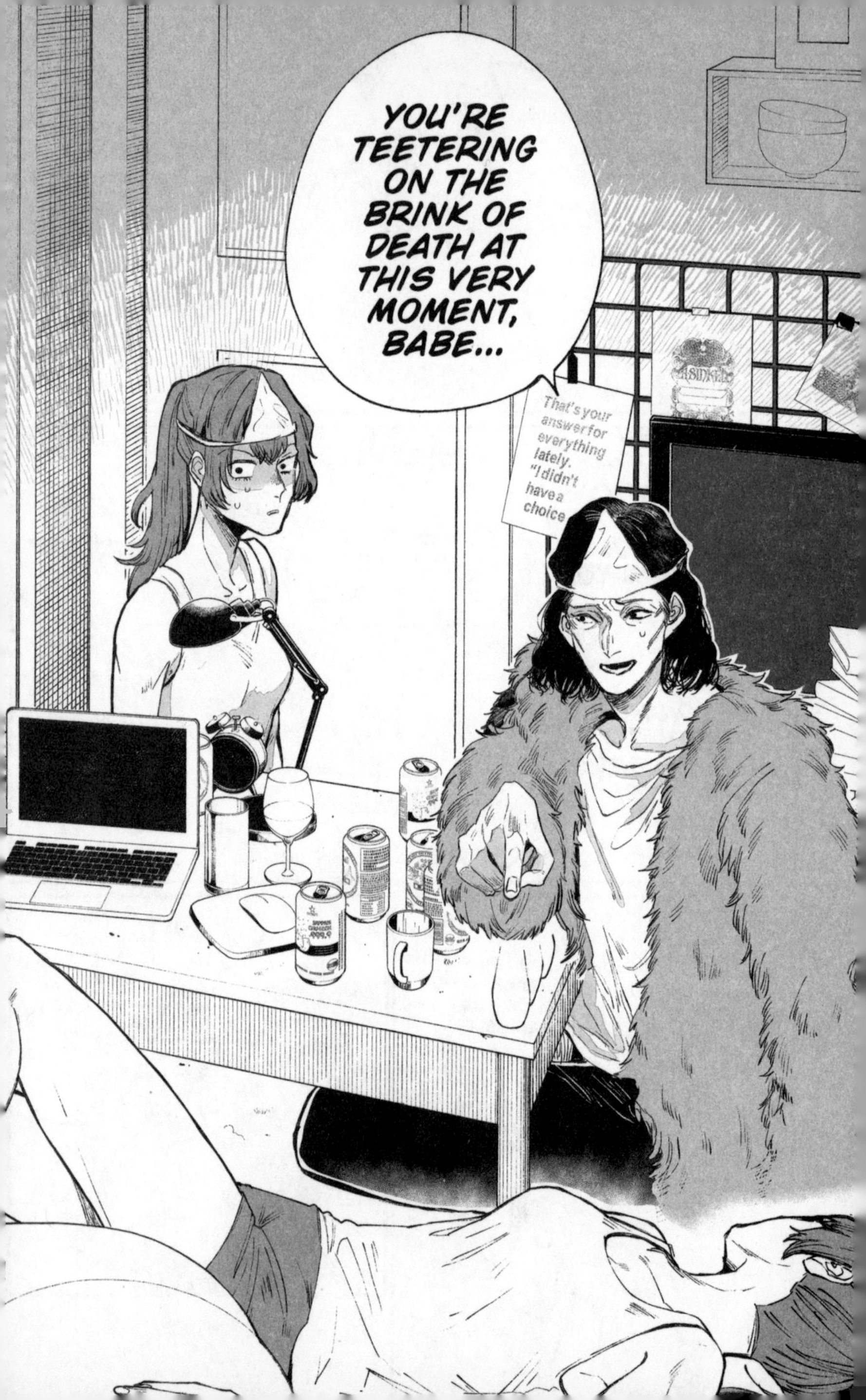
YOU'RE TEETERING ON THE BRINK OF DEATH AT THIS VERY MOMENT, BABE...
That's your answer for everything lately. "I didn't have a choice"

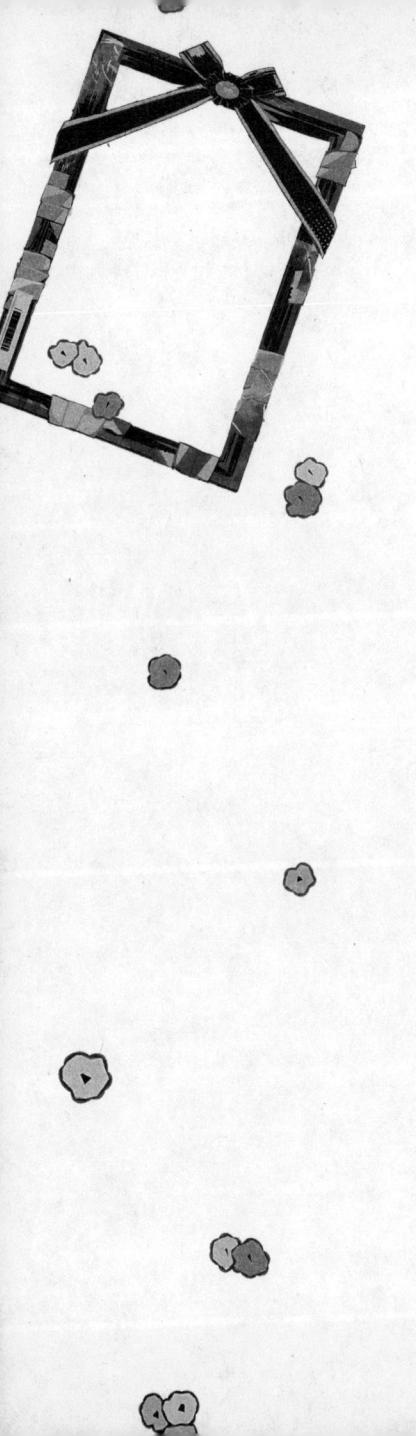

GOGOGOGO-GO-GHOST!

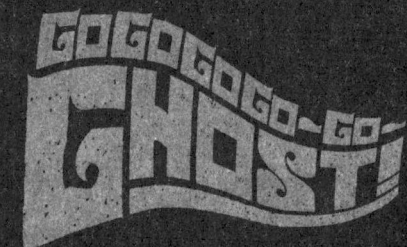

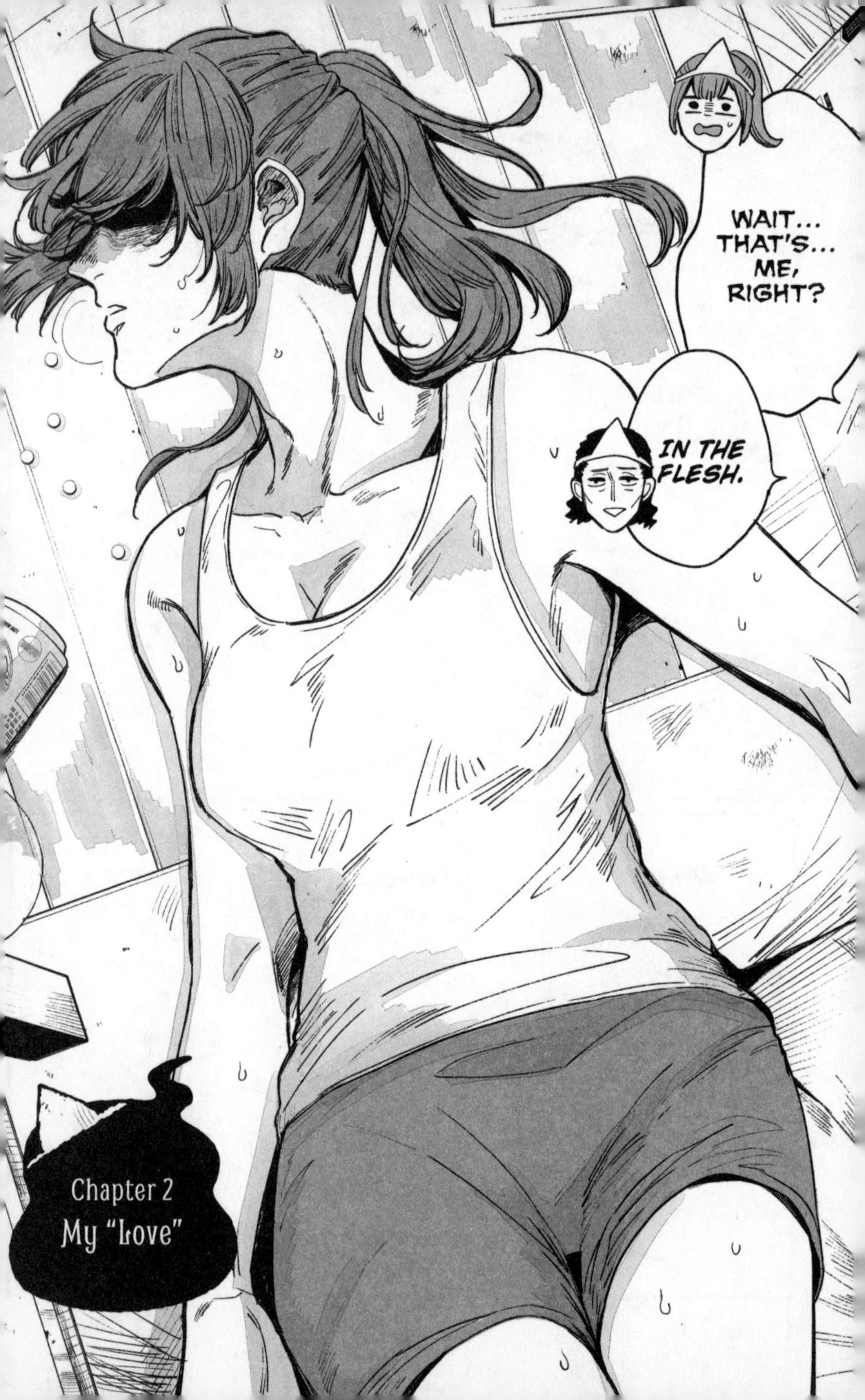
WAIT... THAT'S... ME, RIGHT?
IN THE FLESH.
Chapter 2
My "Love"

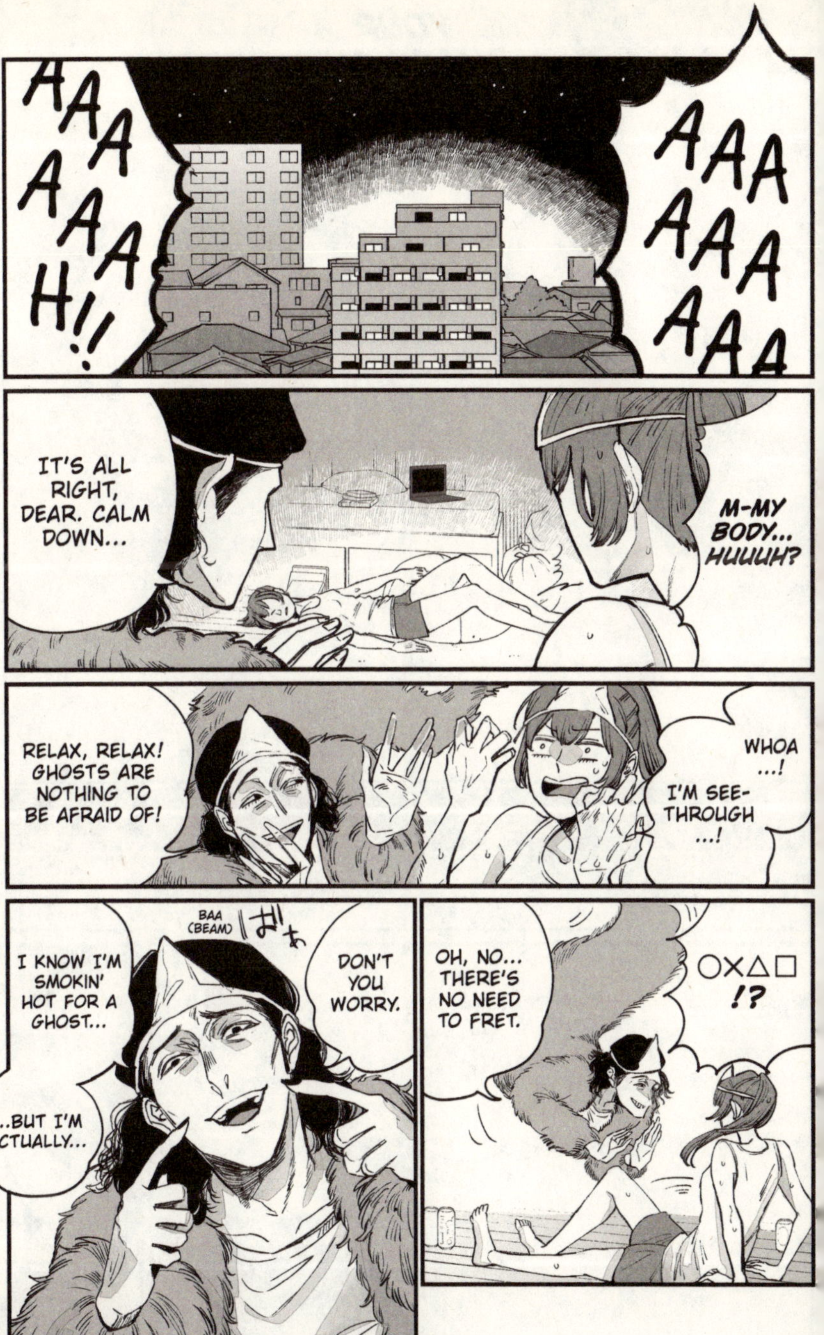
AAAAAAAAAAAA
AAAAAAH!!
M-MY BODY... HUUUH?
IT'S ALL RIGHT, DEAR. CALM DOWN...
WHOA ...! I'M SEE-THROUGH ...!
RELAX, RELAX! GHOSTS ARE NOTHING TO BE AFRAID OF!
○×△□ !?
OH, NO... THERE'S NO NEED TO FRET.
DON'T YOU WORRY.
BAA (BEAM)
I KNOW I'M SMOKIN' HOT FOR A GHOST...
...BUT I'M ACTUALLY...

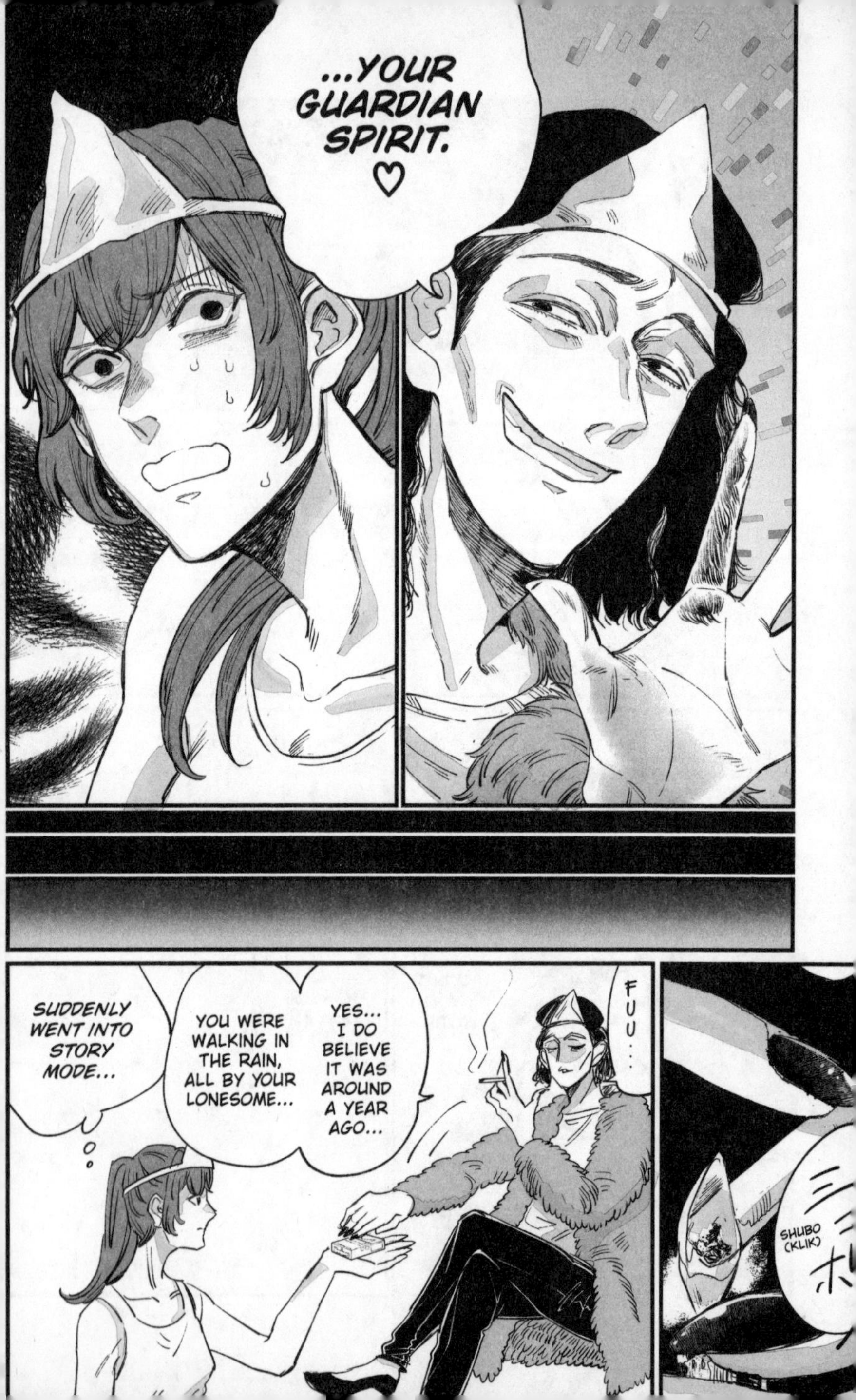
...YOUR GUARDIAN SPIRIT. ♡
SHUBO (KLIK)
FUU...
YES... I DO BELIEVE IT WAS AROUND A YEAR AGO...
YOU WERE WALKING IN THE RAIN, ALL BY YOUR LONESOME...
SUDDENLY WENT INTO STORY MODE...

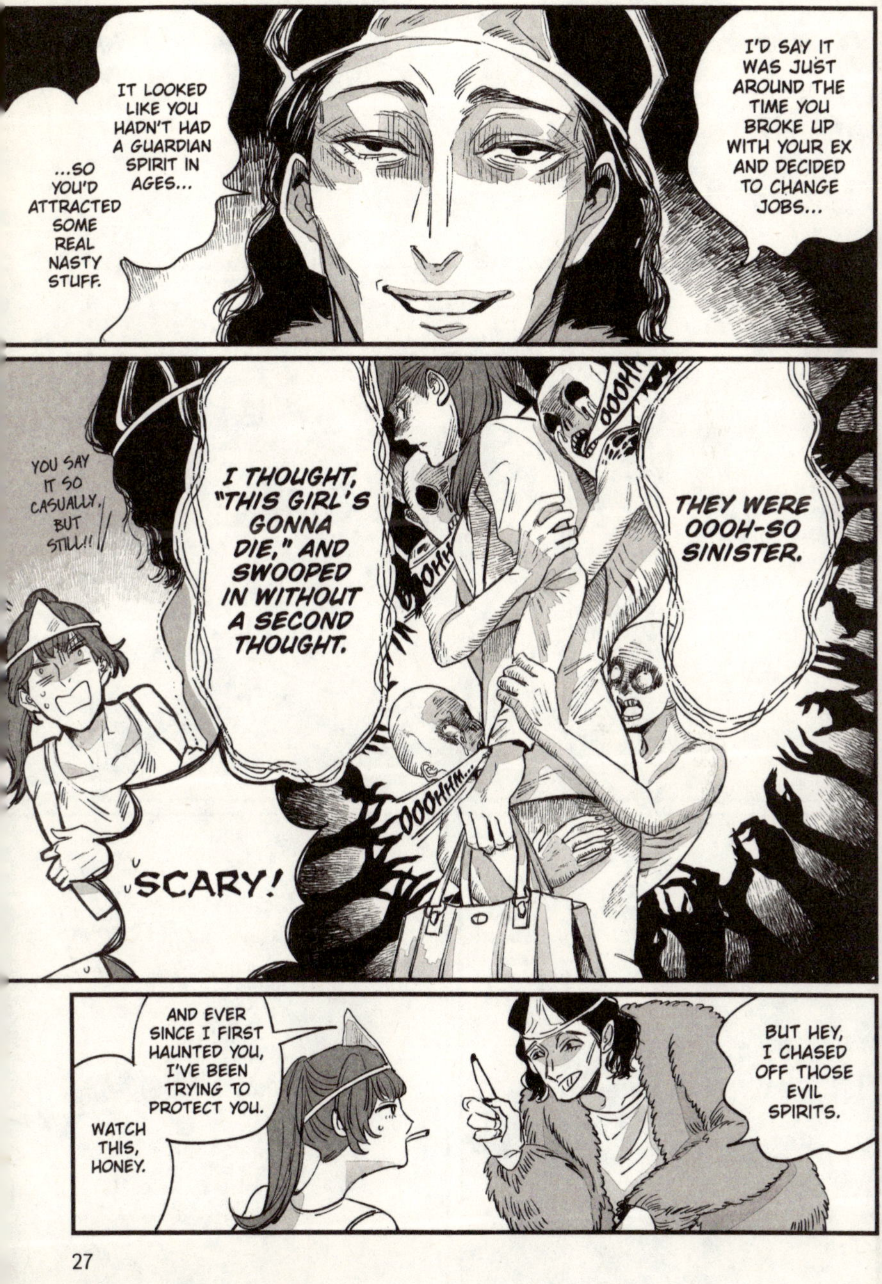
I'D SAY IT WAS JUST AROUND THE TIME YOU BROKE UP WITH YOUR EX AND DECIDED TO CHANGE JOBS...
IT LOOKED LIKE YOU HADN'T HAD A GUARDIAN SPIRIT IN AGES...
...SO YOU'D ATTRACTED SOME REAL NASTY STUFF.
THEY WERE OOOH-SO SINISTER.
I THOUGHT, "THIS GIRL'S GONNA DIE," AND SWOOPED IN WITHOUT A SECOND THOUGHT.
OOOHHM...
YOU SAY IT SO CASUALLY, BUT STILL!!
SCARY!
BUT HEY, I CHASED OFF THOSE EVIL SPIRITS.
AND EVER SINCE I FIRST HAUNTED YOU, I'VE BEEN TRYING TO PROTECT YOU.
WATCH THIS, HONEY.

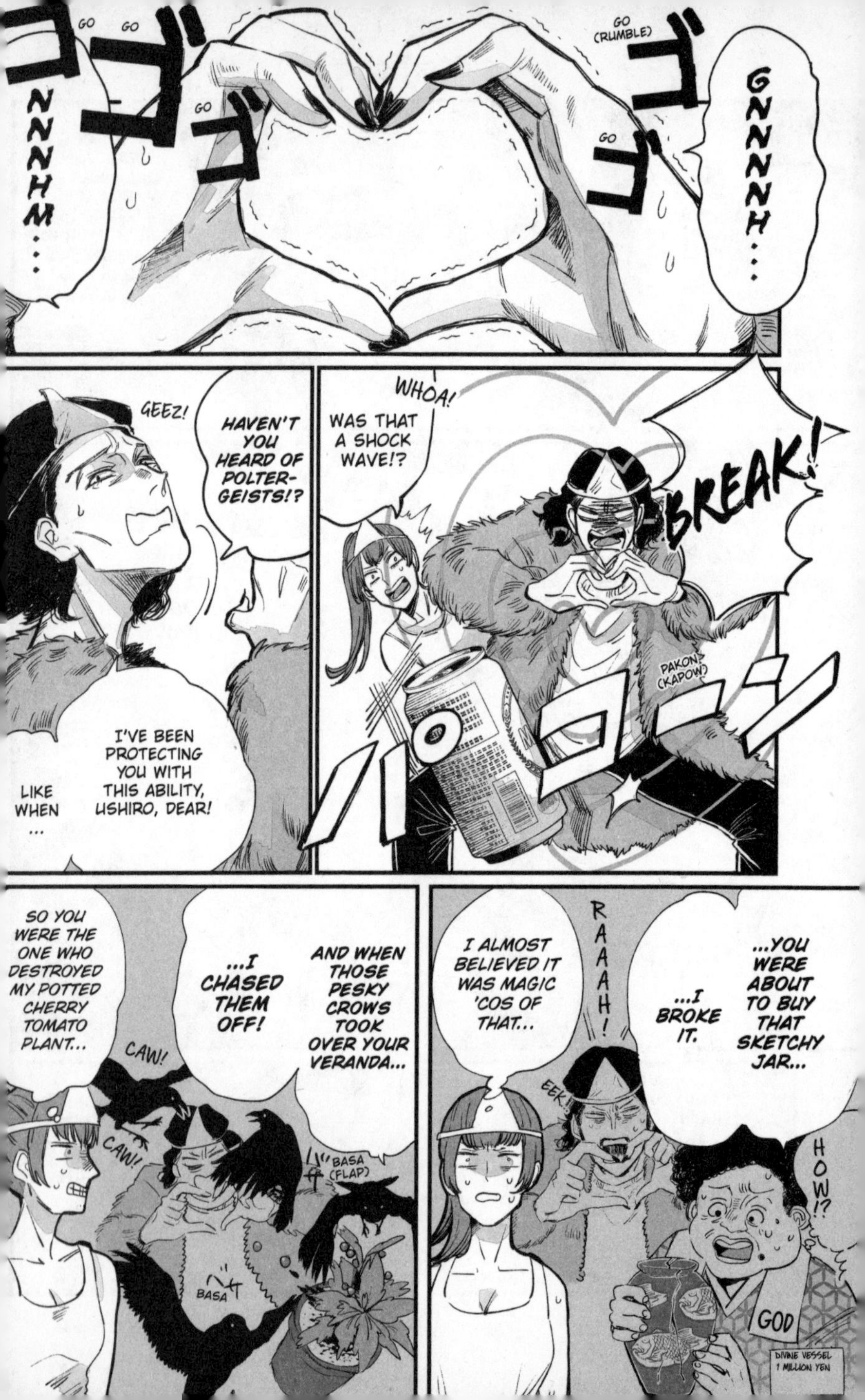
GO (RUMBLE)
GO
GNNNNH...
GO
GO
GO
NNNHM...
BREAK!
WHOA!
WAS THAT A SHOCK WAVE!?
PAKON (KAPOW)
HAVEN'T YOU HEARD OF POLTER-GEISTS!?
GEEZ!
I'VE BEEN PROTECTING YOU WITH THIS ABILITY, USHIRO, DEAR!
LIKE WHEN ...
...YOU WERE ABOUT TO BUY THAT SKETCHY JAR...
...I BROKE IT.
RAAAH!
I ALMOST BELIEVED IT WAS MAGIC 'COS OF THAT...
EEK!
HOW!?
GOD
DIVINE VESSEL 1 MILLION YEN
AND WHEN THOSE PESKY CROWS TOOK OVER YOUR VERANDA...
...I CHASED THEM OFF!
SO YOU WERE THE ONE WHO DESTROYED MY POTTED CHERRY TOMATO PLANT...
CAW!
CAW!
BASA (FLAP)
BASA

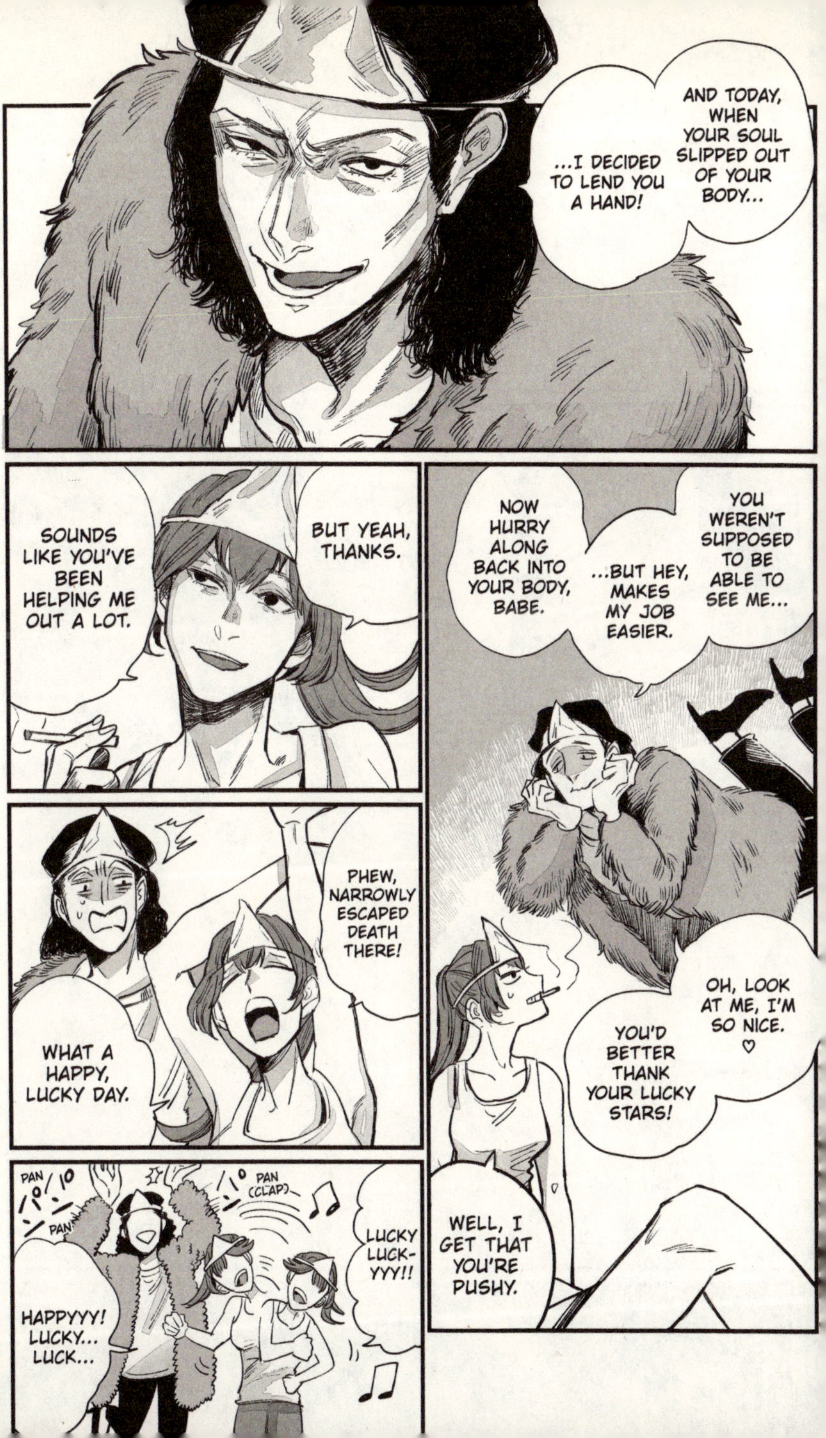
AND TODAY, WHEN YOUR SOUL SLIPPED OUT OF YOUR BODY...
...I DECIDED TO LEND YOU A HAND!
YOU WEREN'T SUPPOSED TO BE ABLE TO SEE ME...
...BUT HEY, MAKES MY JOB EASIER.
NOW HURRY ALONG BACK INTO YOUR BODY, BABE.
OH, LOOK AT ME, I'M SO NICE. ♡
YOU'D BETTER THANK YOUR LUCKY STARS!
WELL, I GET THAT YOU'RE PUSHY.
SOUNDS LIKE YOU'VE BEEN HELPING ME OUT A LOT.
BUT YEAH, THANKS.
PHEW, NARROWLY ESCAPED DEATH THERE!
WHAT A HAPPY, LUCKY DAY.
PAN (CLAP)
PAN
PAN
HAPPYYY! LUCKY... LUCK...
LUCKY LUCK-YYY!!

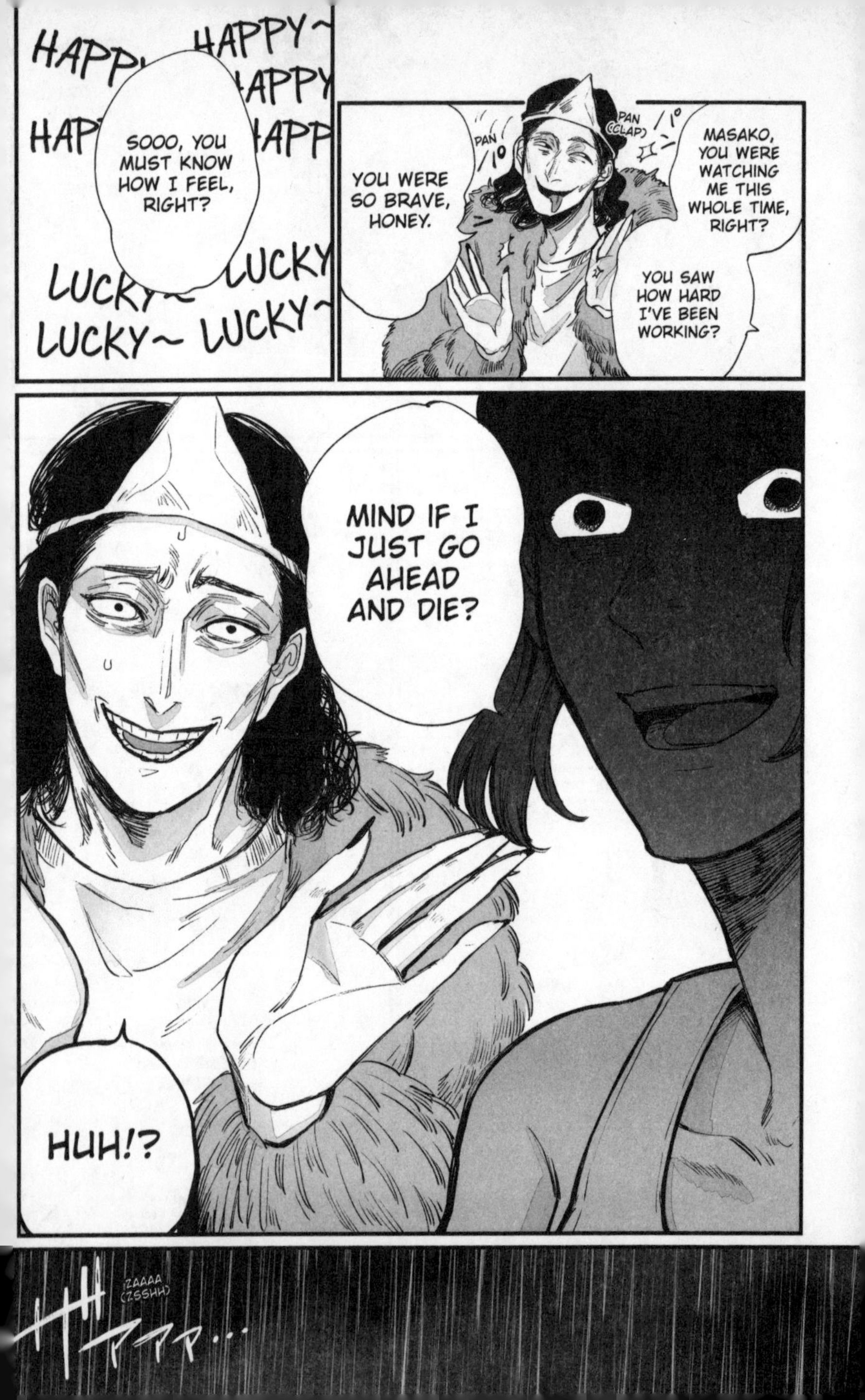
MASAKO, YOU WERE WATCHING ME THIS WHOLE TIME, RIGHT?
PAN (CLAP)
PAN
YOU SAW HOW HARD I'VE BEEN WORKING?
YOU WERE SO BRAVE, HONEY.
HAPPY~
SOOO, YOU MUST KNOW HOW I FEEL, RIGHT?
LUCKY~ LUCKY~
MIND IF I JUST GO AHEAD AND DIE?
HUH!?
ZAAAA (ZSSHH)

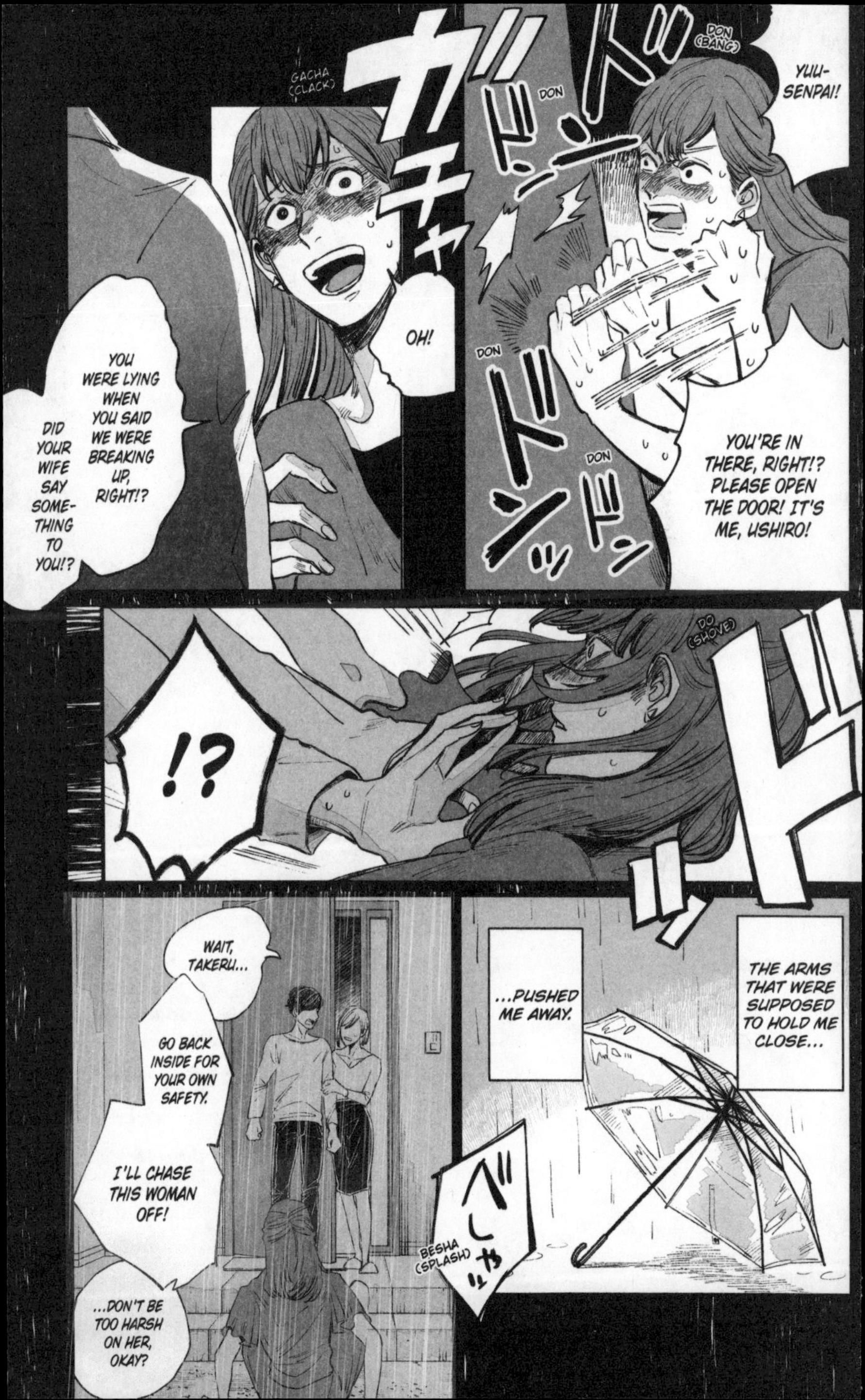
DON (BANG)
YUU-SENPAI!
DON
DON
DON
YOU'RE IN THERE, RIGHT!? PLEASE OPEN THE DOOR! IT'S ME, USHIRO!
GACHA (CLACK)
OH!
YOU WERE LYING WHEN YOU SAID WE WERE BREAKING UP, RIGHT!?
DID YOUR WIFE SAY SOME-THING TO YOU!?
DO (SHOVE)
!?
THE ARMS THAT WERE SUPPOSED TO HOLD ME CLOSE...
...PUSHED ME AWAY.
BESHA (SPLASH)
WAIT, TAKERU...
GO BACK INSIDE FOR YOUR OWN SAFETY.
I'LL CHASE THIS WOMAN OFF!
...DON'T BE TOO HARSH ON HER, OKAY?

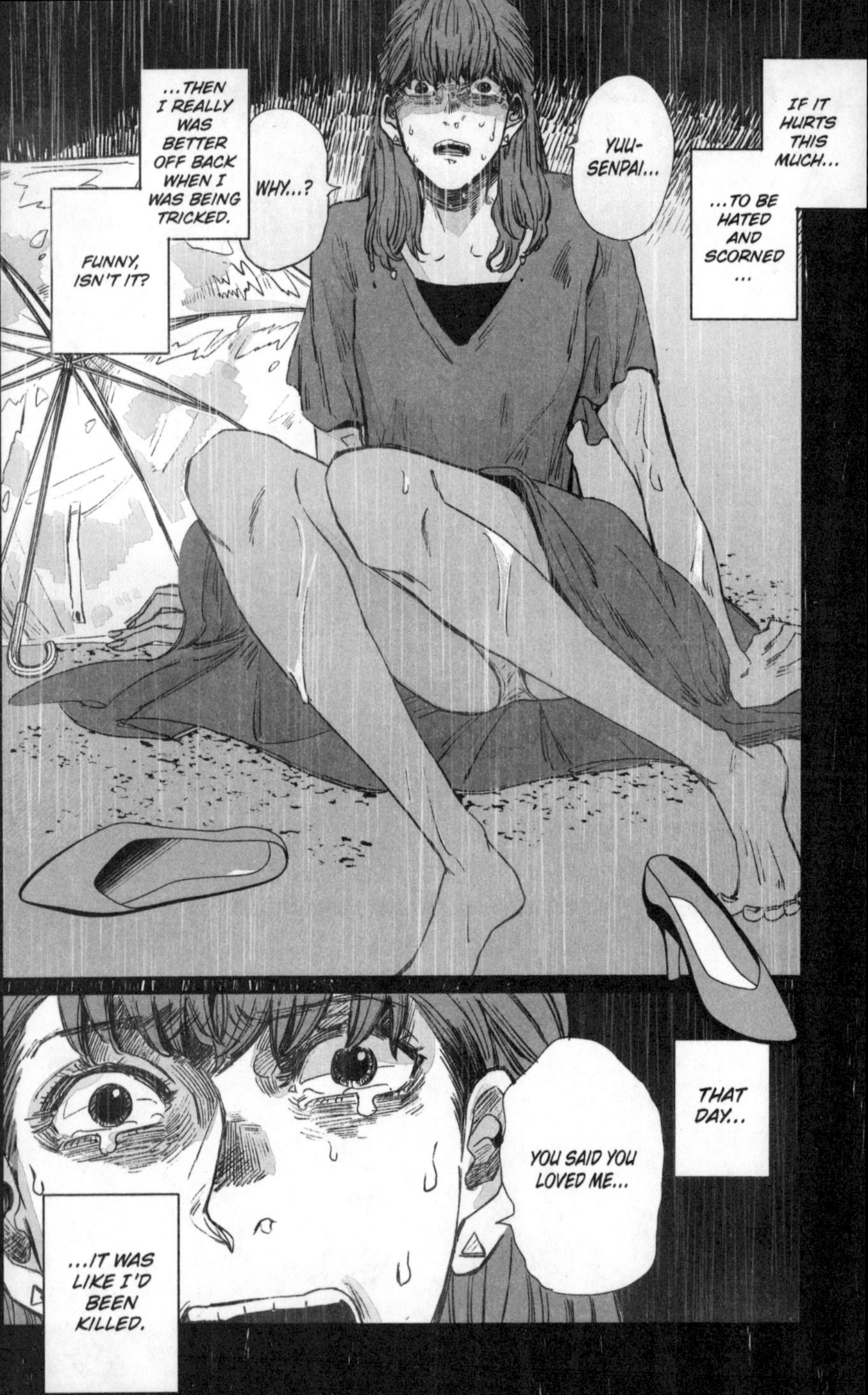
IF IT HURTS THIS MUCH...
...TO BE HATED AND SCORNED...
YUU-SENPAI...
WHY...?
...THEN I REALLY WAS BETTER OFF BACK WHEN I WAS BEING TRICKED.
FUNNY, ISN'T IT?
THAT DAY...
YOU SAID YOU LOVED ME...
...IT WAS LIKE I'D BEEN KILLED.

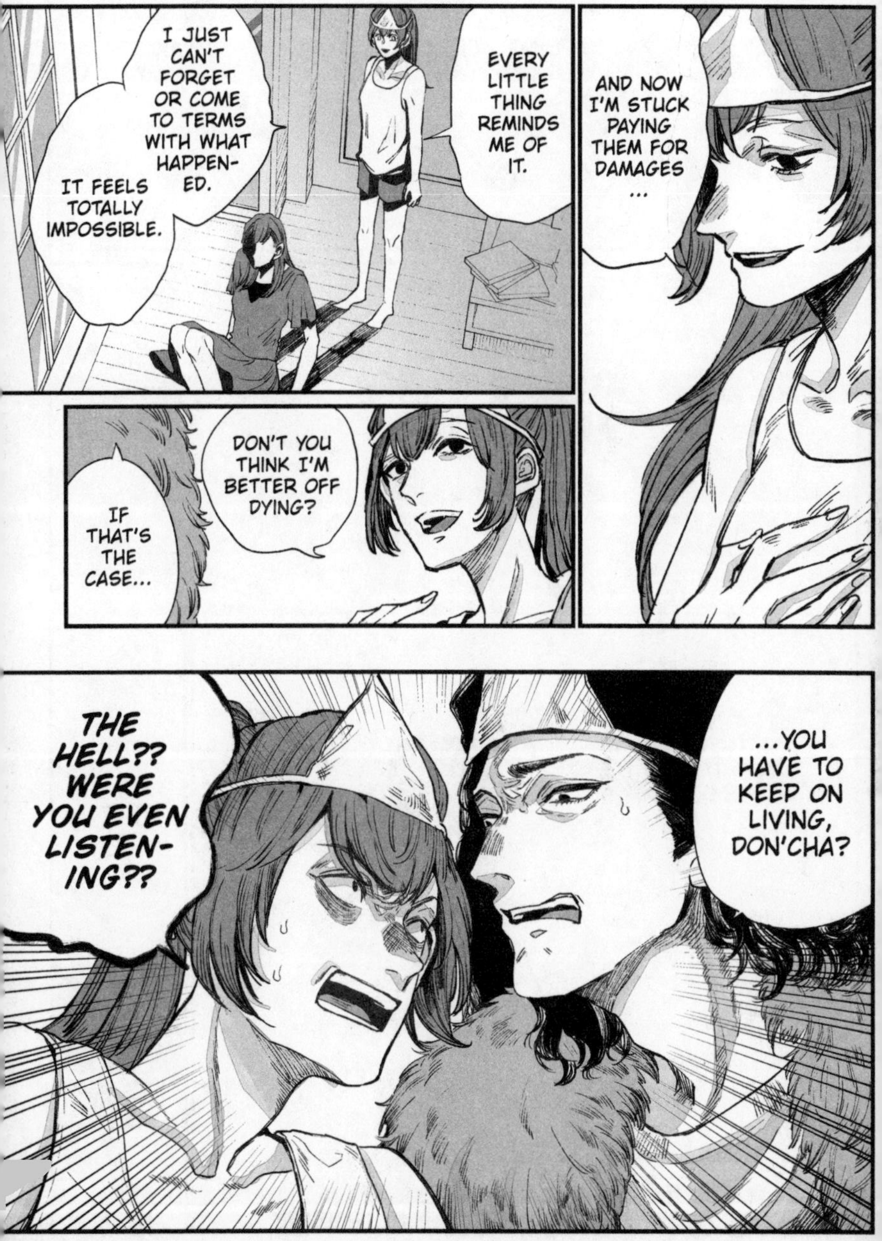
AND NOW I'M STUCK PAYING THEM FOR DAMAGES...
EVERY LITTLE THING REMINDS ME OF IT.
I JUST CAN'T FORGET OR COME TO TERMS WITH WHAT HAPPEN-ED.
IT FEELS TOTALLY IMPOSSIBLE.
DON'T YOU THINK I'M BETTER OFF DYING?
IF THAT'S THE CASE...
...YOU HAVE TO KEEP ON LIVING, DON'CHA?
THE HELL?? WERE YOU EVEN LISTEN-ING??

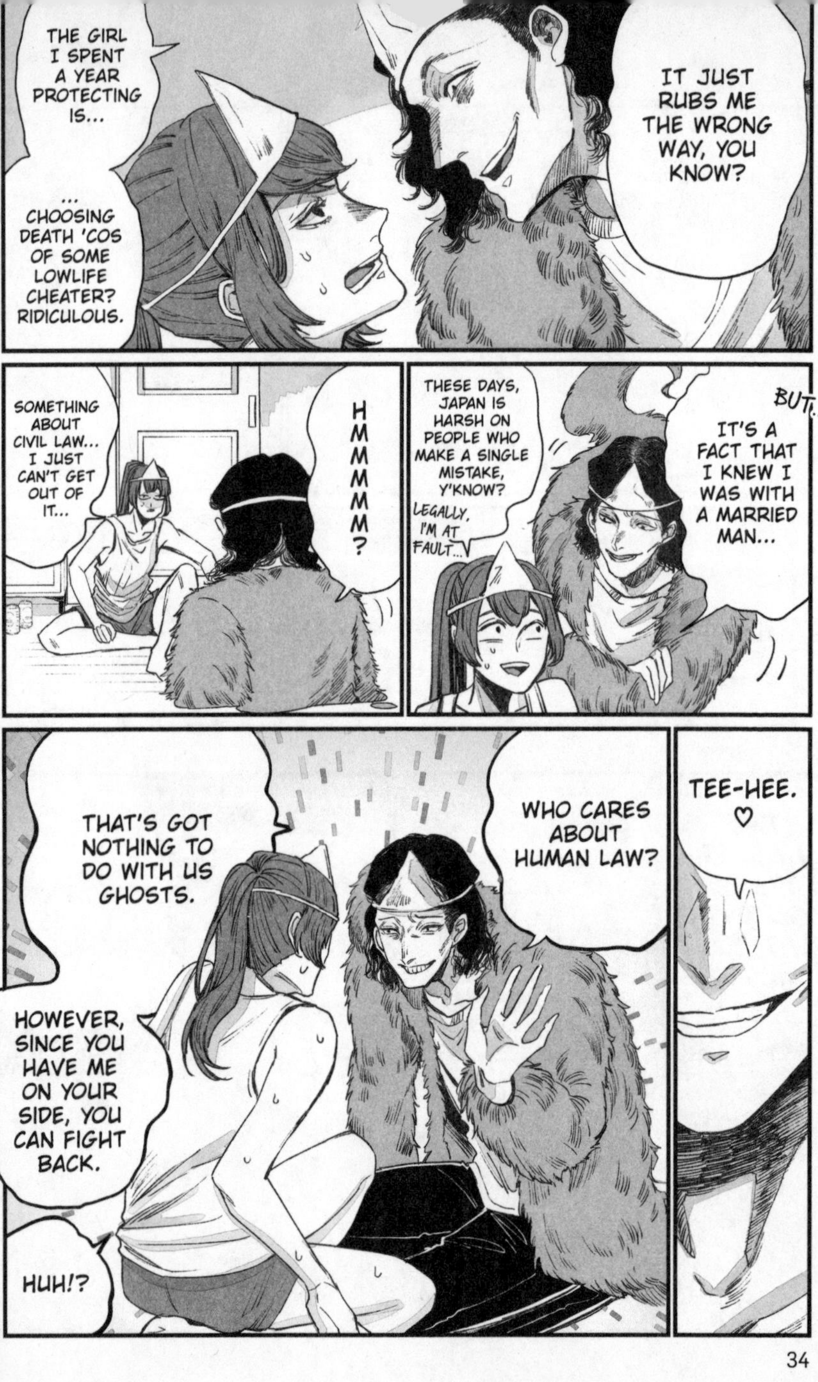
IT JUST RUBS ME THE WRONG WAY, YOU KNOW?
THE GIRL I SPENT A YEAR PROTECTING IS...
...CHOOSING DEATH 'COS OF SOME LOWLIFE CHEATER? RIDICULOUS.
BUT...
IT'S A FACT THAT I KNEW I WAS WITH A MARRIED MAN...
THESE DAYS, JAPAN IS HARSH ON PEOPLE WHO MAKE A SINGLE MISTAKE, Y'KNOW?
LEGALLY, I'M AT FAULT...
HMMMMMM?
SOMETHING ABOUT CIVIL LAW... I JUST CAN'T GET OUT OF IT...
TEE-HEE. ♡
WHO CARES ABOUT HUMAN LAW?
THAT'S GOT NOTHING TO DO WITH US GHOSTS.
HOWEVER, SINCE YOU HAVE ME ON YOUR SIDE, YOU CAN FIGHT BACK.
HUH!?

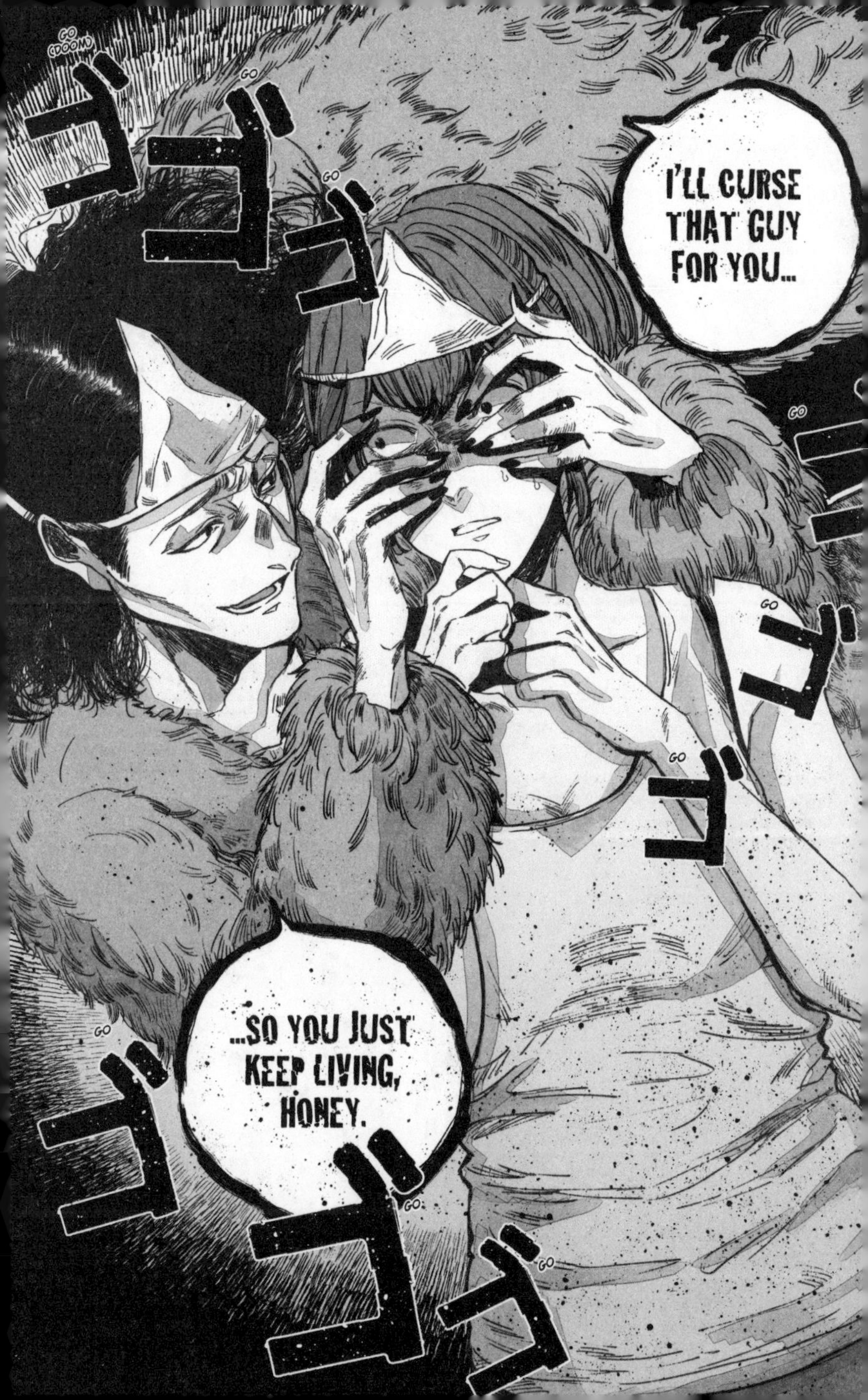
I'LL CURSE THAT GUY FOR YOU...
GO (DOOM)
GO
GO
GO
GO
GO
...SO YOU JUST KEEP LIVING, HONEY.
GO
GO
GO

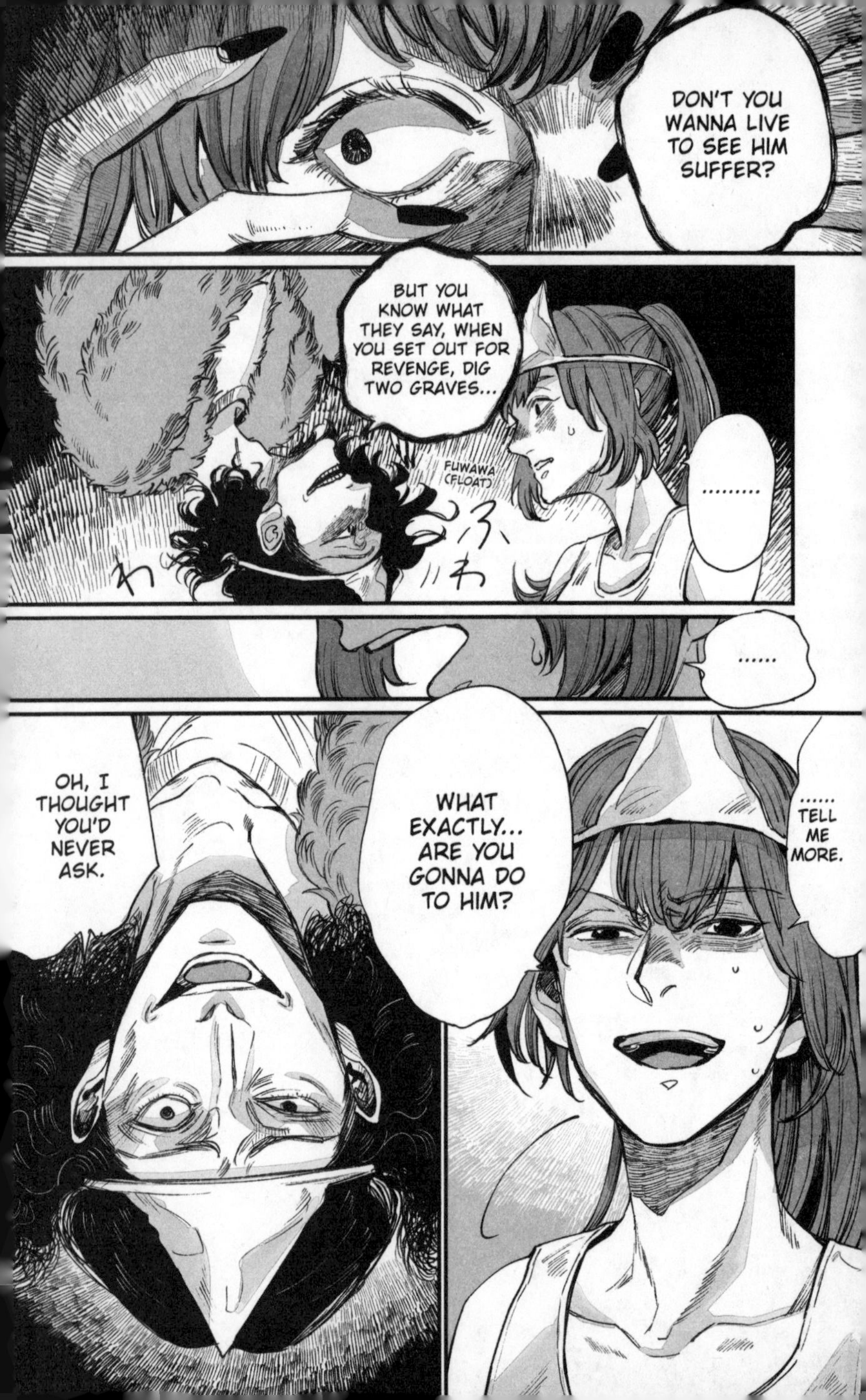
DON'T YOU WANNA LIVE TO SEE HIM SUFFER?
BUT YOU KNOW WHAT THEY SAY, WHEN YOU SET OUT FOR REVENGE, DIG TWO GRAVES...
....
FUWAWA (FLOAT)
ふわわ
......
...... TELL ME MORE.
WHAT EXACTLY... ARE YOU GONNA DO TO HIM?
OH, I THOUGHT YOU'D NEVER ASK.

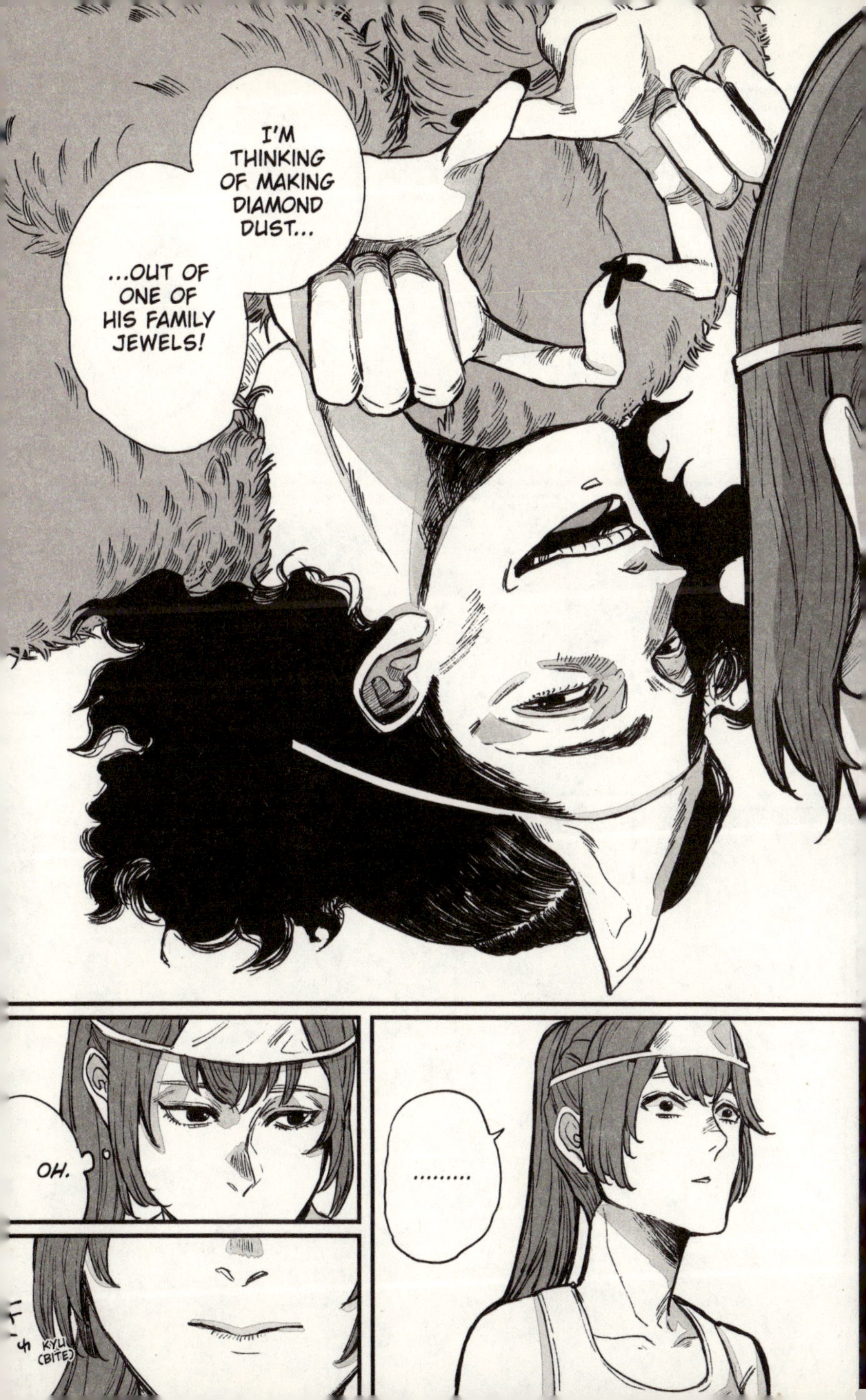
I'M THINKING OF MAKING DIAMOND DUST...
...OUT OF ONE OF HIS FAMILY JEWELS!
....
OH.
KYU (BITE)

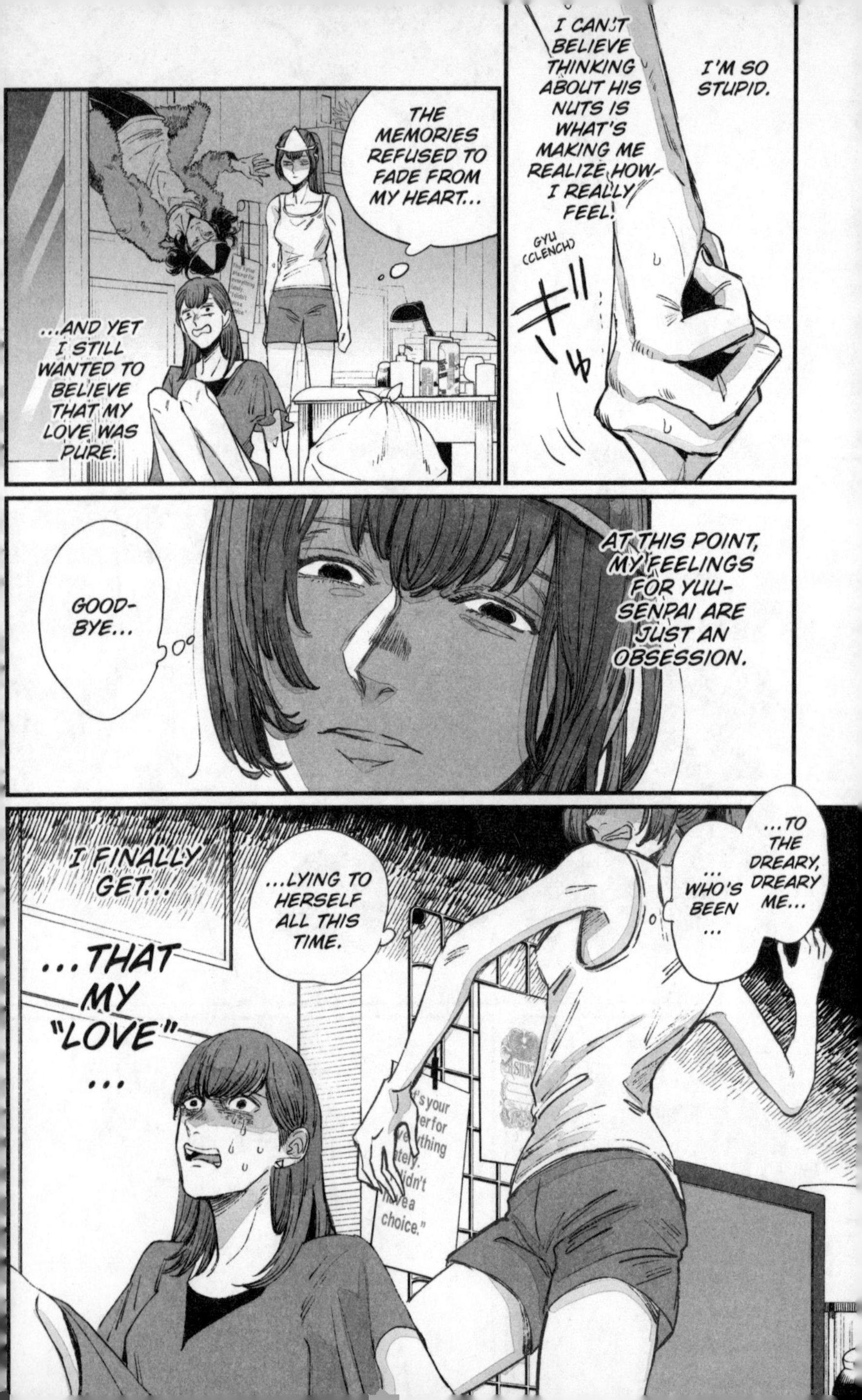
I'M SO STUPID.
I CAN'T BELIEVE THINKING ABOUT HIS NUTS IS WHAT'S MAKING ME REALIZE HOW I REALLY FEEL!
GYU (CLENCH)
THE MEMORIES REFUSED TO FADE FROM MY HEART...
...AND YET I STILL WANTED TO BELIEVE THAT MY LOVE WAS PURE.
AT THIS POINT, MY FEELINGS FOR YUU-SENPAI ARE JUST AN OBSESSION.
GOOD-BYE...
...TO THE DREARY, DREARY ME...
...WHO'S BEEN...
...LYING TO HERSELF ALL THIS TIME.
I FINALLY GET...
...THAT MY "LOVE"...

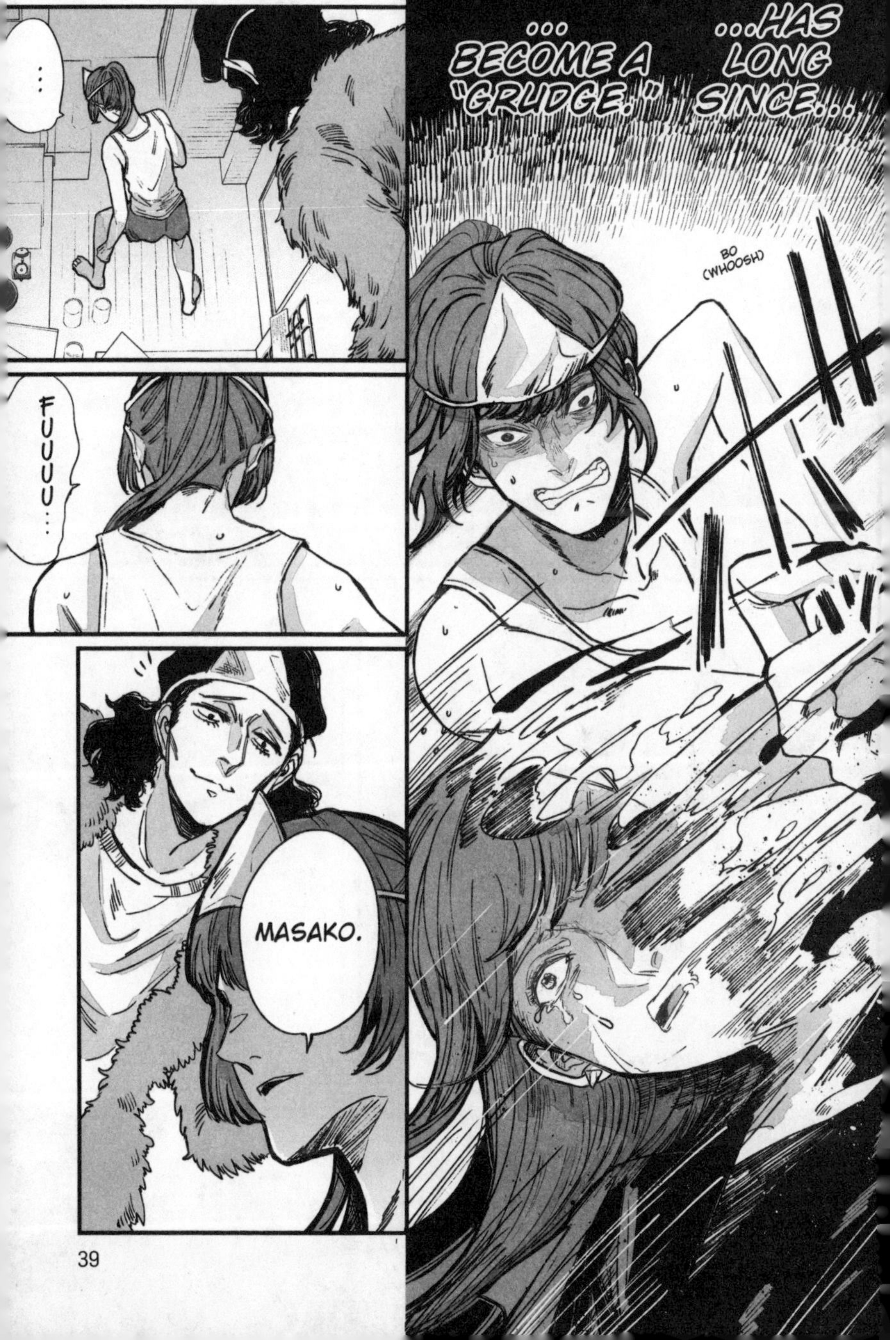
...HAS LONG SINCE...
...BECOME A "GRUDGE."
BO (WHOOSH)
...
FUUUU...
MASAKO.

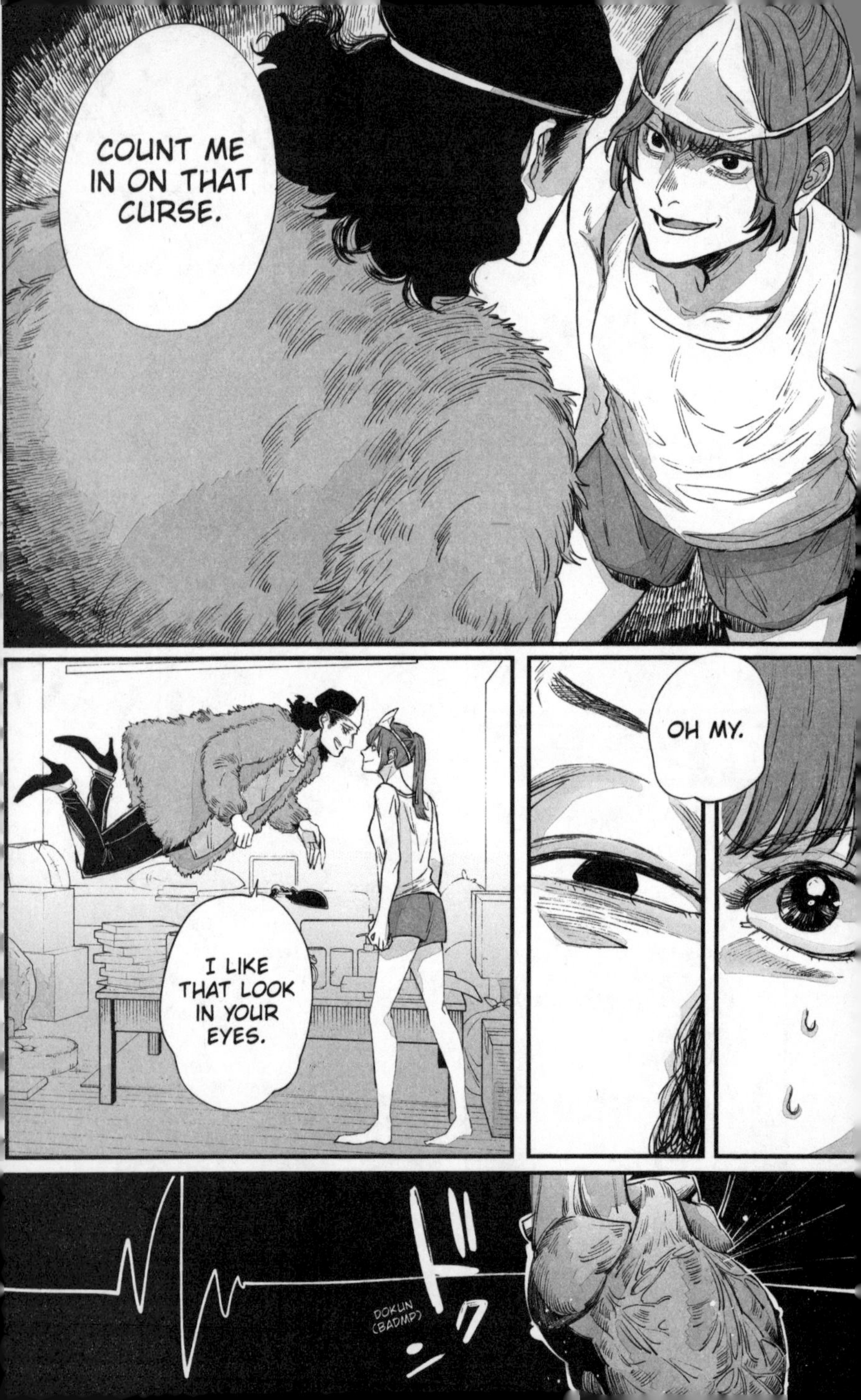
COUNT ME IN ON THAT CURSE.
OH MY.
I LIKE THAT LOOK IN YOUR EYES.
DOKUN (BADMP)

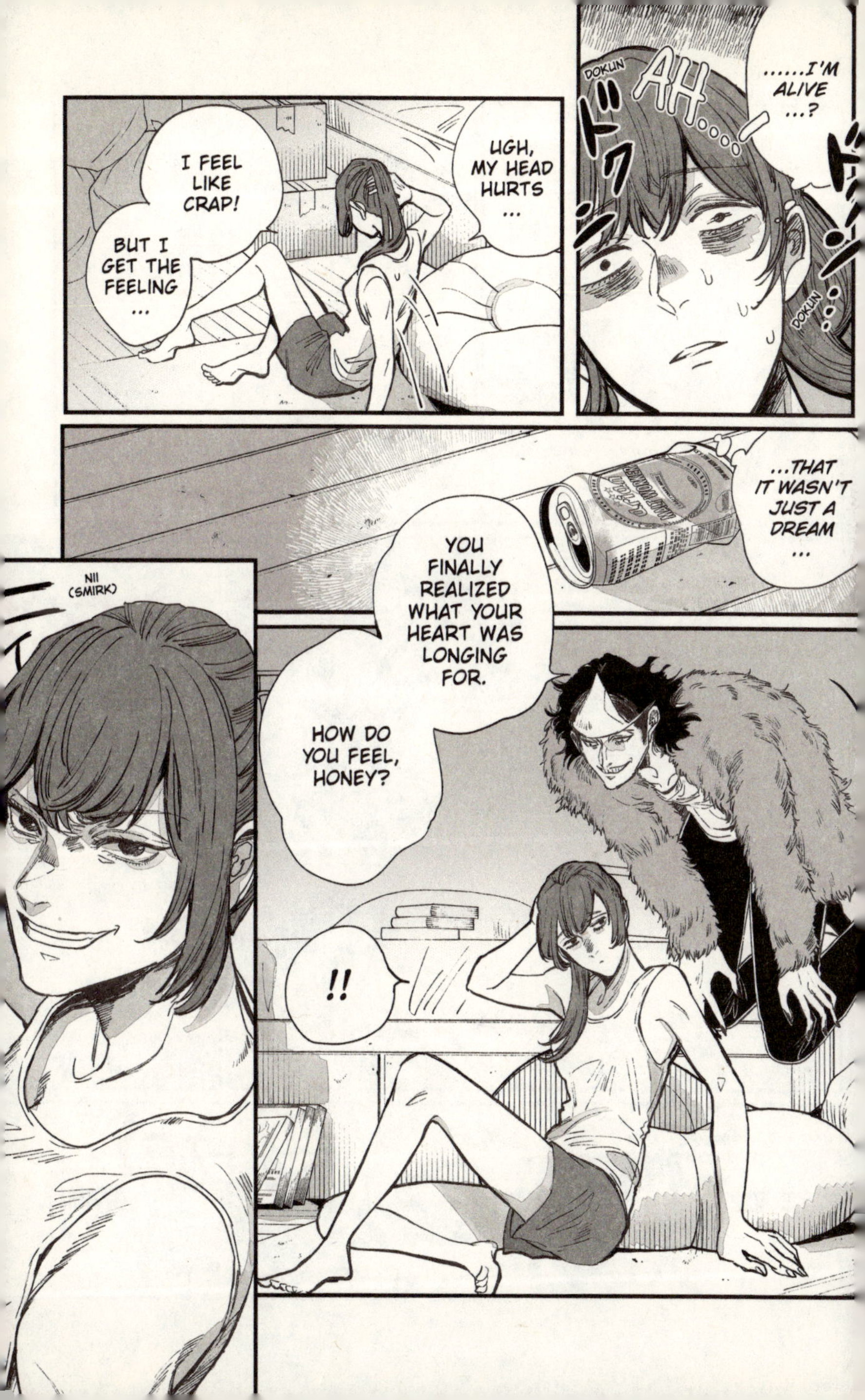

DOKUN
AH....!
......I'M ALIVE ...?
DOKUN
UGH, MY HEAD HURTS ...
I FEEL LIKE CRAP!
BUT I GET THE FEELING ...
...THAT IT WASN'T JUST A DREAM ...
YOU FINALLY REALIZED WHAT YOUR HEART WAS LONGING FOR.
HOW DO YOU FEEL, HONEY?
!!
NII (SMIRK)

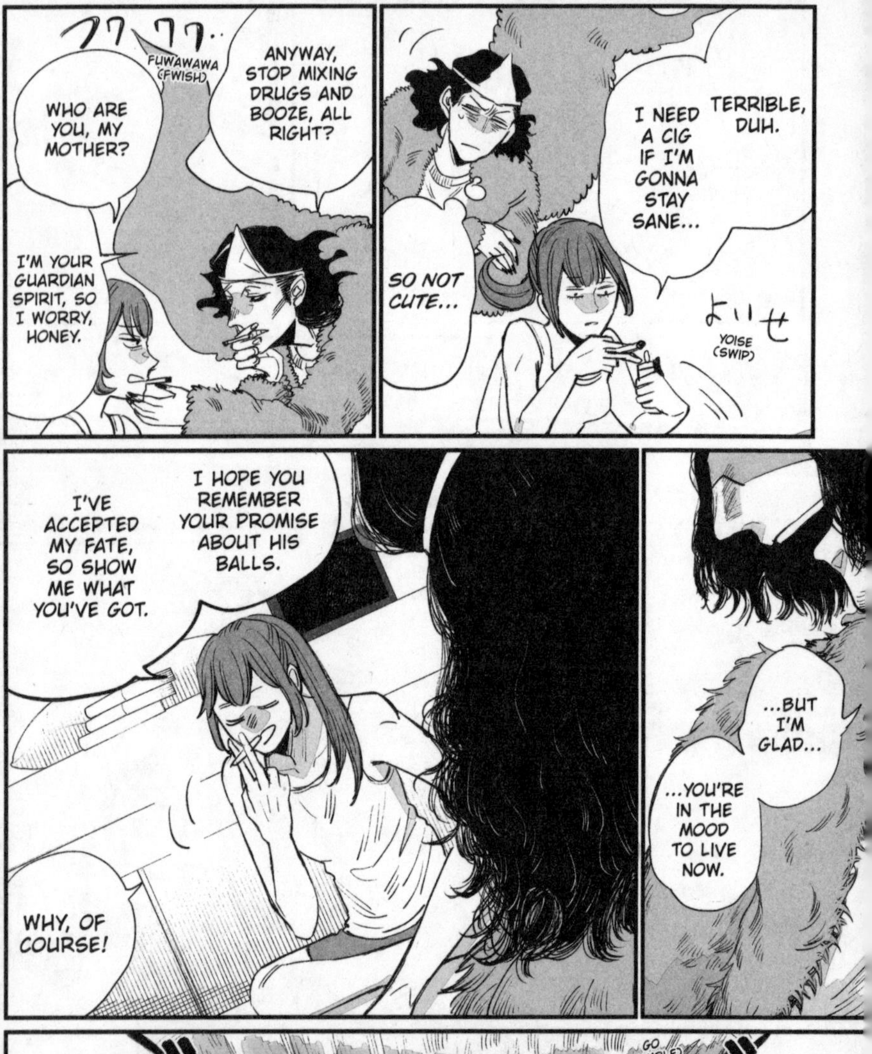
TERRIBLE, DUH.
I NEED A CIG IF I'M GONNA STAY SANE...
SO NOT CUTE...
よいせ
YOISE (SWIP)
ANYWAY, STOP MIXING DRUGS AND BOOZE, ALL RIGHT?
フワワワ…
FUWAWAWA (FWISH)
WHO ARE YOU, MY MOTHER?
I'M YOUR GUARDIAN SPIRIT, SO I WORRY, HONEY.
...BUT I'M GLAD...
...YOU'RE IN THE MOOD TO LIVE NOW.
I HOPE YOU REMEMBER YOUR PROMISE ABOUT HIS BALLS.
I'VE ACCEPTED MY FATE, SO SHOW ME WHAT YOU'VE GOT.
WHY, OF COURSE!
A CURSE...
GO (RUMBLE)
A CURSE...

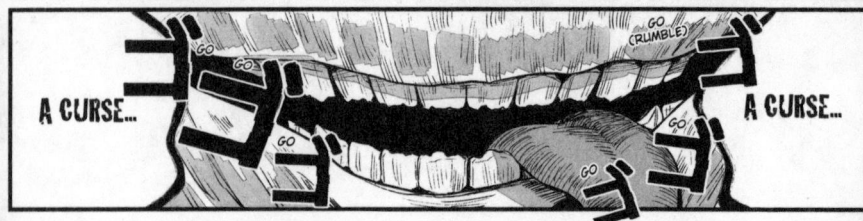

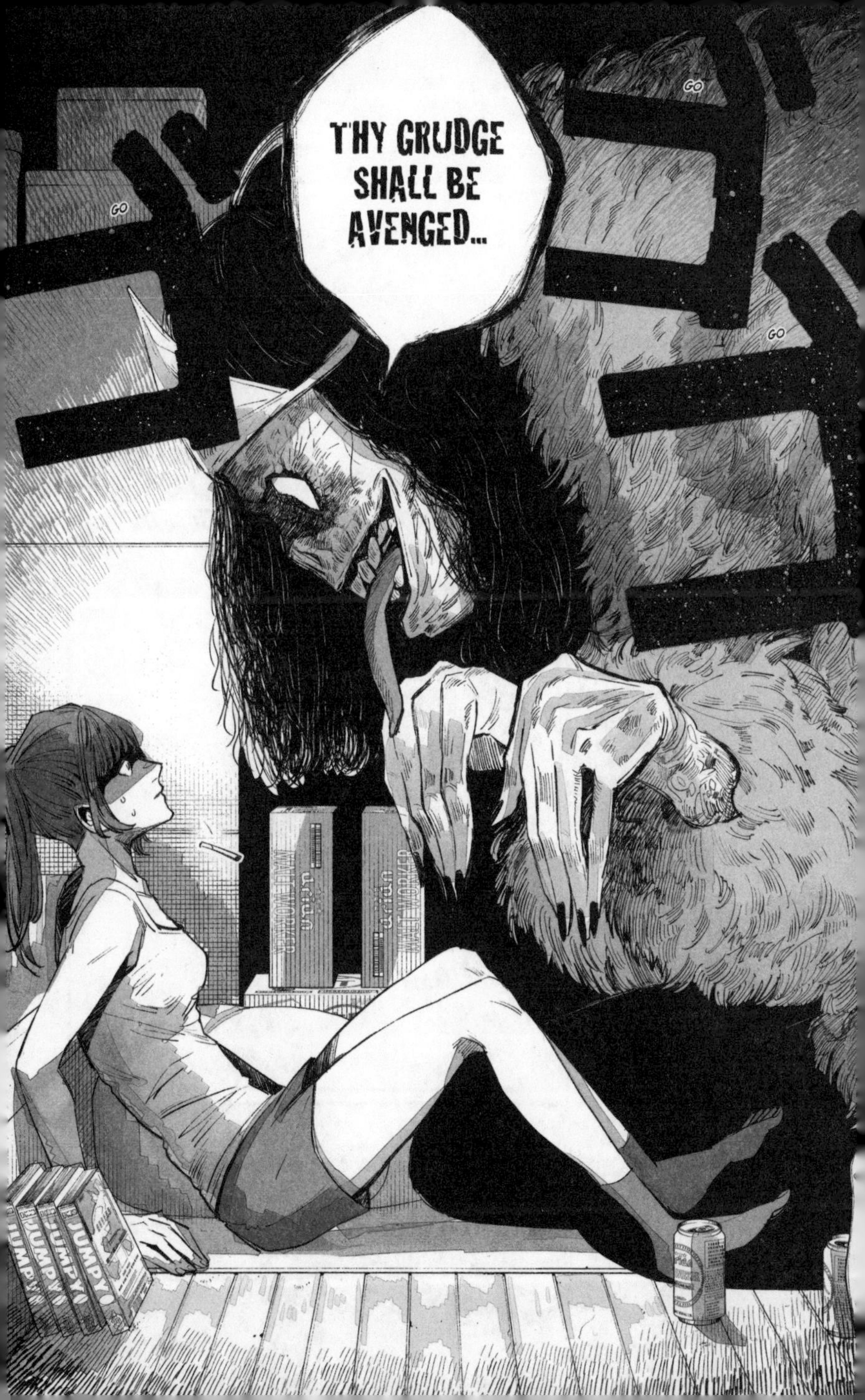
THY GRUDGE SHALL BE AVENGED...
GO
GO
GO

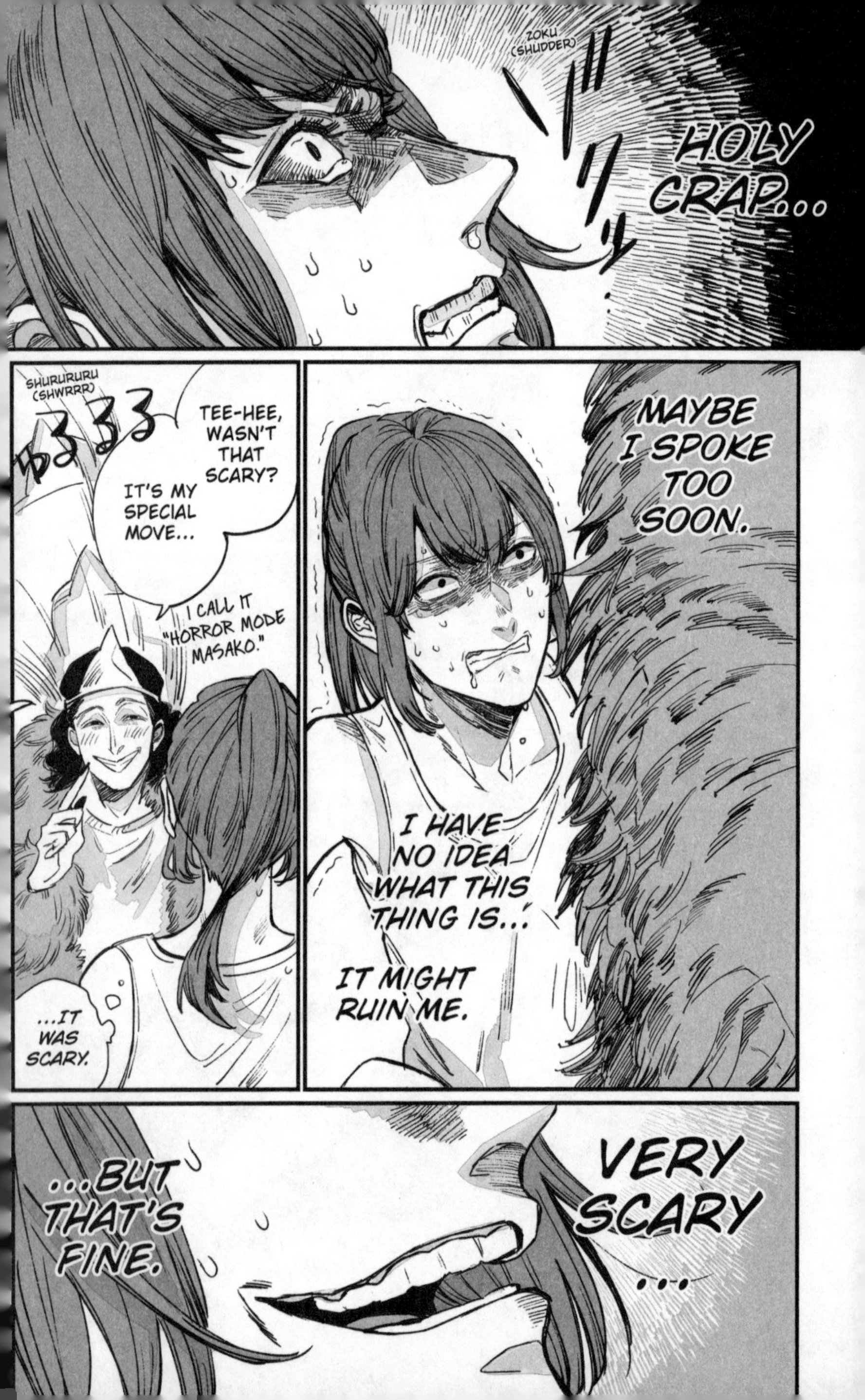
ZOKU (SHUDDER)
HOLY CRAP...
MAYBE I SPOKE TOO SOON.
I HAVE NO IDEA WHAT THIS THING IS...
IT MIGHT RUIN ME.
SHURURURU (SHWRRR)
TEE-HEE, WASN'T THAT SCARY?
IT'S MY SPECIAL MOVE...
I CALL IT "HORROR MODE MASAKO."
...IT WAS SCARY.
VERY SCARY...
...BUT THAT'S FINE.

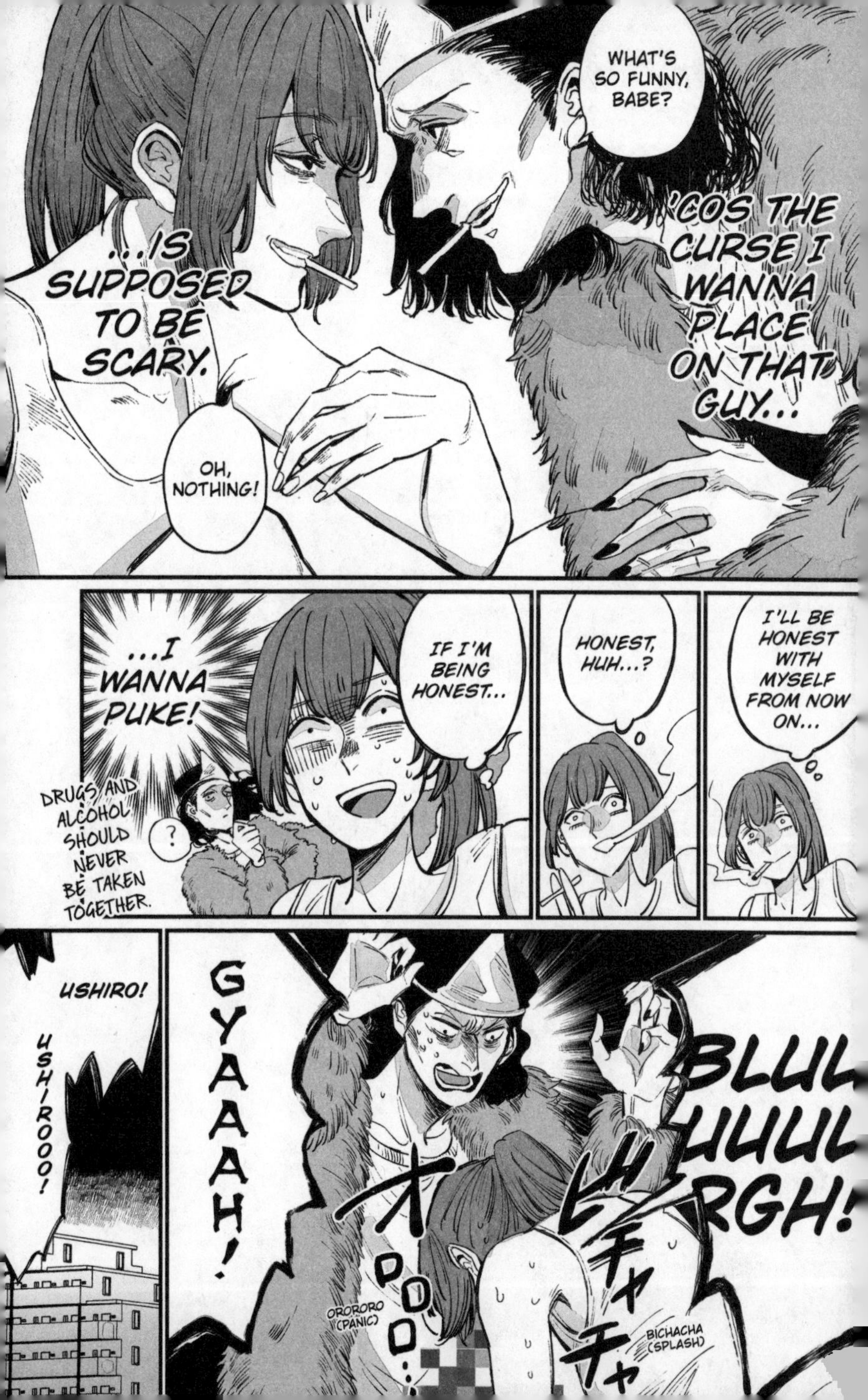
WHAT'S SO FUNNY, BABE?
'COS THE CURSE I WANNA PLACE ON THAT GUY...
...IS SUPPOSED TO BE SCARY.
OH, NOTHING!
I'LL BE HONEST WITH MYSELF FROM NOW ON...
HONEST, HUH...?
IF I'M BEING HONEST...
...I WANNA PUKE!
?
DRUGS AND ALCOHOL SHOULD NEVER BE TAKEN TOGETHER.
BLULUUULRGH!
ビチャチャ
BICHACHA (SPLASH)
GYAAAH!
オ
ORORORO (PANIC)
USHIRO!
USHIROOOO!

GOGOGOGO-GO-GHOST!

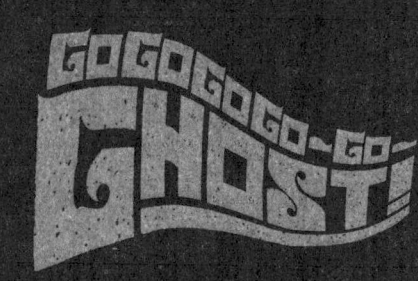

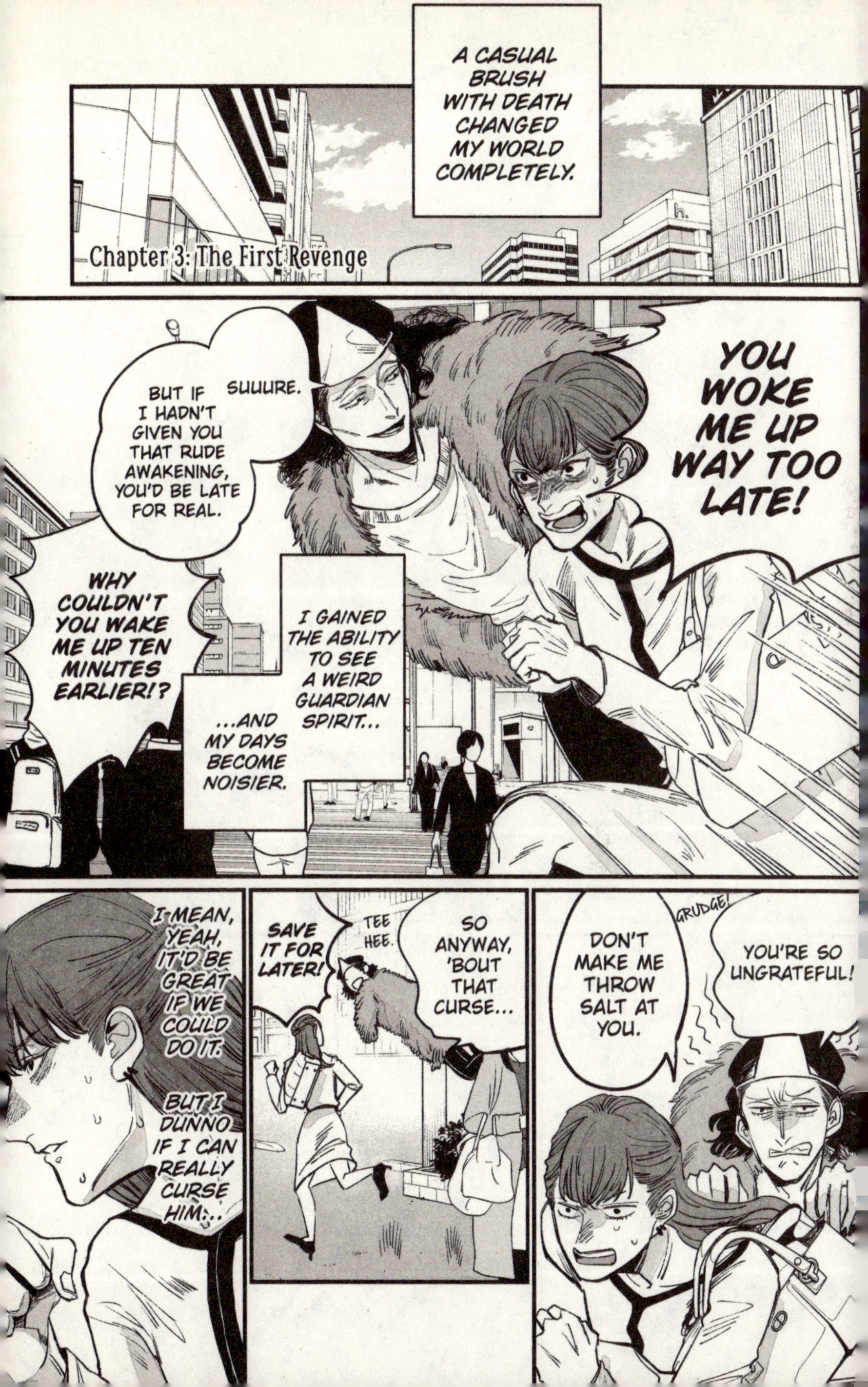
A CASUAL BRUSH WITH DEATH CHANGED MY WORLD COMPLETELY.
Chapter 3: The First Revenge
YOU WOKE ME UP WAY TOO LATE!
SUUURE.
BUT IF I HADN'T GIVEN YOU THAT RUDE AWAKENING, YOU'D BE LATE FOR REAL.
I GAINED THE ABILITY TO SEE A WEIRD GUARDIAN SPIRIT...
...AND MY DAYS BECOME NOISIER.
WHY COULDN'T YOU WAKE ME UP TEN MINUTES EARLIER!?
YOU'RE SO UNGRATEFUL!
GRUDGE!
DON'T MAKE ME THROW SALT AT YOU.
SO ANYWAY, 'BOUT THAT CURSE...
TEE HEE.
SAVE IT FOR LATER!
I MEAN, YEAH, IT'D BE GREAT IF WE COULD DO IT.
BUT I DUNNO IF I CAN REALLY CURSE HIM...

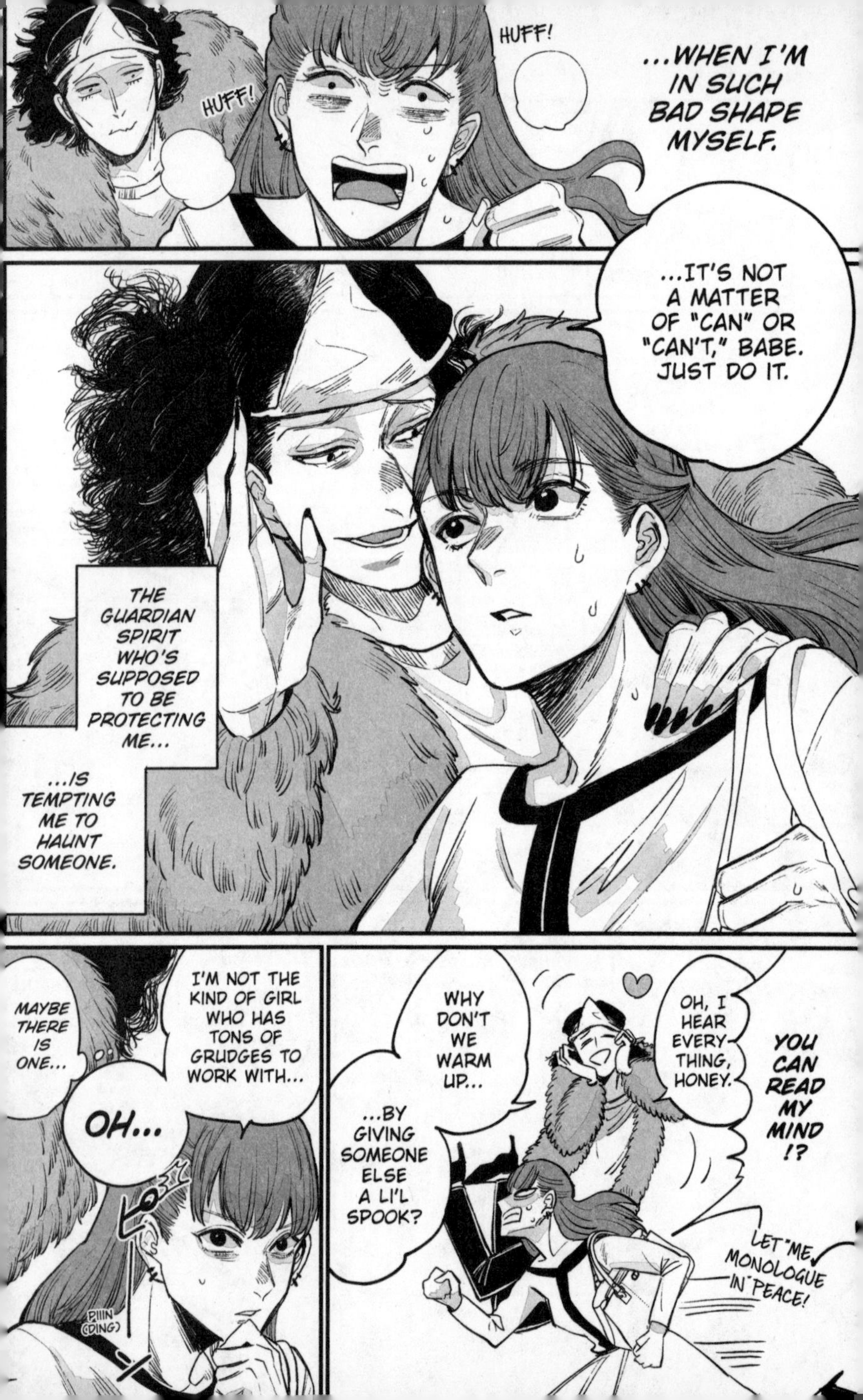
HUFF!
HUFF!
...WHEN I'M IN SUCH BAD SHAPE MYSELF.
...IT'S NOT A MATTER OF "CAN" OR "CAN'T," BABE. JUST DO IT.
THE GUARDIAN SPIRIT WHO'S SUPPOSED TO BE PROTECTING ME...
...IS TEMPTING ME TO HAUNT SOMEONE.
I'M NOT THE KIND OF GIRL WHO HAS TONS OF GRUDGES TO WORK WITH...
MAYBE THERE IS ONE...
OH...
PIIIN (DING)
WHY DON'T WE WARM UP...
...BY GIVING SOMEONE ELSE A LI'L SPOOK?
OH, I HEAR EVERYTHING, HONEY.
YOU CAN READ MY MIND!?
LET ME MONOLOGUE IN PEACE!

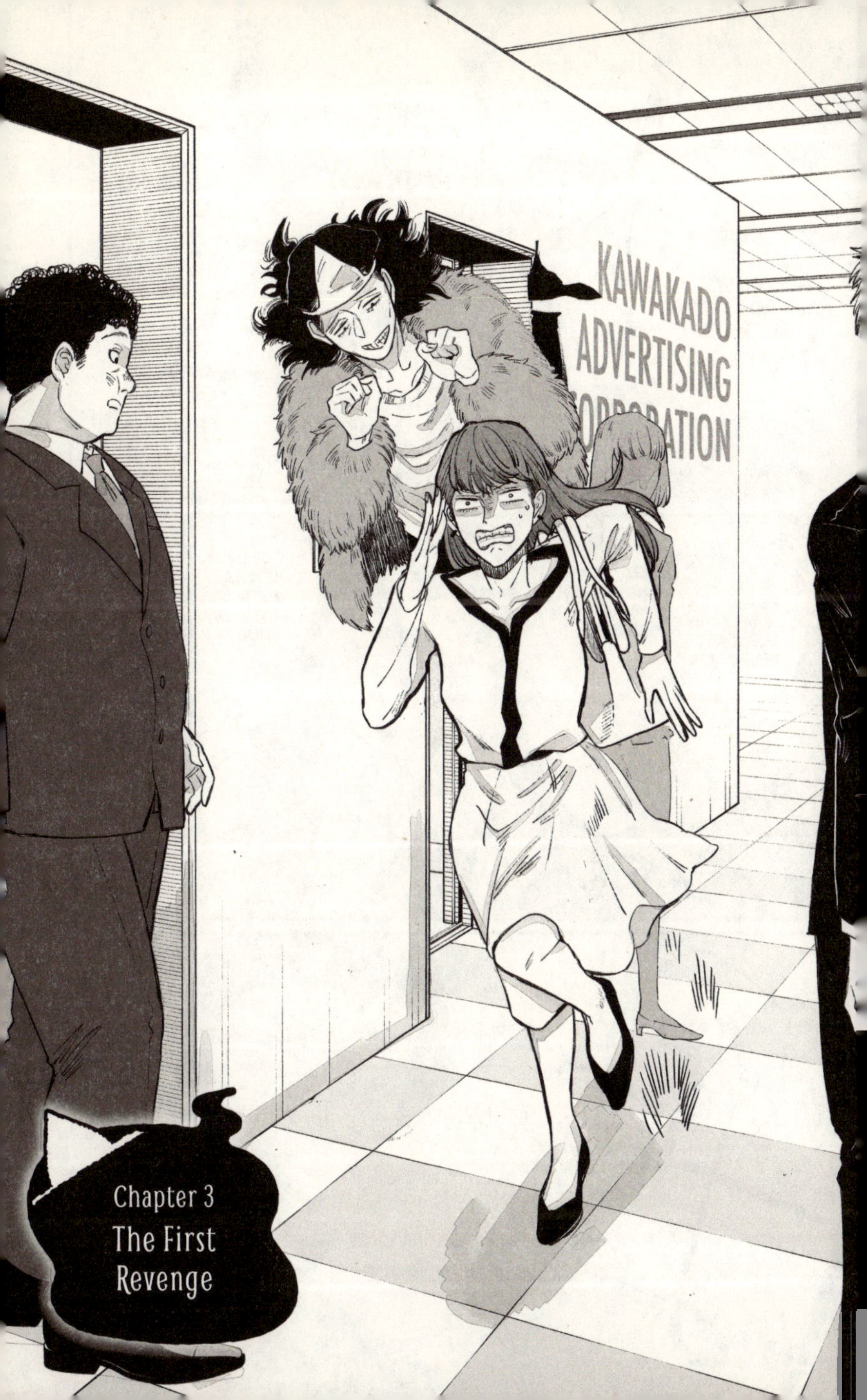
KAWAKADO
ADVERTISING
CORPORATION
Chapter 3
The First
Revenge

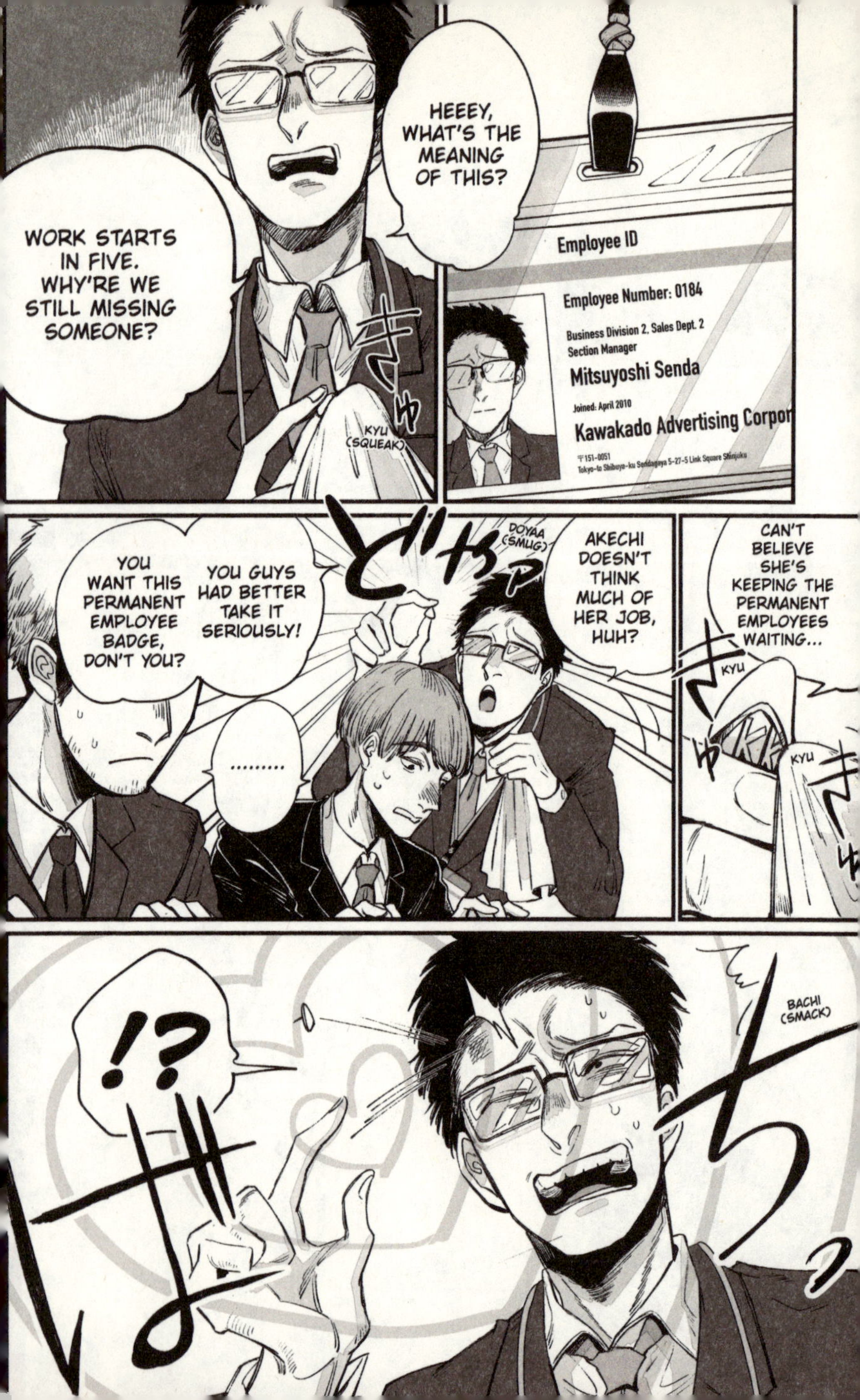
Employee ID
Employee Number: 0184
Business Division 2, Sales Dept. 2
Section Manager
Mitsuyoshi Senda
Joined: April 2010
Kawakado Advertising Corpor
〒151-0051
Tokyo-to Shibuya-ku Sendagaya 5-27-5 Link Square Shinjuku
HEEEY, WHAT'S THE MEANING OF THIS?
KYU (SQUEAK)
WORK STARTS IN FIVE. WHY'RE WE STILL MISSING SOMEONE?
CAN'T BELIEVE SHE'S KEEPING THE PERMANENT EMPLOYEES WAITING...
KYU
KYU
AKECHI DOESN'T THINK MUCH OF HER JOB, HUH?
DOYAA (SMUG)
YOU GUYS HAD BETTER TAKE IT SERIOUSLY!
YOU WANT THIS PERMANENT EMPLOYEE BADGE, DON'T YOU?
....
BACHI (SMACK)
!?

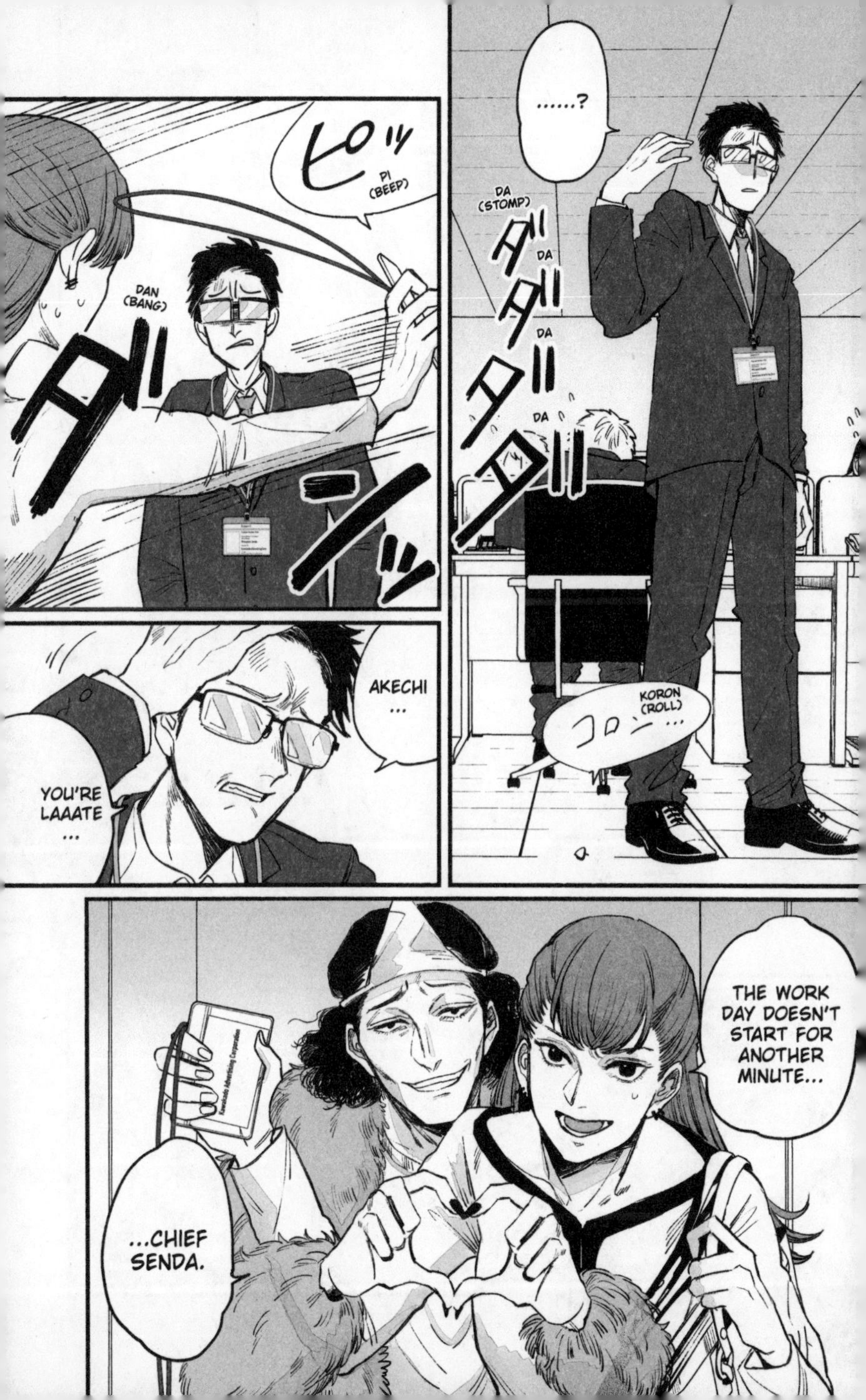
......?
DA (STOMP)
ダダダダ
DA
DA
DA
KORON (ROLL)
コロン…
ピッ
PI (BEEP)
DAN (BANG)
ダーンッ
AKECHI ...
YOU'RE LAAATE ...
THE WORK DAY DOESN'T START FOR ANOTHER MINUTE...
...CHIEF SENDA.

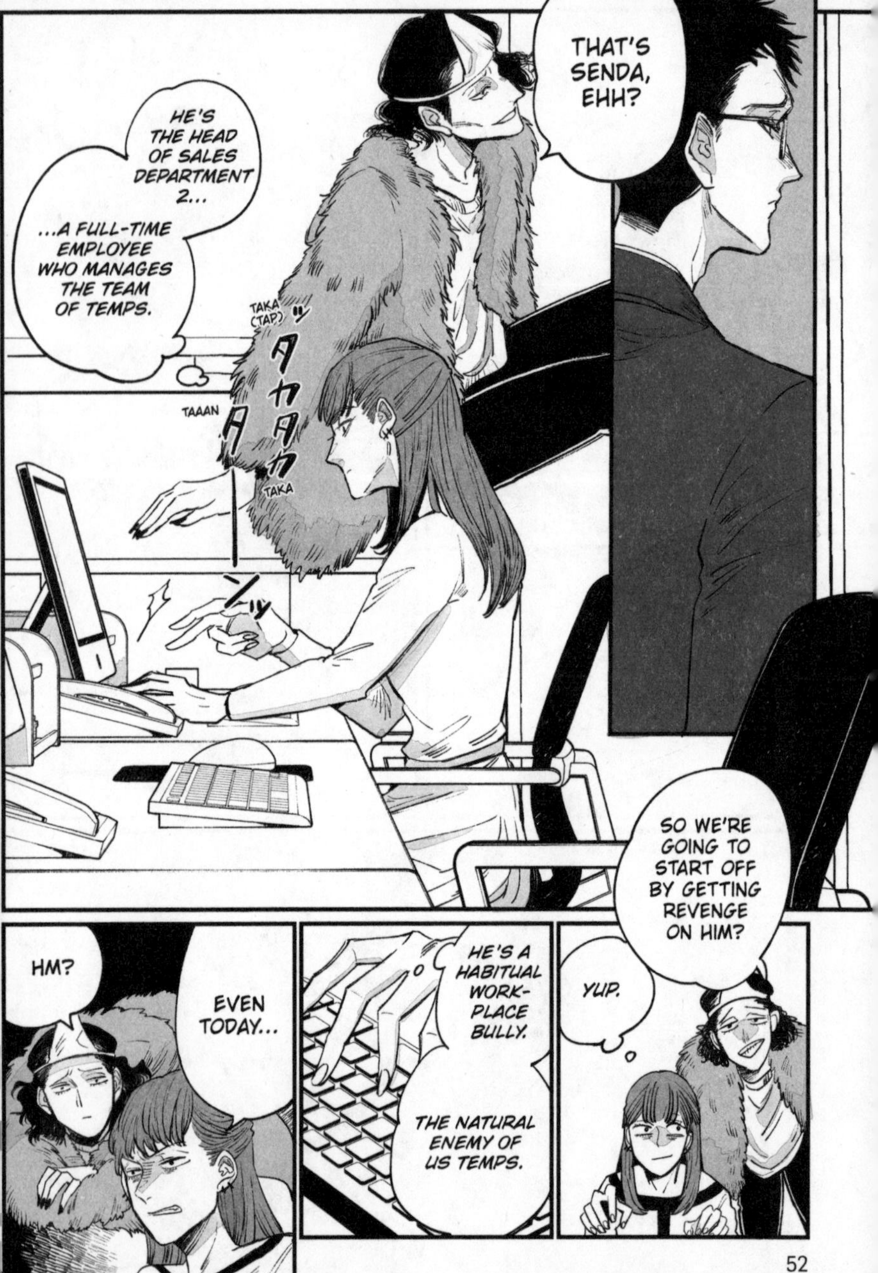
THAT'S SENDA, EHH?
HE'S THE HEAD OF SALES DEPARTMENT 2...
...A FULL-TIME EMPLOYEE WHO MANAGES THE TEAM OF TEMPS.
TAKA (TAP)
TAKA
TAAAN
SO WE'RE GOING TO START OFF BY GETTING REVENGE ON HIM?
YUP.
HE'S A HABITUAL WORK-PLACE BULLY.
THE NATURAL ENEMY OF US TEMPS.
EVEN TODAY...
HM?

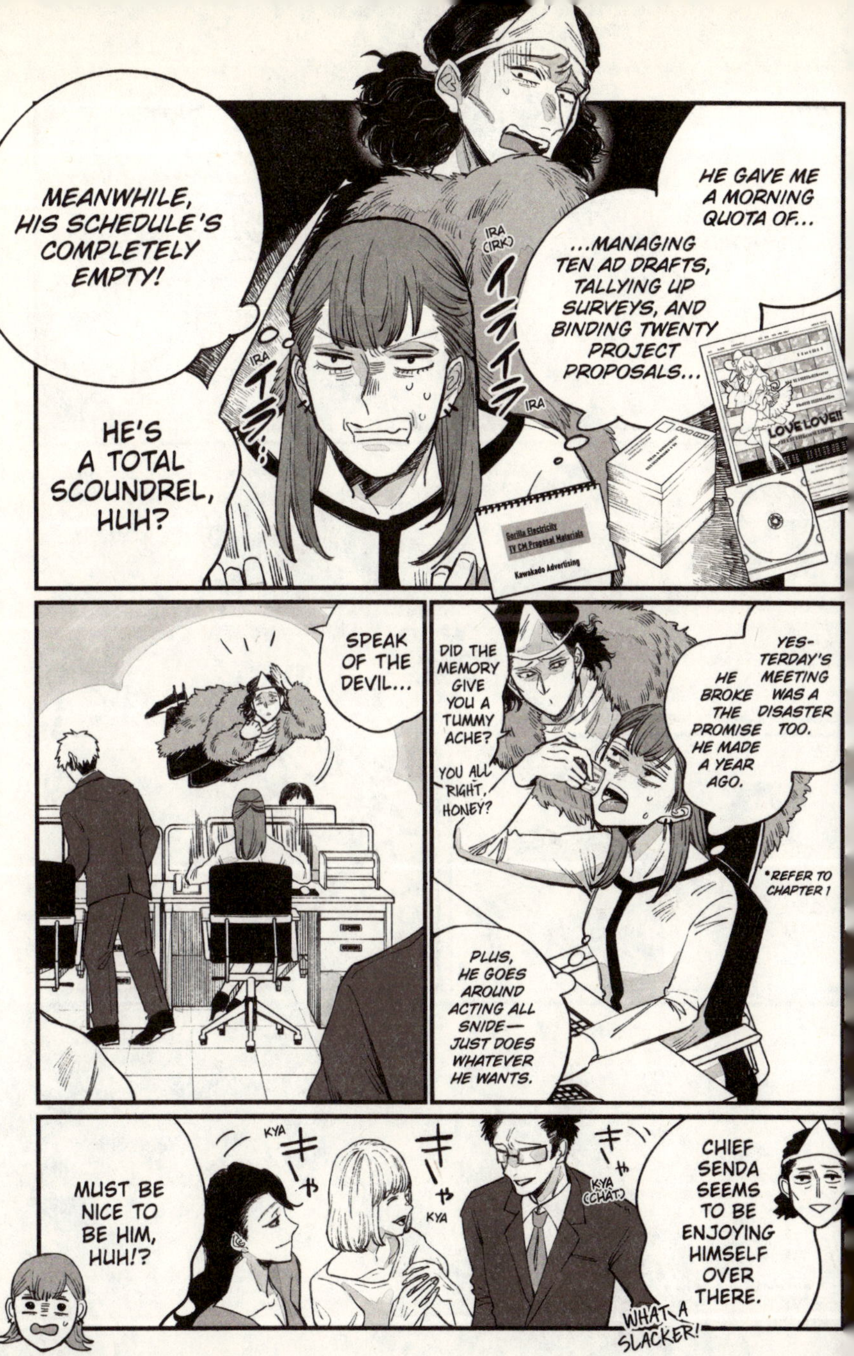
HE GAVE ME A MORNING QUOTA OF...
...MANAGING TEN AD DRAFTS, TALLYING UP SURVEYS, AND BINDING TWENTY PROJECT PROPOSALS...
IRA (IRK)
IRA
LOVE LOVE!!
Gorilla Electricity TV CM Proposal Materials
Kawakado Advertising
MEANWHILE, HIS SCHEDULE'S COMPLETELY EMPTY!
IRA
HE'S A TOTAL SCOUNDREL, HUH?
YES-TERDAY'S MEETING WAS A DISASTER TOO.
HE BROKE THE PROMISE HE MADE A YEAR AGO.
*REFER TO CHAPTER 1
DID THE MEMORY GIVE YOU A TUMMY ACHE?
YOU ALL RIGHT, HONEY?
PLUS, HE GOES AROUND ACTING ALL SNIDE—JUST DOES WHATEVER HE WANTS.
SPEAK OF THE DEVIL...
CHIEF SENDA SEEMS TO BE ENJOYING HIMSELF OVER THERE.
WHAT A SLACKER!
KYA (CHAT)
KYA
KYA
MUST BE NICE TO BE HIM, HUH!?

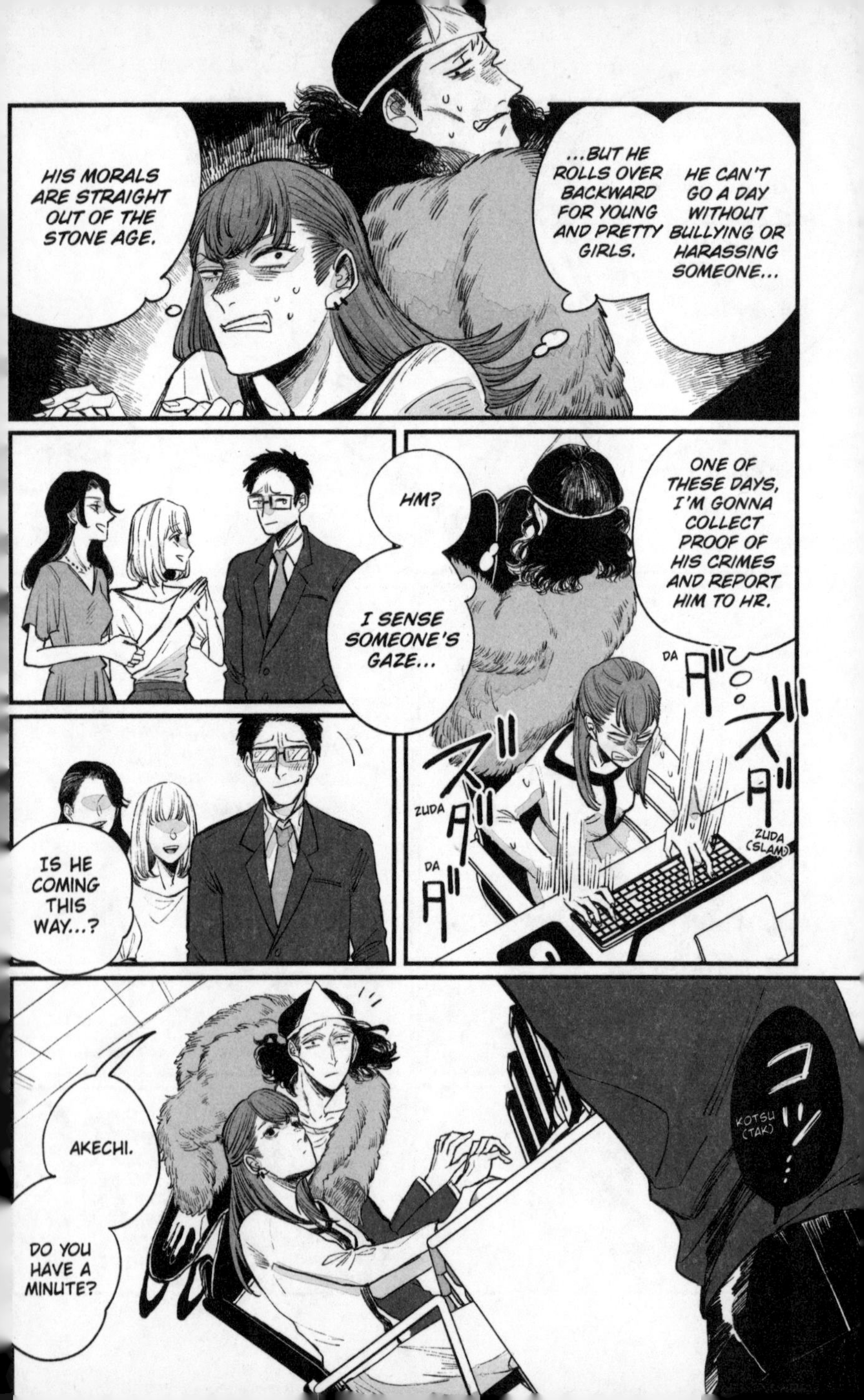
HE CAN'T GO A DAY WITHOUT BULLYING OR HARASSING SOMEONE...
...BUT HE ROLLS OVER BACKWARD FOR YOUNG AND PRETTY GIRLS.
HIS MORALS ARE STRAIGHT OUT OF THE STONE AGE.
ONE OF THESE DAYS, I'M GONNA COLLECT PROOF OF HIS CRIMES AND REPORT HIM TO HR.
DA
ZUDA (SLAM)
ZUDA
DA
HM?
I SENSE SOMEONE'S GAZE...
IS HE COMING THIS WAY...?
KOTSU (TAK)
AKECHI.
DO YOU HAVE A MINUTE?

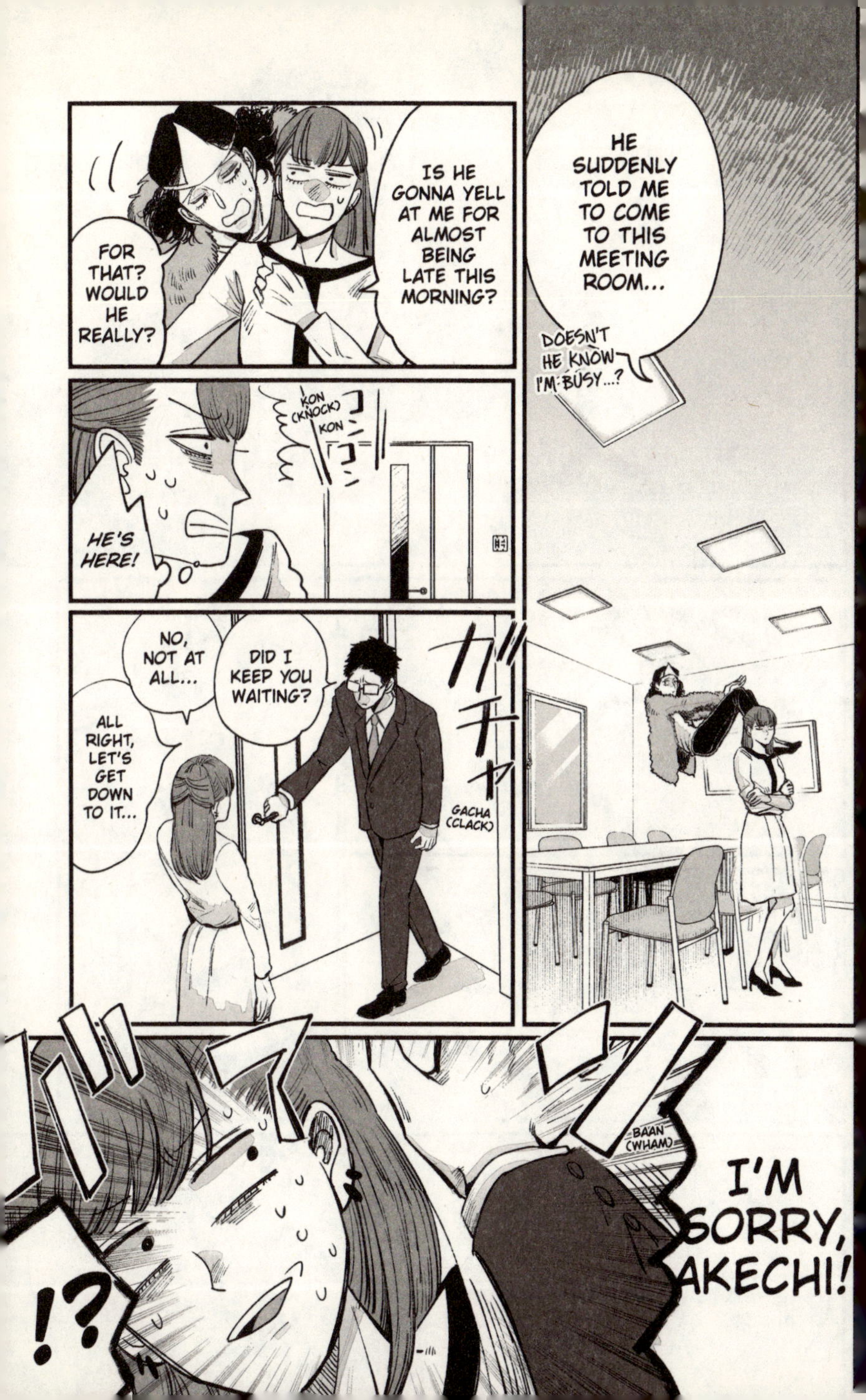
HE SUDDENLY TOLD ME TO COME TO THIS MEETING ROOM...
DOESN'T HE KNOW I'M BUSY...?
IS HE GONNA YELL AT ME FOR ALMOST BEING LATE THIS MORNING?
FOR THAT? WOULD HE REALLY?
KON (KNOCK) KON
HE'S HERE!
GACHA (CLACK)
DID I KEEP YOU WAITING?
NO, NOT AT ALL...
ALL RIGHT, LET'S GET DOWN TO IT...
BA'AN (WHAM)
I'M SORRY, AKECHI!
!?

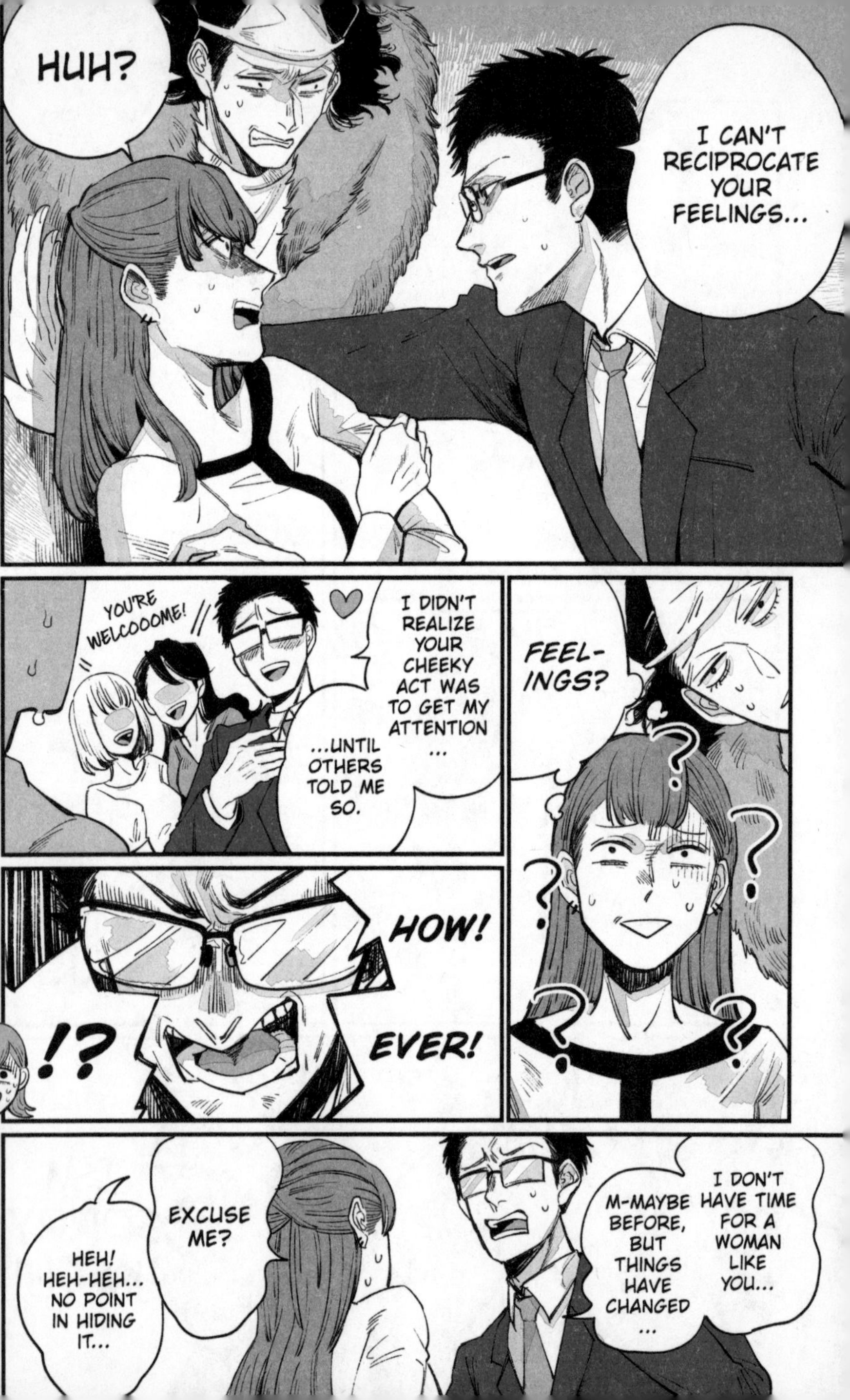
I CAN'T RECIPROCATE YOUR FEELINGS...
HUH?
FEEL-INGS?
I DIDN'T REALIZE YOUR CHEEKY ACT WAS TO GET MY ATTENTION ...
...UNTIL OTHERS TOLD ME SO.
YOU'RE WELCOOOME!
HOW! EVER!
!?
I DON'T HAVE TIME FOR A WOMAN LIKE YOU...
M-MAYBE BEFORE, BUT THINGS HAVE CHANGED ...
EXCUSE ME?
HEH! HEH-HEH... NO POINT IN HIDING IT...

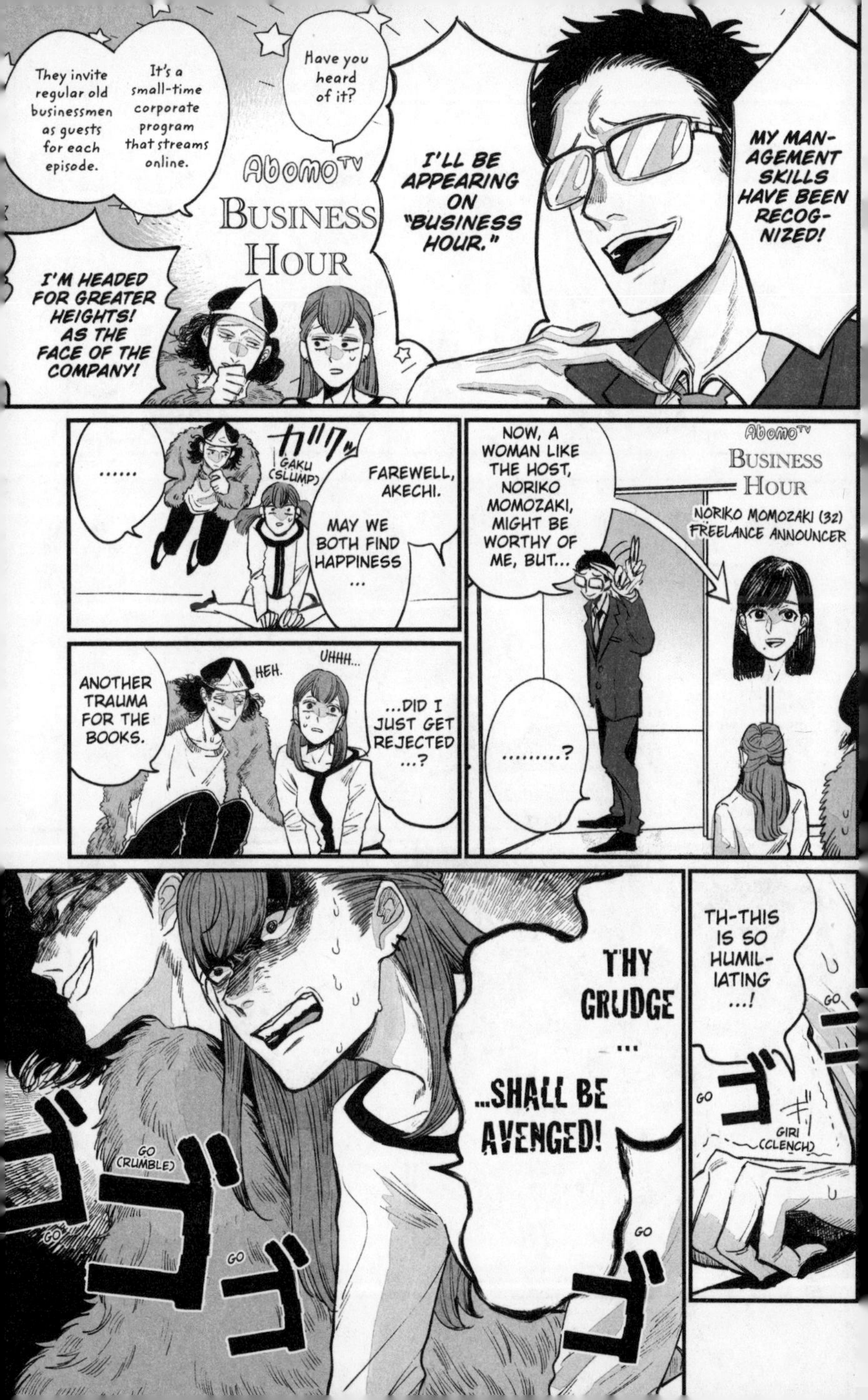
MY MANAGEMENT SKILLS HAVE BEEN RECOGNIZED!
I'LL BE APPEARING ON "BUSINESS HOUR."
Have you heard of it?
It's a small-time corporate program that streams online.
They invite regular old businessmen as guests for each episode.
Abomo TV BUSINESS HOUR
I'M HEADED FOR GREATER HEIGHTS! AS THE FACE OF THE COMPANY!
Abomo TV BUSINESS HOUR
NORIKO MOMOZAKI (32) FREELANCE ANNOUNCER
NOW, A WOMAN LIKE THE HOST, NORIKO MOMOZAKI, MIGHT BE WORTHY OF ME, BUT...
.........?
FAREWELL, AKECHI.
MAY WE BOTH FIND HAPPINESS ...
GAKU (SLUMP)
......
UHHH...
...DID I JUST GET REJECTED ...?
HEH.
ANOTHER TRAUMA FOR THE BOOKS.
TH-THIS IS SO HUMILIATING ...!
GO
GO
GIRI (CLENCH)
THY GRUDGE ...
...SHALL BE AVENGED!
GO (RUMBLE)
GO
GO
GO

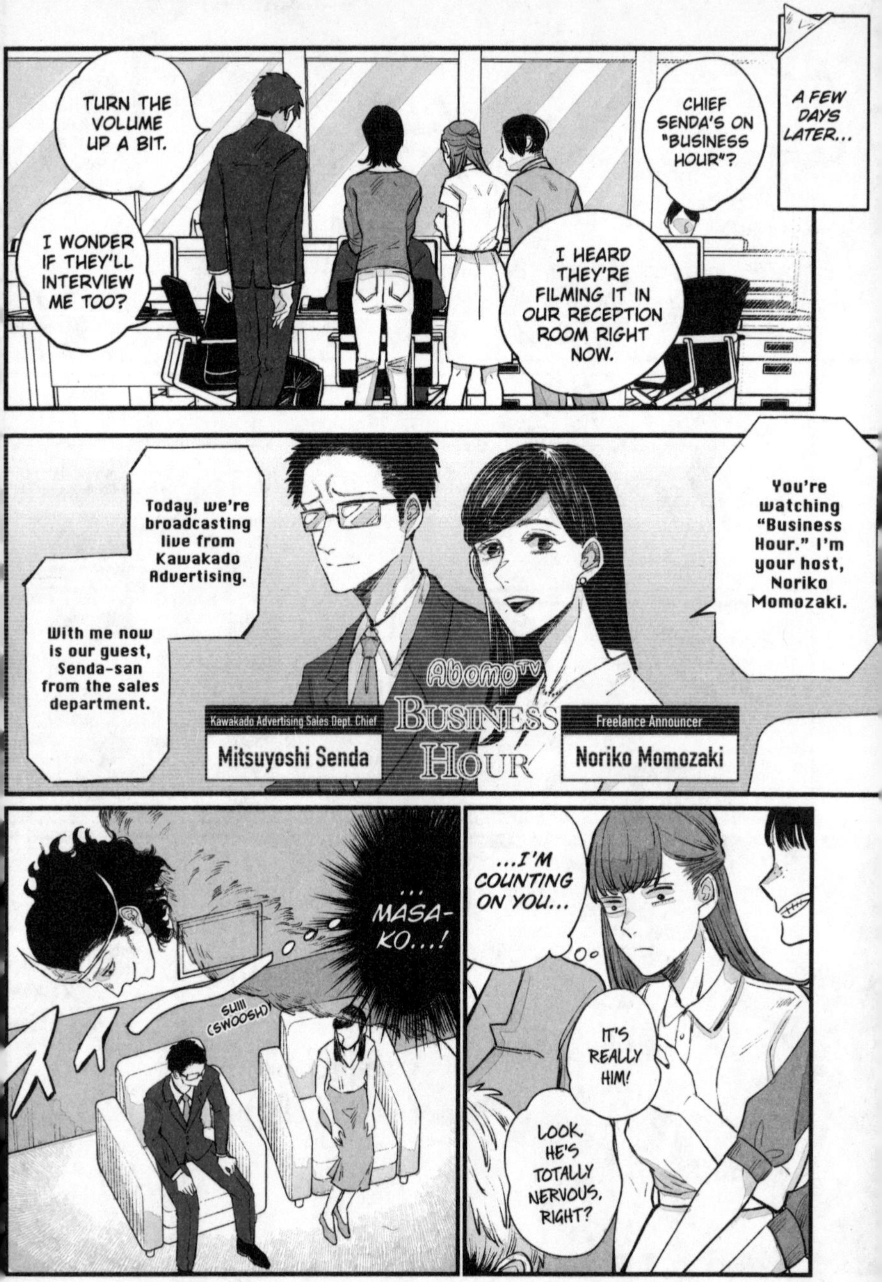
A FEW DAYS LATER...
CHIEF SENDA'S ON "BUSINESS HOUR"?
TURN THE VOLUME UP A BIT.
I HEARD THEY'RE FILMING IT IN OUR RECEPTION ROOM RIGHT NOW.
I WONDER IF THEY'LL INTERVIEW ME TOO?
You're watching "Business Hour." I'm your host, Noriko Momozaki.
Today, we're broadcasting live from Kawakado Advertising.
With me now is our guest, Senda-san from the sales department.
AbomoTV
BUSINESS HOUR
Freelance Announcer
Noriko Momozaki
Kawakado Advertising Sales Dept. Chief
Mitsuyoshi Senda
...I'M COUNTING ON YOU...
IT'S REALLY HIM!
LOOK. HE'S TOTALLY NERVOUS, RIGHT?
...MASA-KO...!
SUIII (SWOOSH)

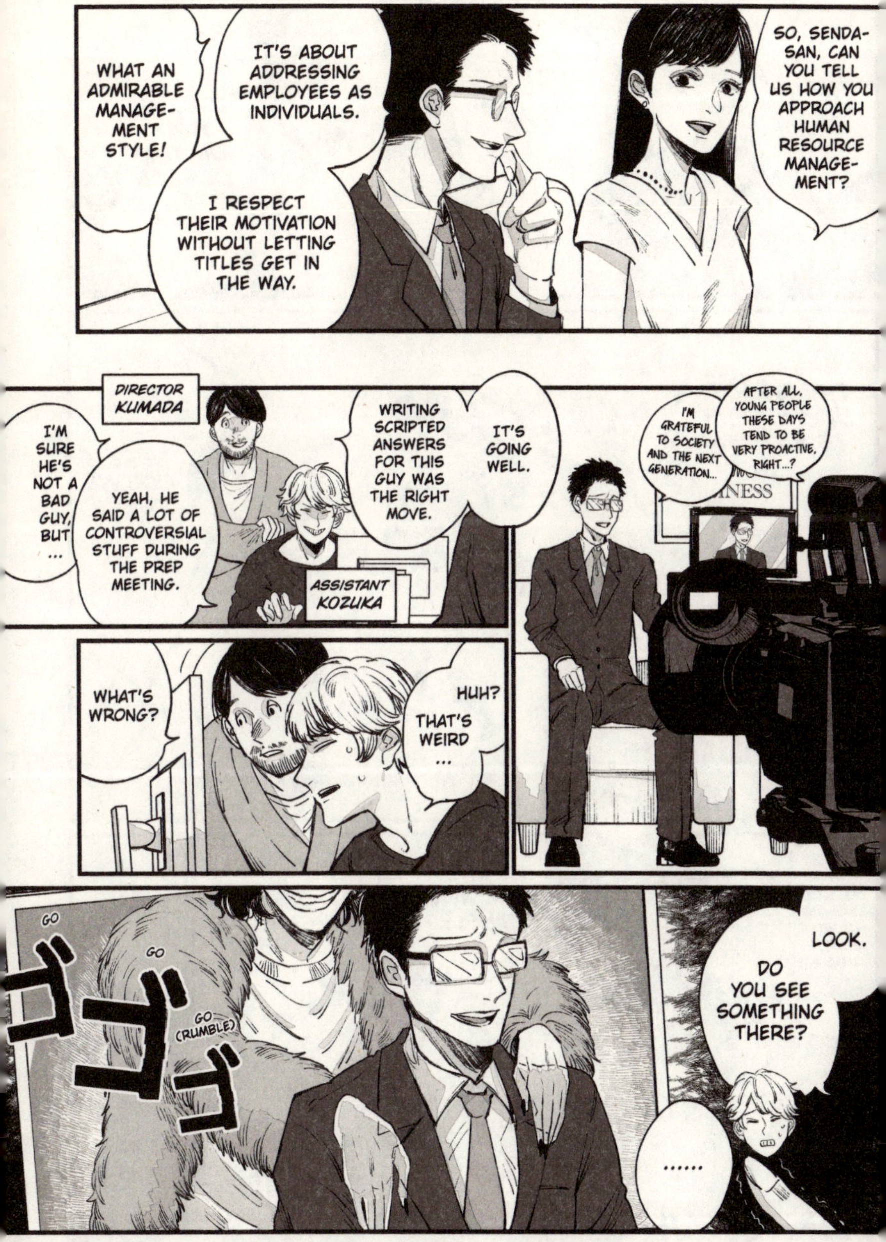
SO, SENDA-SAN, CAN YOU TELL US HOW YOU APPROACH HUMAN RESOURCE MANAGEMENT?
IT'S ABOUT ADDRESSING EMPLOYEES AS INDIVIDUALS.
I RESPECT THEIR MOTIVATION WITHOUT LETTING TITLES GET IN THE WAY.
WHAT AN ADMIRABLE MANAGEMENT STYLE!
AFTER ALL, YOUNG PEOPLE THESE DAYS TEND TO BE VERY PROACTIVE, RIGHT...?
I'M GRATEFUL TO SOCIETY AND THE NEXT GENERATION...
IT'S GOING WELL.
WRITING SCRIPTED ANSWERS FOR THIS GUY WAS THE RIGHT MOVE.
DIRECTOR KUMADA
ASSISTANT KOZUKA
YEAH, HE SAID A LOT OF CONTROVERSIAL STUFF DURING THE PREP MEETING.
I'M SURE HE'S NOT A BAD GUY, BUT...
HUH?
THAT'S WEIRD...
WHAT'S WRONG?
LOOK.
DO YOU SEE SOMETHING THERE?
......
ゴゴゴ
GO GO GO (RUMBLE)

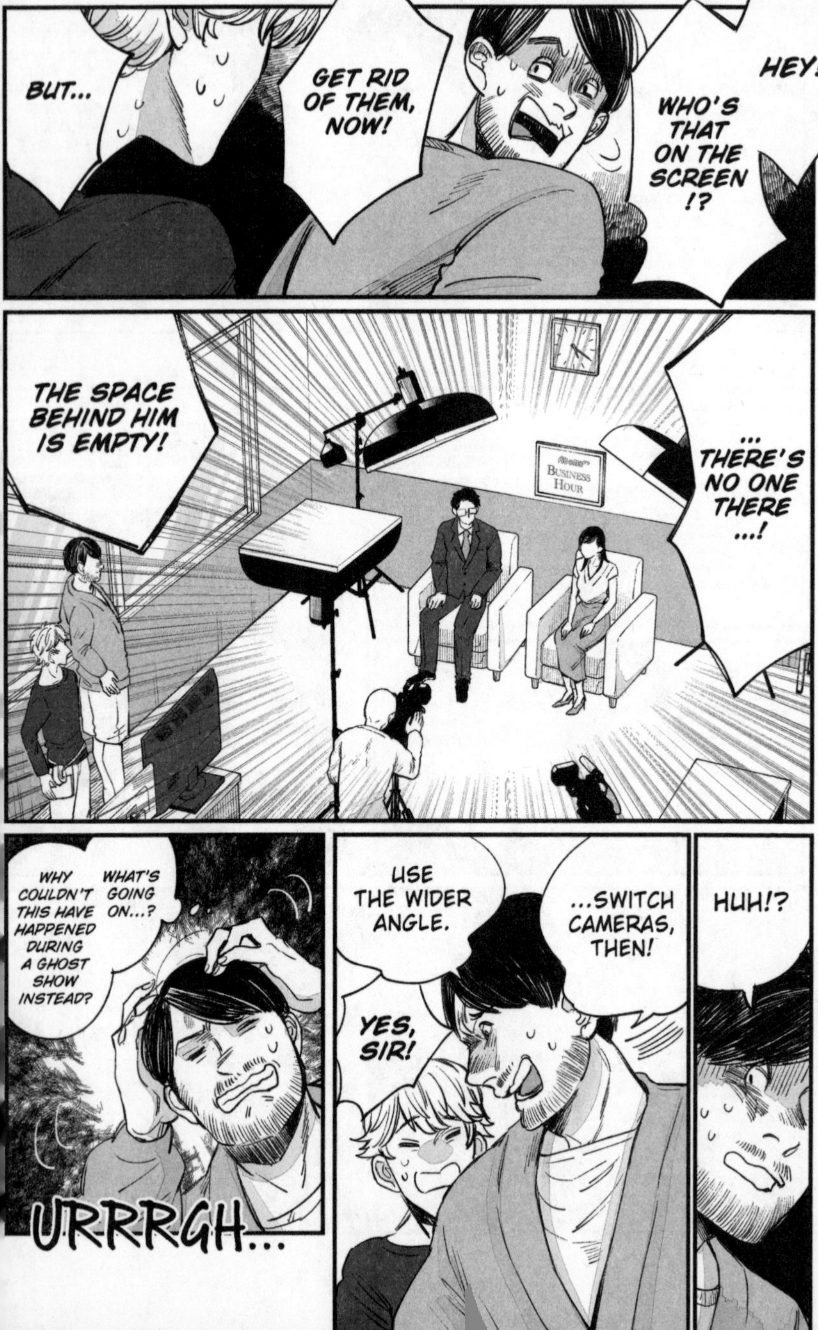
HEY!
WHO'S THAT ON THE SCREEN!?
GET RID OF THEM, NOW!
BUT...
...THERE'S NO ONE THERE...!
BUSINESS HOUR
THE SPACE BEHIND HIM IS EMPTY!
HUH!?
...SWITCH CAMERAS, THEN!
USE THE WIDER ANGLE.
YES, SIR!
WHAT'S GOING ON...?
WHY COULDN'T THIS HAVE HAPPENED DURING A GHOST SHOW INSTEAD?
URRRGH...

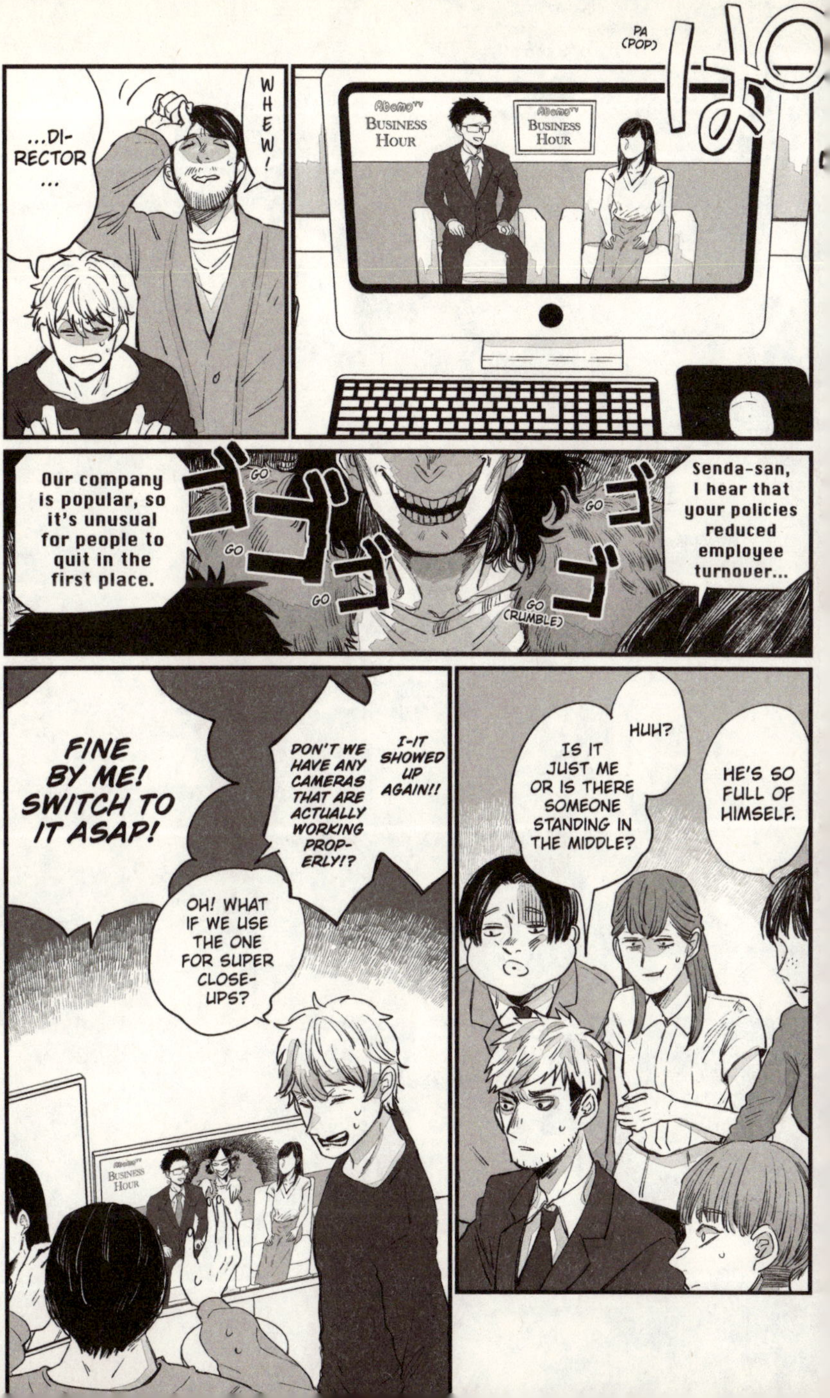
PA
(POP)
WHEW!
...DI-RECTOR ...
Senda-san, I hear that your policies reduced employee turnover...
GO GO GO GO GO
(RUMBLE)
Our company is popular, so it's unusual for people to quit in the first place.
HE'S SO FULL OF HIMSELF.
HUH?
IS IT JUST ME OR IS THERE SOMEONE STANDING IN THE MIDDLE?
I-IT SHOWED UP AGAIN!!
DON'T WE HAVE ANY CAMERAS THAT ARE ACTUALLY WORKING PROP-ERLY!?
FINE BY ME! SWITCH TO IT ASAP!
OH! WHAT IF WE USE THE ONE FOR SUPER CLOSE-UPS?

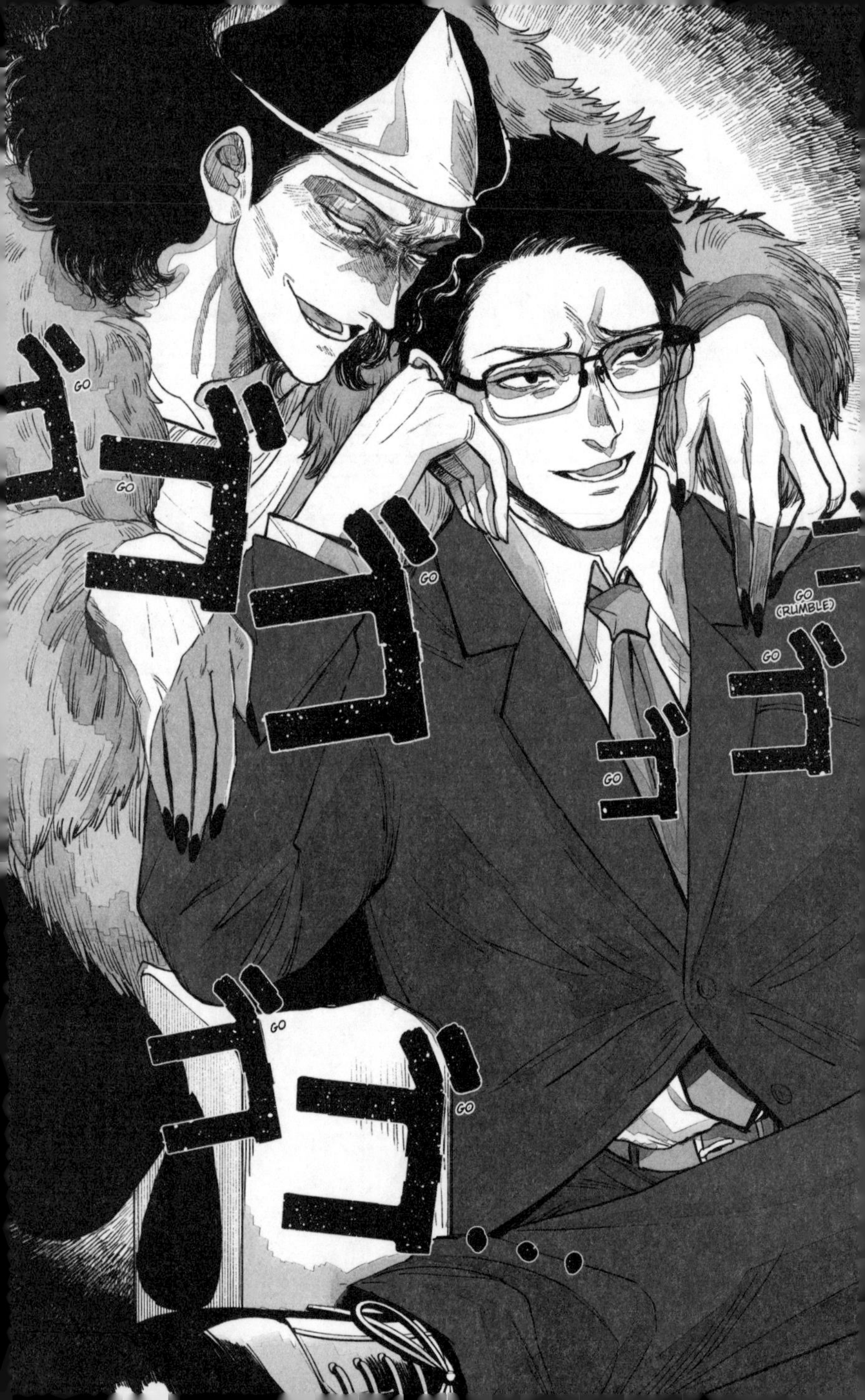
GO (RUMBLE)
GO
GO
GO
GO
GO
GO
GO

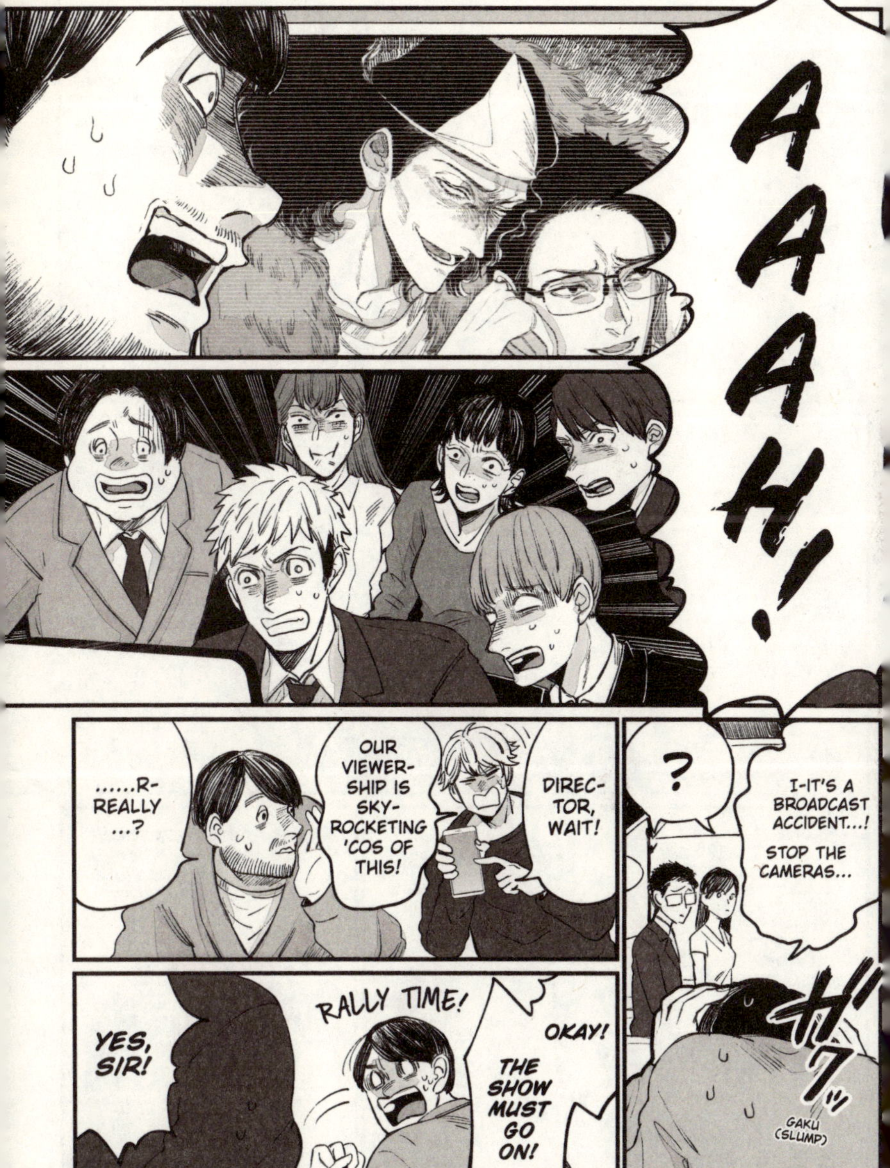
AAAAH!
I-IT'S A BROADCAST ACCIDENT...!
STOP THE CAMERAS...
?
GAKU (SLUMP)
DIREC-TOR, WAIT!
OUR VIEWER-SHIP IS SKY-ROCKETING 'COS OF THIS!
......R-REALLY ...?
OKAY!
THE SHOW MUST GO ON!
RALLY TIME!
YES, SIR!

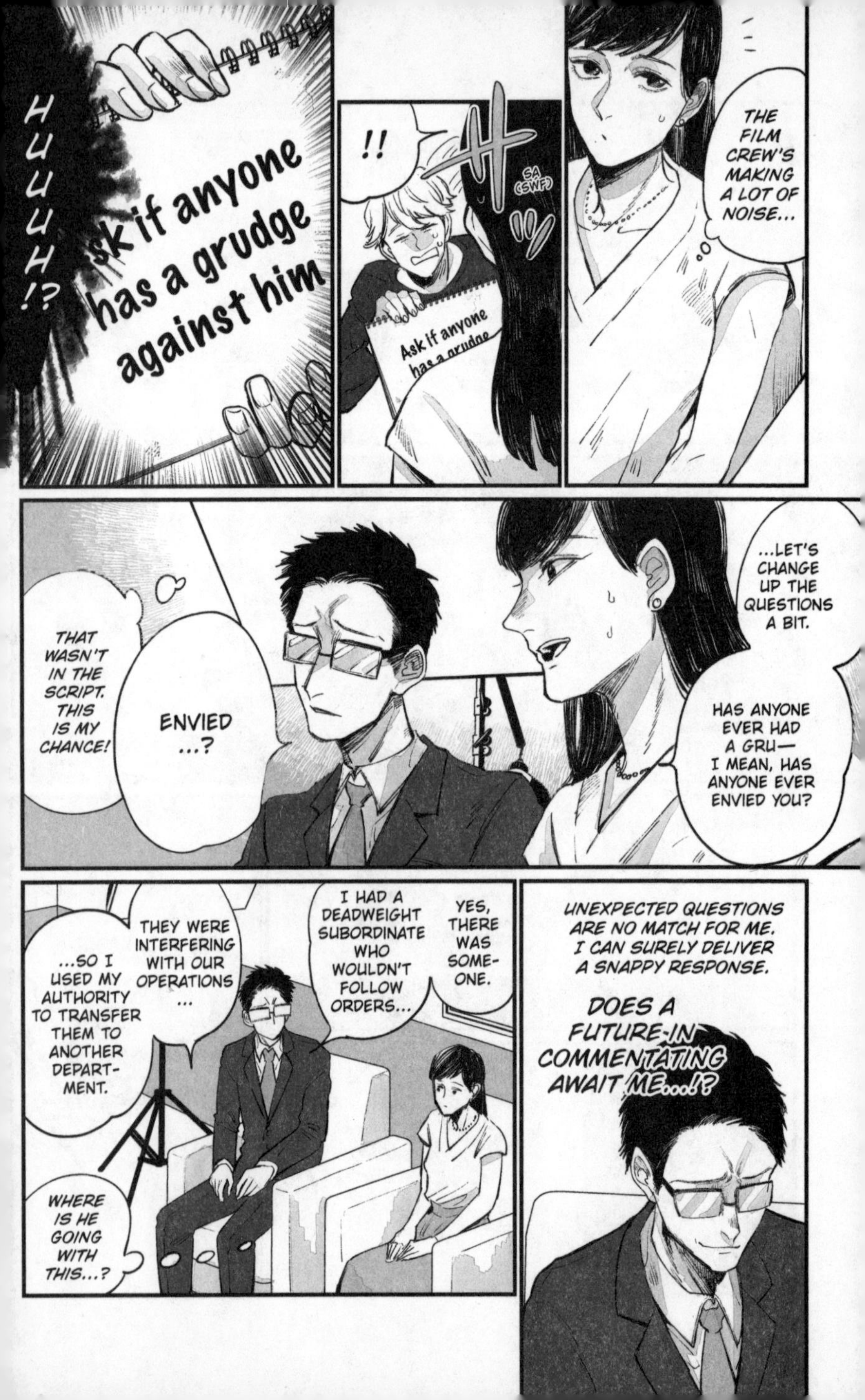
THE FILM CREW'S MAKING A LOT OF NOISE...
!!
SA (SWF)
Ask if anyone has a grudge
HUUUUH!?
sk if anyone has a grudge against him
...LET'S CHANGE UP THE QUESTIONS A BIT.
HAS ANYONE EVER HAD A GRU— I MEAN, HAS ANYONE EVER ENVIED YOU?
ENVIED ...?
THAT WASN'T IN THE SCRIPT. THIS IS MY CHANCE!
UNEXPECTED QUESTIONS ARE NO MATCH FOR ME. I CAN SURELY DELIVER A SNAPPY RESPONSE.
DOES A FUTURE IN COMMENTATING AWAIT ME...!?
YES, THERE WAS SOME-ONE.
I HAD A DEADWEIGHT SUBORDINATE WHO WOULDN'T FOLLOW ORDERS...
THEY WERE INTERFERING WITH OUR OPERATIONS...
...SO I USED MY AUTHORITY TO TRANSFER THEM TO ANOTHER DEPART-MENT.
WHERE IS HE GOING WITH THIS...?

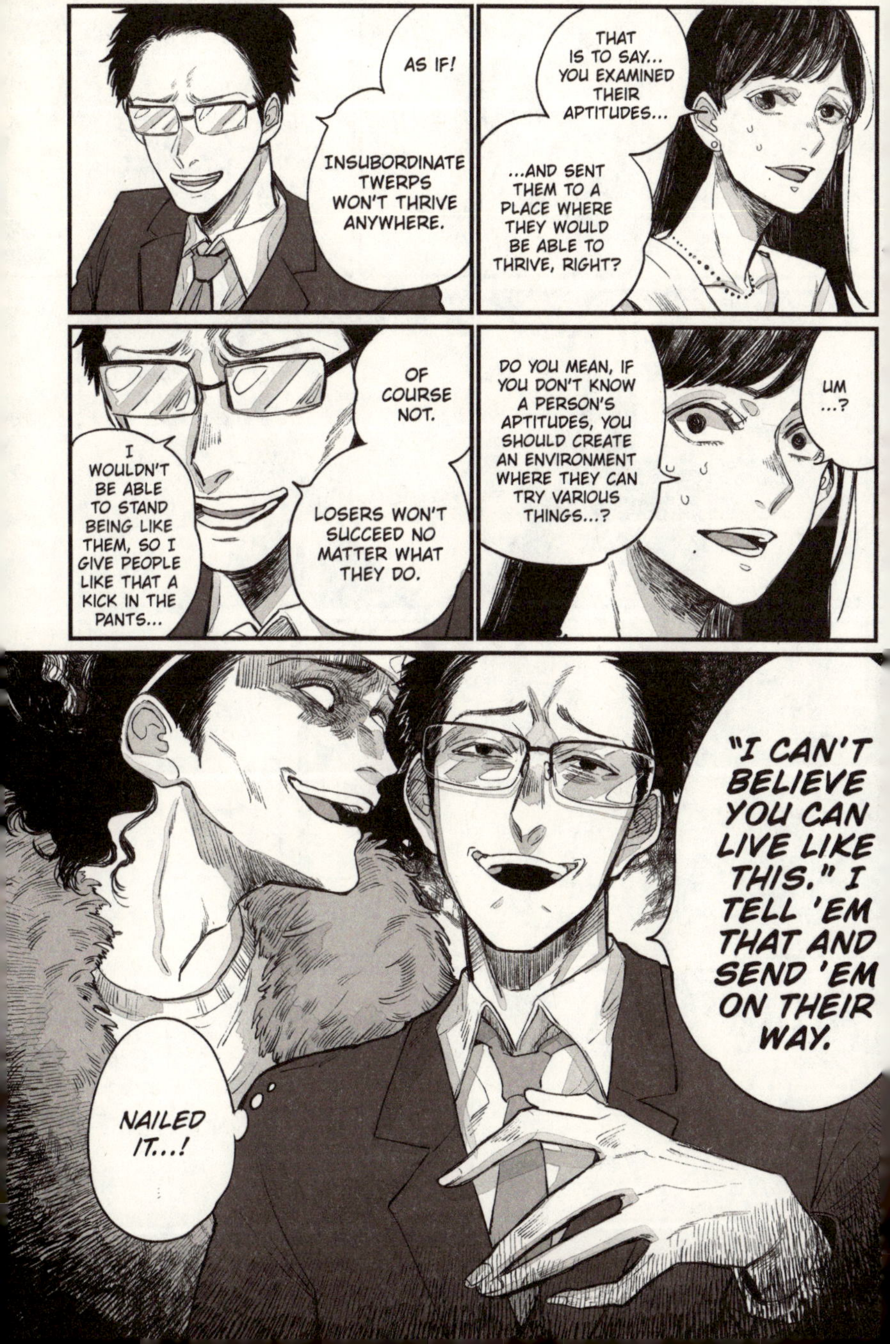
THAT IS TO SAY... YOU EXAMINED THEIR APTITUDES...
...AND SENT THEM TO A PLACE WHERE THEY WOULD BE ABLE TO THRIVE, RIGHT?
AS IF!
INSUBORDINATE TWERPS WON'T THRIVE ANYWHERE.
UM ...?
DO YOU MEAN, IF YOU DON'T KNOW A PERSON'S APTITUDES, YOU SHOULD CREATE AN ENVIRONMENT WHERE THEY CAN TRY VARIOUS THINGS...?
OF COURSE NOT.
LOSERS WON'T SUCCEED NO MATTER WHAT THEY DO.
I WOULDN'T BE ABLE TO STAND BEING LIKE THEM, SO I GIVE PEOPLE LIKE THAT A KICK IN THE PANTS...
"I CAN'T BELIEVE YOU CAN LIVE LIKE THIS." I TELL 'EM THAT AND SEND 'EM ON THEIR WAY.
NAILED IT...!

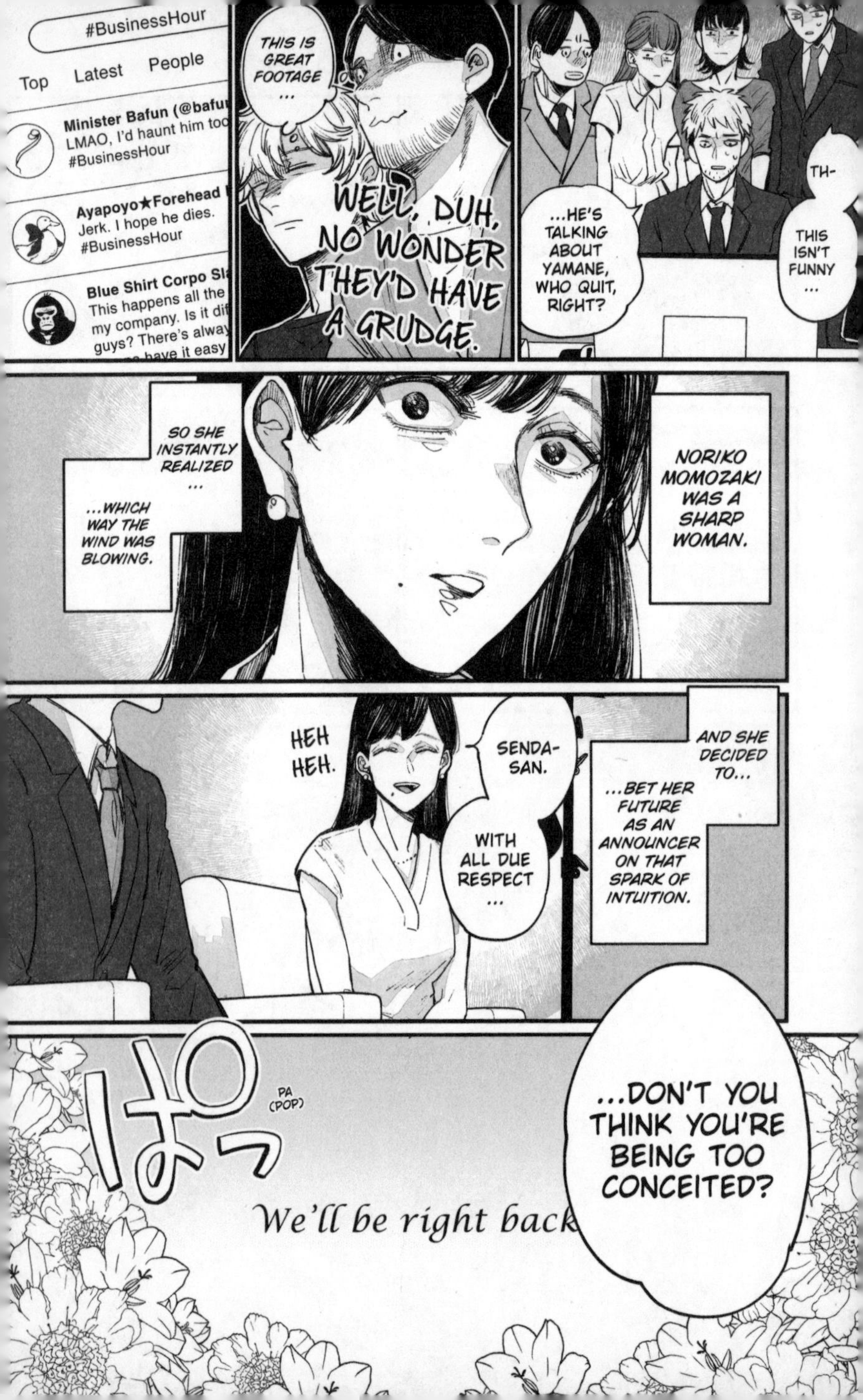
TH-
THIS ISN'T FUNNY...
...HE'S TALKING ABOUT YAMANE, WHO QUIT, RIGHT?
THIS IS GREAT FOOTAGE...
WELL, DUH, NO WONDER THEY'D HAVE A GRUDGE.
#BusinessHour
Top Latest People
Minister Bafun (@bafu
LMAO, I'd haunt him too
#BusinessHour
Ayapoyo★Forehead
Jerk. I hope he dies.
#BusinessHour
Blue Shirt Corpo Sl
This happens all the
my company. Is it dif
guys? There's alway
NORIKO MOMOZAKI WAS A SHARP WOMAN.
SO SHE INSTANTLY REALIZED...
...WHICH WAY THE WIND WAS BLOWING.
AND SHE DECIDED TO...
...BET HER FUTURE AS AN ANNOUNCER ON THAT SPARK OF INTUITION.
SENDA-SAN.
WITH ALL DUE RESPECT...
HEH HEH.
...DON'T YOU THINK YOU'RE BEING TOO CONCEITED?
ぱっ
PA (POP)
We'll be right back

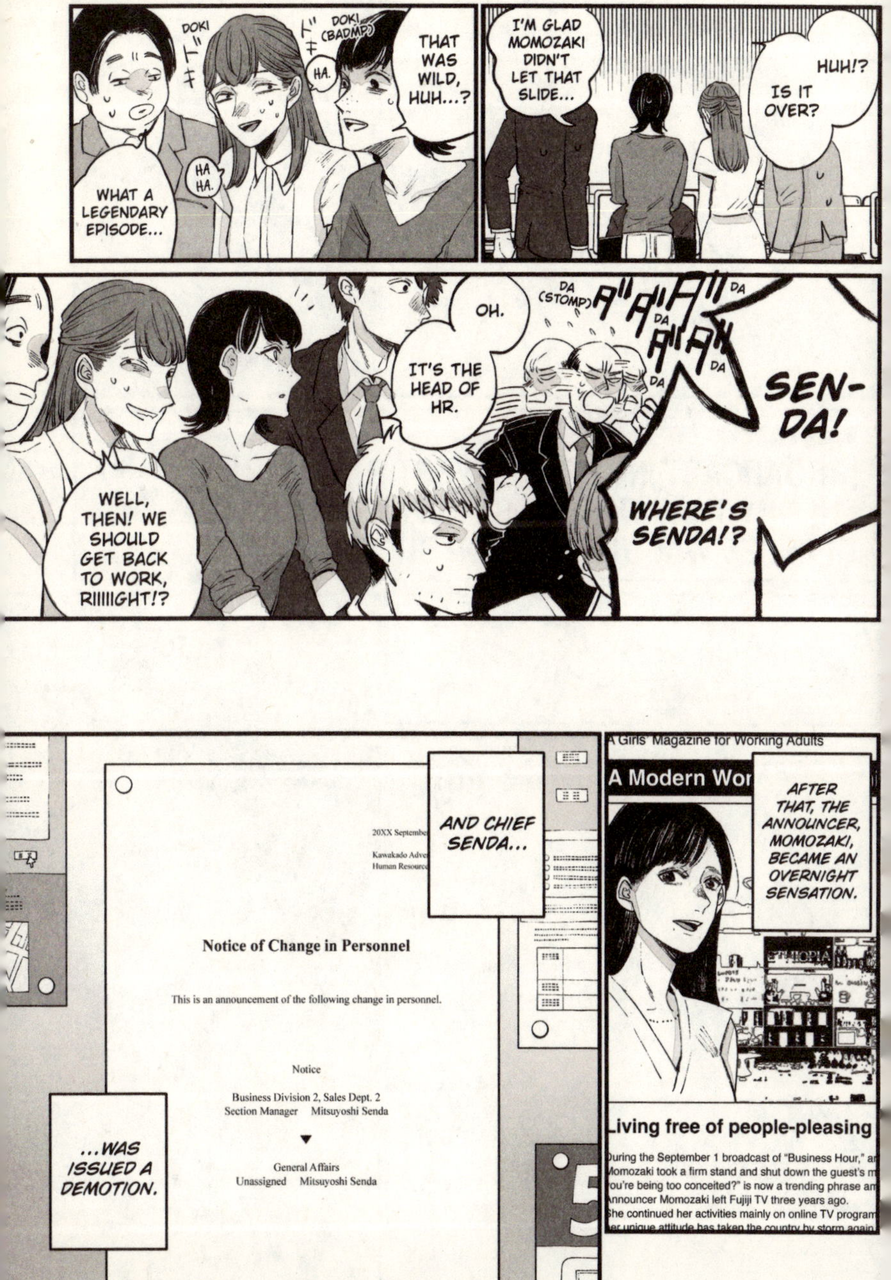
HUH!? IS IT OVER?
I'M GLAD MOMOZAKI DIDN'T LET THAT SLIDE...
DOKI (BADMP)
DOKI
THAT WAS WILD, HUH...?
HA.
HA HA.
WHAT A LEGENDARY EPISODE...
SEN-DA!
WHERE'S SENDA!?
DA
DA (STOMP)
DA
DA
DA
OH.
IT'S THE HEAD OF HR.
WELL, THEN! WE SHOULD GET BACK TO WORK, RIIIIGHT!?
A Girls' Magazine for Working Adults
A Modern Wor
AFTER THAT, THE ANNOUNCER, MOMOZAKI, BECAME AN OVERNIGHT SENSATION.
Living free of people-pleasing
During the September 1 broadcast of "Business Hour," a
Momozaki took a firm stand and shut down the guest's m
You're being too conceited?" is now a trending phrase an
Announcer Momozaki left Fujiji TV three years ago.
She continued her activities mainly on online TV program
AND CHIEF SENDA...
20XX September
Kawakado Adver
Human Resource
Notice of Change in Personnel
This is an announcement of the following change in personnel.
Notice
Business Division 2, Sales Dept. 2
Section Manager Mitsuyoshi Senda
General Affairs
Unassigned Mitsuyoshi Senda
...WAS ISSUED A DEMOTION.

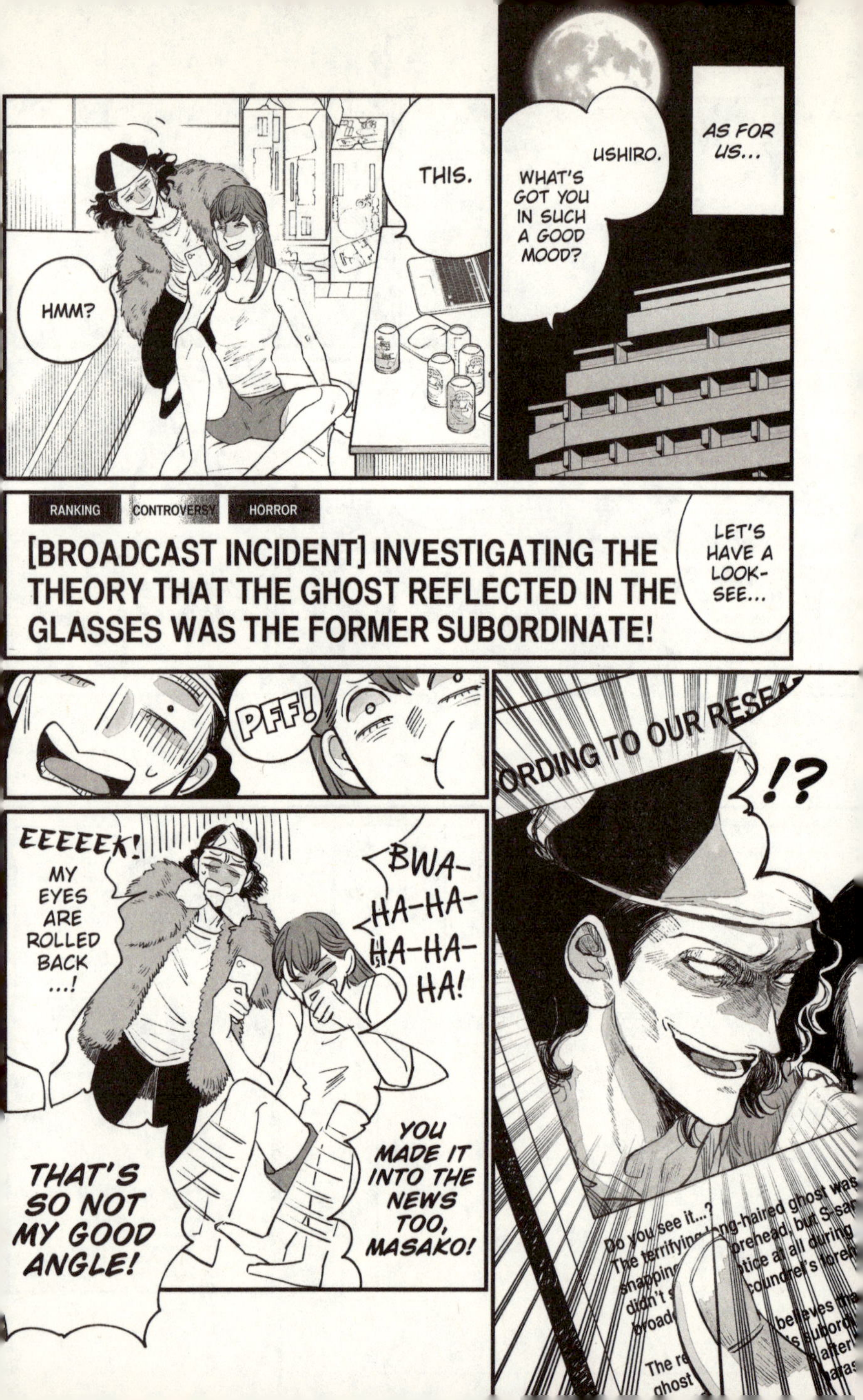
AS FOR US...
USHIRO.
WHAT'S GOT YOU IN SUCH A GOOD MOOD?
THIS.
HMM?
LET'S HAVE A LOOK-SEE...
RANKING
CONTROVERSY
HORROR
[BROADCAST INCIDENT] INVESTIGATING THE THEORY THAT THE GHOST REFLECTED IN THE GLASSES WAS THE FORMER SUBORDINATE!
!?
ORDING TO OUR RESE
Do you see it...?
PFF!
EEEEEK!
MY EYES ARE ROLLED BACK ...!
BWA-HA-HA-HA-HA-HA!
YOU MADE IT INTO THE NEWS TOO, MASAKO!
THAT'S SO NOT MY GOOD ANGLE!

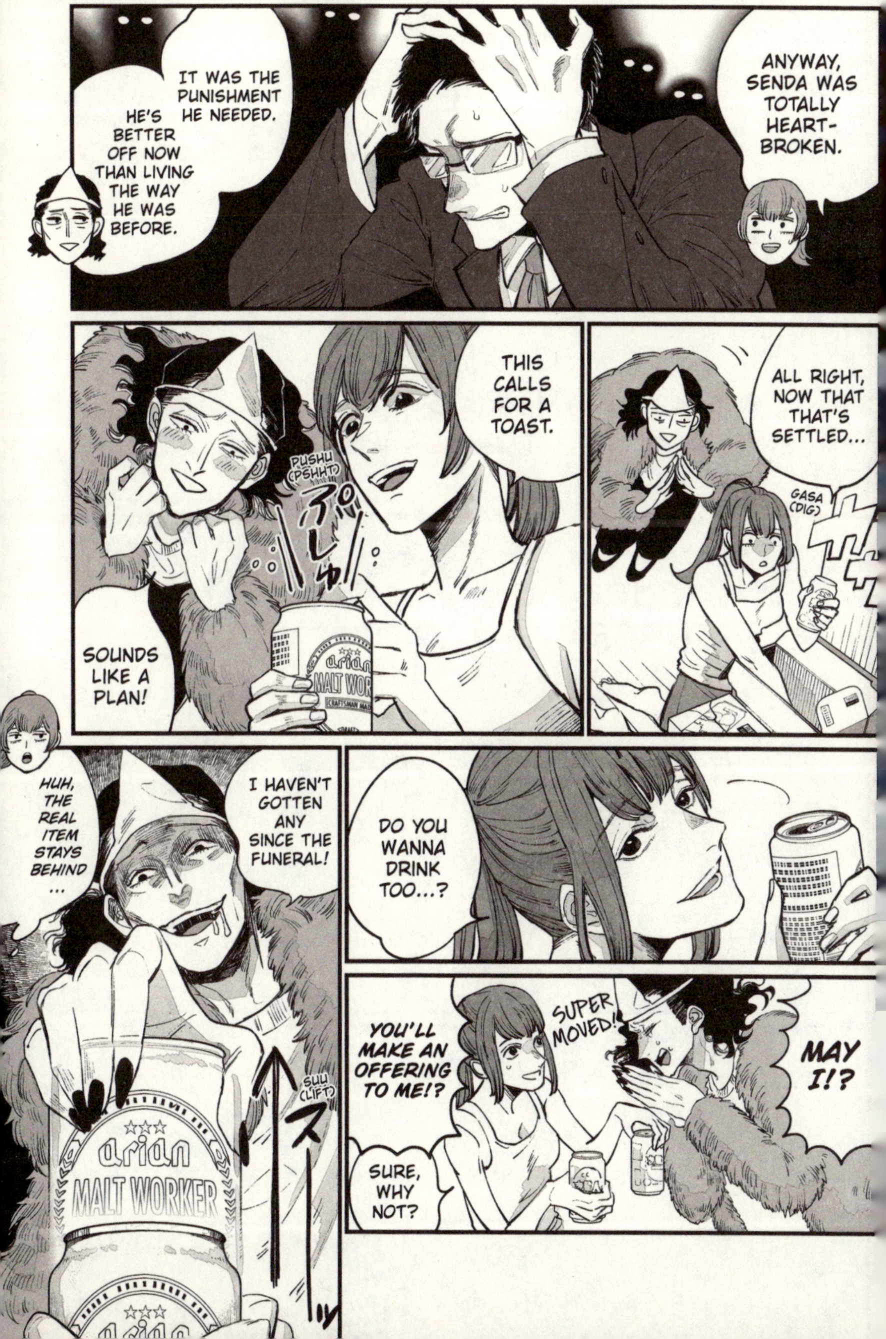
ANYWAY, SENDA WAS TOTALLY HEART-BROKEN.
IT WAS THE PUNISHMENT HE NEEDED.
HE'S BETTER OFF NOW THAN LIVING THE WAY HE WAS BEFORE.
ALL RIGHT, NOW THAT THAT'S SETTLED...
GASA (DIG)
THIS CALLS FOR A TOAST.
PUSHU (PSHHT)
SOUNDS LIKE A PLAN!
DO YOU WANNA DRINK TOO...?
MAY I!?
SUPER MOVED!
YOU'LL MAKE AN OFFERING TO ME!?
SURE, WHY NOT?
I HAVEN'T GOTTEN ANY SINCE THE FUNERAL!
HUH, THE REAL ITEM STAYS BEHIND...
SUU (LIFT)
arian
MALT WORKER

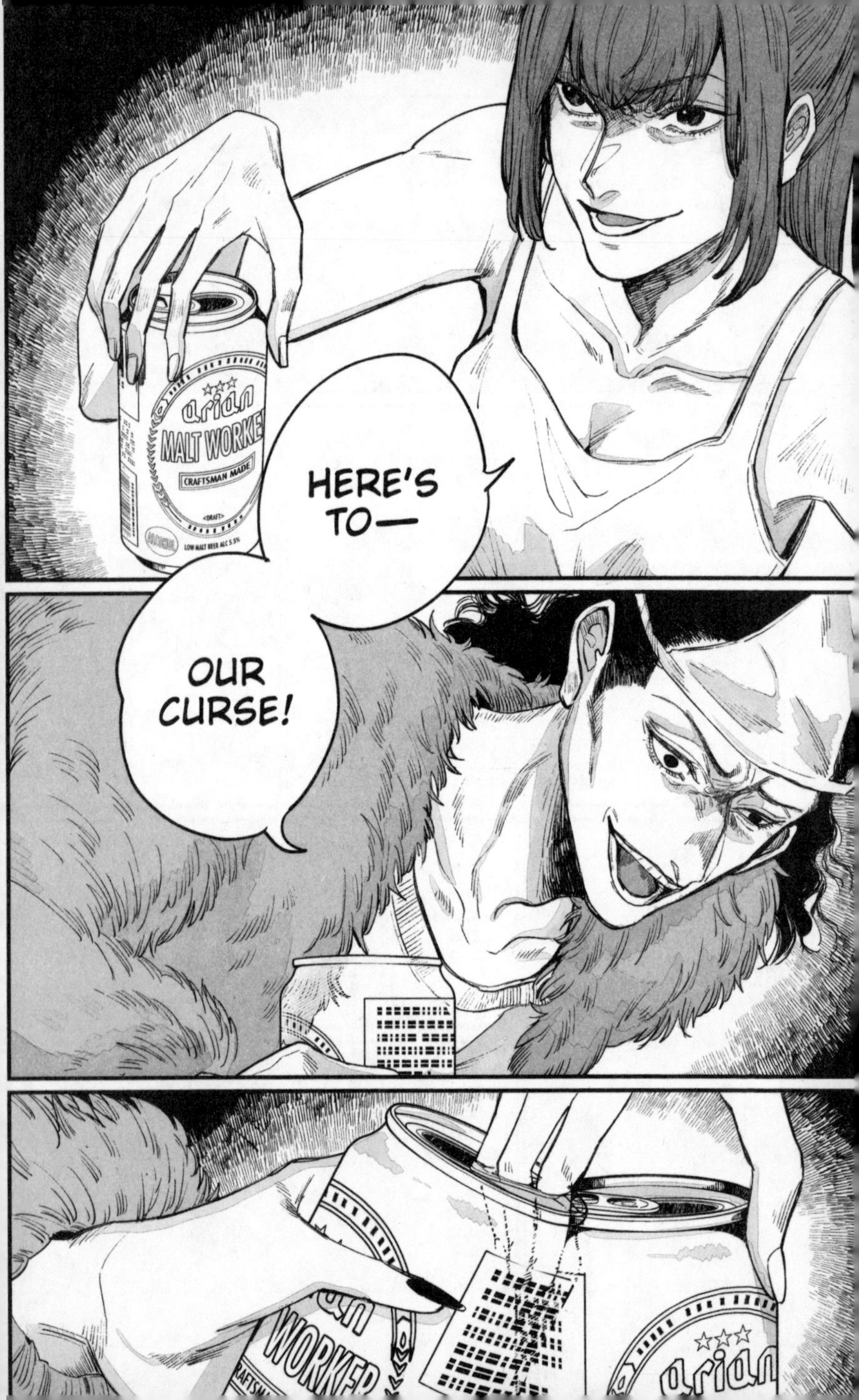
HERE'S TO—
OUR CURSE!
arian
CRAFTSMAN MADE

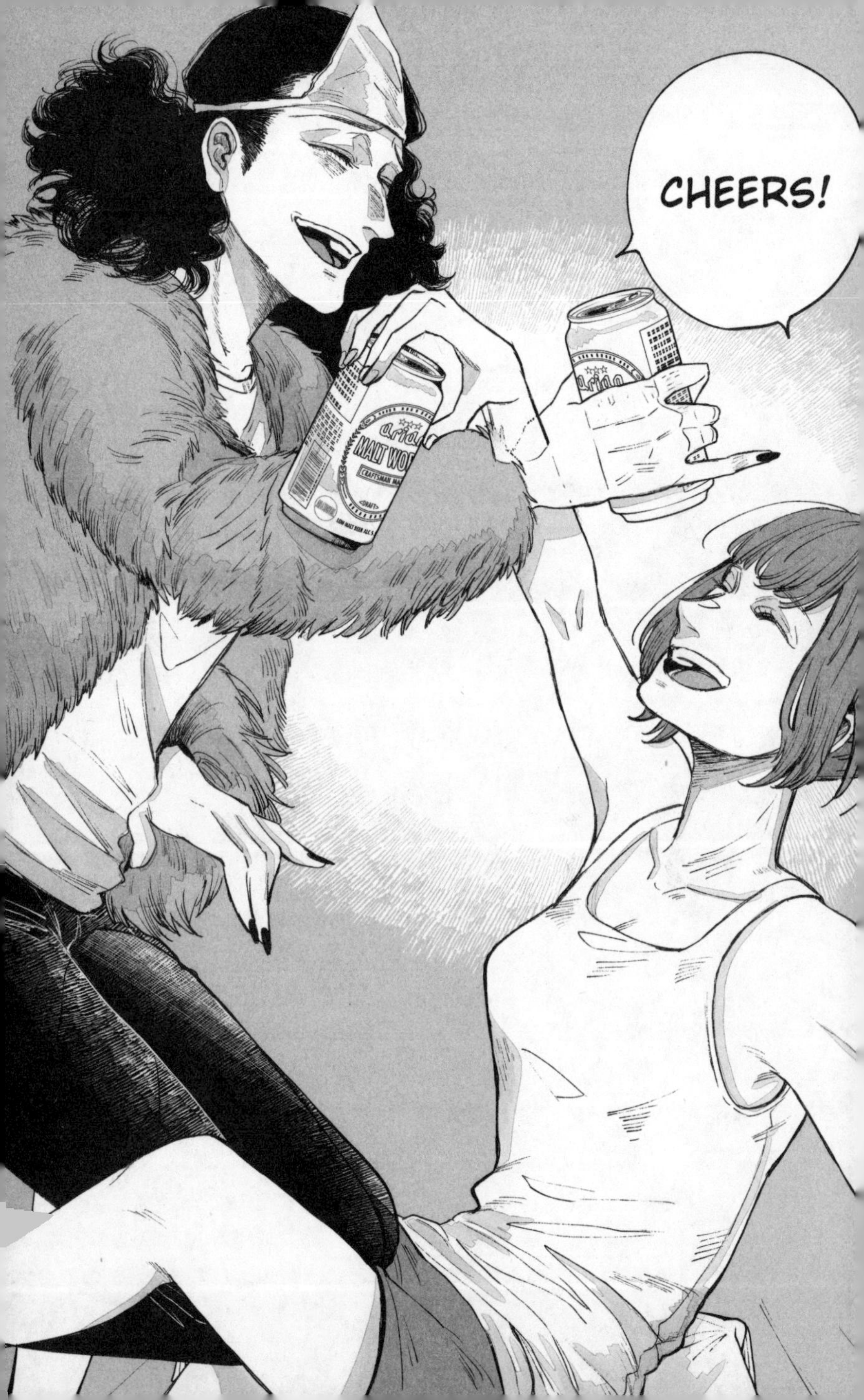
CHEERS!

GOGOGOGO-GO-GHOST!

Chapter 4: Hardcore Neighbor

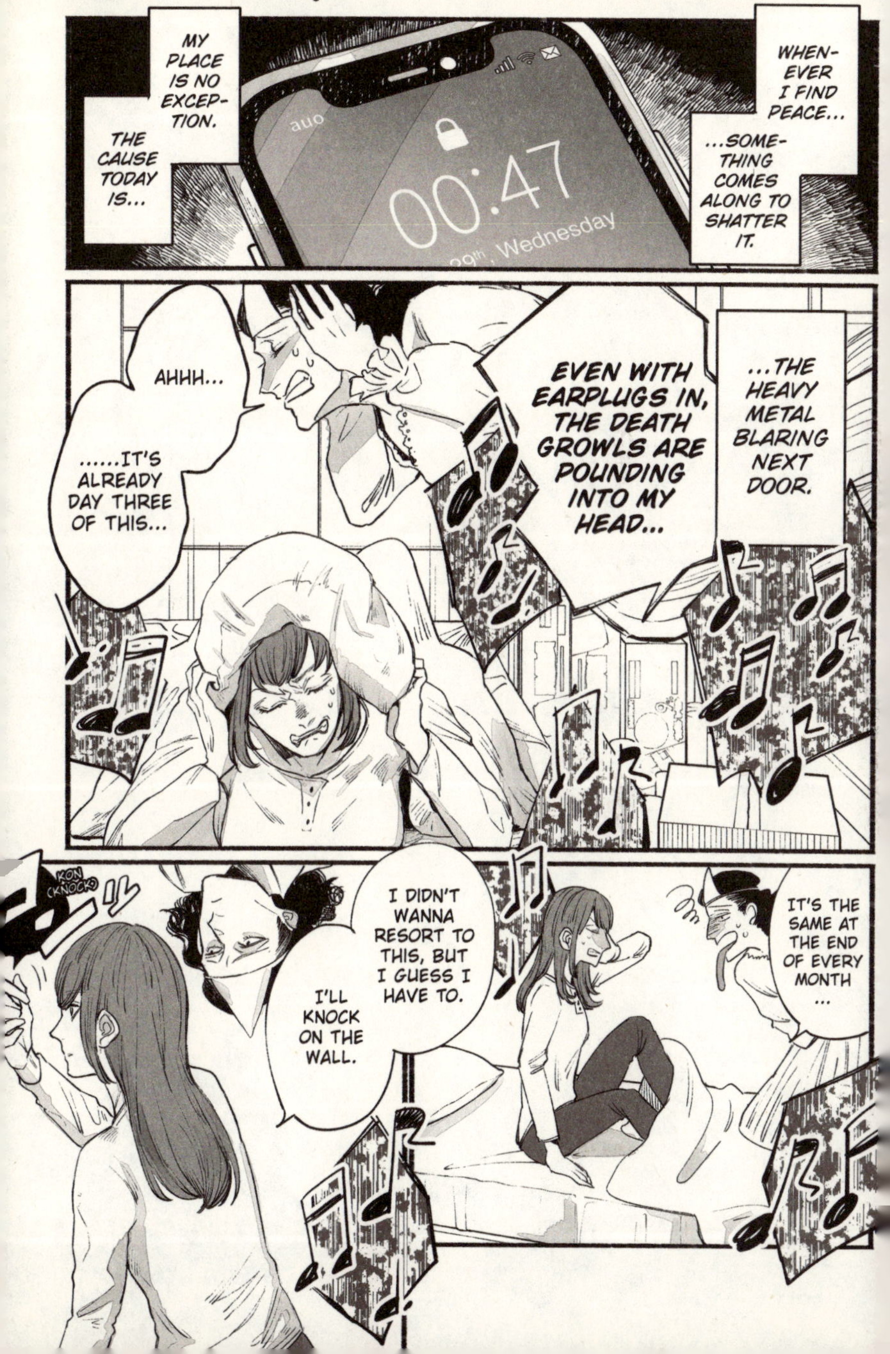
WHENEVER I FIND PEACE...
...SOMETHING COMES ALONG TO SHATTER IT.
MY PLACE IS NO EXCEPTION.
THE CAUSE TODAY IS...
00:47
Wednesday
...THE HEAVY METAL BLARING NEXT DOOR.
EVEN WITH EARPLUGS IN, THE DEATH GROWLS ARE POUNDING INTO MY HEAD...
AHHH...
......IT'S ALREADY DAY THREE OF THIS...
IT'S THE SAME AT THE END OF EVERY MONTH ...
I DIDN'T WANNA RESORT TO THIS, BUT I GUESS I HAVE TO.
I'LL KNOCK ON THE WALL.
KON (KNOCK)

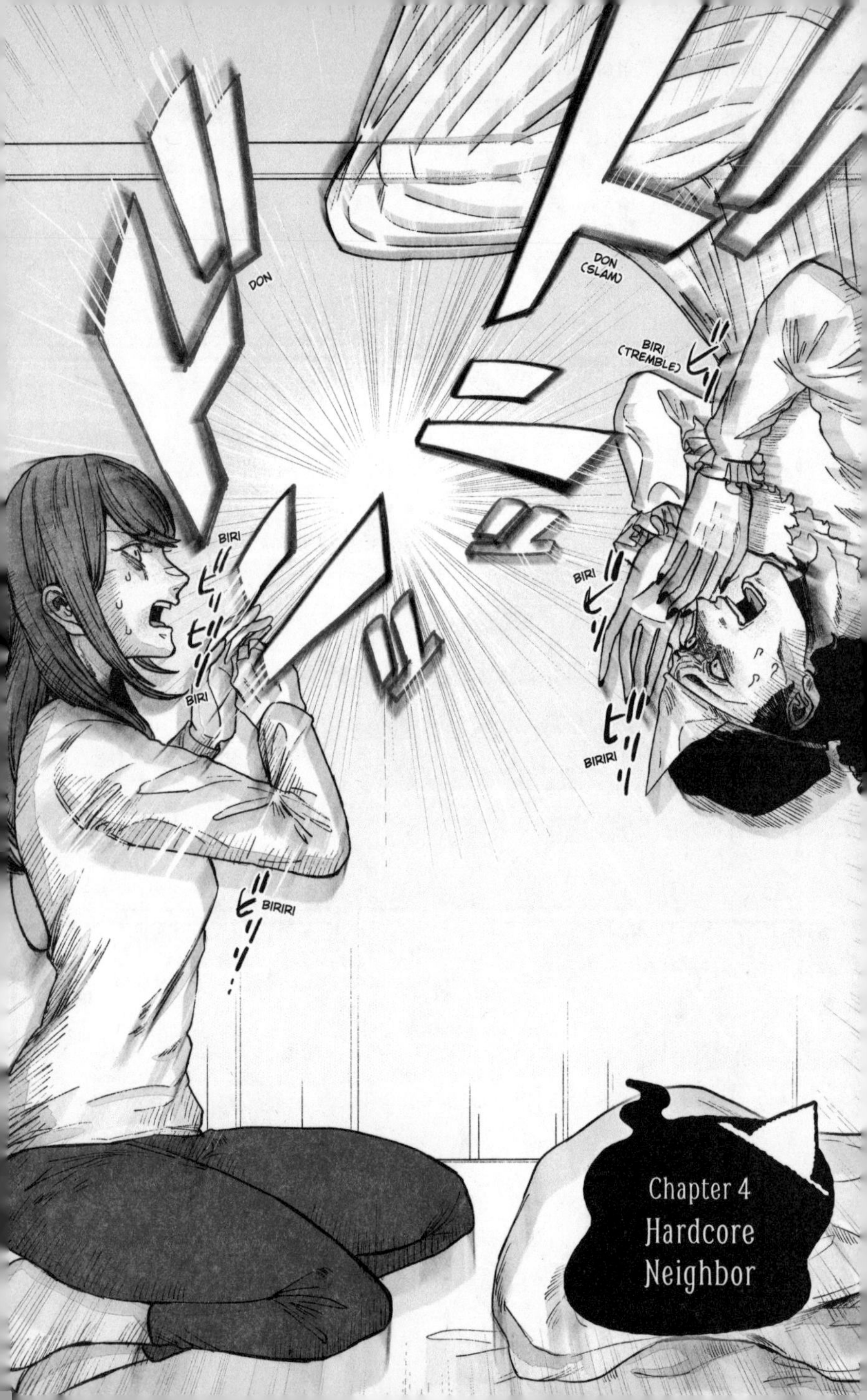
DON (SLAM)
BIRI (TREMBLE)
BIRI
BIRIRI
DON
BIRI
BIRI
BIRIRI
Chapter 4
Hardcore Neighbor

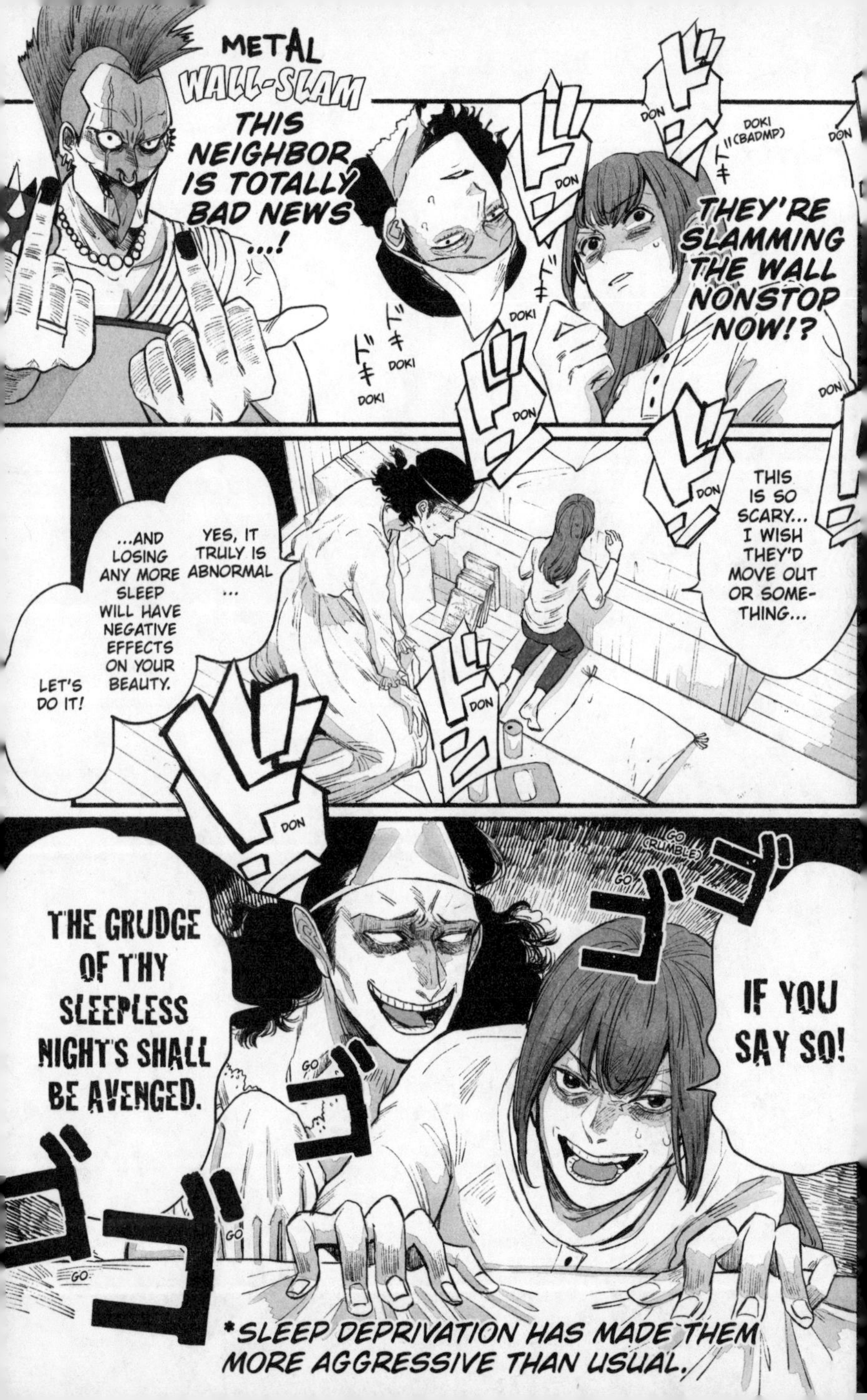
DON
DOKI (BADMP)
DON
THEY'RE SLAMMING THE WALL NONSTOP NOW!?
DON
DOKI
DOKI
DOKI
METAL WALL-SLAM
THIS NEIGHBOR IS TOTALLY BAD NEWS...!
DON
DON
THIS IS SO SCARY... I WISH THEY'D MOVE OUT OR SOME-THING...
DON
YES, IT TRULY IS ABNORMAL...
...AND LOSING ANY MORE SLEEP WILL HAVE NEGATIVE EFFECTS ON YOUR BEAUTY.
LET'S DO IT!
DON
GO (RUMBLE)
GO
IF YOU SAY SO!
THE GRUDGE OF THY SLEEPLESS NIGHT'S SHALL BE AVENGED.
GO
GO
GO
*SLEEP DEPRIVATION HAS MADE THEM MORE AGGRESSIVE THAN USUAL.

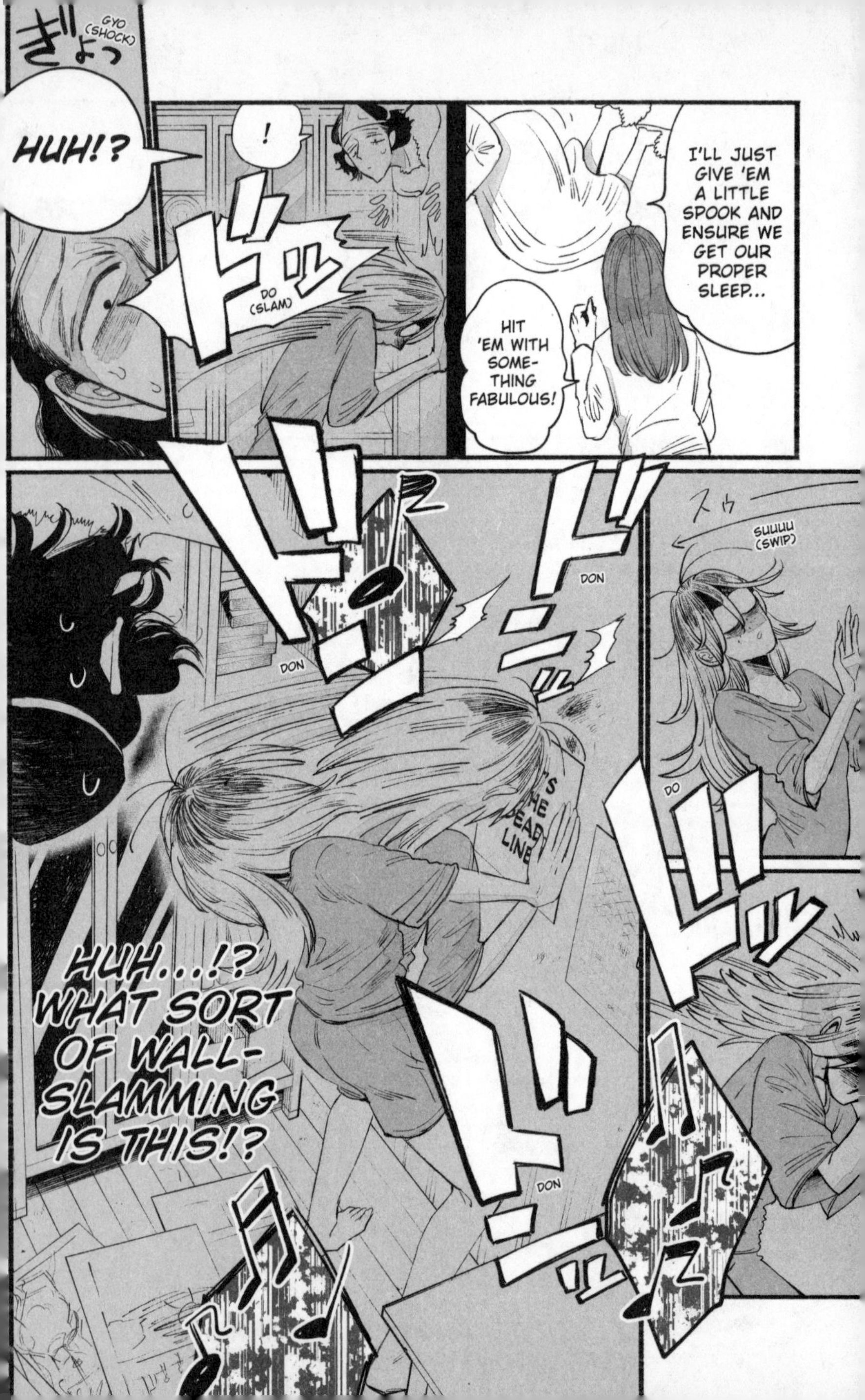
I'LL JUST GIVE 'EM A LITTLE SPOOK AND ENSURE WE GET OUR PROPER SLEEP...
HIT 'EM WITH SOME-THING FABULOUS!
!
DO (SLAM)
ぎょっ
GYO (SHOCK)
HUH!?
スゥ
SUUUU (SWIP)
DO
DON
DON
DON
HUH...!? WHAT SORT OF WALL-SLAMMING IS THIS!?

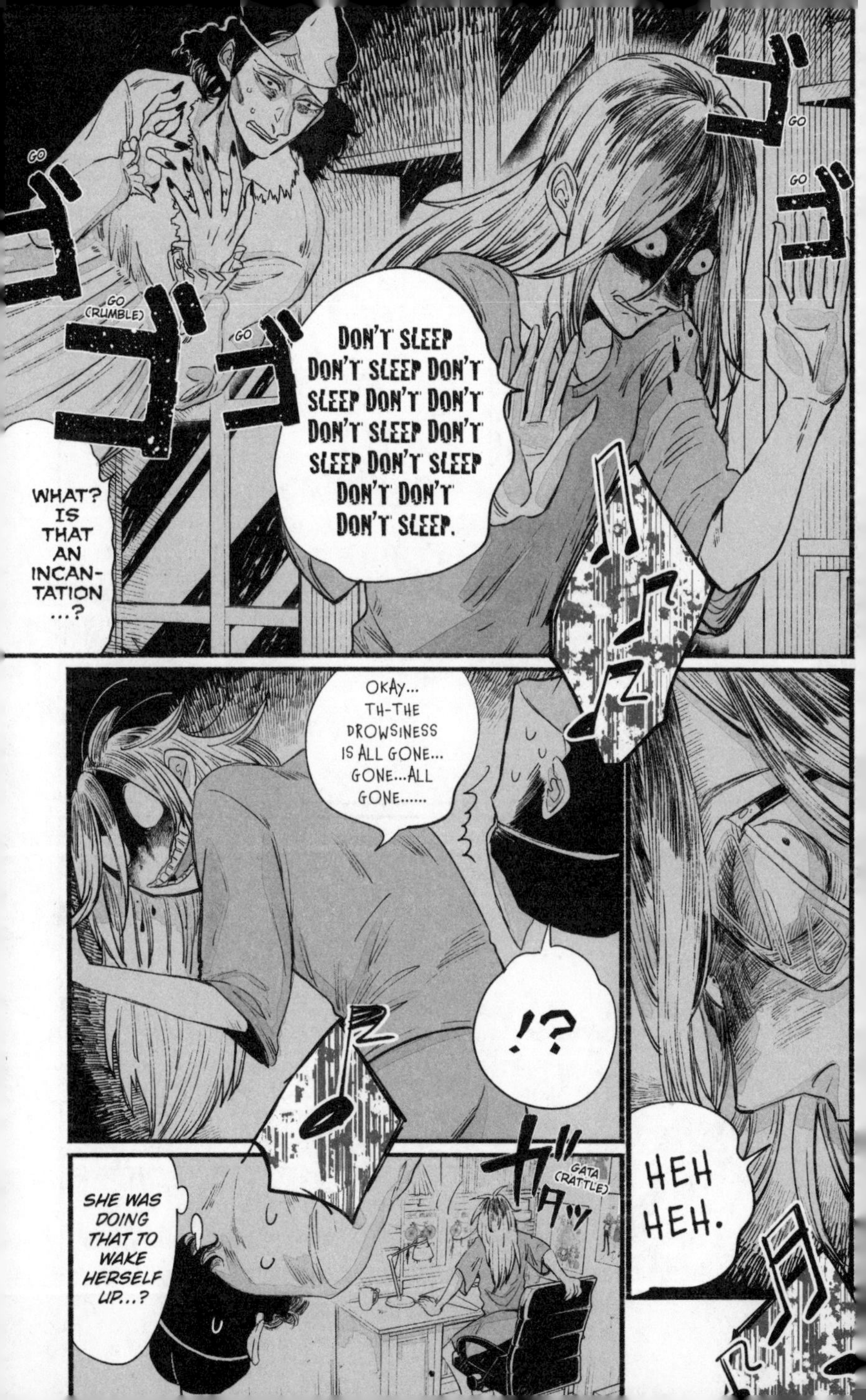
GO
GO
DON'T SLEEP DON'T SLEEP DON'T SLEEP DON'T DON'T DON'T SLEEP DON'T SLEEP DON'T SLEEP DON'T DON'T DON'T SLEEP.
GO (RUMBLE)
GO
GO
WHAT? IS THAT AN INCANTATION...?
HEH HEH.
OKAY... TH-THE DROWSINESS IS ALL GONE... GONE...ALL GONE......
!?
GATA (RATTLE)
SHE WAS DOING THAT TO WAKE HERSELF UP...?

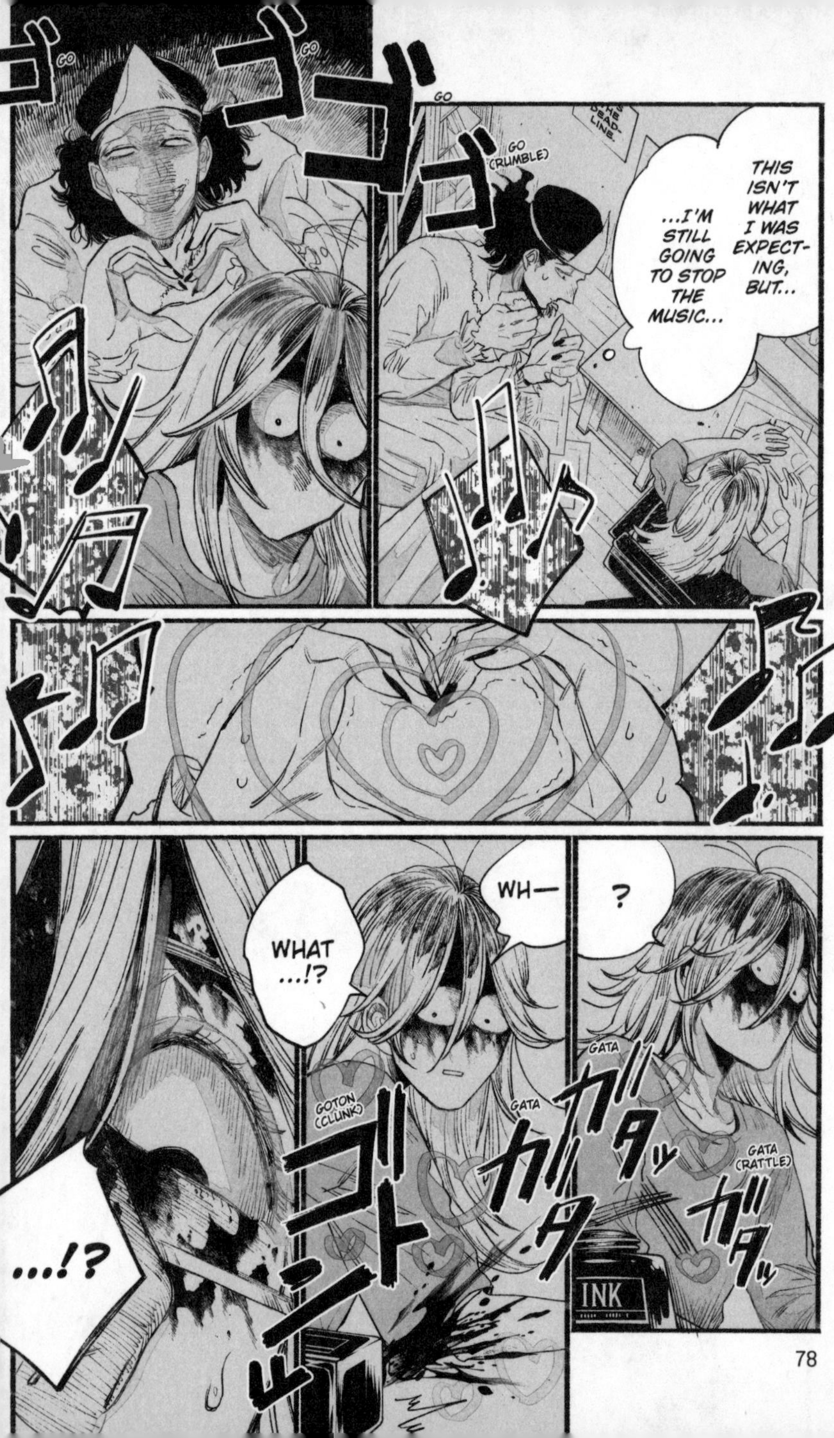
GO
GO (RUMBLE)
THE DEAD-LINE.
THIS ISN'T WHAT I WAS EXPECT-ING, BUT...
...I'M STILL GOING TO STOP THE MUSIC...
GO
GO
?
GATA
GATA (RATTLE)
INK
WH—
WHAT ...!?
GOTON (CLUNK)
GATA
...!?

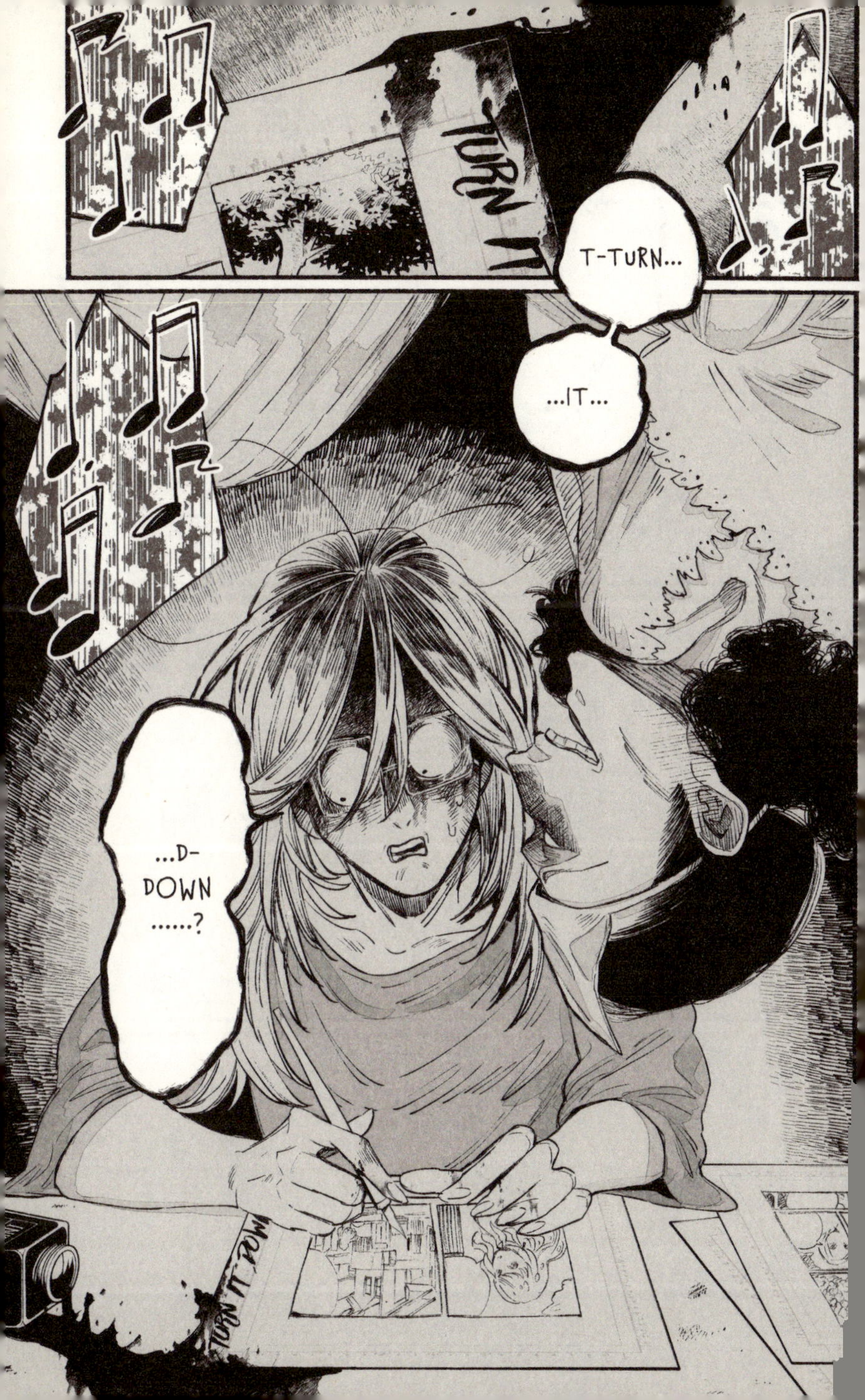
TURN IT
T-TURN...
...IT...
...D-
DOWN
......?
TURN IT DOWN

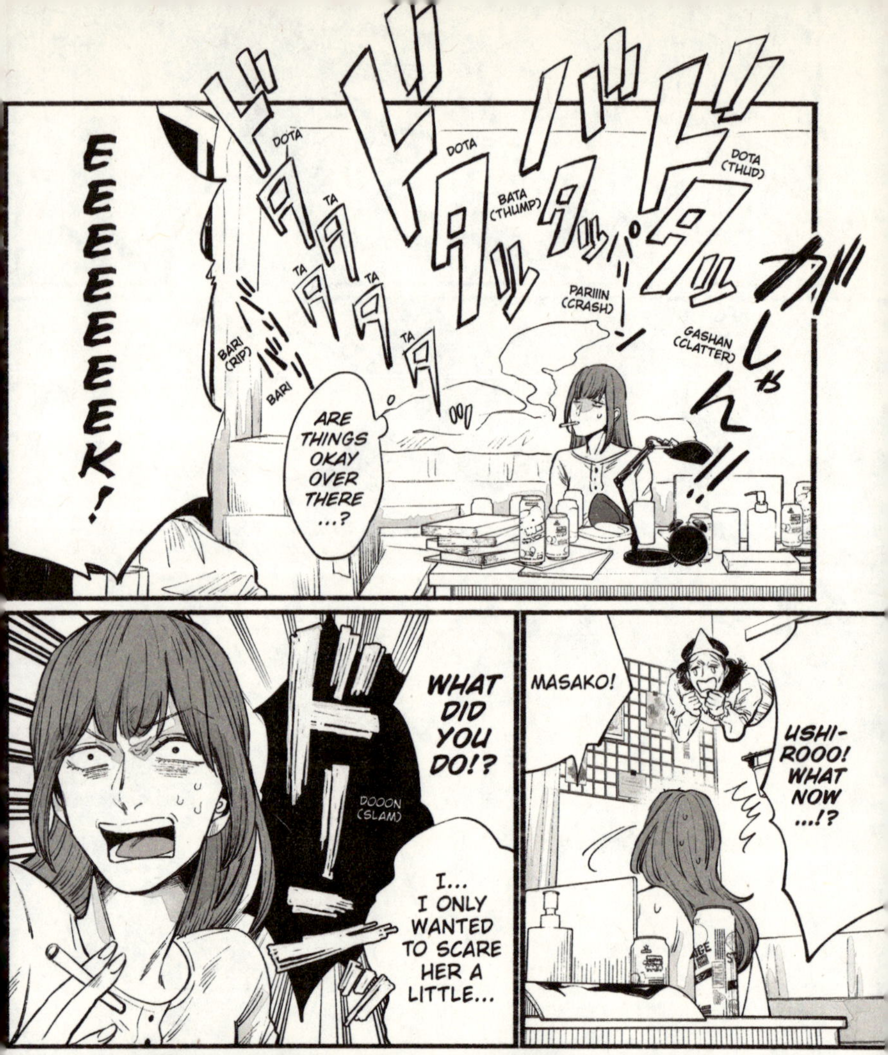
DOTA (THUD)
BATA (THUMP)
DOTA
DOTA
TA
TA
TA
TA
PARIIIN (CRASH)
GASHAN (CLATTER)
ARE THINGS OKAY OVER THERE ...?
BARI (RIP)
BARI
EEEEEEEEEEK!
MASAKO!
USHI-ROOO! WHAT NOW ...!?
WHAT DID YOU DO!?
DOOON (SLAM)
I... I ONLY WANTED TO SCARE HER A LITTLE...
HUH ...!?
....
IT SUDDENLY WENT QUIET...
DON'T TELL ME......
....
IS SHE DEAD?

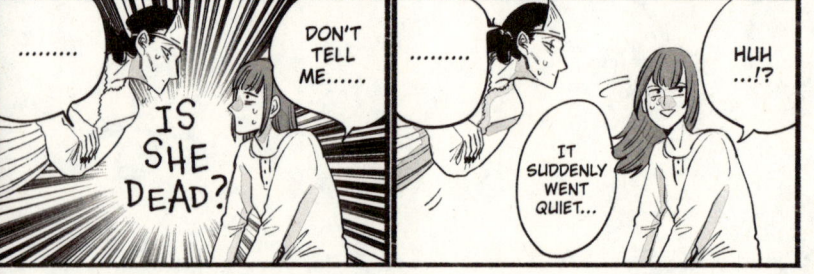

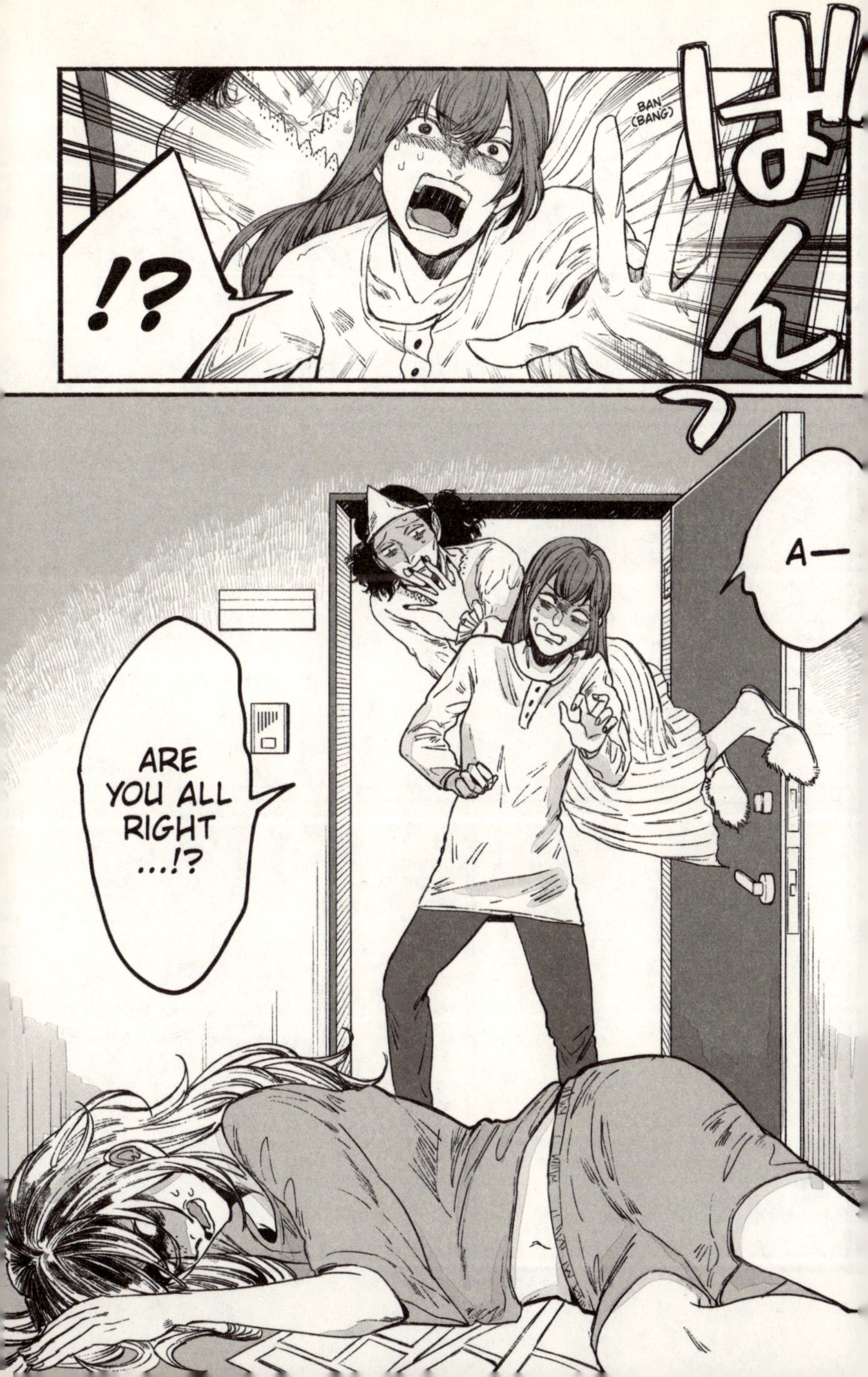
ばんっ
BAN (BANG)
!?
A—
ARE YOU ALL RIGHT ...!?

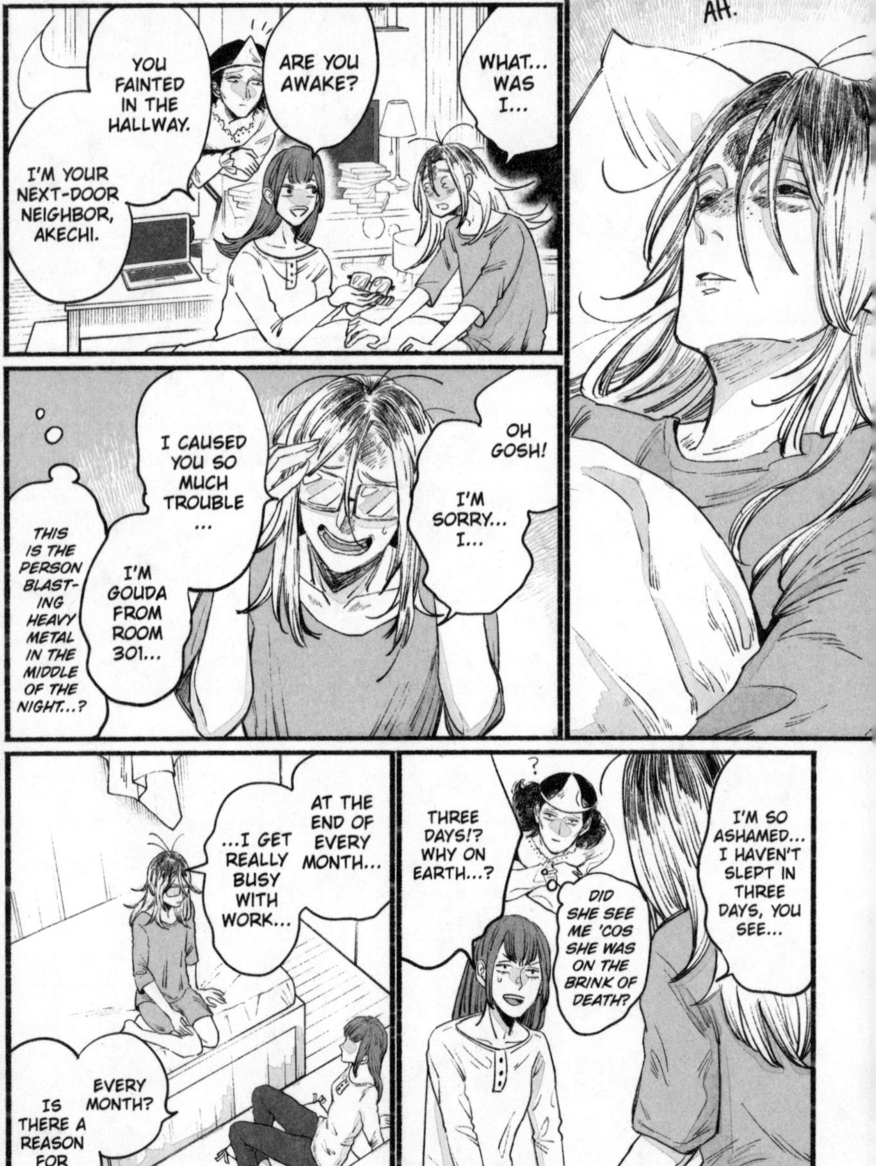
AH.
WHAT... WAS I...
ARE YOU AWAKE?
YOU FAINTED IN THE HALLWAY.
I'M YOUR NEXT-DOOR NEIGHBOR, AKECHI.
OH GOSH! I'M SORRY... I...
I CAUSED YOU SO MUCH TROUBLE...
I'M GOUDA FROM ROOM 301...
THIS IS THE PERSON BLASTING HEAVY METAL IN THE MIDDLE OF THE NIGHT...?
I'M SO ASHAMED... I HAVEN'T SLEPT IN THREE DAYS, YOU SEE...
THREE DAYS!? WHY ON EARTH...?
?
DID SHE SEE ME 'COS SHE WAS ON THE BRINK OF DEATH?
AT THE END OF EVERY MONTH...
...I GET REALLY BUSY WITH WORK...
EVERY MONTH?
IS THERE A REASON FOR THAT?

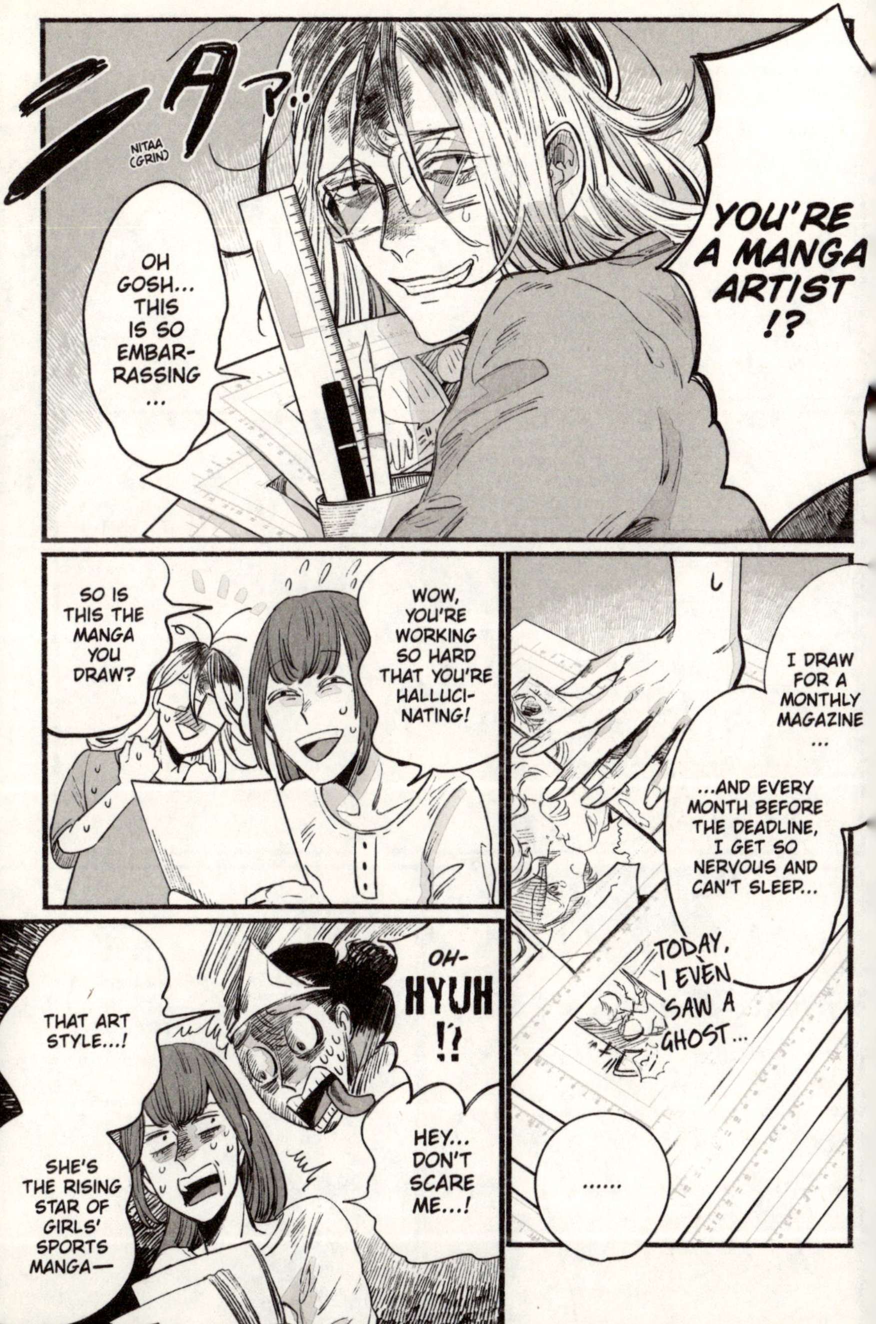
YOU'RE A MANGA ARTIST!?
ニタァ..
NITAA (GRIN)
OH GOSH... THIS IS SO EMBARRASSING...
I DRAW FOR A MONTHLY MAGAZINE...
...AND EVERY MONTH BEFORE THE DEADLINE, I GET SO NERVOUS AND CAN'T SLEEP...
TODAY, I EVEN SAW A GHOST...
......
WOW, YOU'RE WORKING SO HARD THAT YOU'RE HALLUCINATING!
SO IS THIS THE MANGA YOU DRAW?
OH-HYUH!?
THAT ART STYLE...!
HEY... DON'T SCARE ME...!
SHE'S THE RISING STAR OF GIRLS' SPORTS MANGA—

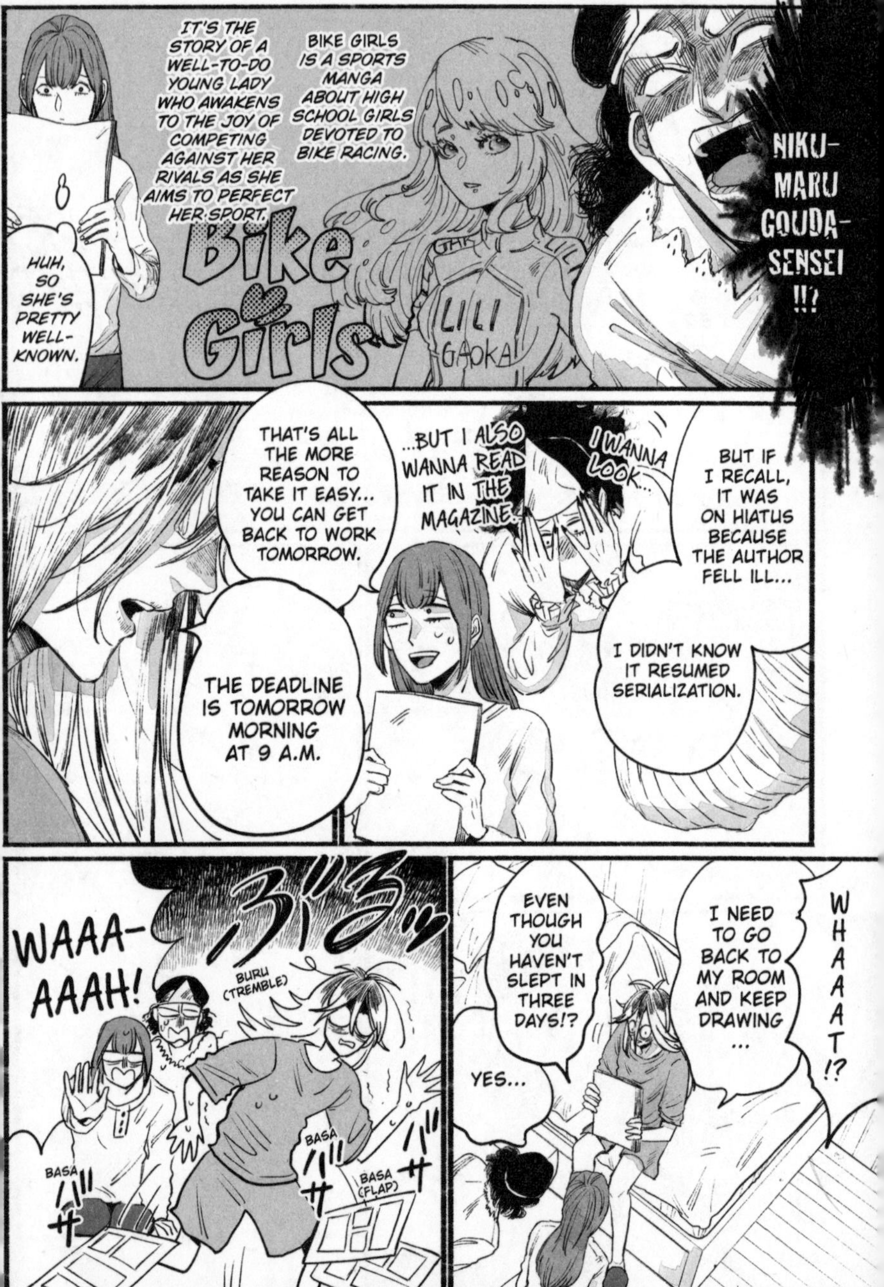
NIKU-MARU GOUDA-SENSEI!!?
BIKE GIRLS IS A SPORTS MANGA ABOUT HIGH SCHOOL GIRLS DEVOTED TO BIKE RACING.
IT'S THE STORY OF A WELL-TO-DO YOUNG LADY WHO AWAKENS TO THE JOY OF COMPETING AGAINST HER RIVALS AS SHE AIMS TO PERFECT HER SPORT.
Bike Girls
HUH, SO SHE'S PRETTY WELL-KNOWN.
BUT IF I RECALL, IT WAS ON HIATUS BECAUSE THE AUTHOR FELL ILL...
I DIDN'T KNOW IT RESUMED SERIALIZATION.
I WANNA LOOK...
...BUT I ALSO WANNA READ IT IN THE MAGAZINE.
THAT'S ALL THE MORE REASON TO TAKE IT EASY... YOU CAN GET BACK TO WORK TOMORROW.
THE DEADLINE IS TOMORROW MORNING AT 9 A.M.
WHAAAAT!?
I NEED TO GO BACK TO MY ROOM AND KEEP DRAWING...
EVEN THOUGH YOU HAVEN'T SLEPT IN THREE DAYS!?
YES...
BURU (TREMBLE)
WAAA-AAAH!
BASA
BASA (FLAP)
BASA

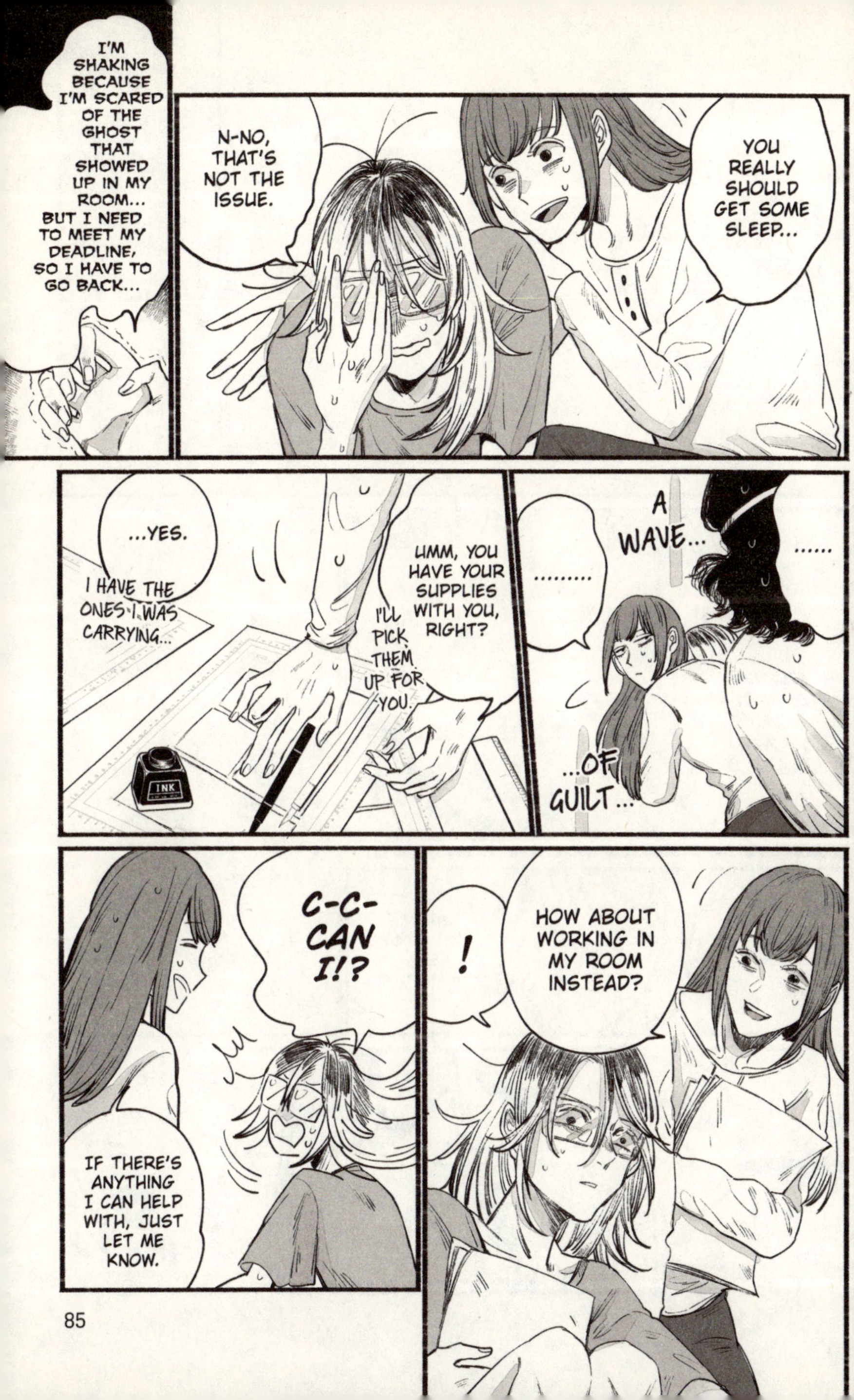
YOU REALLY SHOULD GET SOME SLEEP...
N-NO, THAT'S NOT THE ISSUE.
I'M SHAKING BECAUSE I'M SCARED OF THE GHOST THAT SHOWED UP IN MY ROOM... BUT I NEED TO MEET MY DEADLINE, SO I HAVE TO GO BACK...
......
A WAVE...
....
...OF GUILT...
UMM, YOU HAVE YOUR SUPPLIES WITH YOU, RIGHT?
I'LL PICK THEM UP FOR YOU.
...YES.
I HAVE THE ONES I WAS CARRYING...
INK
HOW ABOUT WORKING IN MY ROOM INSTEAD?
!
C-C-CAN I!?
IF THERE'S ANYTHING I CAN HELP WITH, JUST LET ME KNOW.

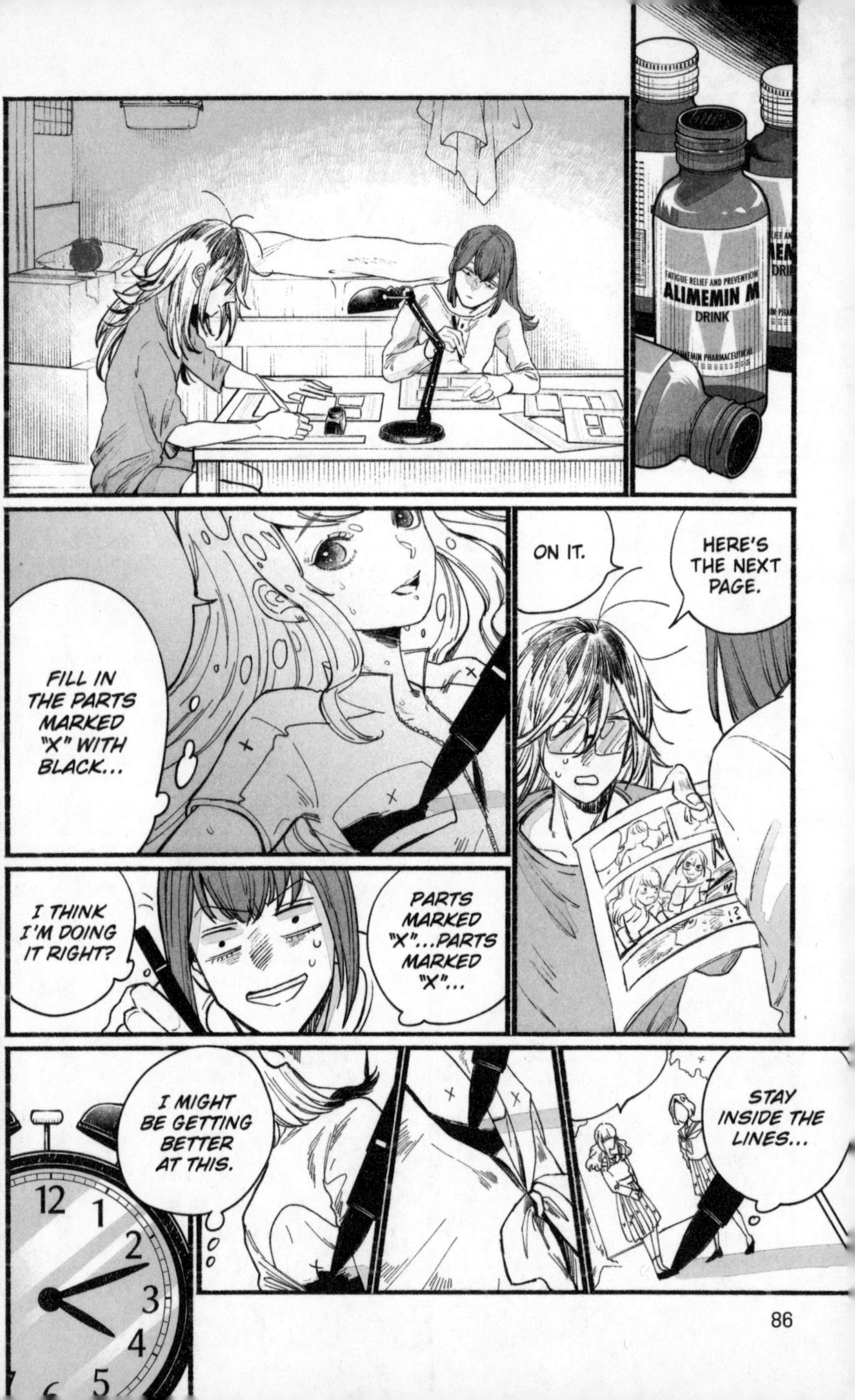
FATIGUE RELIEF AND PREVENTION
ALIMEMIN M
DRINK
HERE'S THE NEXT PAGE.
ON IT.
FILL IN THE PARTS MARKED "X" WITH BLACK...
PARTS MARKED "X"...PARTS MARKED "X"...
I THINK I'M DOING IT RIGHT?
STAY INSIDE THE LINES...
I MIGHT BE GETTING BETTER AT THIS.

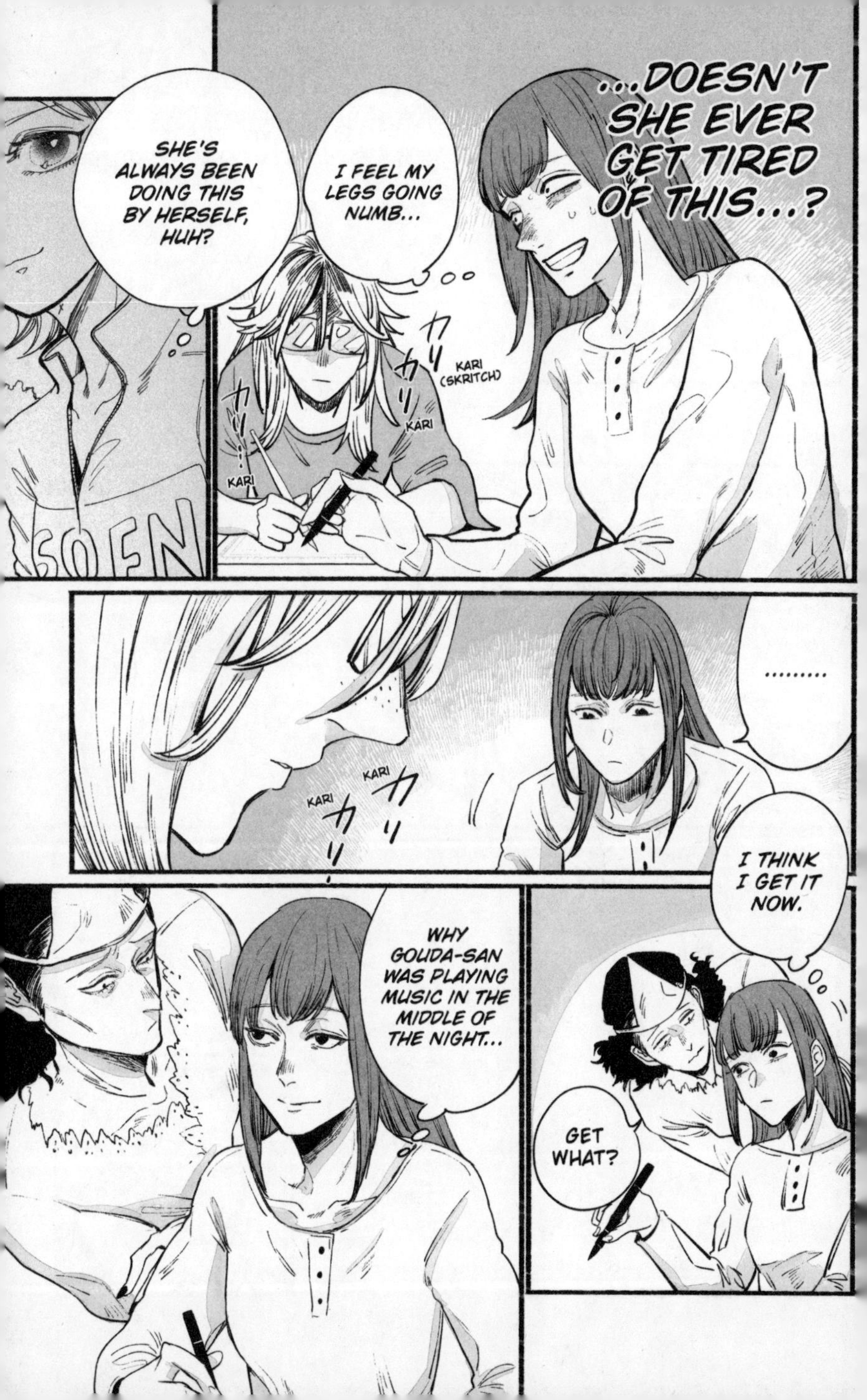
...DOESN'T SHE EVER GET TIRED OF THIS...?
I FEEL MY LEGS GOING NUMB...
KARI (SKRITCH)
KARI
KARI
SHE'S ALWAYS BEEN DOING THIS BY HERSELF, HUH?
....
KARI
KARI
I THINK I GET IT NOW.
GET WHAT?
WHY GOUDA-SAN WAS PLAYING MUSIC IN THE MIDDLE OF THE NIGHT...

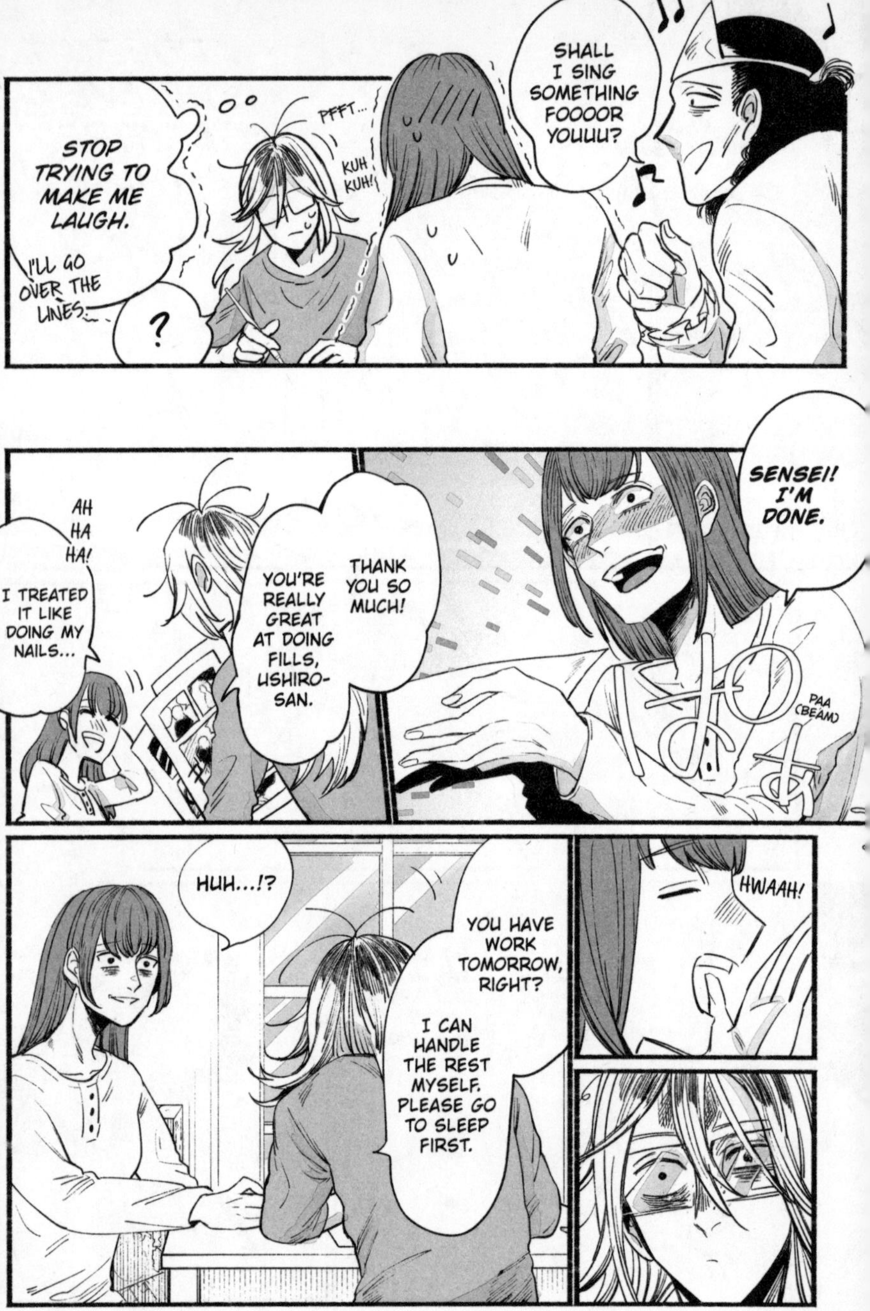
SHALL I SING SOMETHING FOOOOR YOUUU?
PFFT...
KUH KUH!
STOP TRYING TO MAKE ME LAUGH.
I'LL GO OVER THE LINES
?
SENSEI! I'M DONE.
PAA (BEAM)
THANK YOU SO MUCH!
YOU'RE REALLY GREAT AT DOING FILLS, USHIRO-SAN.
AH HA HA!
I TREATED IT LIKE DOING MY NAILS...
HWAAH!
YOU HAVE WORK TOMORROW, RIGHT?
I CAN HANDLE THE REST MYSELF. PLEASE GO TO SLEEP FIRST.
HUH...!?

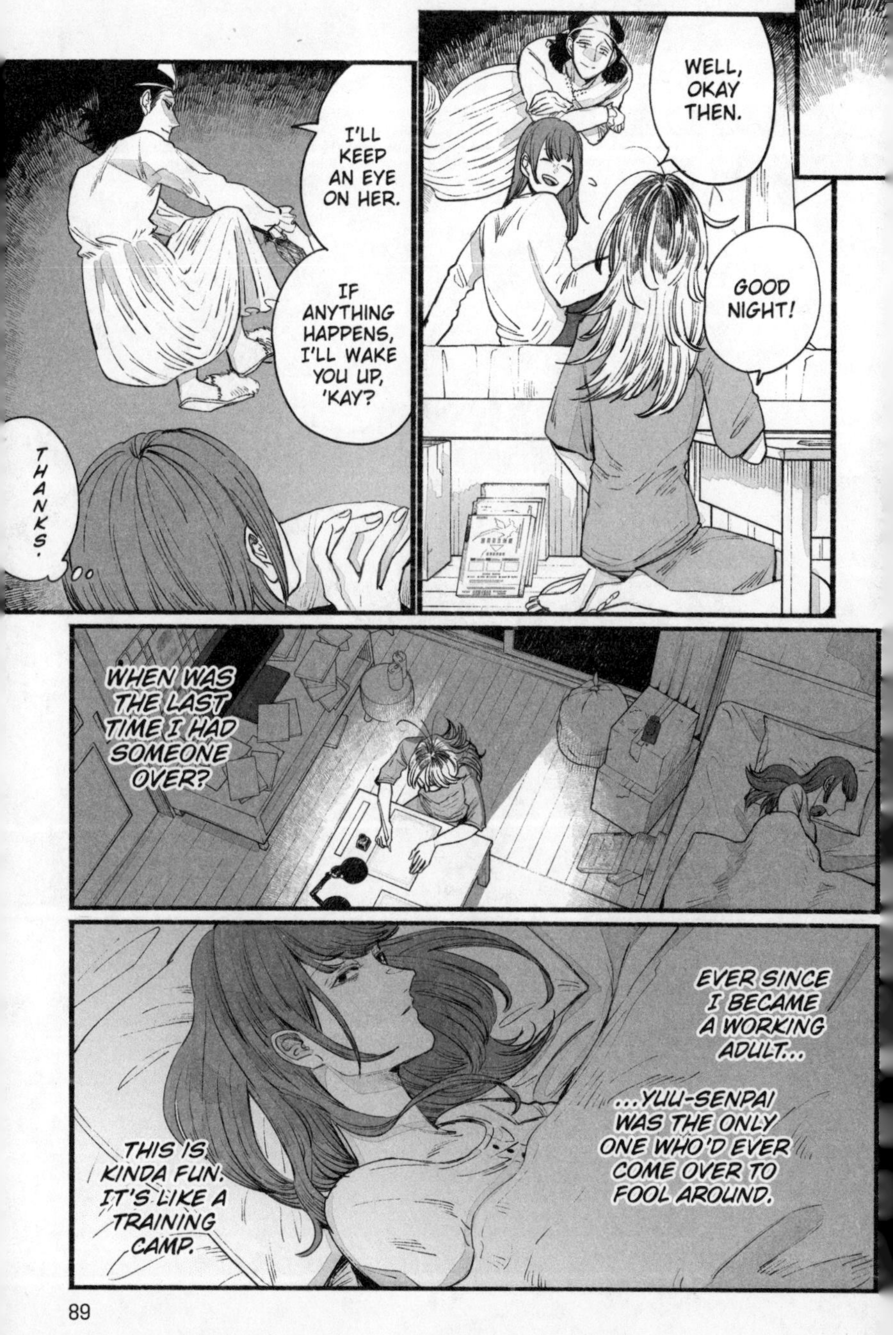
WELL, OKAY THEN.
GOOD NIGHT!
I'LL KEEP AN EYE ON HER.
IF ANYTHING HAPPENS, I'LL WAKE YOU UP, 'KAY?
THANKS.
WHEN WAS THE LAST TIME I HAD SOMEONE OVER?
EVER SINCE I BECAME A WORKING ADULT...
...YUU-SENPAI WAS THE ONLY ONE WHO'D EVER COME OVER TO FOOL AROUND.
THIS IS KINDA FUN. IT'S LIKE A TRAINING CAMP.

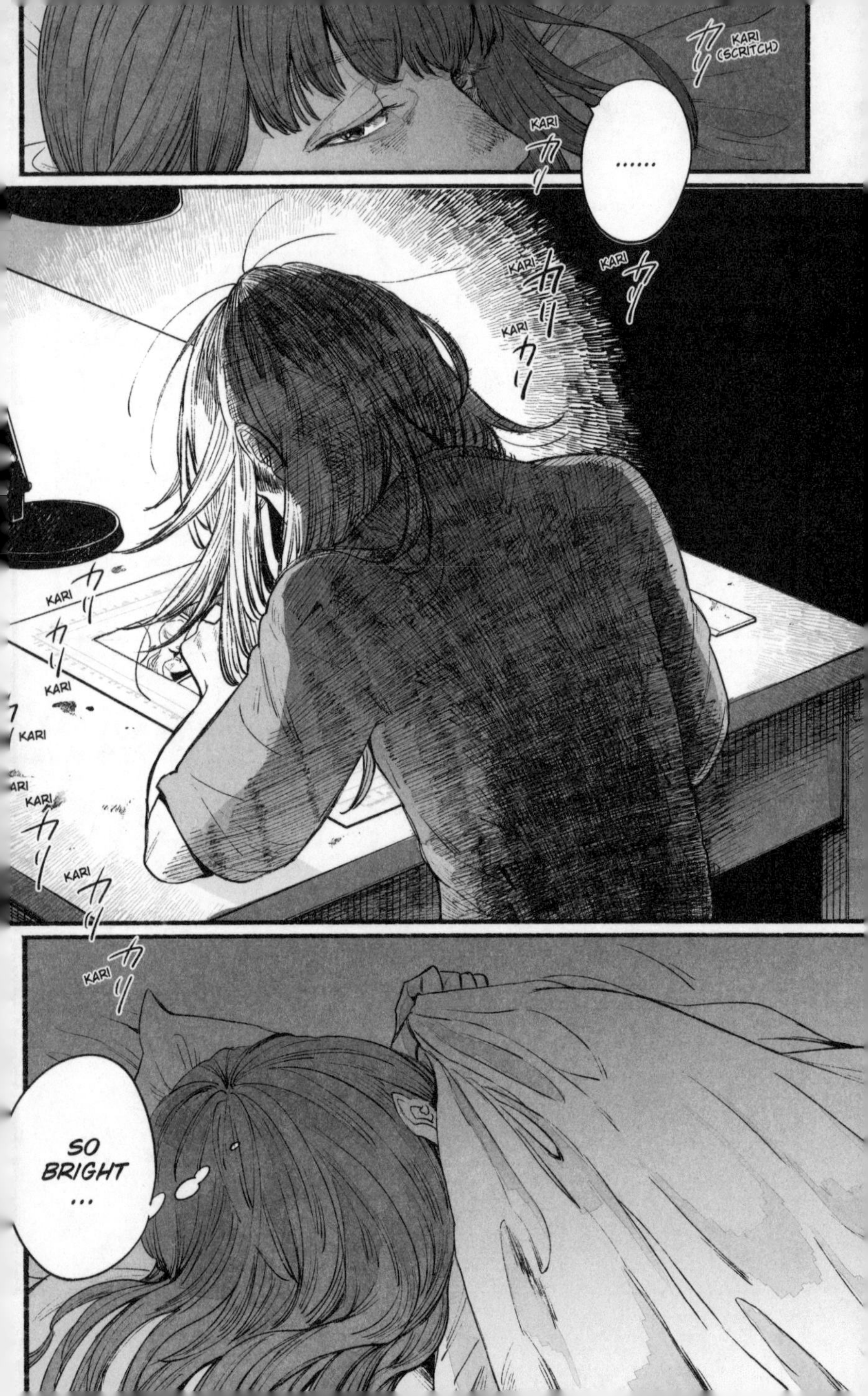

カリ
KARI (SCRITCH)
......
KARI
カリ
KARI
カリ
KARI
カリ
KARI
カリ
KARI
カリ
カリ
KARI
KARI
KARI
カリ
KARI
カリ
KARI
カリ
SO BRIGHT ...

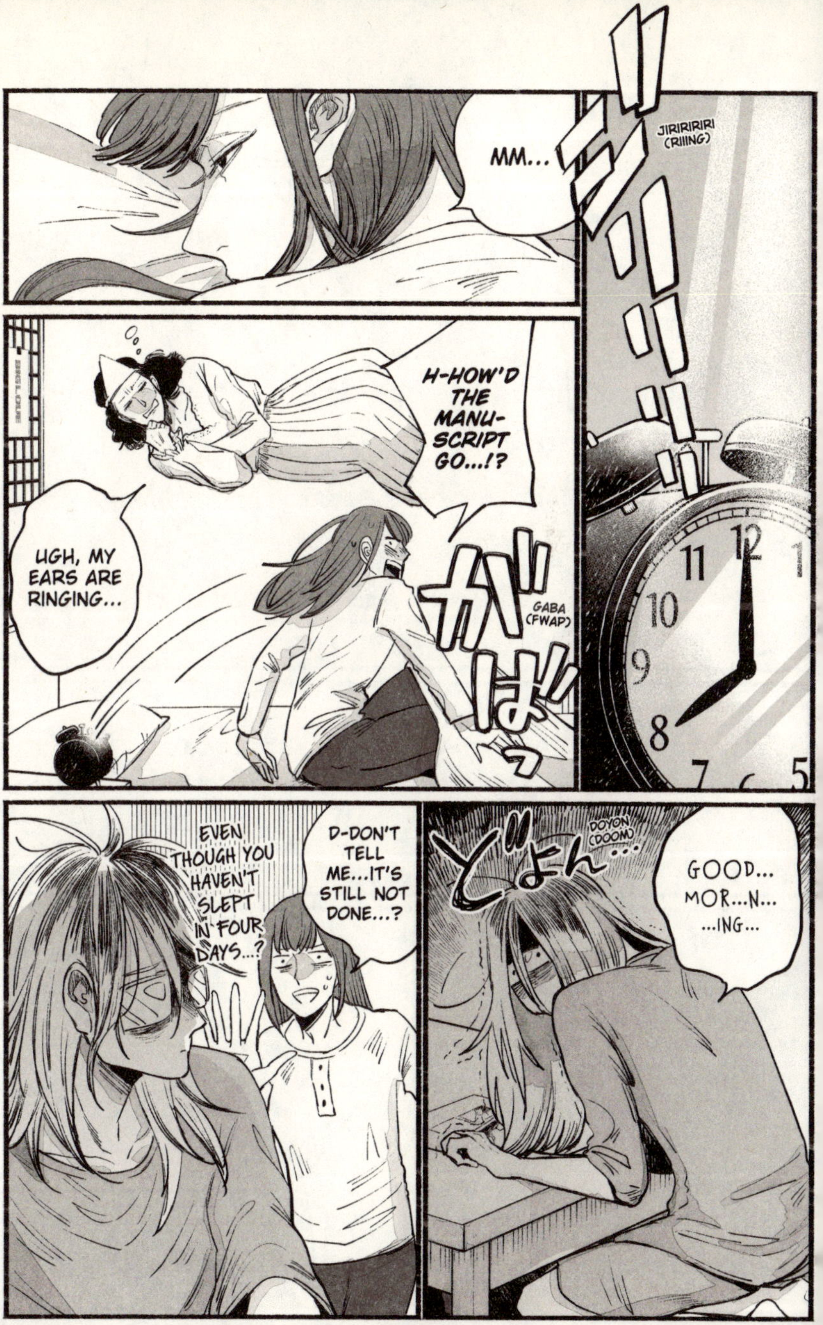
JIRIRIRIRI (RIIING)
MM...
H-HOW'D THE MANU-SCRIPT GO...!?
GABA (FWAP)
UGH, MY EARS ARE RINGING...
DOYON (DOOM)
GOOD... MOR...N... ...ING...
D-DON'T TELL ME...IT'S STILL NOT DONE...?
EVEN THOUGH YOU HAVEN'T SLEPT IN FOUR DAYS...?

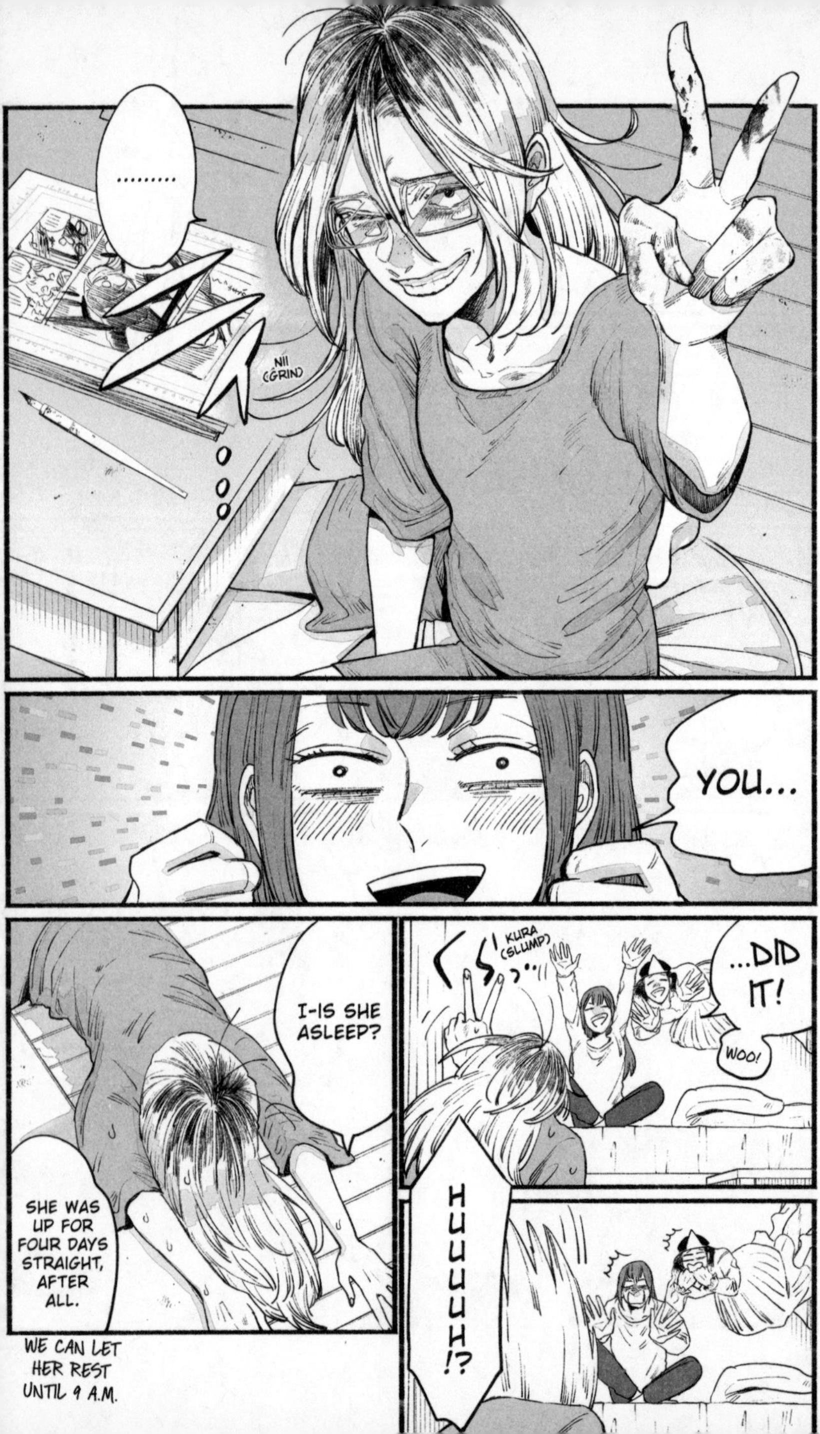
....
NII (GRIN)
YOU...
...DID IT!
KURA (SLUMP)
WOO!
HUUUUUH!?
I-IS SHE ASLEEP?
SHE WAS UP FOR FOUR DAYS STRAIGHT, AFTER ALL.
WE CAN LET HER REST UNTIL 9 A.M.

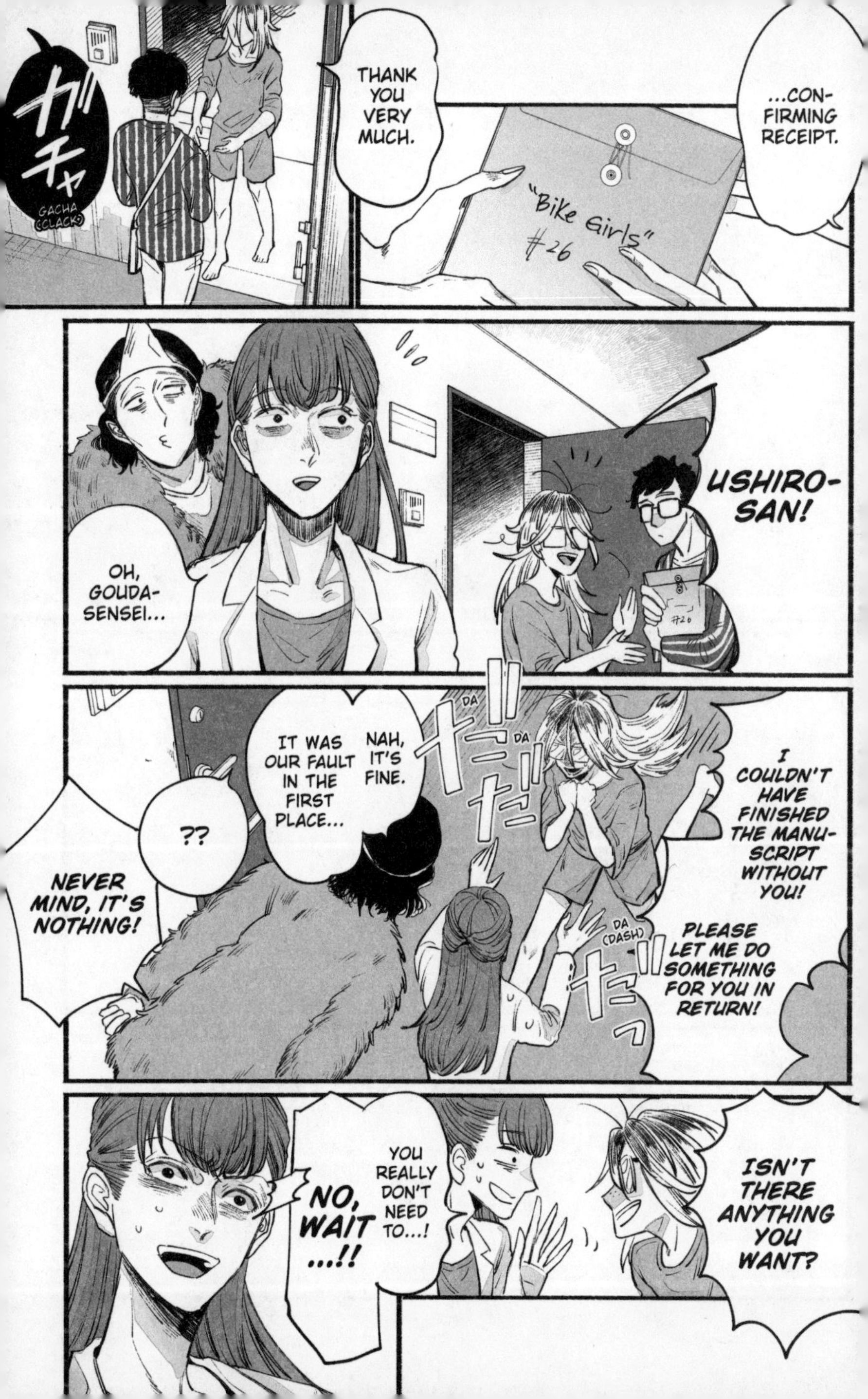
...CON-FIRMING RECEIPT.
"Bike Girls" #26
THANK YOU VERY MUCH.
ガチャ
GACHA (CLACK)
USHIRO-SAN!
#26
OH, GOUDA-SENSEI...
I COULDN'T HAVE FINISHED THE MANU-SCRIPT WITHOUT YOU!
PLEASE LET ME DO SOMETHING FOR YOU IN RETURN!
DA
DA
DA (DASH)
NAH, IT'S FINE.
IT WAS OUR FAULT IN THE FIRST PLACE...
??
NEVER MIND, IT'S NOTHING!
ISN'T THERE ANYTHING YOU WANT?
YOU REALLY DON'T NEED TO...!
NO, WAIT ...!!

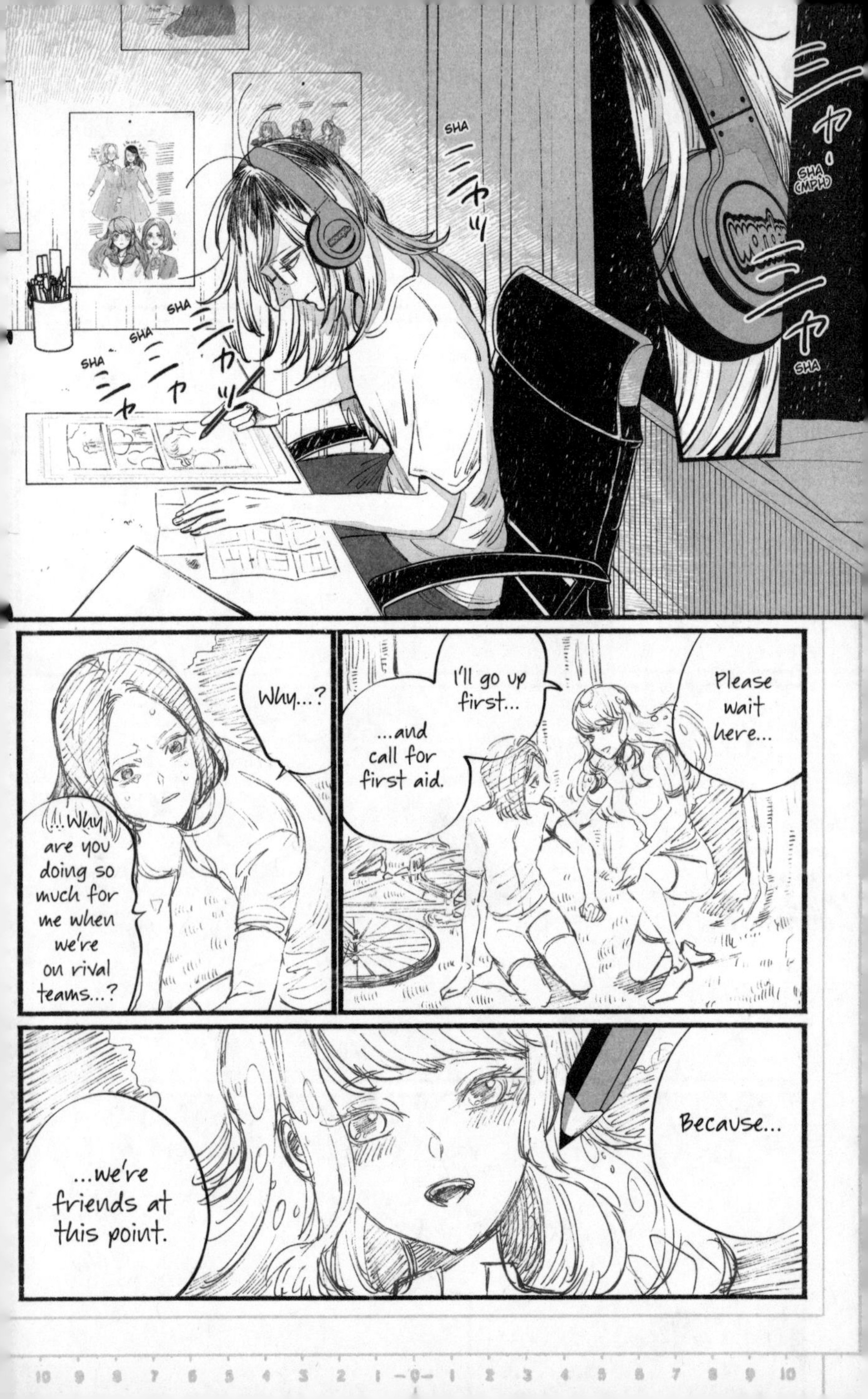
SHA (MPHD)
SHA
SHA
SHA
SHA
SHA
Please wait here...
I'll go up first...
...and call for first aid.
Why...?
...Why are you doing so much for me when we're on rival teams...?
Because...
...we're friends at this point.

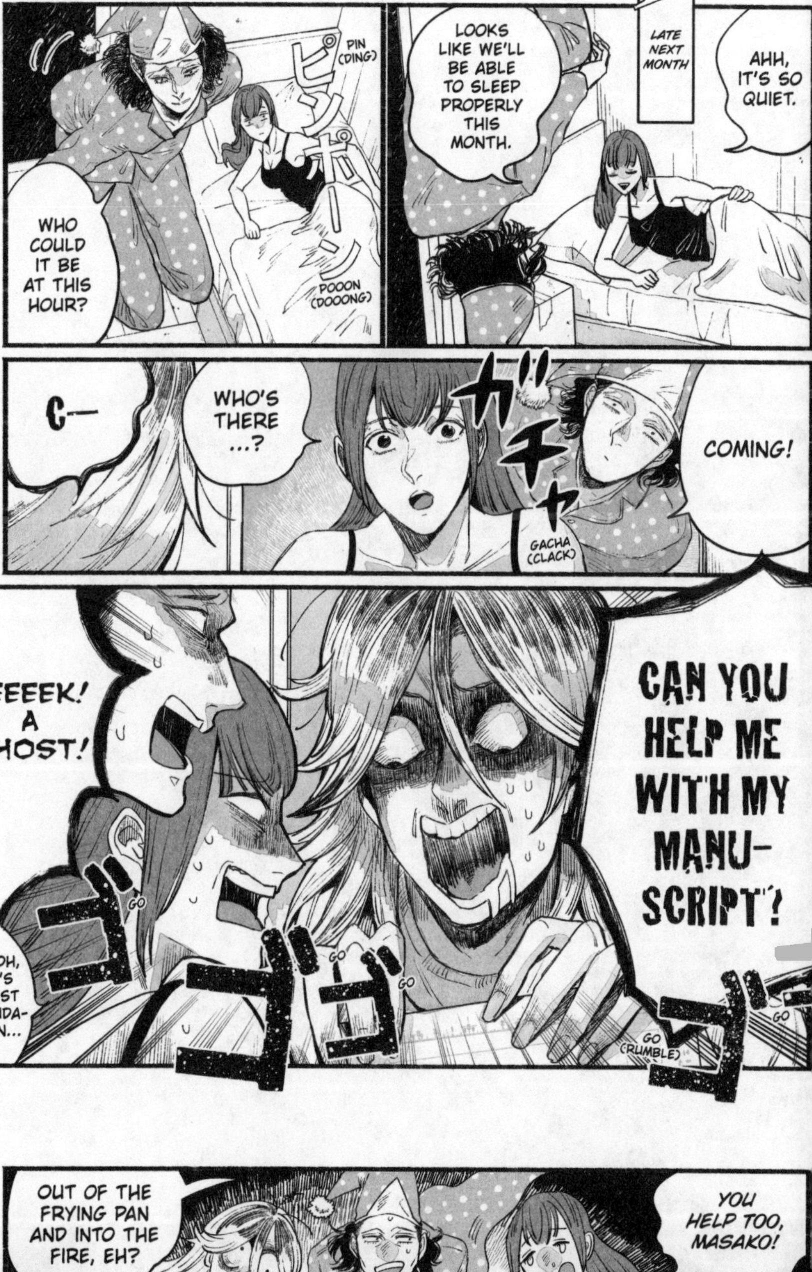
LATE NEXT MONTH
AHH, IT'S SO QUIET.
LOOKS LIKE WE'LL BE ABLE TO SLEEP PROPERLY THIS MONTH.
PIN (DING)
POOON (DOOONG)
WHO COULD IT BE AT THIS HOUR?
COMING!
GACHA (CLACK)
WHO'S THERE ...?
C—
CAN YOU HELP ME WITH MY MANU-SCRIPT?
EEEEEK! A GHOST!
GO GO GO GO (RUMBLE)
...OH, IT'S JUST GOUDA-SAN...
YOU HELP TOO, MASAKO!
OUT OF THE FRYING PAN AND INTO THE FIRE, EH?

GOGOGOGO-GO-GHOST!

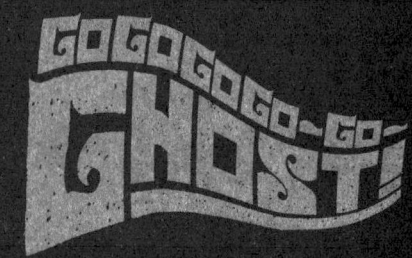

Chapter 5: Regarding That Faithful Dog

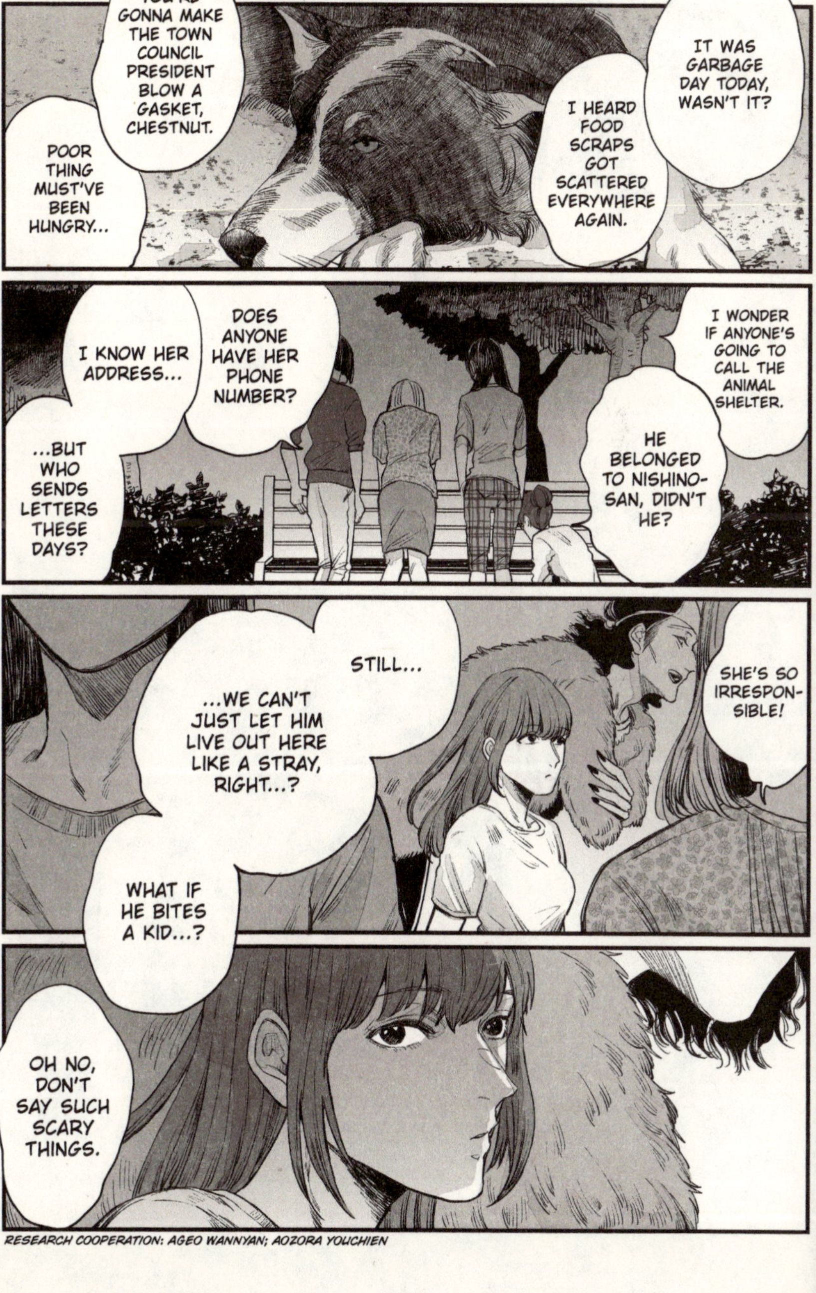
IT WAS GARBAGE DAY TODAY, WASN'T IT?
I HEARD FOOD SCRAPS GOT SCATTERED EVERYWHERE AGAIN.
YOU'RE GONNA MAKE THE TOWN COUNCIL PRESIDENT BLOW A GASKET, CHESTNUT.
POOR THING MUST'VE BEEN HUNGRY...
I WONDER IF ANYONE'S GOING TO CALL THE ANIMAL SHELTER.
HE BELONGED TO NISHINO-SAN, DIDN'T HE?
DOES ANYONE HAVE HER PHONE NUMBER?
I KNOW HER ADDRESS...
...BUT WHO SENDS LETTERS THESE DAYS?
SHE'S SO IRRESPONSIBLE!
STILL...
...WE CAN'T JUST LET HIM LIVE OUT HERE LIKE A STRAY, RIGHT...?
WHAT IF HE BITES A KID...?
OH NO, DON'T SAY SUCH SCARY THINGS.

RESEARCH COOPERATION: AGEO WANNYAN; AOZORA YOUCHIEN

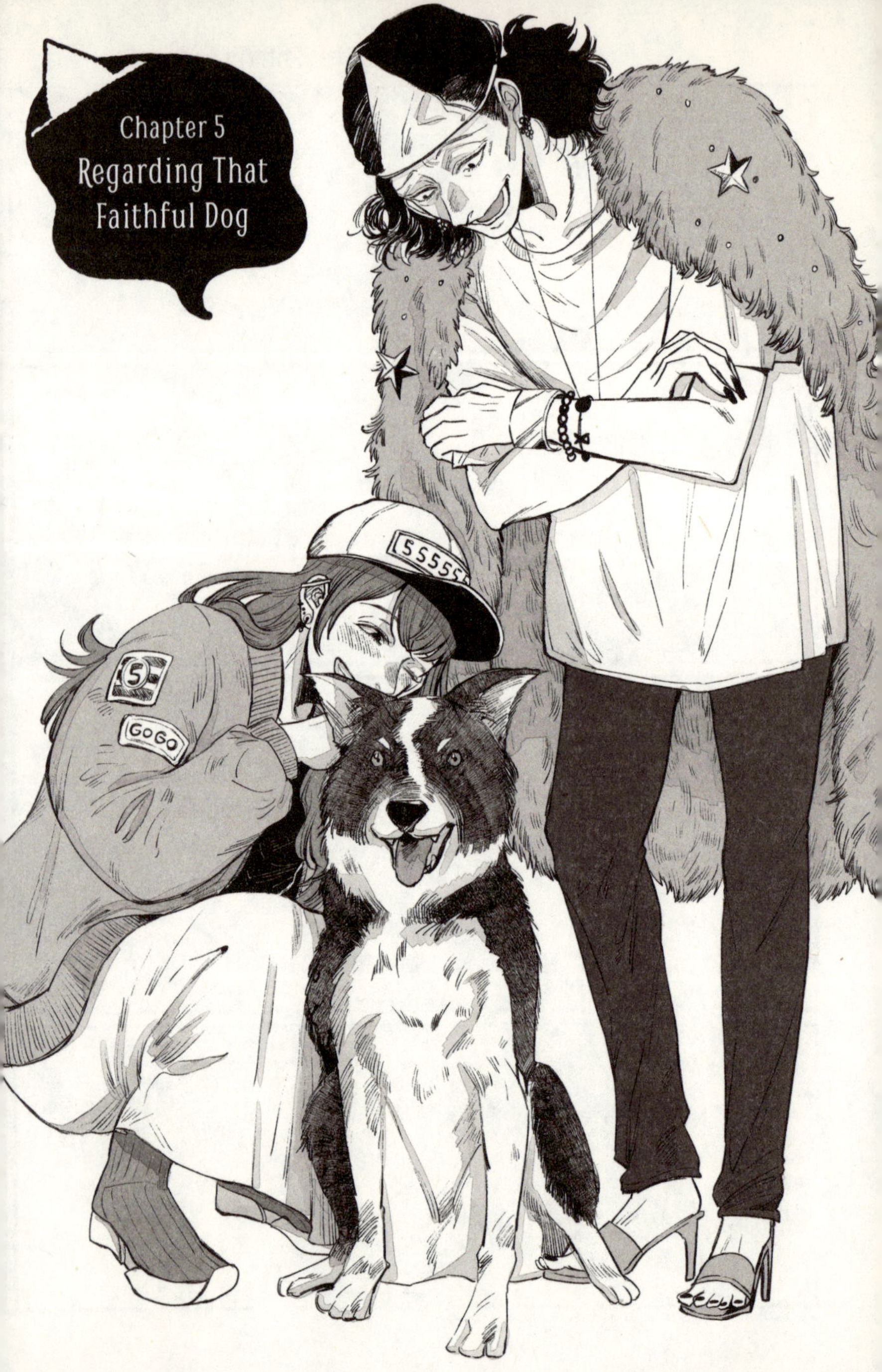
Chapter 5
Regarding That Faithful Dog
5
GoGo

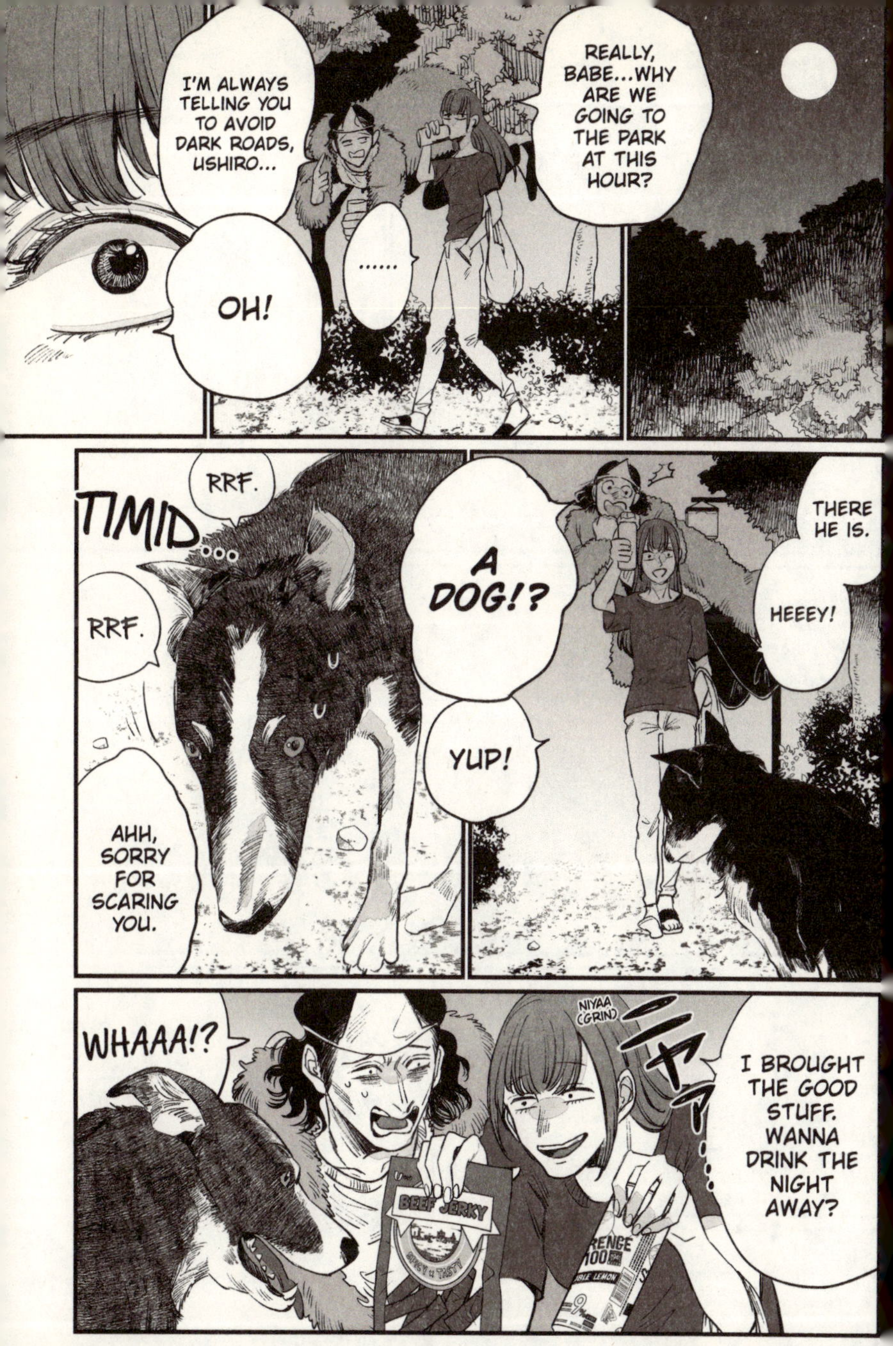
REALLY, BABE...WHY ARE WE GOING TO THE PARK AT THIS HOUR?
......
I'M ALWAYS TELLING YOU TO AVOID DARK ROADS, USHIRO...
OH!
THERE HE IS.
HEEEY!
A DOG!?
YUP!
RRF.
TIMID...
RRF.
AHH, SORRY FOR SCARING YOU.
NIYAA (GRIN)
I BROUGHT THE GOOD STUFF. WANNA DRINK THE NIGHT AWAY?
WHAAA!?
BEEF JERKY

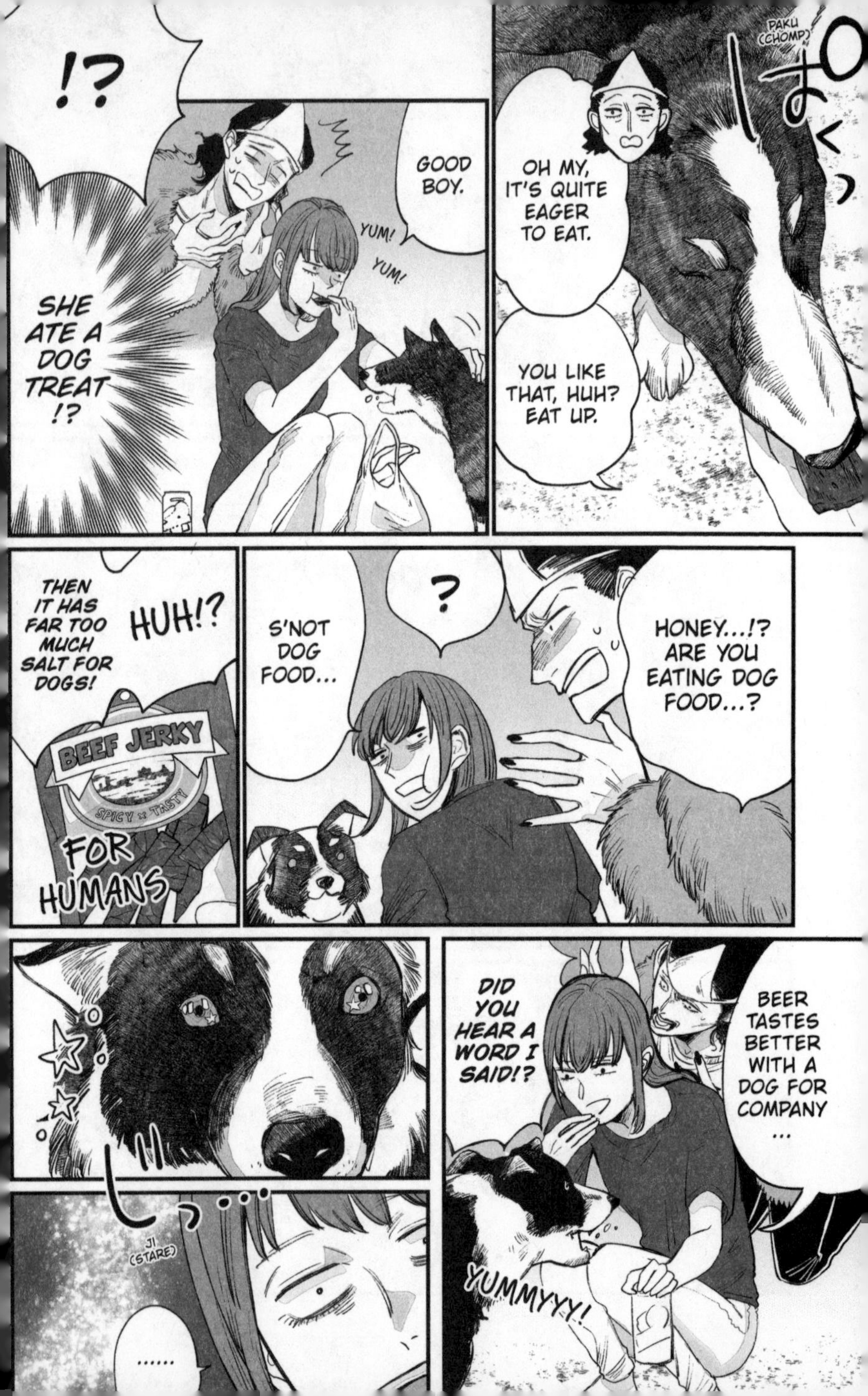
PAKU (CHOMP)
ぱくっ
OH MY, IT'S QUITE EAGER TO EAT.
YOU LIKE THAT, HUH? EAT UP.
!?
GOOD BOY.
YUM!
YUM!
SHE ATE A DOG TREAT !?
HONEY...!? ARE YOU EATING DOG FOOD...?
?
S'NOT DOG FOOD...
THEN IT HAS FAR TOO MUCH SALT FOR DOGS!
HUH!?
BEEF JERKY
SPICY × TASTY
FOR HUMANS
BEER TASTES BETTER WITH A DOG FOR COMPANY ...
DID YOU HEAR A WORD I SAID!?
YUMMYYY!
...
じっ
JI (STARE)
......

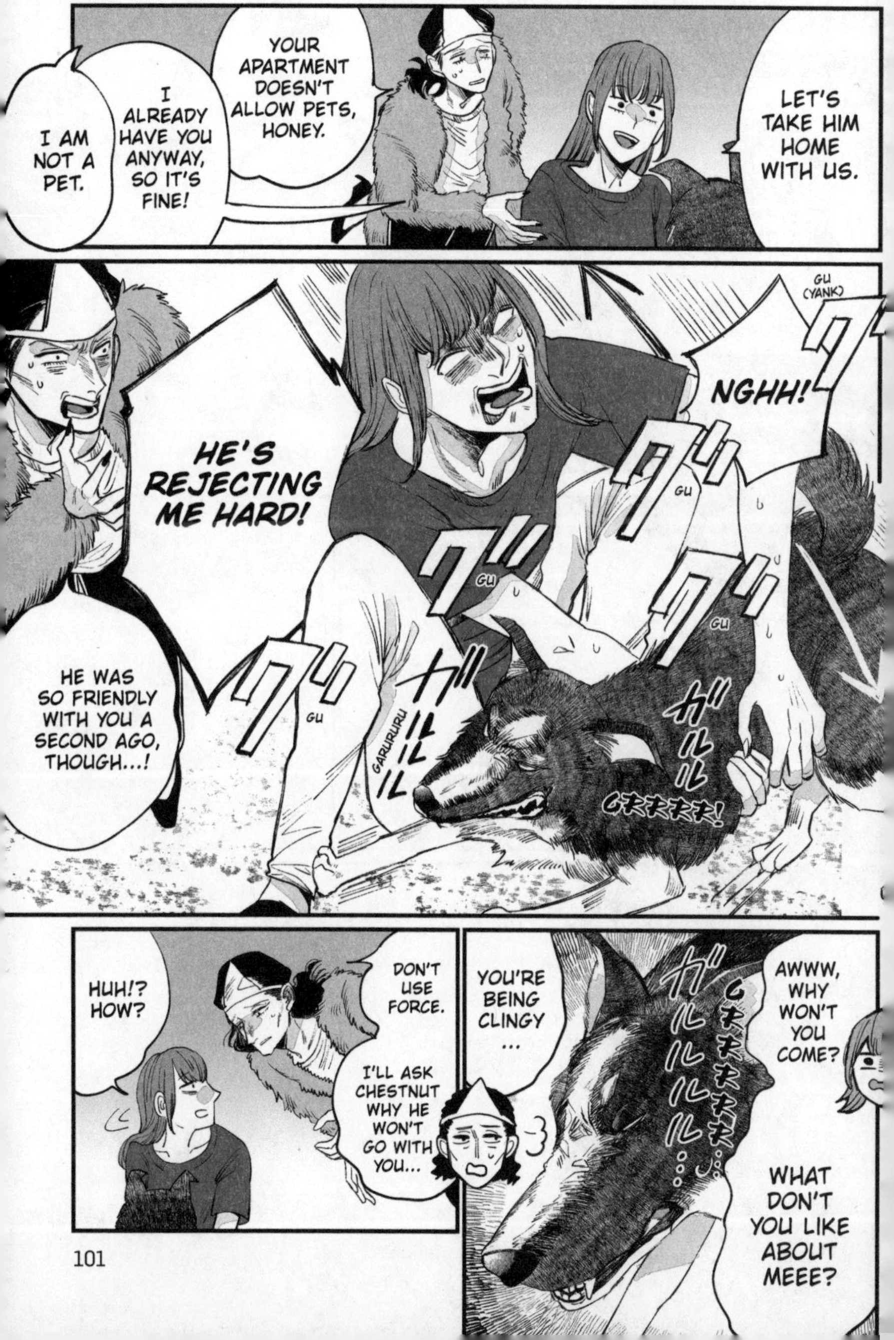
LET'S TAKE HIM HOME WITH US.
YOUR APARTMENT DOESN'T ALLOW PETS, HONEY.
I ALREADY HAVE YOU ANYWAY, SO IT'S FINE!
I AM NOT A PET.
GU (YANK)
NGHH!
GU
GU
GU
GU
GARURURU
GRRRRR!
HE'S REJECTING ME HARD!
HE WAS SO FRIENDLY WITH YOU A SECOND AGO, THOUGH...!
AWWW, WHY WON'T YOU COME?
GRRRRR...
WHAT DON'T YOU LIKE ABOUT MEEE?
YOU'RE BEING CLINGY...
DON'T USE FORCE.
HUH!? HOW?
I'LL ASK CHESTNUT WHY HE WON'T GO WITH YOU...

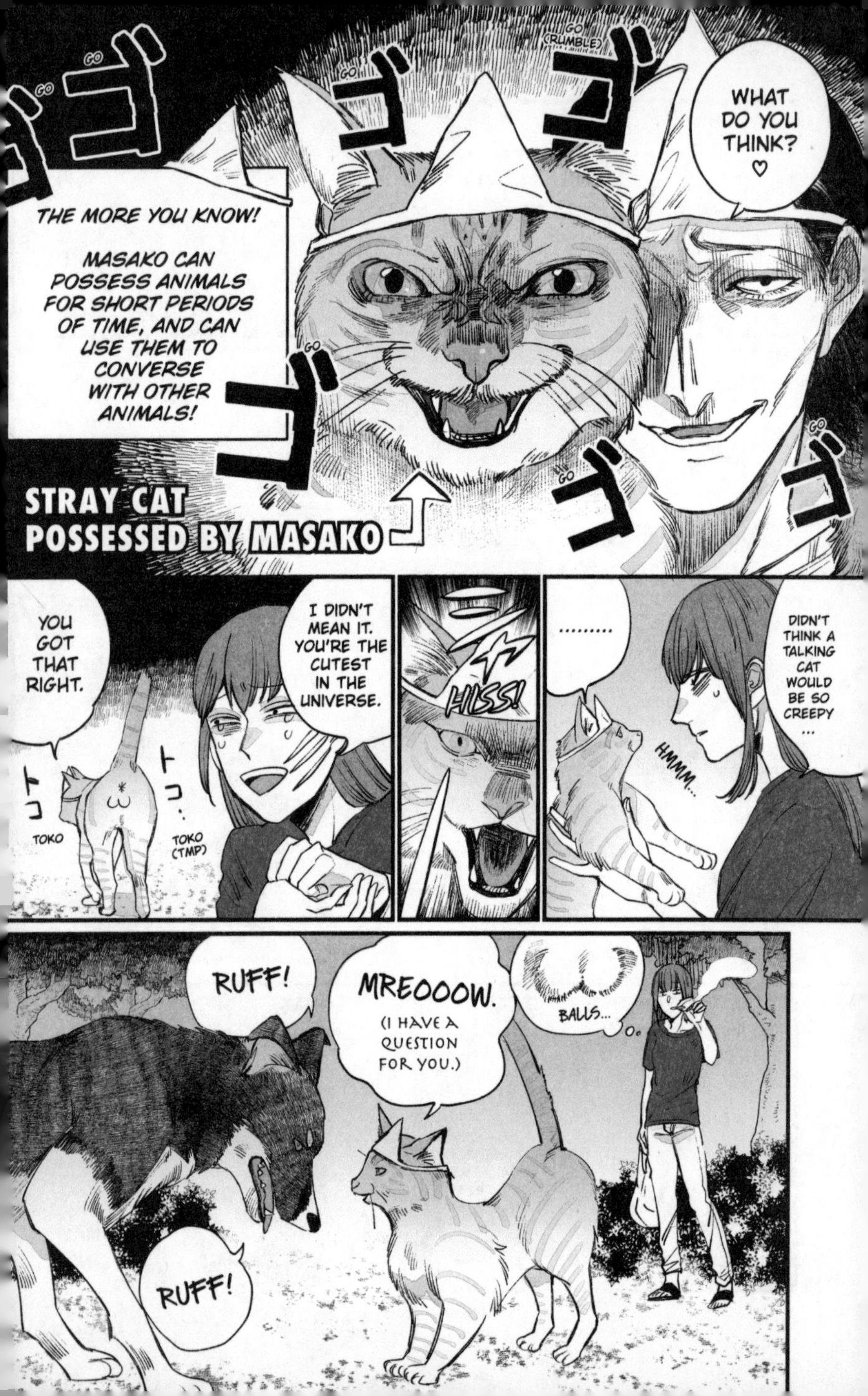
GO (RUMBLE)
GO
WHAT DO YOU THINK? ♡
GO
GO
THE MORE YOU KNOW!
MASAKO CAN POSSESS ANIMALS FOR SHORT PERIODS OF TIME, AND CAN USE THEM TO CONVERSE WITH OTHER ANIMALS!
GO
GO
GO
STRAY CAT POSSESSED BY MASAKO
DIDN'T THINK A TALKING CAT WOULD BE SO CREEPY ...
....
HMMM...
HISS!
I DIDN'T MEAN IT. YOU'RE THE CUTEST IN THE UNIVERSE.
YOU GOT THAT RIGHT.
TOKO (TMP)
TOKO
BALLS...
MREOOOW. (I HAVE A QUESTION FOR YOU.)
RUFF!
RUFF!

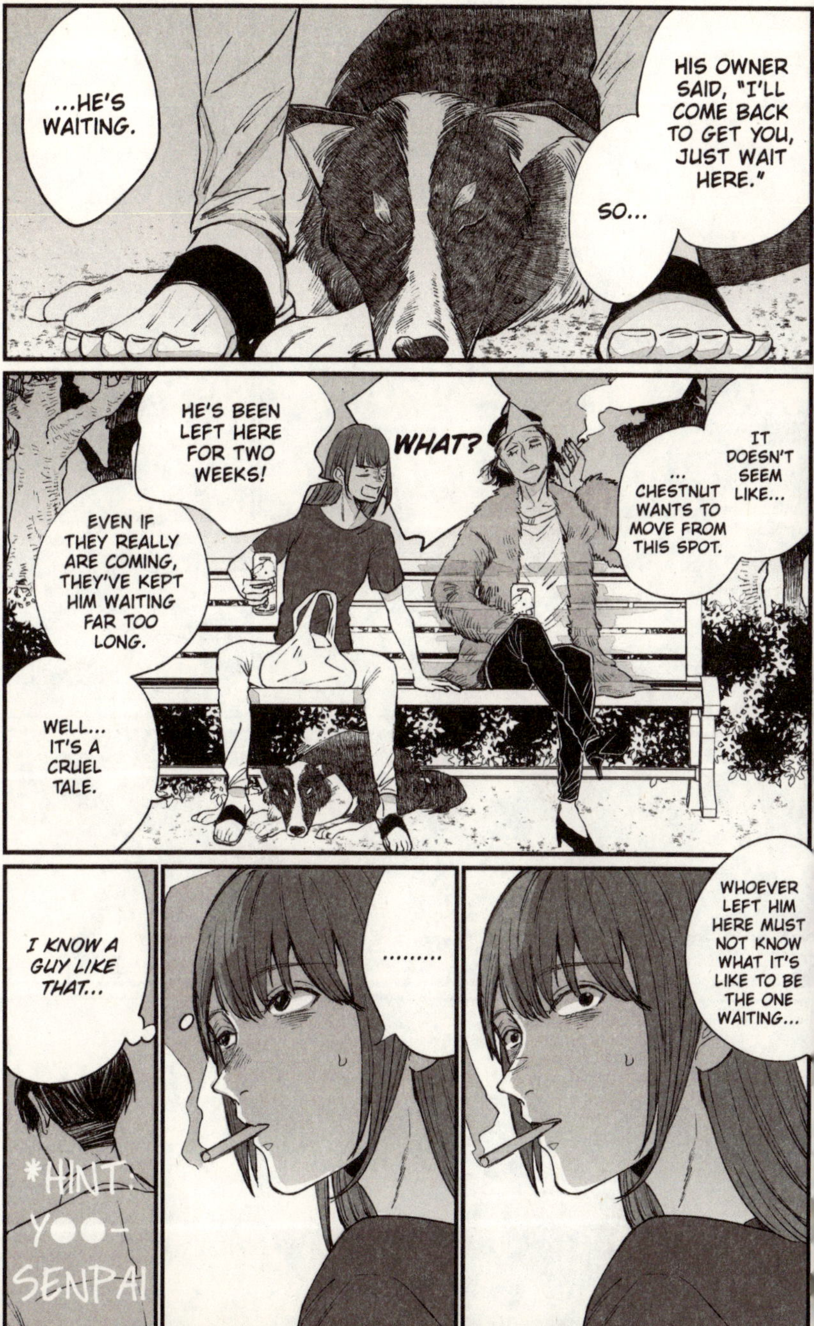
HIS OWNER SAID, "I'LL COME BACK TO GET YOU, JUST WAIT HERE."
SO...
...HE'S WAITING.
IT DOESN'T SEEM LIKE...
...CHESTNUT WANTS TO MOVE FROM THIS SPOT.
WHAT?
HE'S BEEN LEFT HERE FOR TWO WEEKS!
EVEN IF THEY REALLY ARE COMING, THEY'VE KEPT HIM WAITING FAR TOO LONG.
WELL... IT'S A CRUEL TALE.
WHOEVER LEFT HIM HERE MUST NOT KNOW WHAT IT'S LIKE TO BE THE ONE WAITING...
....
I KNOW A GUY LIKE THAT...
*HINT: YOO-SENPAI

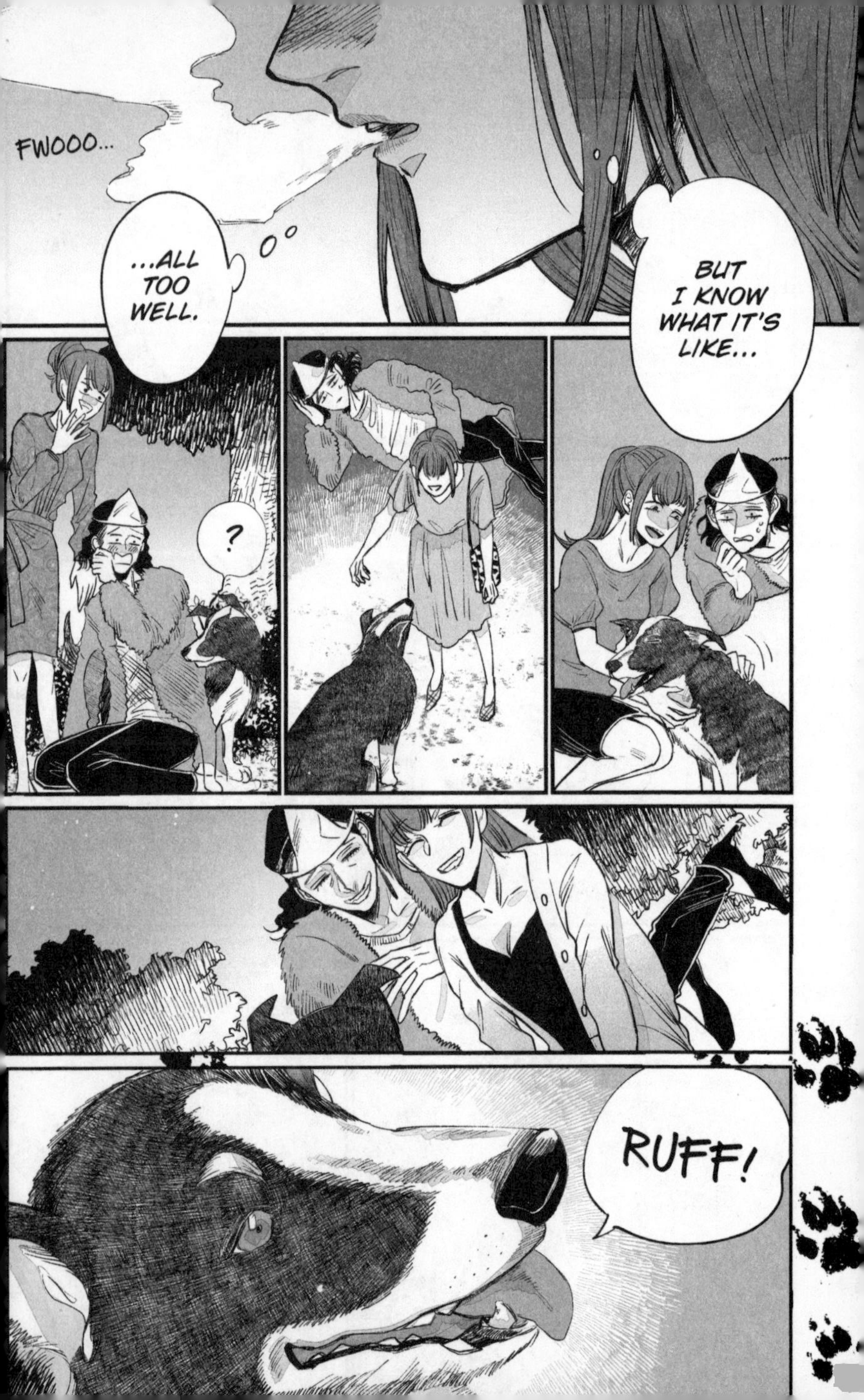
BUT I KNOW WHAT IT'S LIKE...
...ALL TOO WELL.
FWOOO...
?
RUFF!

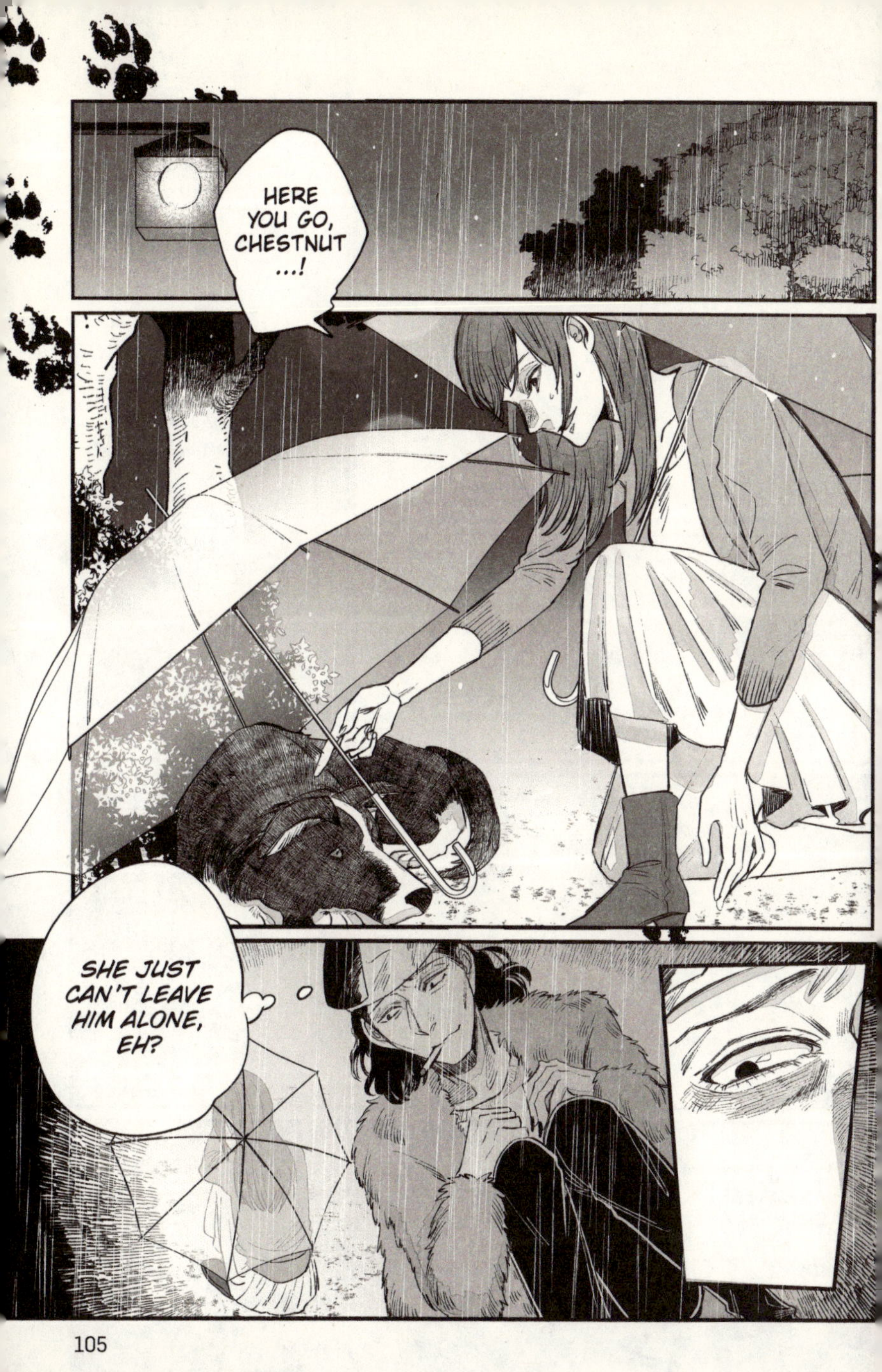
HERE YOU GO, CHESTNUT ...!
SHE JUST CAN'T LEAVE HIM ALONE, EH?

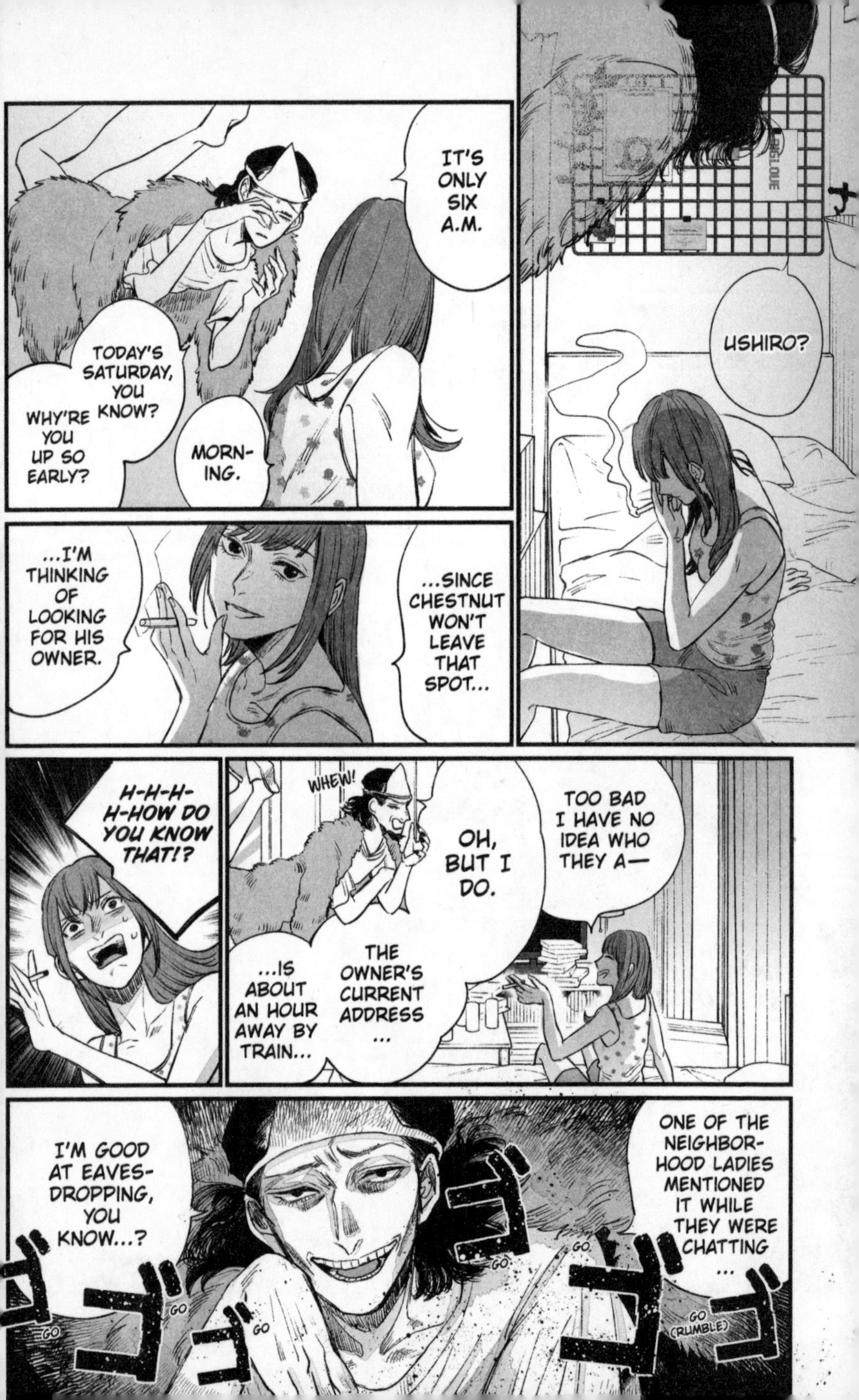
USHIRO?
IT'S ONLY SIX A.M.
TODAY'S SATURDAY, YOU KNOW?
WHY'RE YOU UP SO EARLY?
MORNING.
...SINCE CHESTNUT WON'T LEAVE THAT SPOT...
...I'M THINKING OF LOOKING FOR HIS OWNER.
TOO BAD I HAVE NO IDEA WHO THEY A—
OH, BUT I DO.
WHEW!
THE OWNER'S CURRENT ADDRESS...
...IS ABOUT AN HOUR AWAY BY TRAIN...
H-H-H-H-HOW DO YOU KNOW THAT!?
ONE OF THE NEIGHBORHOOD LADIES MENTIONED IT WHILE THEY WERE CHATTING...
I'M GOOD AT EAVES-DROPPING, YOU KNOW...?
GO GO
GO (RUMBLE)
GO GO GO

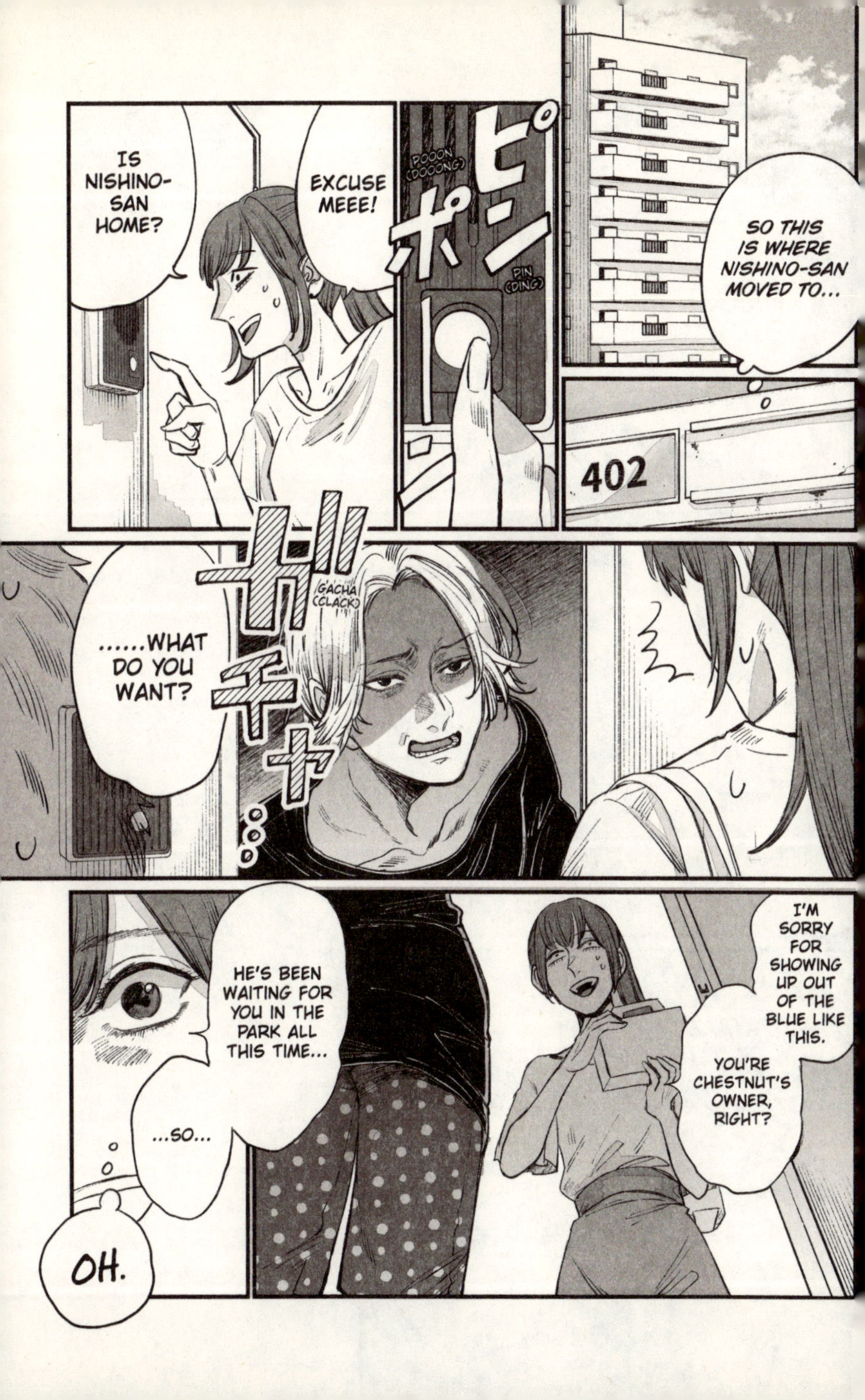
SO THIS IS WHERE NISHINO-SAN MOVED TO...
402
PIN (DING)
POOON (DOOONG)
EXCUSE MEEE!
IS NISHINO-SAN HOME?
ガチャ
GACHA (CLACK)
......WHAT DO YOU WANT?
I'M SORRY FOR SHOWING UP OUT OF THE BLUE LIKE THIS.
YOU'RE CHESTNUT'S OWNER, RIGHT?
HE'S BEEN WAITING FOR YOU IN THE PARK ALL THIS TIME...
...SO...
OH.

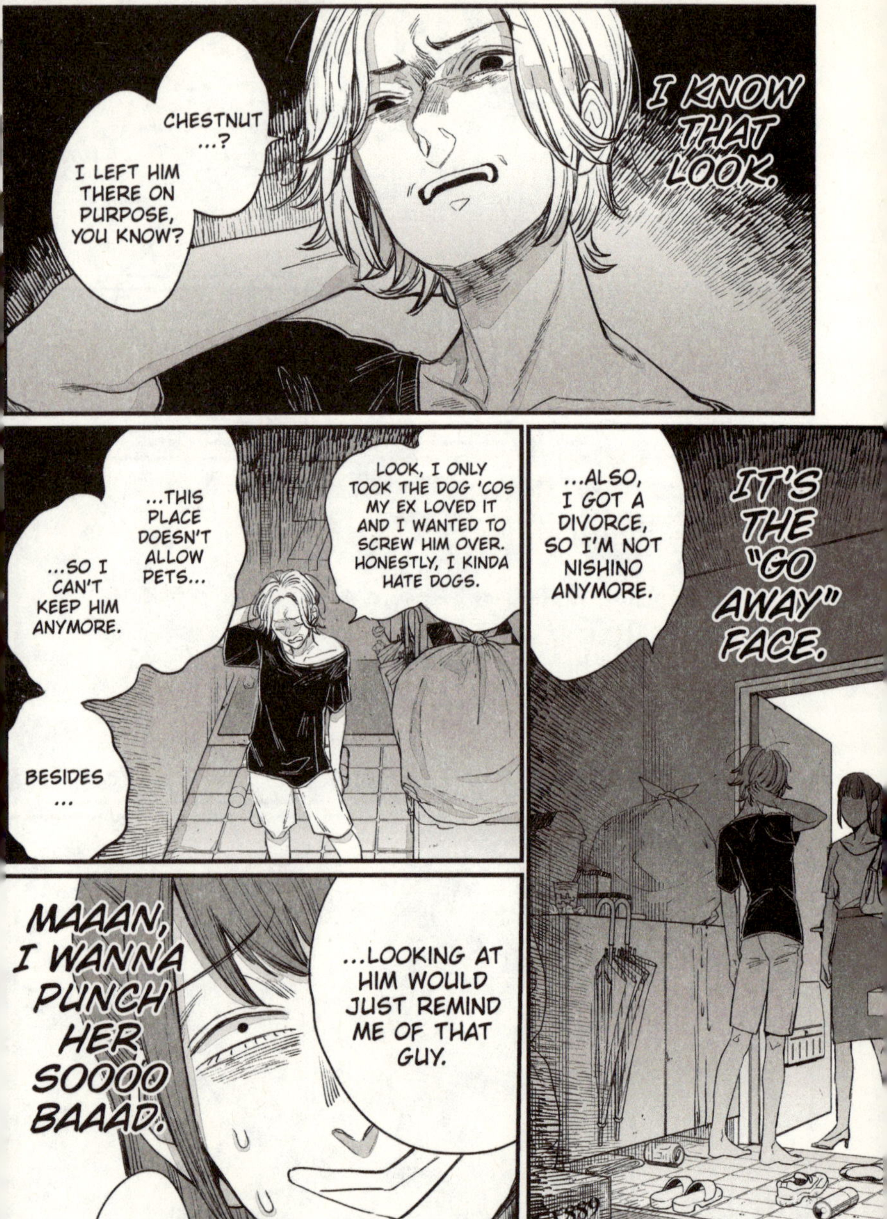
I KNOW THAT LOOK.
CHESTNUT ...?
I LEFT HIM THERE ON PURPOSE, YOU KNOW?
IT'S THE "GO AWAY" FACE.
...ALSO, I GOT A DIVORCE, SO I'M NOT NISHINO ANYMORE.
LOOK, I ONLY TOOK THE DOG 'COS MY EX LOVED IT AND I WANTED TO SCREW HIM OVER. HONESTLY, I KINDA HATE DOGS.
...THIS PLACE DOESN'T ALLOW PETS...
...SO I CAN'T KEEP HIM ANYMORE.
BESIDES ...
...LOOKING AT HIM WOULD JUST REMIND ME OF THAT GUY.
MAAAN, I WANNA PUNCH HER SOOOO BAAAD.
....

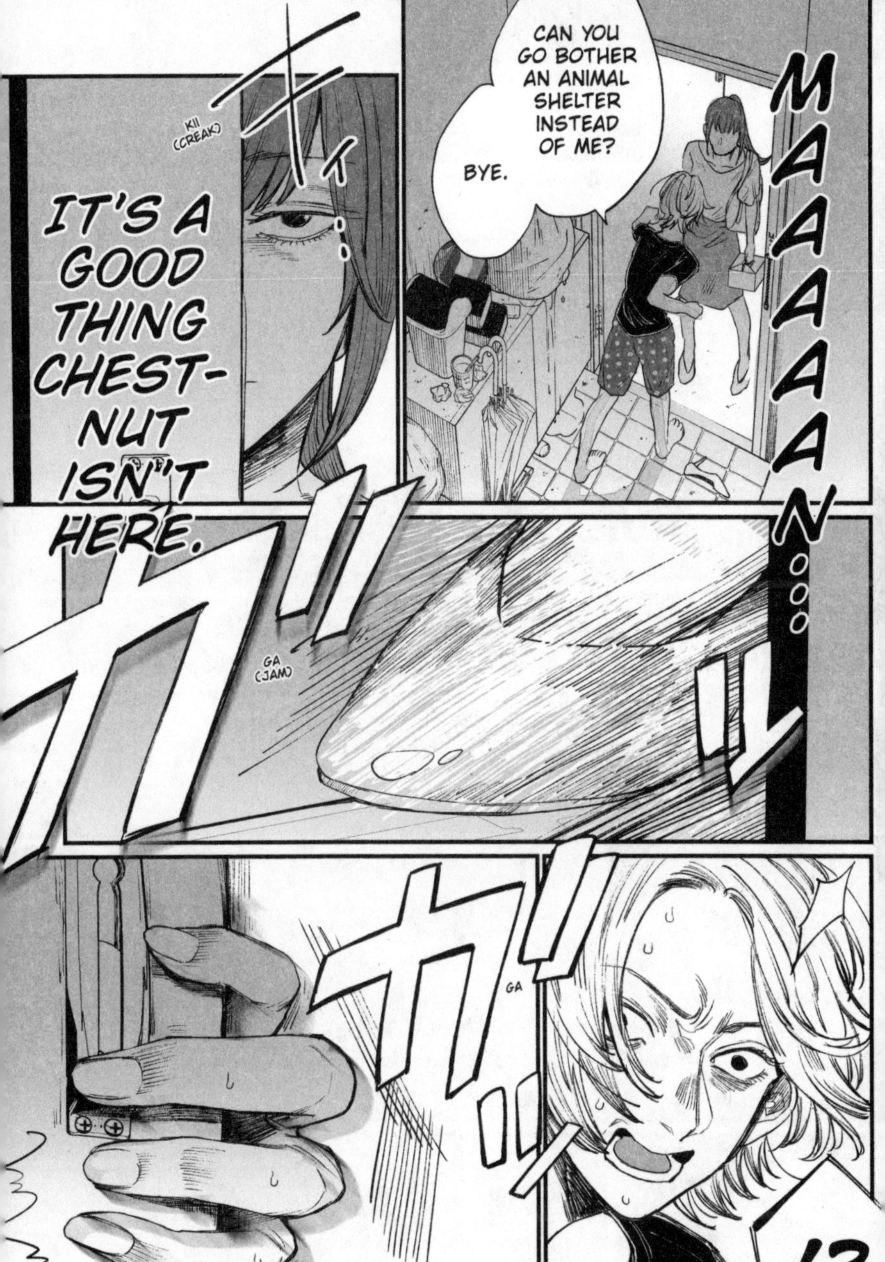
CAN YOU GO BOTHER AN ANIMAL SHELTER INSTEAD OF ME?
BYE.
MAAAAAAN...
KII (CREAK)
IT'S A GOOD THING CHEST-NUT ISN"T HERE.
GA (JAM)
GA
!?

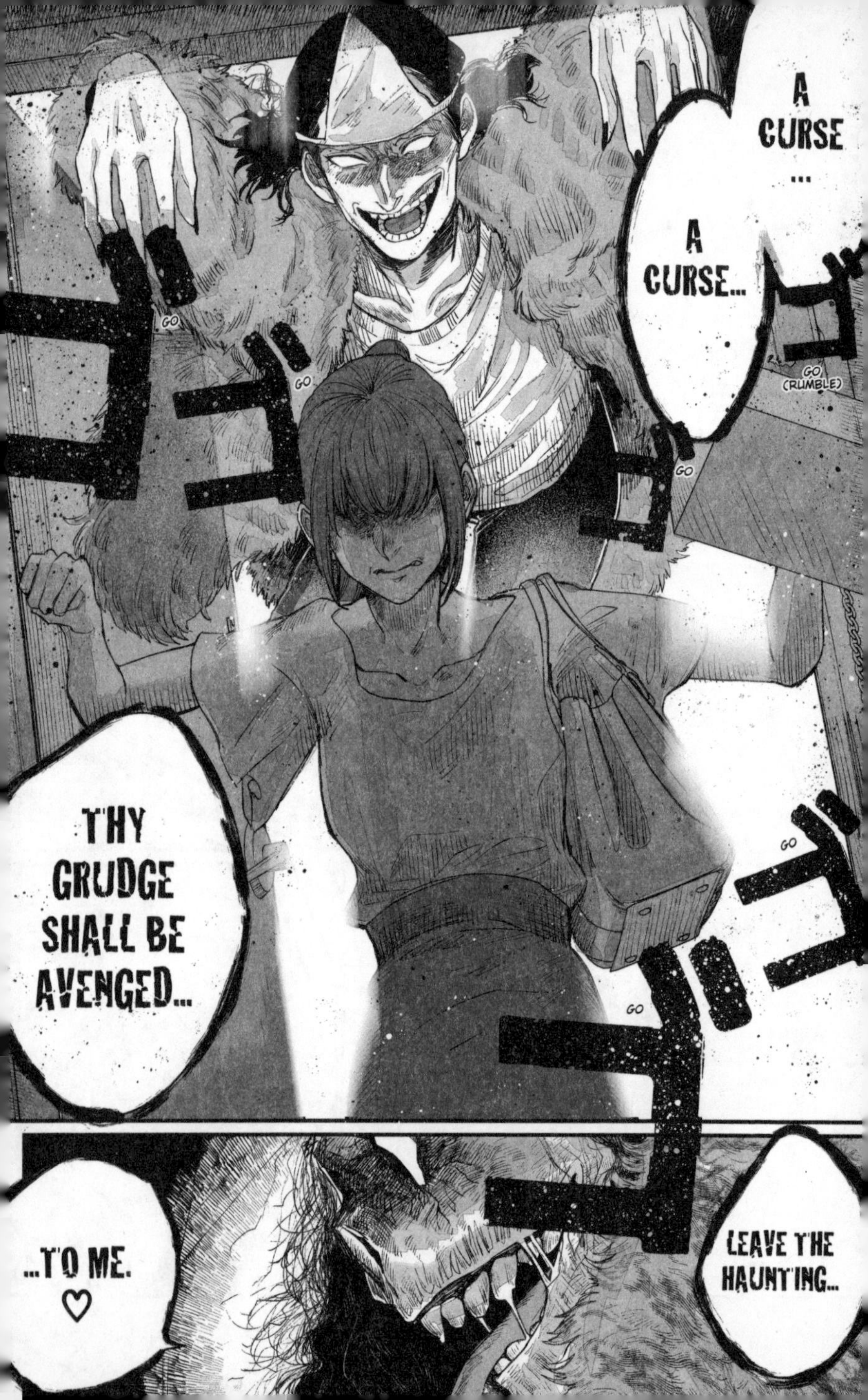
A CURSE ...
A CURSE...
GO (RUMBLE)
GO
GO
GO
GO
THY GRUDGE SHALL BE AVENGED...
GO
LEAVE THE HAUNTING...
...TO ME. ♡

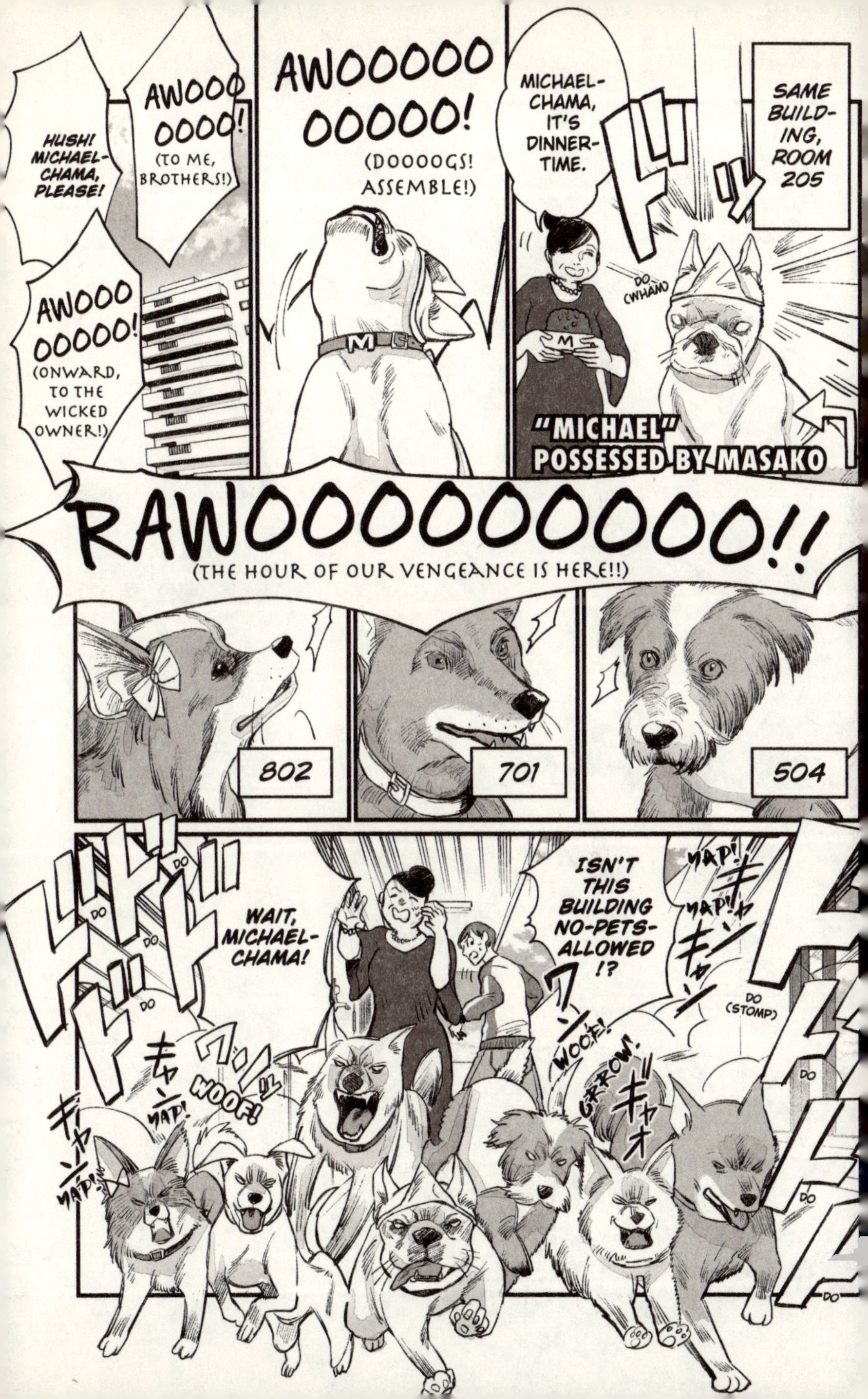

SAME BUILDING, ROOM 205
MICHAEL-CHAMA, IT'S DINNER-TIME.
DO (WHAM)
"MICHAEL" POSSESSED BY MASAKO
AWOOOOOO OOOOO!
(DOOOOGS! ASSEMBLE!)
AWOOOOOOO!
(TO ME, BROTHERS!)
HUSH! MICHAEL-CHAMA, PLEASE!
AWOOOOOOOO!
(ONWARD, TO THE WICKED OWNER!)
RAWOOOOOOOOOO!!
(THE HOUR OF OUR VENGEANCE IS HERE!!)
504
701
802
DO
DO
DO (STOMP)
YAP! YAP!
ISN'T THIS BUILDING NO-PETS-ALLOWED!?
WOOF!
GRROW!
WAIT, MICHAEL-CHAMA!
DO
DO
DO
DO
WOOF!
YAP!
YAP!

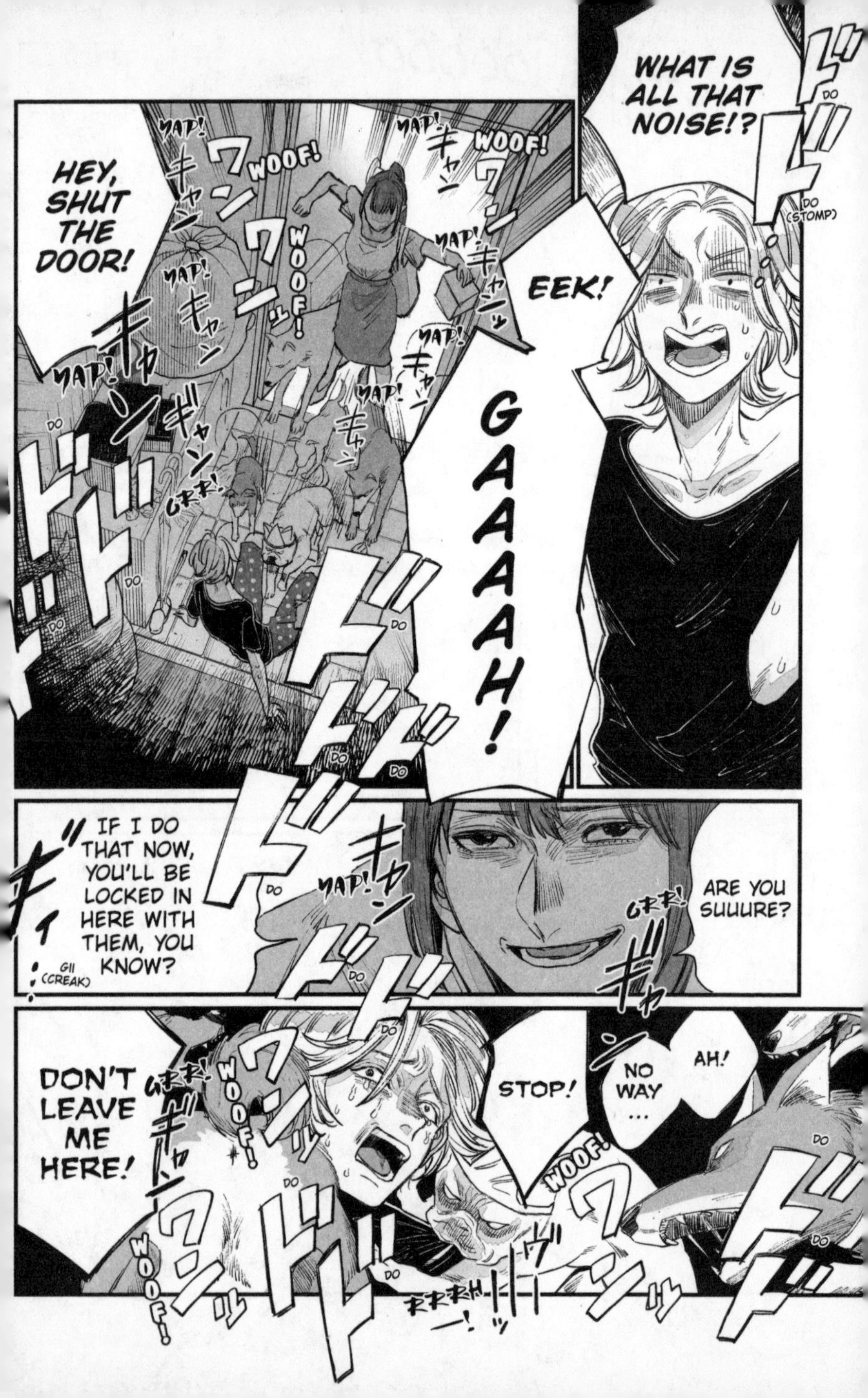
WHAT IS ALL THAT NOISE!?
DO
DO (STOMP)
EEK!
GAAAAAH!
HEY, SHUT THE DOOR!
YAP!
WOOF!
YAP!
WOOF!
YAP!
WOOF!
YAP!
YAP!
YAP!
YAP!
YAP!
GRR!
DO
DO
DO
DO
DO
ARE YOU SUUURE?
GRR!
YAP!
DO
DO
IF I DO THAT NOW, YOU'LL BE LOCKED IN HERE WITH THEM, YOU KNOW?
GII (CREAK)
AH!
NO WAY...
STOP!
DO
DO
WOOF!
RRRH!
DO
DO
GRR!
WOOF!
DON'T LEAVE ME HERE!
WOOF!
DO

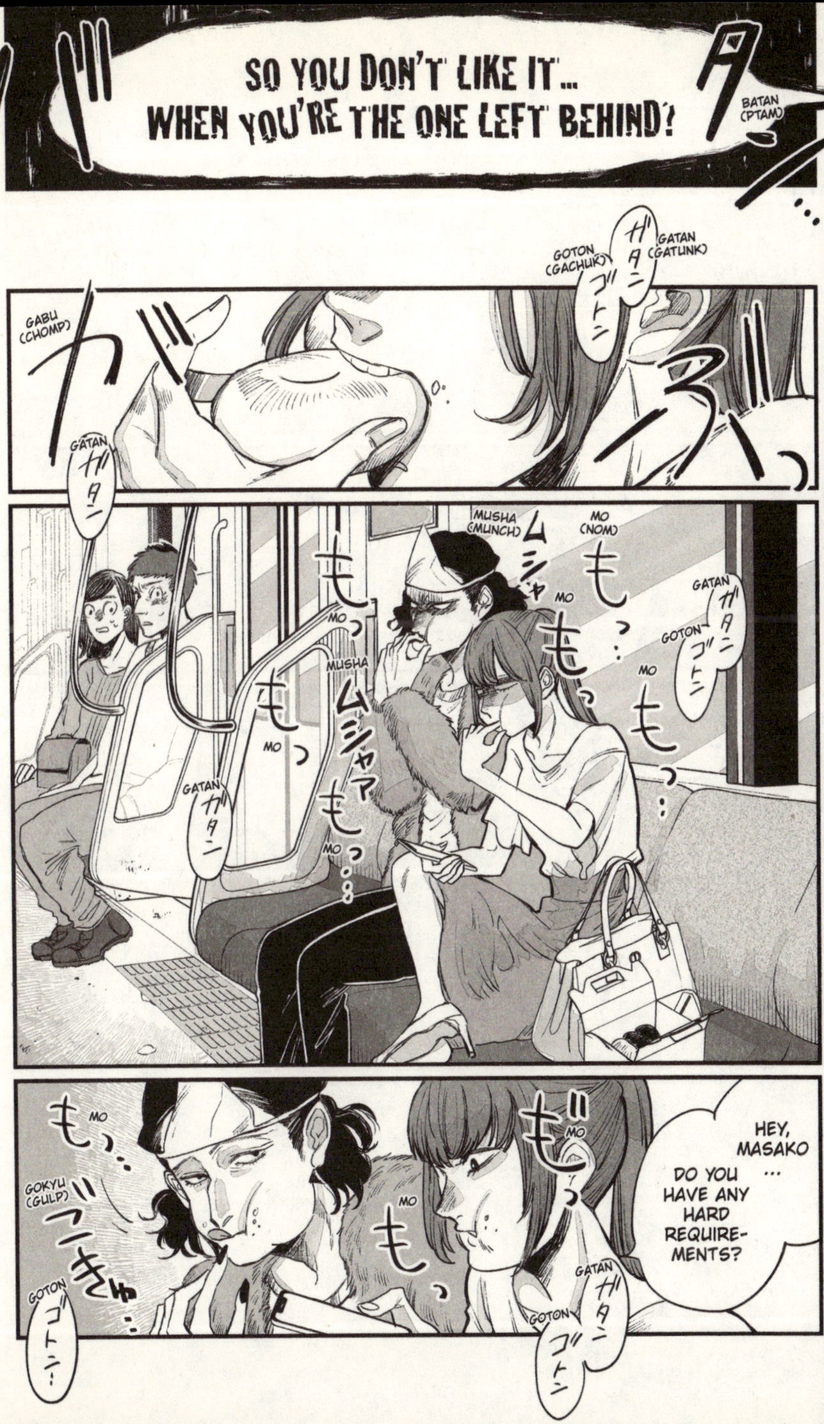

SO YOU DON'T LIKE IT... WHEN YOU'RE THE ONE LEFT BEHIND?
BATAN (PTAM)
GATAN (GATUNK)
GOTON (GACHUK)
GABU (CHOMP)
GATAN
GOTON
MO
MO
MO (NOM)
MUSHA (MUNCH)
MO
MUSHA
MO
MO
GATAN
GATAN
HEY, MASAKO...
DO YOU HAVE ANY HARD REQUIRE-MENTS?
MO
GATAN
GOTON
MO
MO
GOKYU (GULP)
GOTON

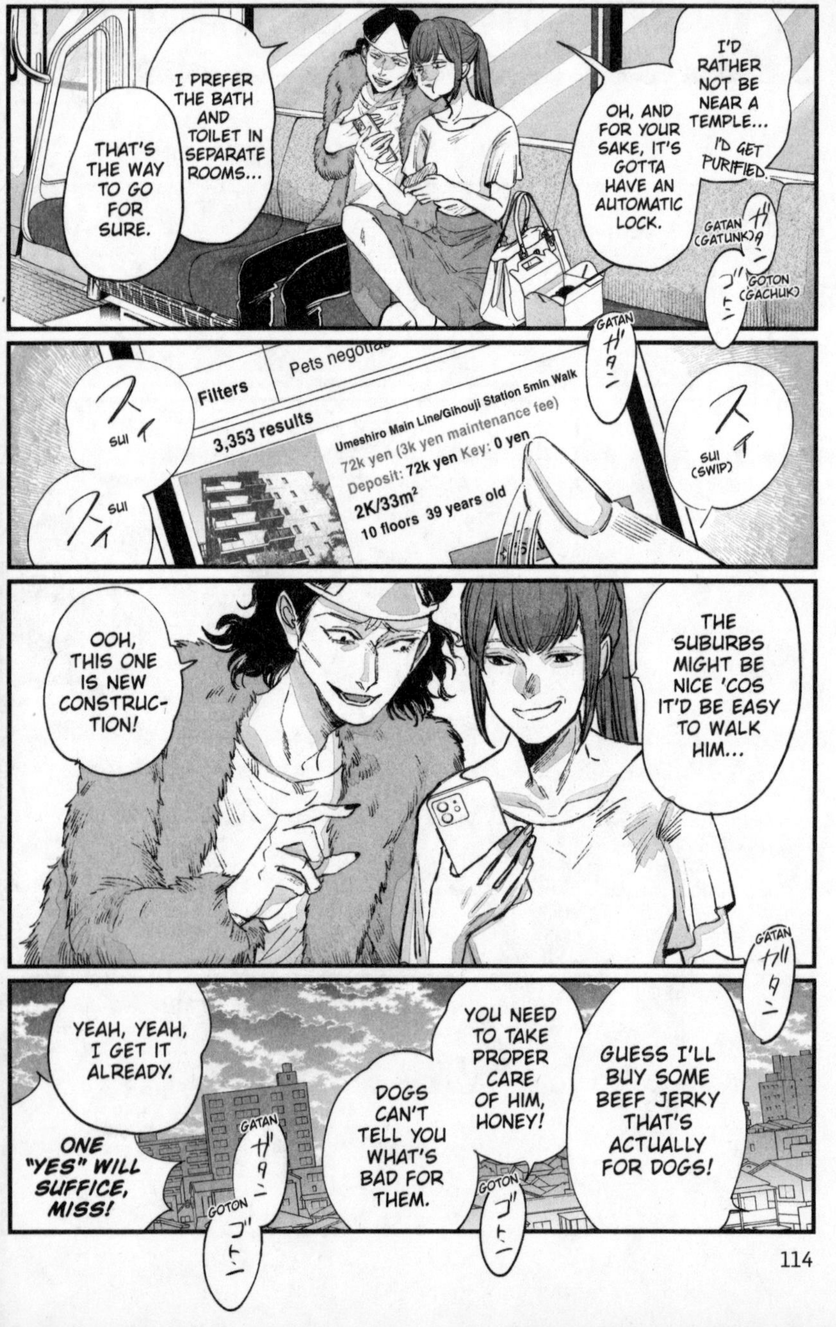
I'D RATHER NOT BE NEAR A TEMPLE... I'D GET PURIFIED.
OH, AND FOR YOUR SAKE, IT'S GOTTA HAVE AN AUTOMATIC LOCK.
I PREFER THE BATH AND TOILET IN SEPARATE ROOMS...
THAT'S THE WAY TO GO FOR SURE.
ガタン GATAN (GATUNK)
ゴトン GOTON (GACHUK)
ガタン GATAN
スィ SUI (SWIP)
Pets negotiab
Filters
3,353 results
Umeshiro Main Line/Gihouji Station 5min Walk
72k yen (3k yen maintenance fee)
Deposit: 72k yen Key: 0 yen
2K/33m²
10 floors 39 years old
スィ SUI
スィ SUI
THE SUBURBS MIGHT BE NICE 'COS IT'D BE EASY TO WALK HIM...
OOH, THIS ONE IS NEW CONSTRUC-TION!
ガタン GATAN
GUESS I'LL BUY SOME BEEF JERKY THAT'S ACTUALLY FOR DOGS!
YOU NEED TO TAKE PROPER CARE OF HIM, HONEY!
ゴトン GOTON
DOGS CAN'T TELL YOU WHAT'S BAD FOR THEM.
YEAH, YEAH, I GET IT ALREADY.
ONE "YES" WILL SUFFICE, MISS!
ガタン GATAN
ゴトン GOTON

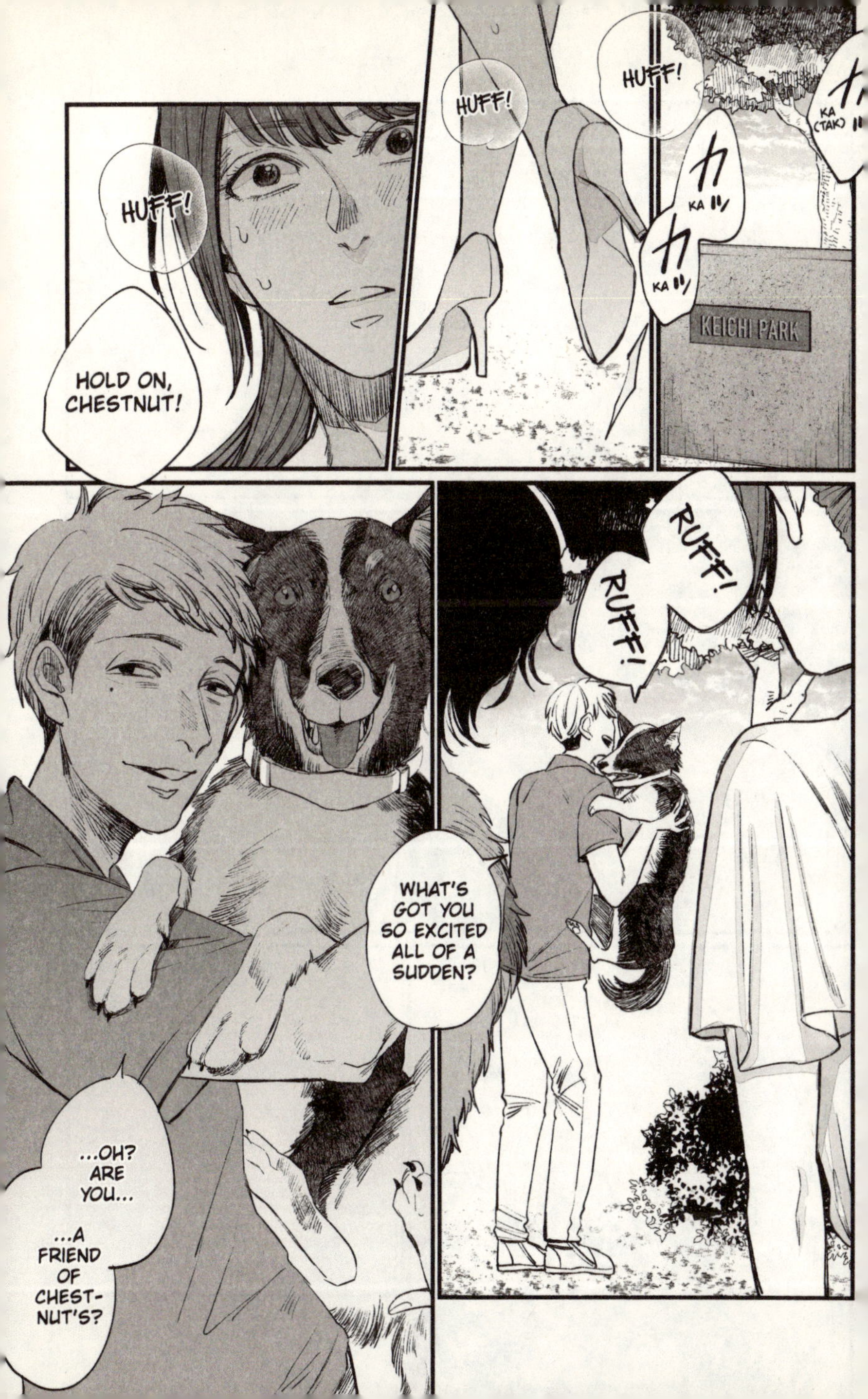
HUFF!
KA (TAK)
KA
KA
KEICHI PARK
HUFF!
HUFF!
HOLD ON, CHESTNUT!
RUFF! RUFF!
WHAT'S GOT YOU SO EXCITED ALL OF A SUDDEN?
...OH? ARE YOU...
...A FRIEND OF CHEST-NUT'S?

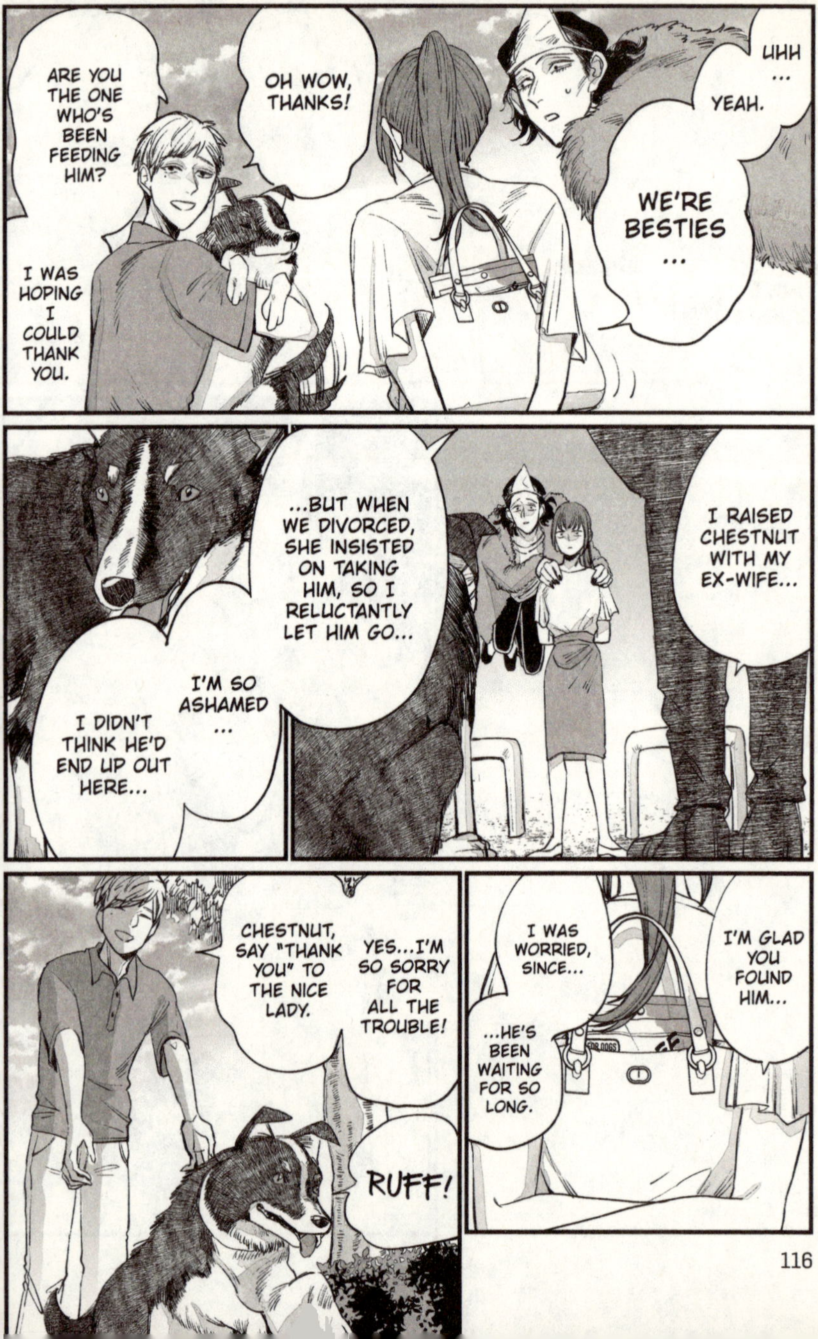
UHH ... YEAH.
WE'RE BESTIES ...
OH WOW, THANKS!
ARE YOU THE ONE WHO'S BEEN FEEDING HIM?
I WAS HOPING I COULD THANK YOU.
I RAISED CHESTNUT WITH MY EX-WIFE...
...BUT WHEN WE DIVORCED, SHE INSISTED ON TAKING HIM, SO I RELUCTANTLY LET HIM GO...
I'M SO ASHAMED ...
I DIDN'T THINK HE'D END UP OUT HERE...
I'M GLAD YOU FOUND HIM...
I WAS WORRIED, SINCE...
...HE'S BEEN WAITING FOR SO LONG.
YES...I'M SO SORRY FOR ALL THE TROUBLE!
CHESTNUT, SAY "THANK YOU" TO THE NICE LADY.
RUFF!

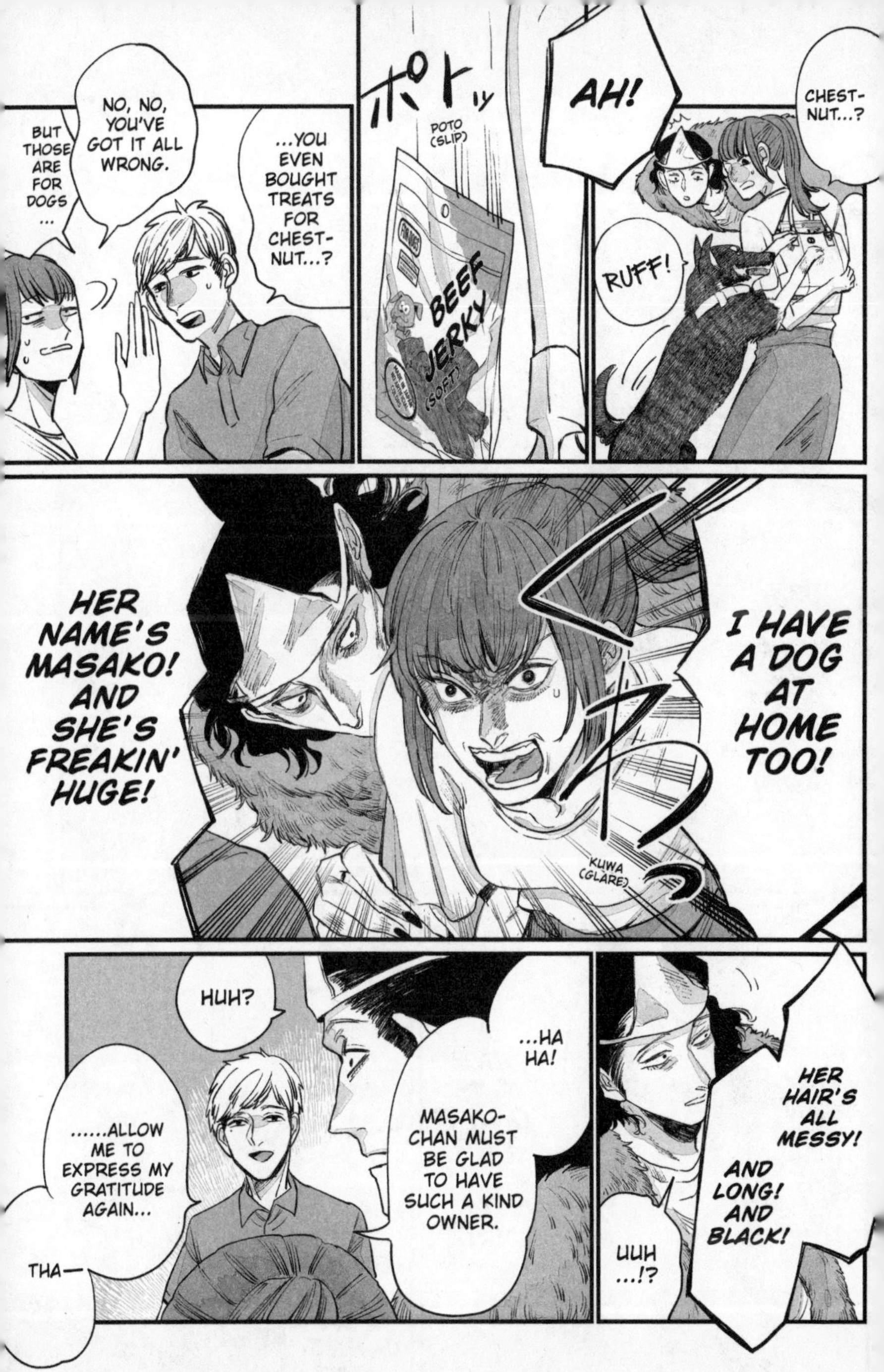
CHEST-NUT...?
AH!
RUFF!
ポト
POTO (SLIP)
BEEF JERKY (SOFT)
...YOU EVEN BOUGHT TREATS FOR CHEST-NUT...?
NO, NO, YOU'VE GOT IT ALL WRONG.
BUT THOSE ARE FOR DOGS ...
I HAVE A DOG AT HOME TOO!
KUWA (GLARE)
HER NAME'S MASAKO! AND SHE'S FREAKIN' HUGE!
HER HAIR'S ALL MESSY!
AND LONG! AND BLACK!
UUH ...!?
...HA HA!
MASAKO-CHAN MUST BE GLAD TO HAVE SUCH A KIND OWNER.
HUH?
......ALLOW ME TO EXPRESS MY GRATITUDE AGAIN...
THA—

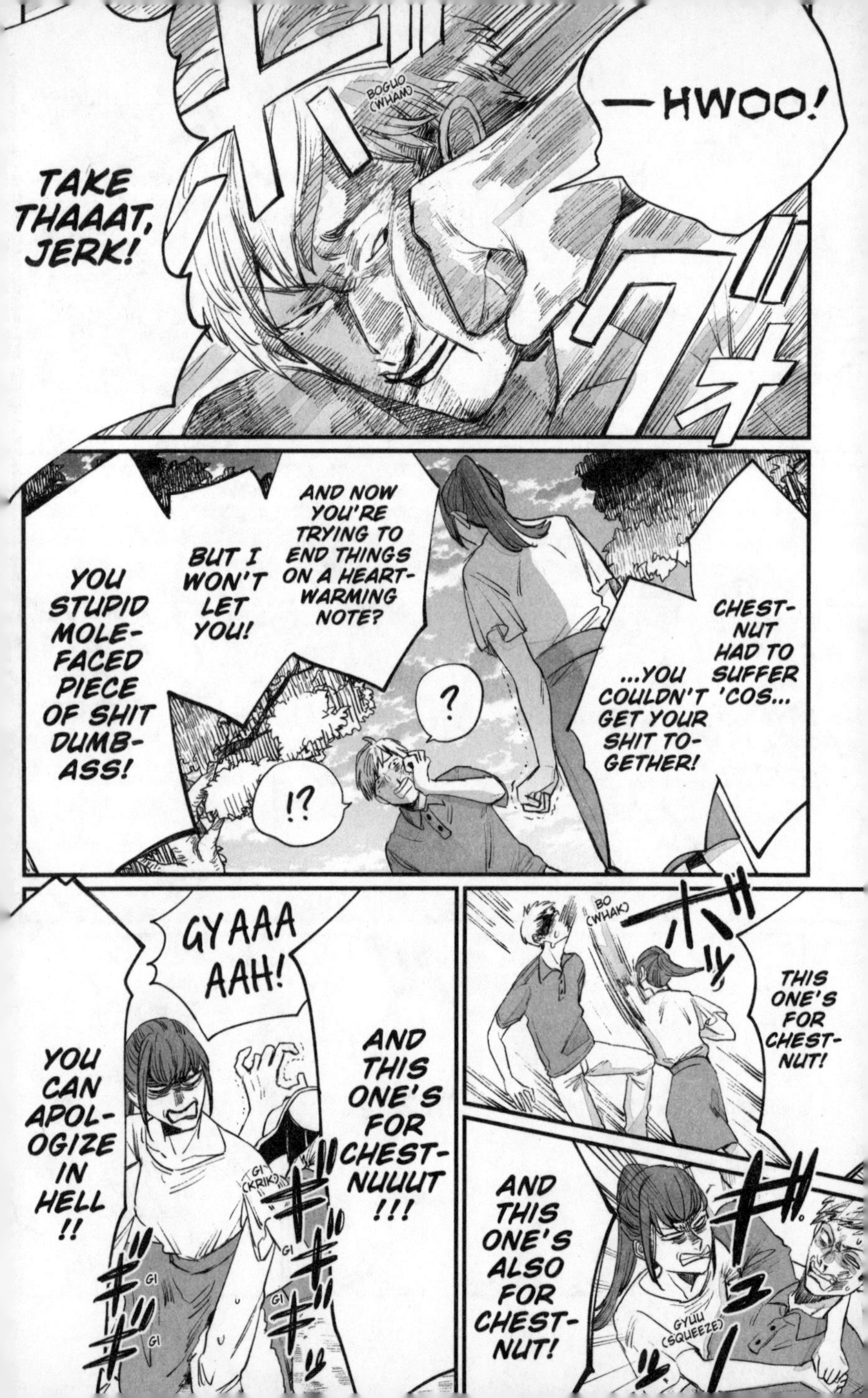
—HWOO!
BOGUO (WHAM)
TAKE THAAAT, JERK!
CHEST-NUT HAD TO SUFFER 'COS...
...YOU COULDN'T GET YOUR SHIT TO-GETHER!
?
!?
AND NOW YOU'RE TRYING TO END THINGS ON A HEART-WARMING NOTE?
BUT I WON'T LET YOU!
YOU STUPID MOLE-FACED PIECE OF SHIT DUMB-ASS!
BO (WHAK)
THIS ONE'S FOR CHEST-NUT!
GYUU (SQUEEZE)
AND THIS ONE'S ALSO FOR CHEST-NUT!
GYAAA AAH!
AND THIS ONE'S FOR CHEST-NUUUT!!!
GI (KRIK)
GI
GI
GI
GI
YOU CAN APOL-OGIZE IN HELL!!

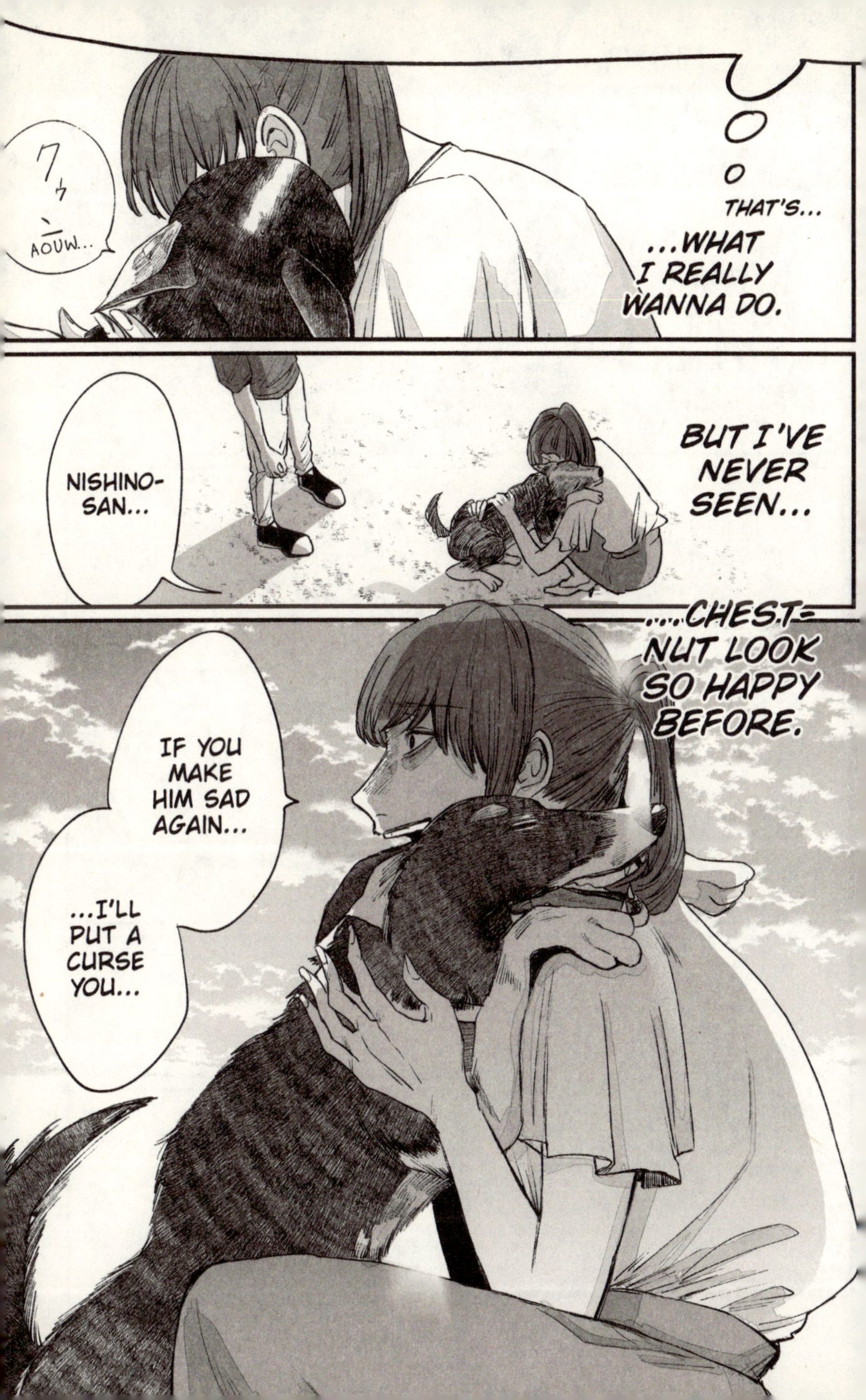
THAT'S...
...WHAT I REALLY WANNA DO.
AOUW...
BUT I'VE NEVER SEEN...
NISHINO-SAN...
...CHEST-NUT LOOK SO HAPPY BEFORE.
IF YOU MAKE HIM SAD AGAIN...
...I'LL PUT A CURSE YOU...

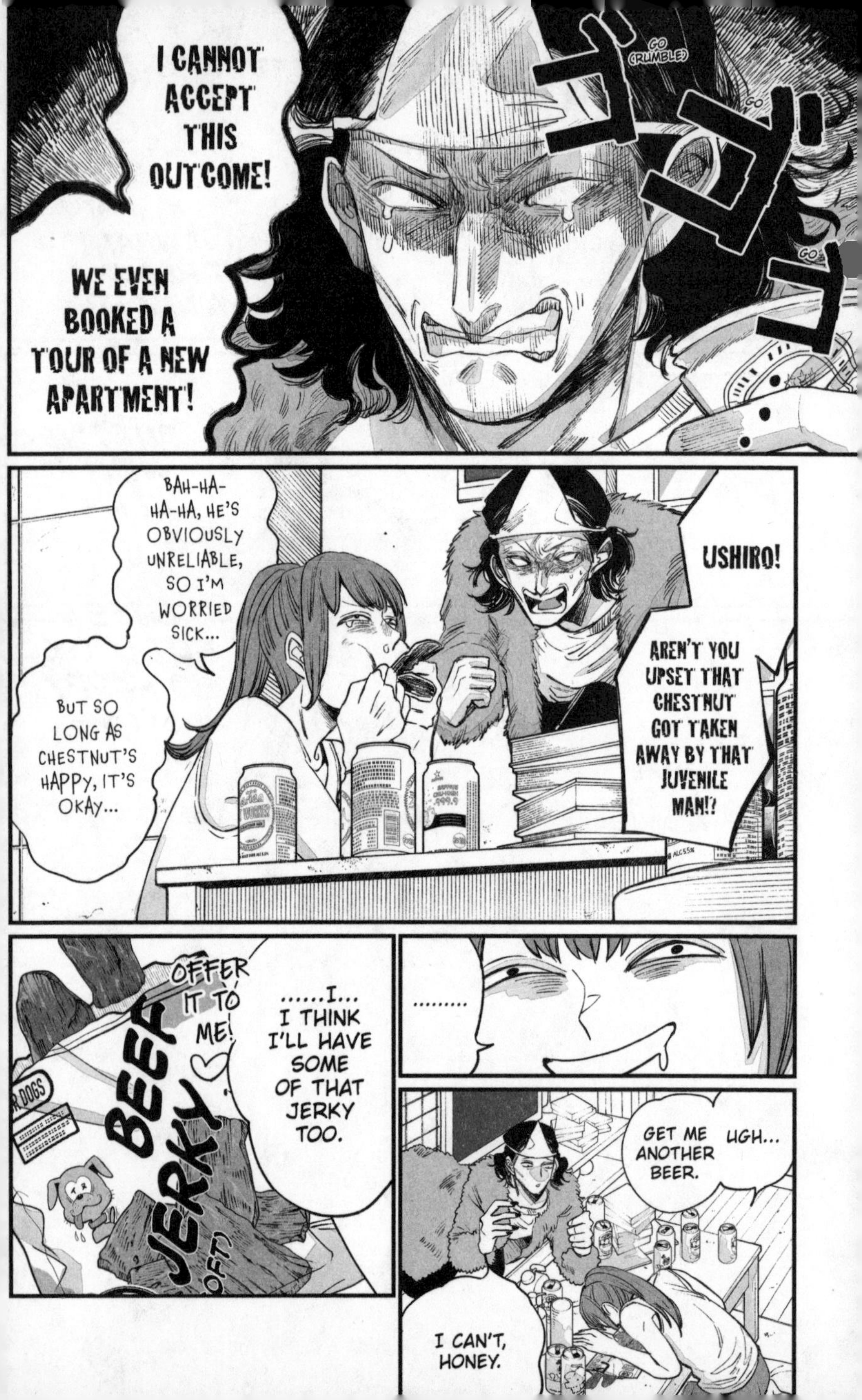
GO (RUMBLE)
GO
GO
I CANNOT ACCEPT THIS OUTCOME!
WE EVEN BOOKED A TOUR OF A NEW APARTMENT!
USHIRO!
AREN'T YOU UPSET THAT CHESTNUT GOT TAKEN AWAY BY THAT JUVENILE MAN!?
BAH-HA-HA-HA, HE'S OBVIOUSLY UNRELIABLE, SO I'M WORRIED SICK...
BUT SO LONG AS CHESTNUT'S HAPPY, IT'S OKAY...
....
UGH...
GET ME ANOTHER BEER.
I CAN'T, HONEY.
......I... I THINK I'LL HAVE SOME OF THAT JERKY TOO.
OFFER IT TO ME!
BEEF JERKY

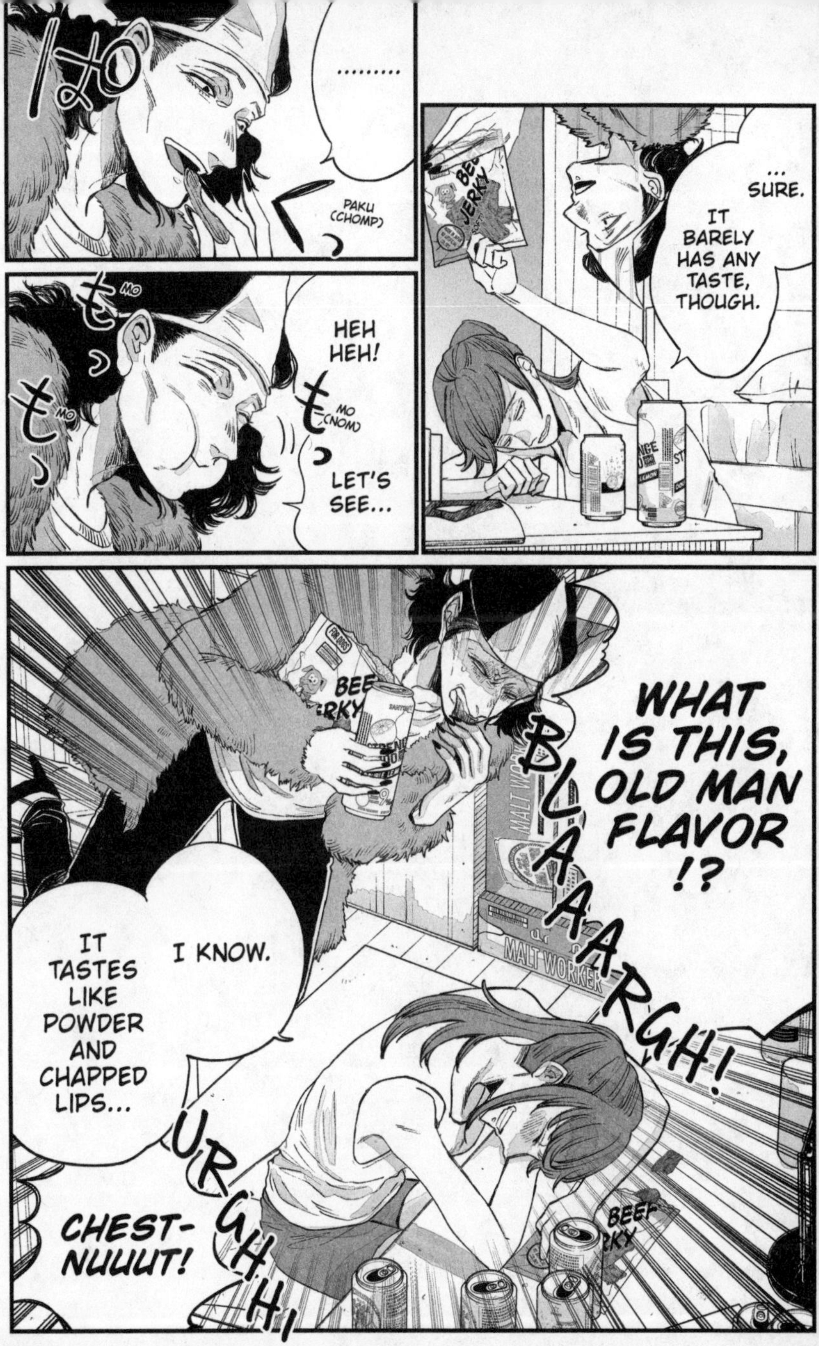
... SURE.
IT BARELY HAS ANY TASTE, THOUGH.
BEEF JERKY
....
はむ
PAKU (CHOMP)
HEH HEH!
も MO
も MO
も MO (NOM)
LET'S SEE...
WHAT IS THIS, OLD MAN FLAVOR !?
BLAAAARGH!
BEEF JERKY
MALT WORKER
I KNOW.
IT TASTES LIKE POWDER AND CHAPPED LIPS...
URGHH!
CHEST-NUUUT!

GOGOGOGO-GO-GHOST!

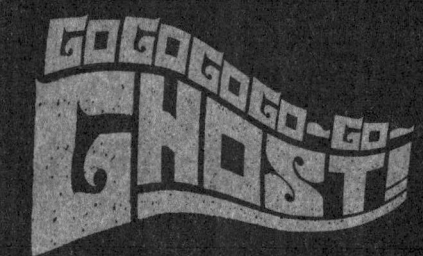

Chapter 6: Café 6th

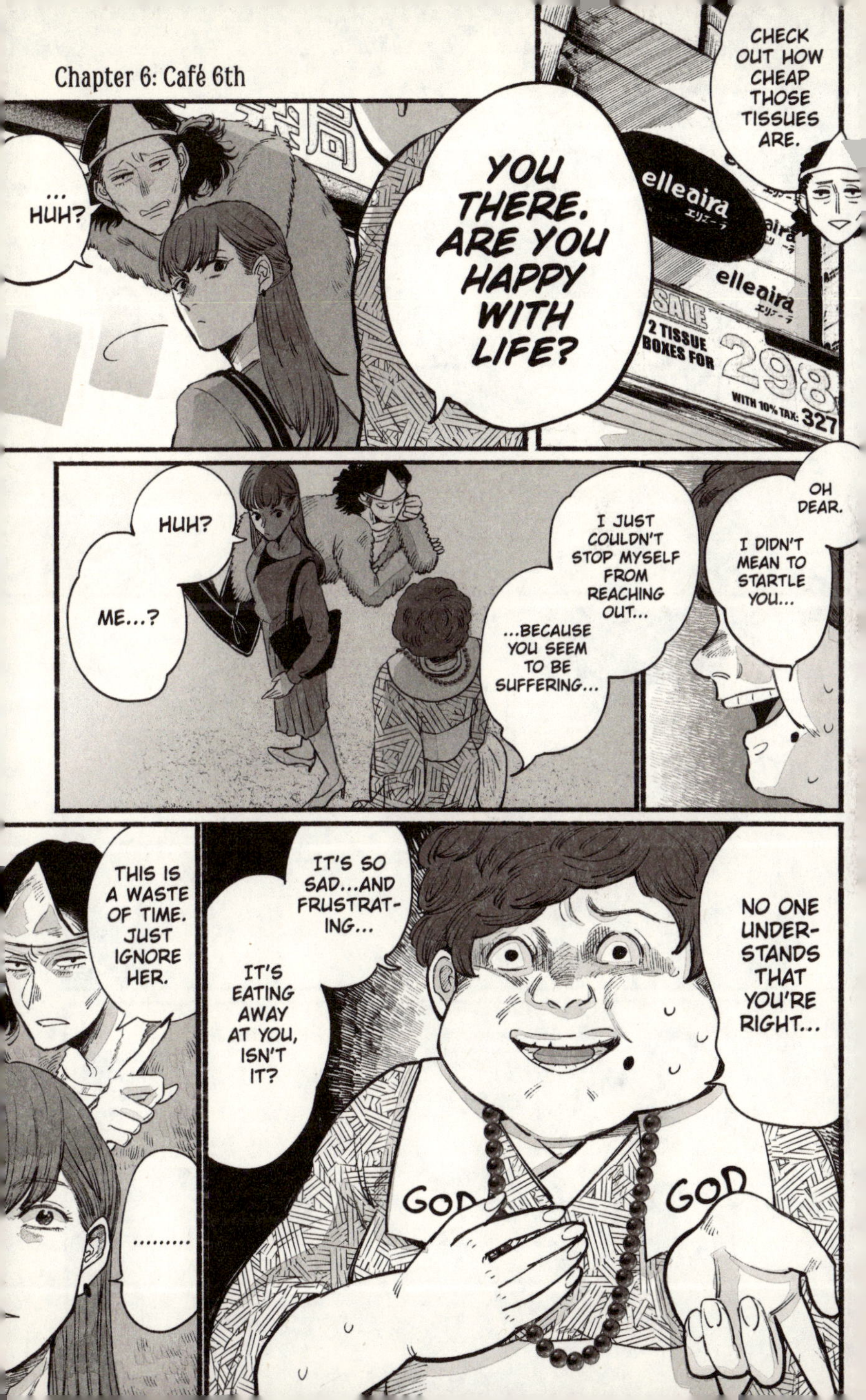
CHECK OUT HOW CHEAP THOSE TISSUES ARE.
YOU THERE. ARE YOU HAPPY WITH LIFE?
elleaira エリエール
elleaira エリエール
SALE
2 TISSUE BOXES FOR 298
WITH 10% TAX: 327
... HUH?
OH DEAR.
I DIDN'T MEAN TO STARTLE YOU...
I JUST COULDN'T STOP MYSELF FROM REACHING OUT...
...BECAUSE YOU SEEM TO BE SUFFERING...
HUH?
ME...?
NO ONE UNDERSTANDS THAT YOU'RE RIGHT...
IT'S SO SAD...AND FRUSTRATING...
IT'S EATING AWAY AT YOU, ISN'T IT?
GOD
GOD
THIS IS A WASTE OF TIME. JUST IGNORE HER.
....

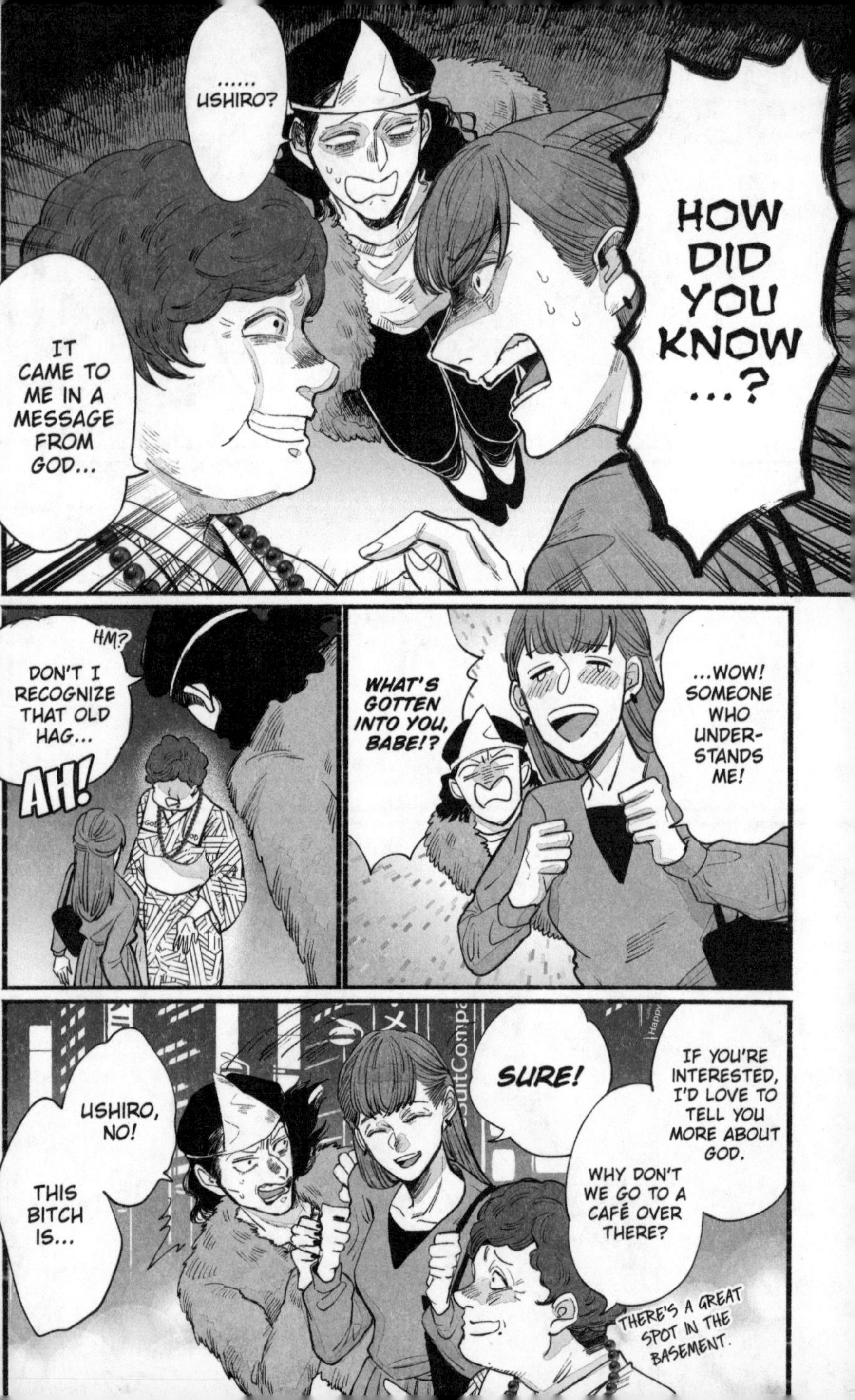
......USHIRO?
HOW DID YOU KNOW...?
IT CAME TO ME IN A MESSAGE FROM GOD...
...WOW! SOMEONE WHO UNDER-STANDS ME!
WHAT'S GOTTEN INTO YOU, BABE!?
HM?
DON'T I RECOGNIZE THAT OLD HAG...
AH!
IF YOU'RE INTERESTED, I'D LOVE TO TELL YOU MORE ABOUT GOD.
WHY DON'T WE GO TO A CAFÉ OVER THERE?
SURE!
THERE'S A GREAT SPOT IN THE BASEMENT.
USHIRO, NO!
THIS BITCH IS...

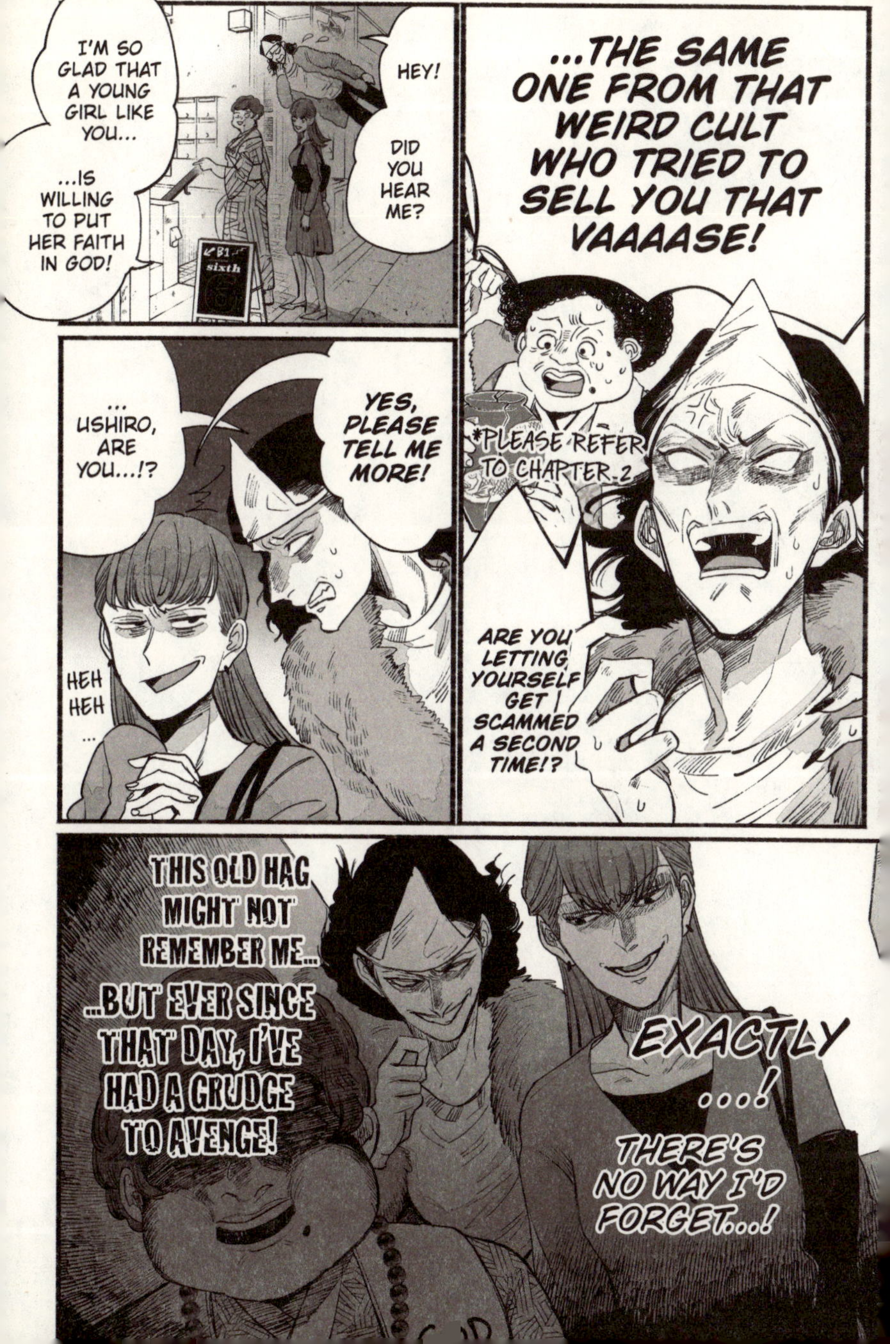
...THE SAME ONE FROM THAT WEIRD CULT WHO TRIED TO SELL YOU THAT VAAAASE!
*PLEASE REFER TO CHAPTER 2
ARE YOU LETTING YOURSELF GET SCAMMED A SECOND TIME!?
HEY!
DID YOU HEAR ME?
I'M SO GLAD THAT A YOUNG GIRL LIKE YOU...
...IS WILLING TO PUT HER FAITH IN GOD!
B1
sixth
YES, PLEASE TELL ME MORE!
... USHIRO, ARE YOU...!?
HEH HEH ...
EXACTLY ...!
THERE'S NO WAY I'D FORGET...!
THIS OLD HAG MIGHT NOT REMEMBER ME...
...BUT EVER SINCE THAT DAY, I'VE HAD A GRUDGE TO AVENGE!

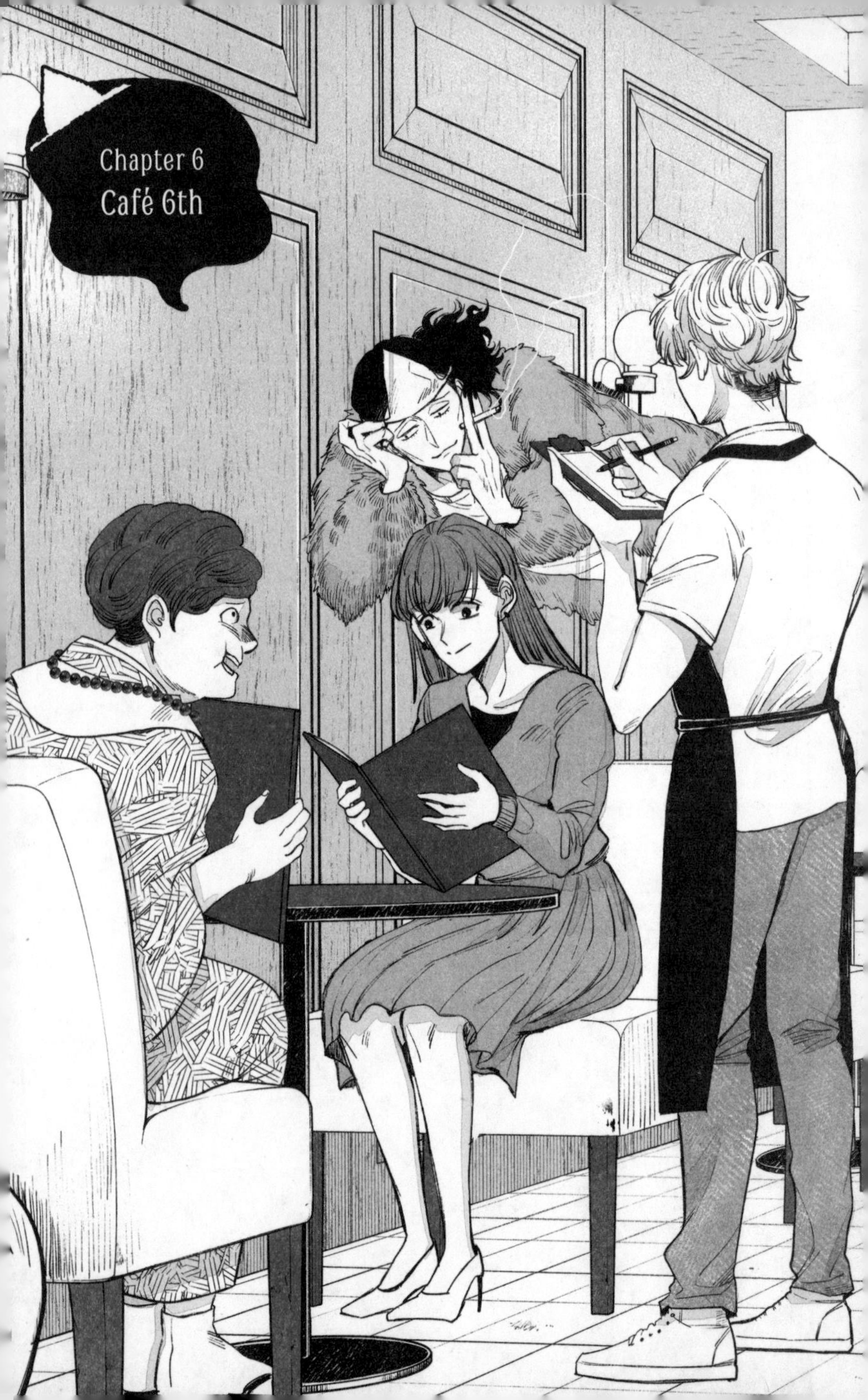
Chapter 6
Café 6th

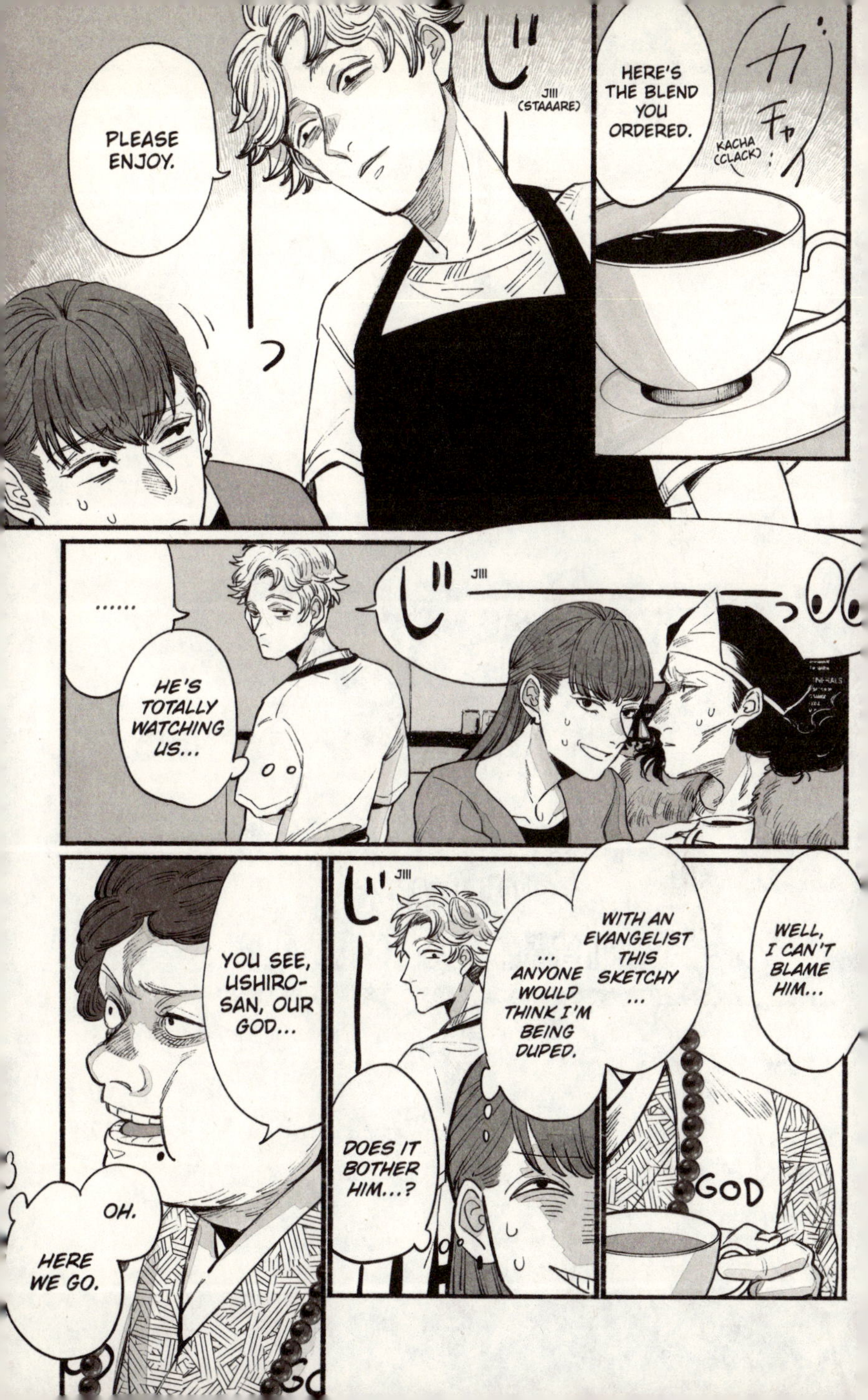
KACHA (CLACK)
HERE'S THE BLEND YOU ORDERED.
JIII (STAAARE)
PLEASE ENJOY.
JIII
......
HE'S TOTALLY WATCHING US...
WELL, I CAN'T BLAME HIM...
GOD
WITH AN EVANGELIST THIS SKETCHY ...
... ANYONE WOULD THINK I'M BEING DUPED.
JIII
DOES IT BOTHER HIM...?
YOU SEE, USHIRO-SAN, OUR GOD...
OH.
HERE WE GO.

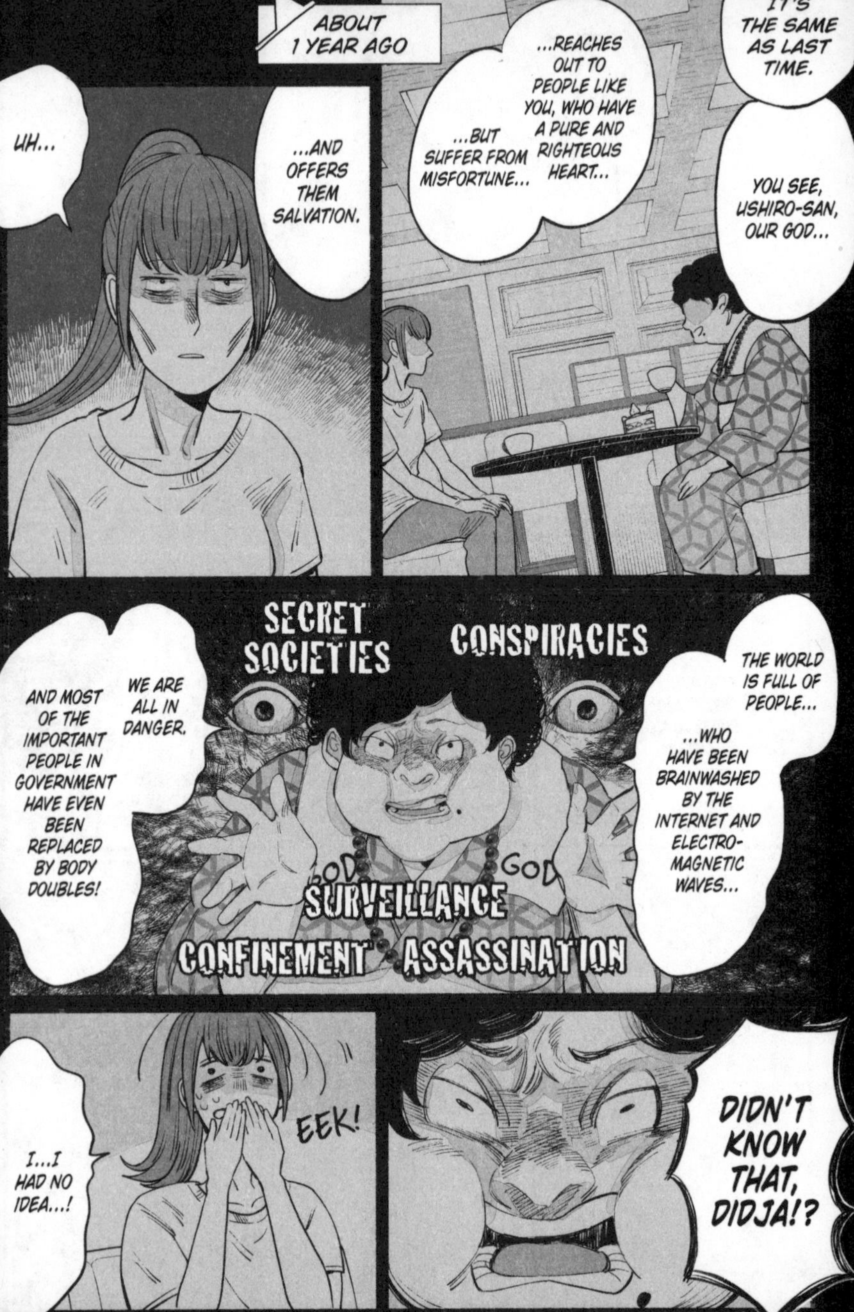
ABOUT 1 YEAR AGO
IT'S THE SAME AS LAST TIME.
YOU SEE, USHIRO-SAN, OUR GOD...
...REACHES OUT TO PEOPLE LIKE YOU, WHO HAVE A PURE AND RIGHTEOUS HEART...
...BUT SUFFER FROM MISFORTUNE...
...AND OFFERS THEM SALVATION.
UH...
THE WORLD IS FULL OF PEOPLE...
...WHO HAVE BEEN BRAINWASHED BY THE INTERNET AND ELECTRO-MAGNETIC WAVES...
CONSPIRACIES
SECRET SOCIETIES
WE ARE ALL IN DANGER.
AND MOST OF THE IMPORTANT PEOPLE IN GOVERNMENT HAVE EVEN BEEN REPLACED BY BODY DOUBLES!
GOD
SURVEILLANCE
ASSASSINATION
CONFINEMENT
DIDN'T KNOW THAT, DIDJA!?
EEK!
I...I HAD NO IDEA...!

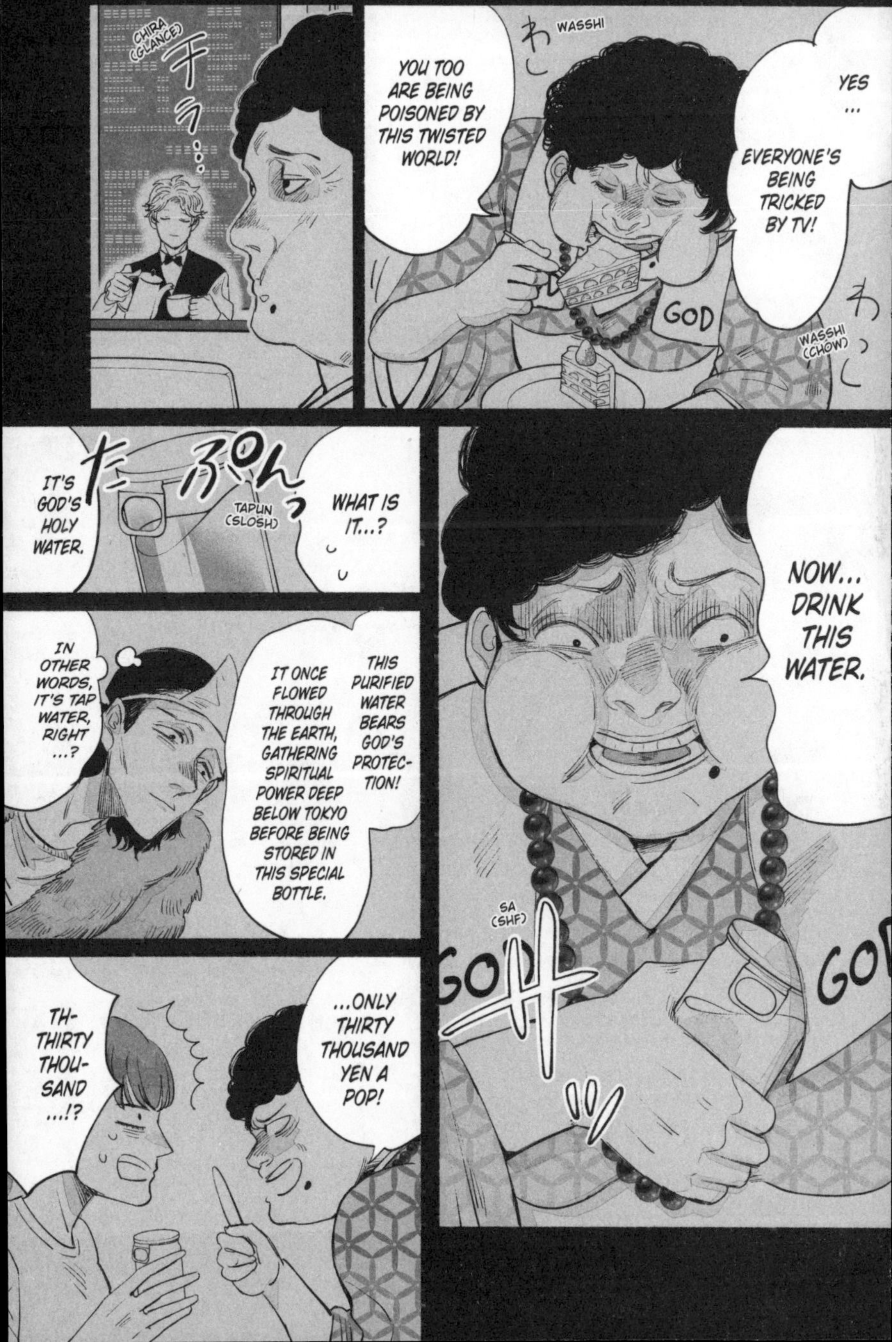
YES ... EVERYONE'S BEING TRICKED BY TV!
WASSHI
WASSHI (CHOW)
YOU TOO ARE BEING POISONED BY THIS TWISTED WORLD!
GOD
CHIRA (GLANCE)
NOW... DRINK THIS WATER.
GOD
GOD
SA (SHF)
WHAT IS IT...?
TAPUN (SLOSH)
IT'S GOD'S HOLY WATER.
THIS PURIFIED WATER BEARS GOD'S PROTEC-TION!
IT ONCE FLOWED THROUGH THE EARTH, GATHERING SPIRITUAL POWER DEEP BELOW TOKYO BEFORE BEING STORED IN THIS SPECIAL BOTTLE.
IN OTHER WORDS, IT'S TAP WATER, RIGHT ...?
...ONLY THIRTY THOUSAND YEN A POP!
TH-THIRTY THOU-SAND ...!?

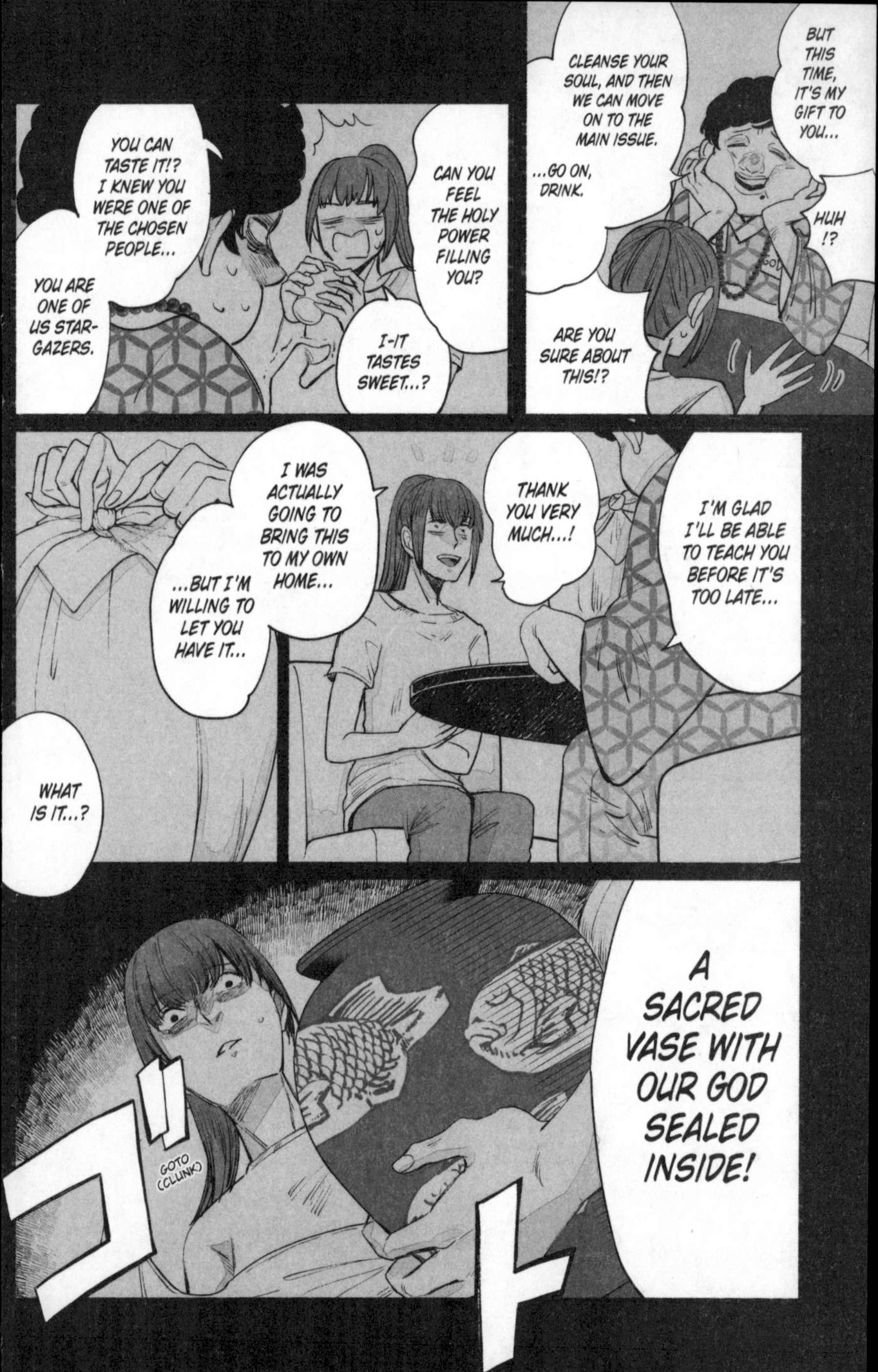
CLEANSE YOUR SOUL, AND THEN WE CAN MOVE ON TO THE MAIN ISSUE.
...GO ON, DRINK.
BUT THIS TIME, IT'S MY GIFT TO YOU...
HUH !?
ARE YOU SURE ABOUT THIS!?
CAN YOU FEEL THE HOLY POWER FILLING YOU?
I-IT TASTES SWEET...?
YOU CAN TASTE IT!? I KNEW YOU WERE ONE OF THE CHOSEN PEOPLE...
YOU ARE ONE OF US STAR-GAZERS.
I'M GLAD I'LL BE ABLE TO TEACH YOU BEFORE IT'S TOO LATE...
THANK YOU VERY MUCH...!
I WAS ACTUALLY GOING TO BRING THIS TO MY OWN HOME...
...BUT I'M WILLING TO LET YOU HAVE IT...
WHAT IS IT...?
A SACRED VASE WITH OUR GOD SEALED INSIDE!
GOTO (CLUNK)

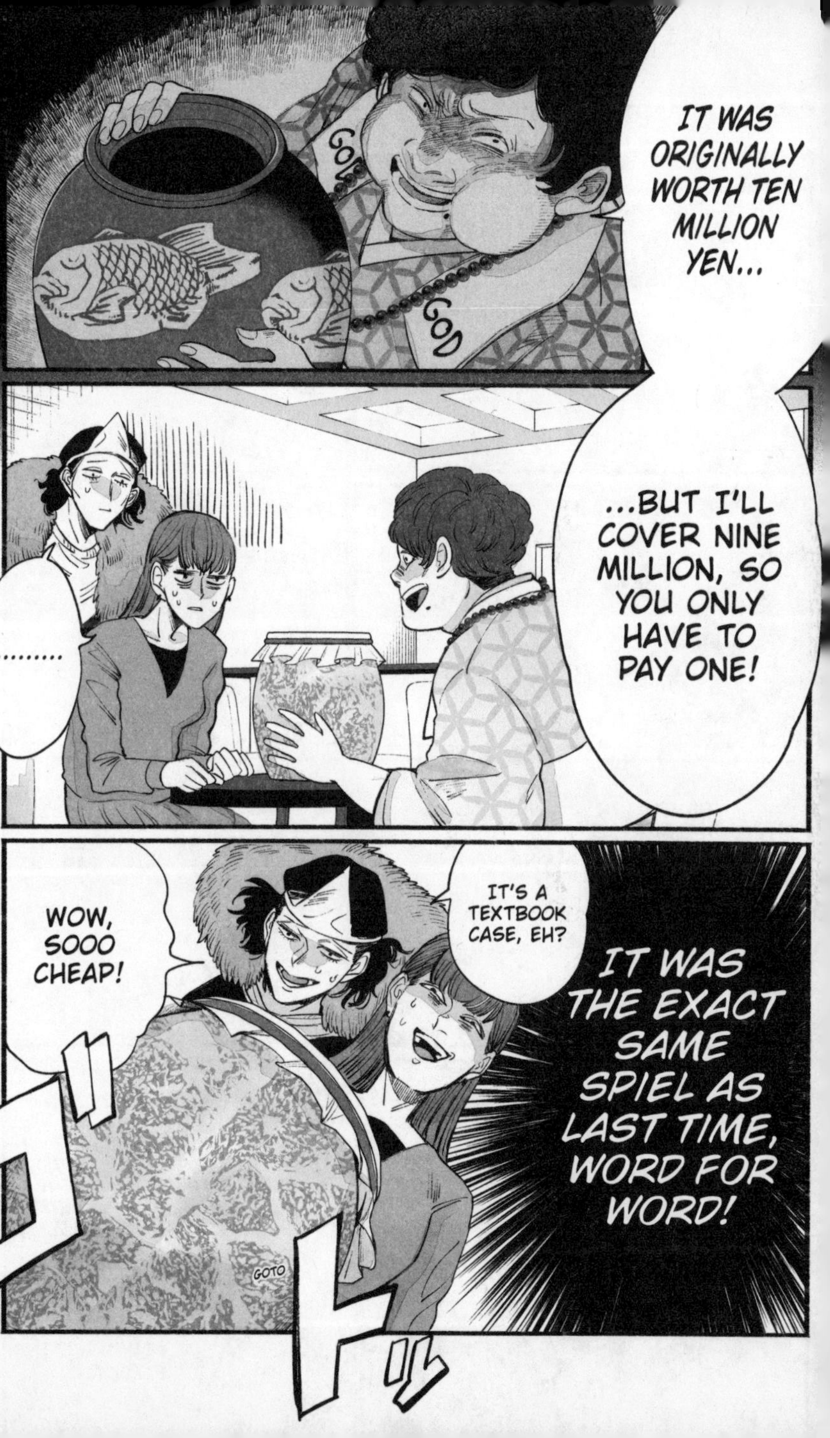
GOD
GOD
IT WAS ORIGINALLY WORTH TEN MILLION YEN...
...BUT I'LL COVER NINE MILLION, SO YOU ONLY HAVE TO PAY ONE!
....
IT WAS THE EXACT SAME SPIEL AS LAST TIME, WORD FOR WORD!
IT'S A TEXTBOOK CASE, EH?
WOW, SOOO CHEAP!
GOTO

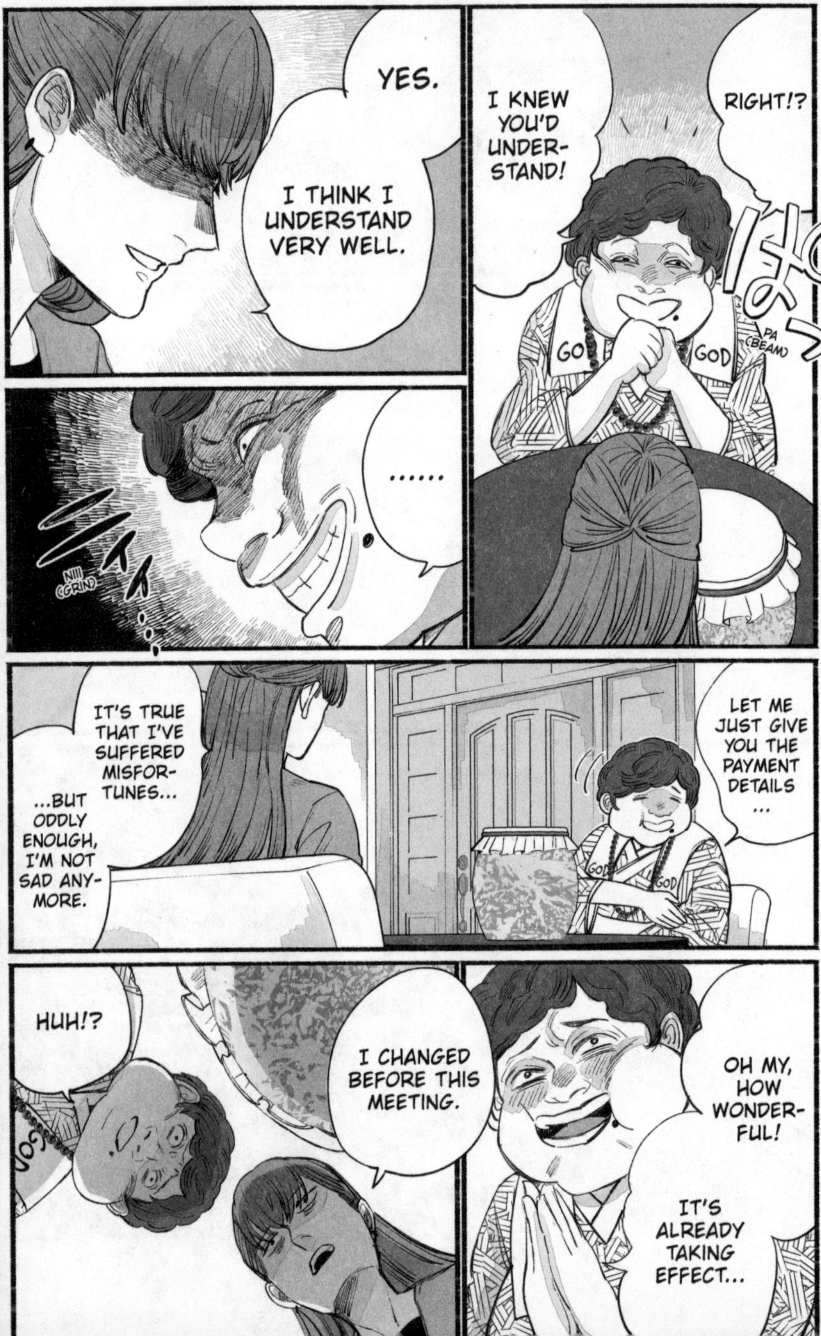
RIGHT!?
I KNEW YOU'D UNDERSTAND!
ぱっ
PA (BEAM)
GOD
GOD
YES.
I THINK I UNDERSTAND VERY WELL.
......
NIII (GRIN)
LET ME JUST GIVE YOU THE PAYMENT DETAILS ...
GOD
GOD
IT'S TRUE THAT I'VE SUFFERED MISFORTUNES...
...BUT ODDLY ENOUGH, I'M NOT SAD ANYMORE.
OH MY, HOW WONDERFUL!
IT'S ALREADY TAKING EFFECT...
I CHANGED BEFORE THIS MEETING.
HUH!?

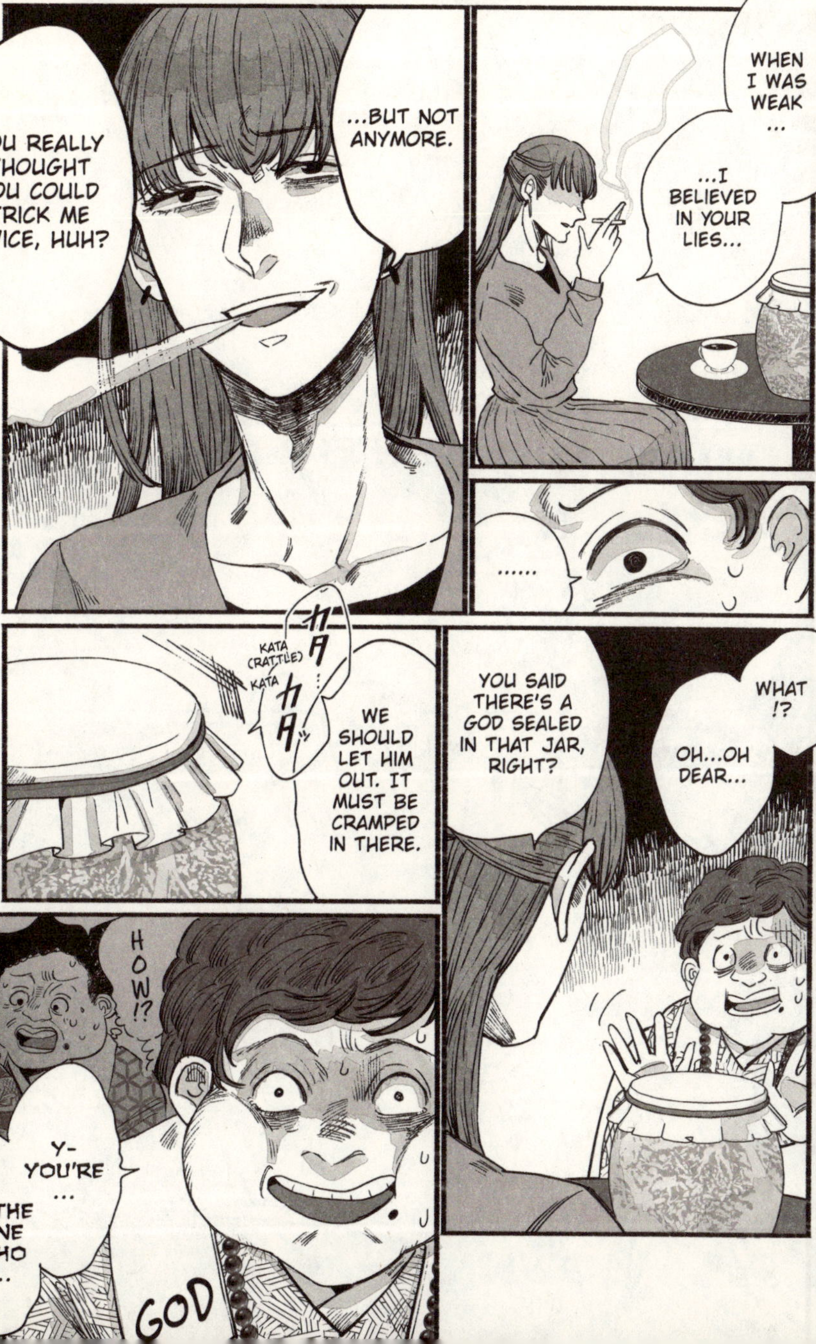
WHEN I WAS WEAK ...
...I BELIEVED IN YOUR LIES...
......
...BUT NOT ANYMORE.
YOU REALLY THOUGHT YOU COULD TRICK ME TWICE, HUH?
YOU SAID THERE'S A GOD SEALED IN THAT JAR, RIGHT?
WHAT !?
OH...OH DEAR...
カタ KATA (RATTLE)
カタッ KATA
WE SHOULD LET HIM OUT. IT MUST BE CRAMPED IN THERE.
HOW!?
Y- YOU'RE ...
...THE ONE WHO ...
GOD

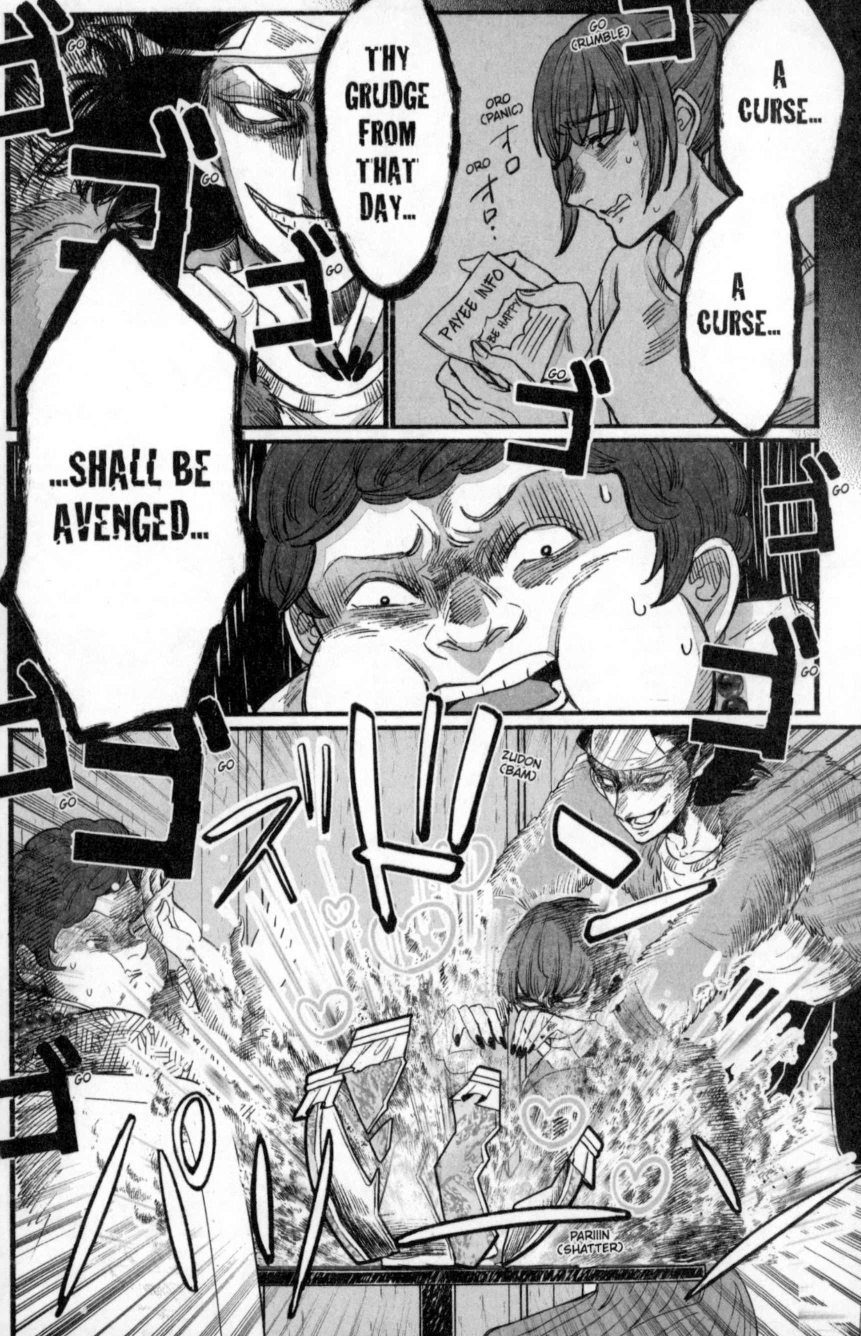
GO (RUMBLE)
A CURSE...
A CURSE...
ORO (PANIC)
ORO
PAYEE INFO
BE HAPPY
GO
GO
GO
THY GRUDGE FROM THAT DAY...
GO
...SHALL BE AVENGED...
GO
GO
ZUDON (BAM)
GO
GO
GO
PARIIN (SHATTER)

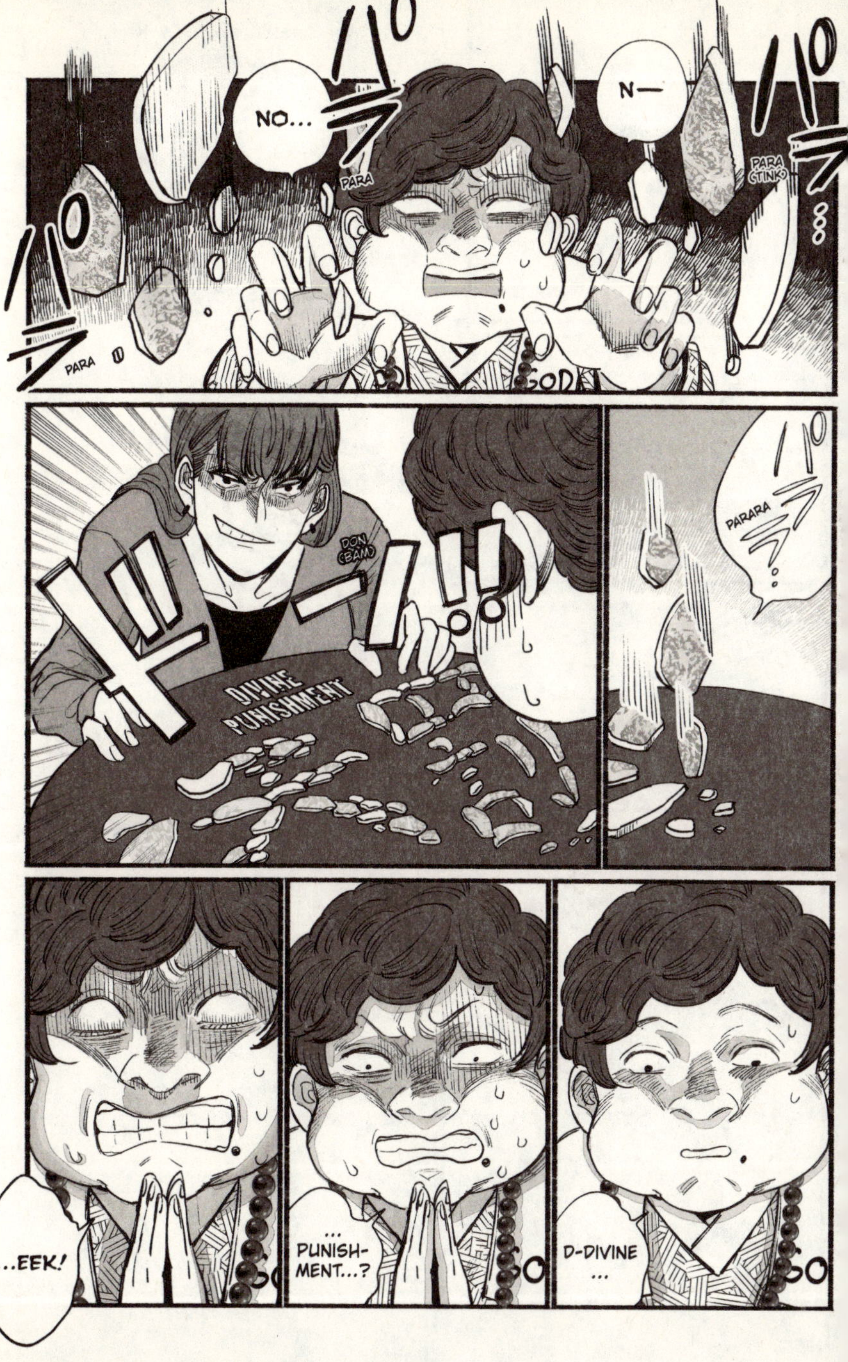

N—
PARA (TINK)
PARA
NO...
PARA
PARARA
DON (BAM)
DIVINE PUNISHMENT
D-DIVINE ...
... PUNISH-MENT...?
...EEK!

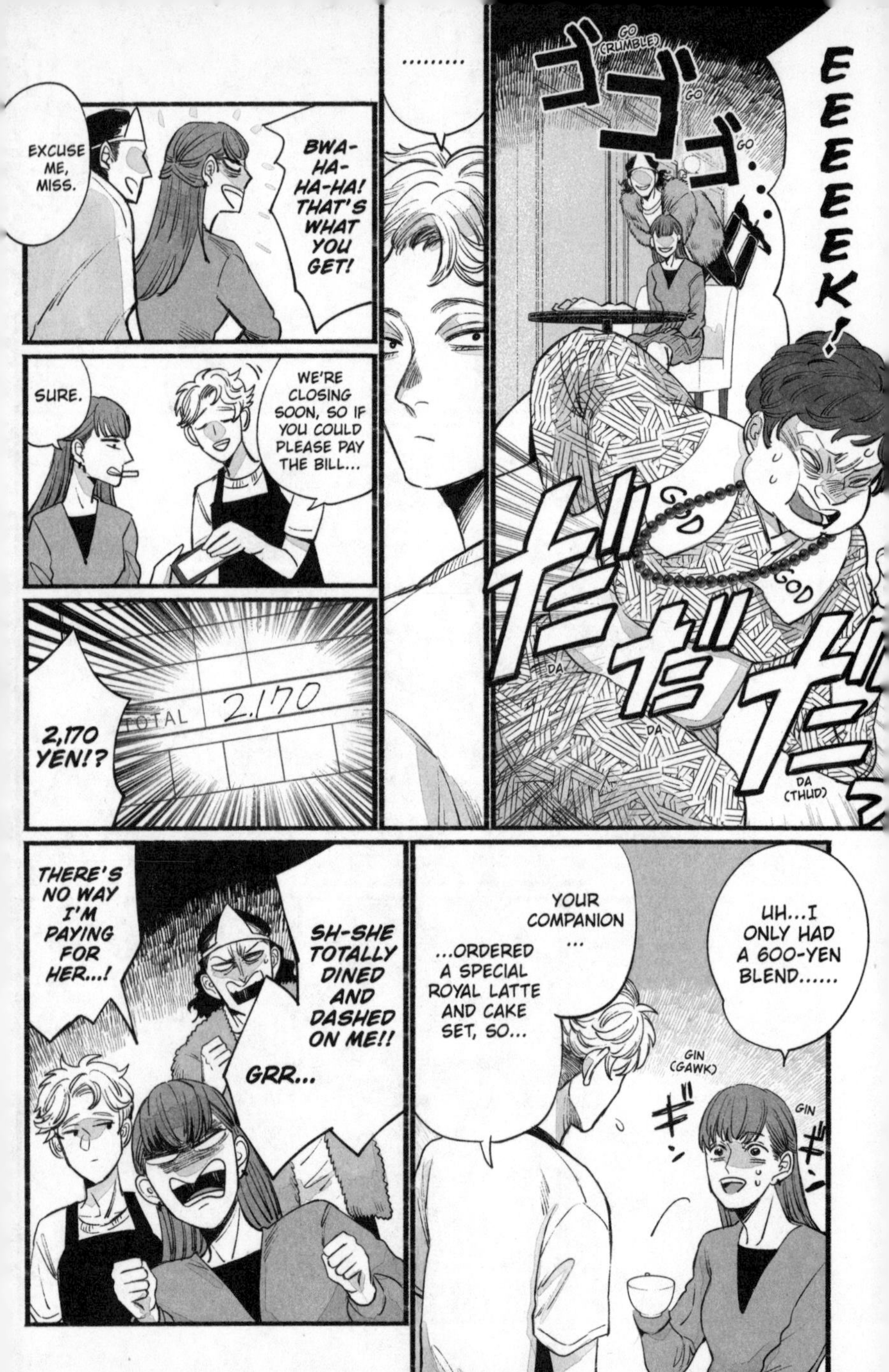
GO (RUMBLE)
GO
GO
EEEEEK!
GOD
GOD
DA
DA
DA (THUD)
....
BWA-HA-HA-HA! THAT'S WHAT YOU GET!
EXCUSE ME, MISS.
WE'RE CLOSING SOON, SO IF YOU COULD PLEASE PAY THE BILL...
SURE.
TOTAL 2,170
2,170 YEN!?
UH...I ONLY HAD A 600-YEN BLEND......
YOUR COMPANION...
...ORDERED A SPECIAL ROYAL LATTE AND CAKE SET, SO...
GIN (GAWK)
GIN
SH-SHE TOTALLY DINED AND DASHED ON ME!!
THERE'S NO WAY I'M PAYING FOR HER...!
GRR...

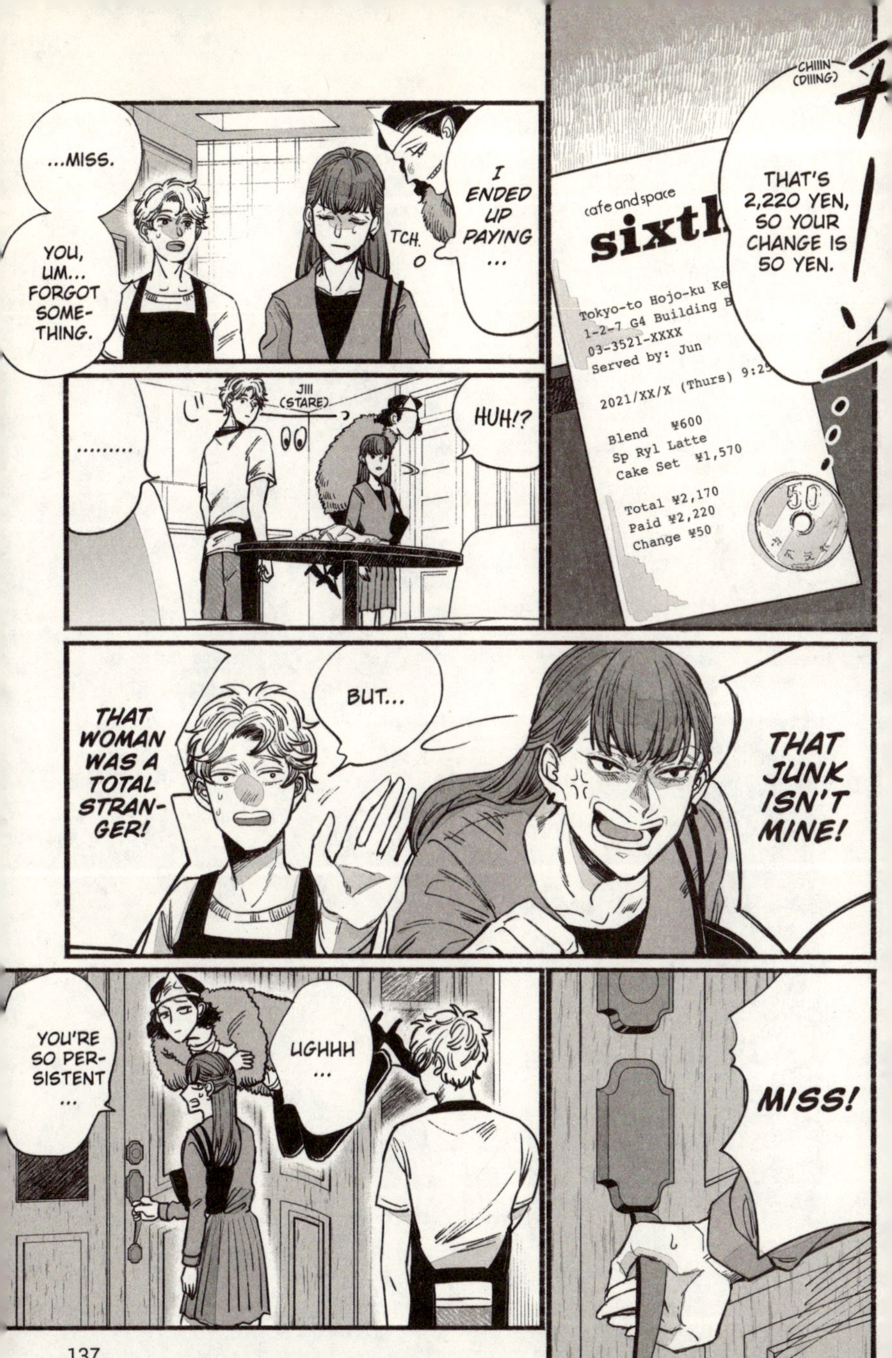
CHIIIN
(DIIING)
THAT'S 2,220 YEN, SO YOUR CHANGE IS 50 YEN.
cafe and space
sixth
Tokyo-to Hojo-ku Ke
1-2-7 G4 Building B
03-3521-XXXX
Served by: Jun
2021/XX/X (Thurs) 9:25
Blend ¥600
Sp Ryl Latte
Cake Set ¥1,570
Total ¥2,170
Paid ¥2,220
Change ¥50
I ENDED UP PAYING...
TCH.
...MISS.
YOU, UM... FORGOT SOMETHING.
HUH!?
JIII
(STARE)
....
THAT JUNK ISN'T MINE!
BUT...
THAT WOMAN WAS A TOTAL STRANGER!
MISS!
UGHHH...
YOU'RE SO PERSISTENT...

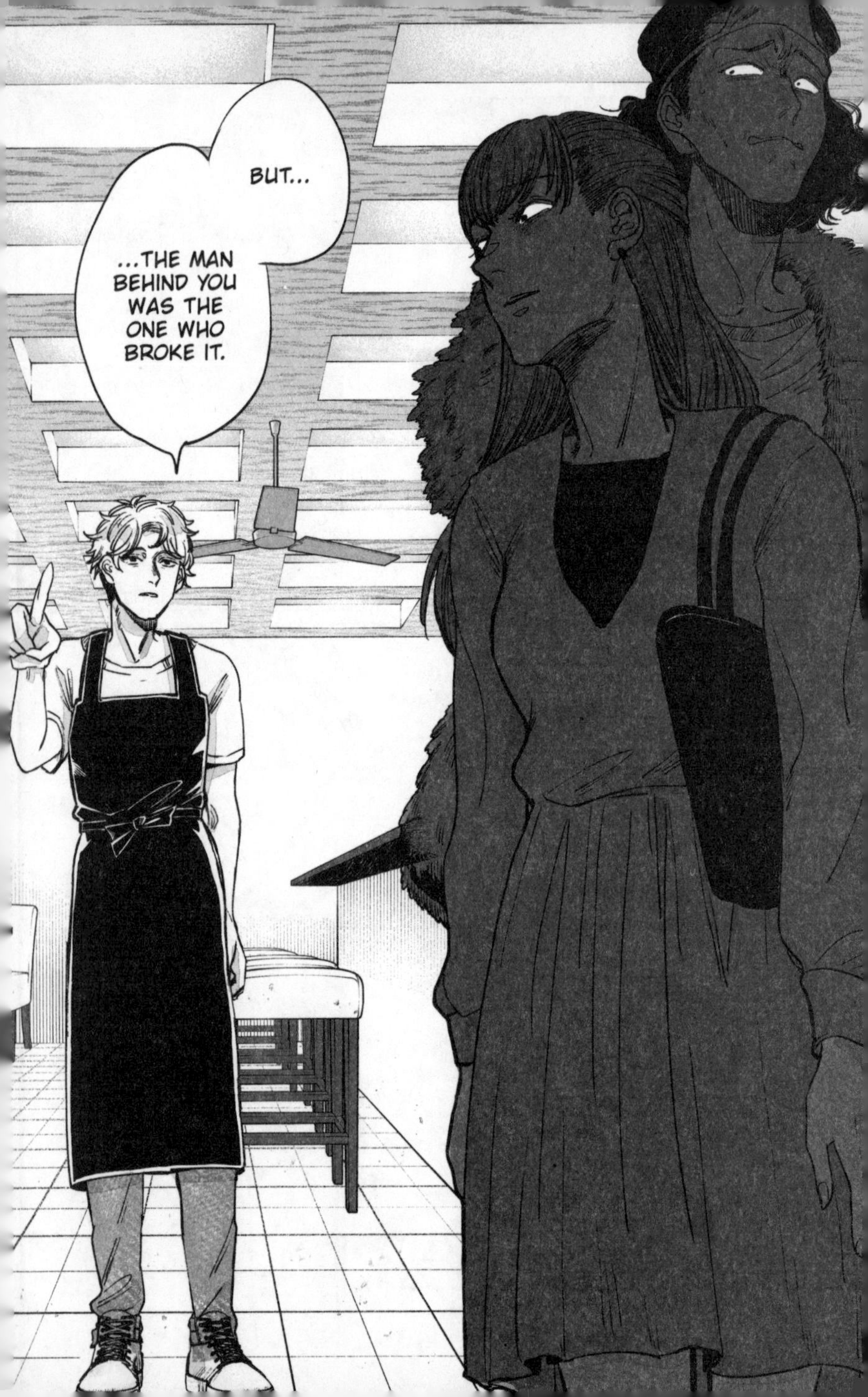
BUT...
...THE MAN BEHIND YOU WAS THE ONE WHO BROKE IT.

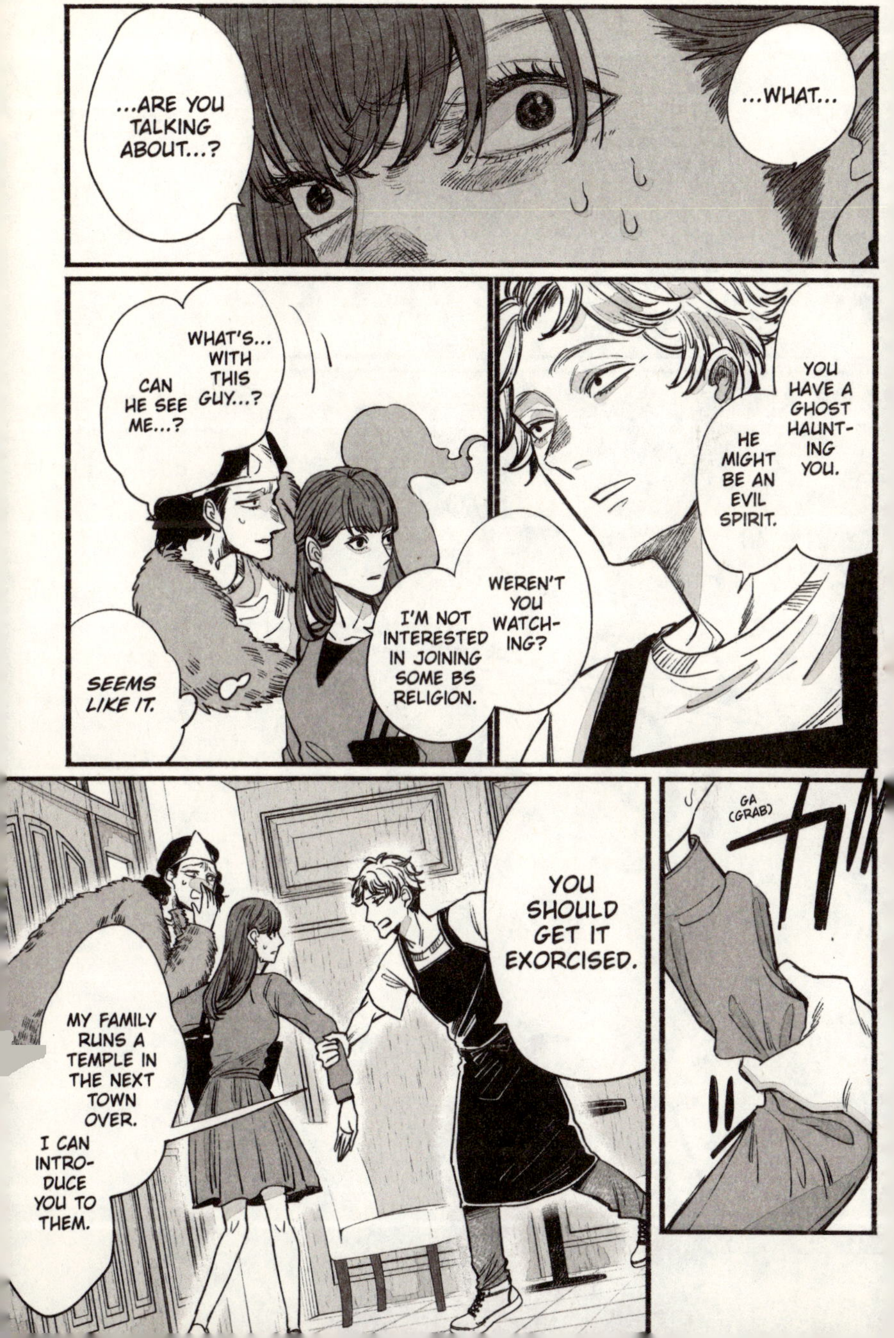
...WHAT...
...ARE YOU TALKING ABOUT...?
YOU HAVE A GHOST HAUNTING YOU.
HE MIGHT BE AN EVIL SPIRIT.
WEREN'T YOU WATCHING?
I'M NOT INTERESTED IN JOINING SOME BS RELIGION.
WHAT'S... WITH THIS GUY...?
CAN HE SEE ME...?
SEEMS LIKE IT.
GA (GRAB)
YOU SHOULD GET IT EXORCISED.
MY FAMILY RUNS A TEMPLE IN THE NEXT TOWN OVER.
I CAN INTRODUCE YOU TO THEM.

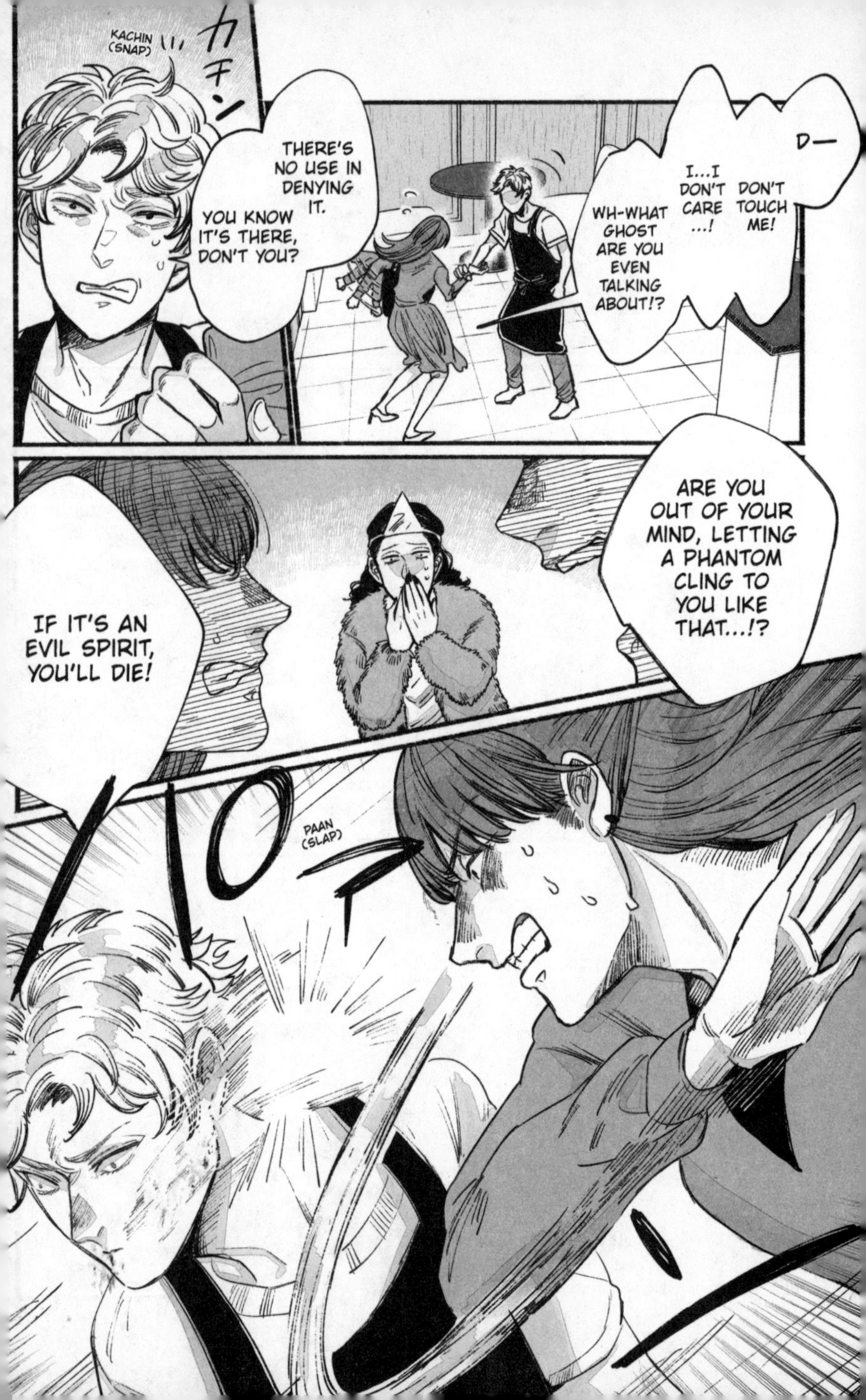
D—
DON'T TOUCH ME!
I...I DON'T CARE ...!
WH-WHAT GHOST ARE YOU EVEN TALKING ABOUT!?
THERE'S NO USE IN DENYING IT.
YOU KNOW IT'S THERE, DON'T YOU?
KACHIN (SNAP)
ARE YOU OUT OF YOUR MIND, LETTING A PHANTOM CLING TO YOU LIKE THAT...!?
IF IT'S AN EVIL SPIRIT, YOU'LL DIE!
PAAN (SLAP)

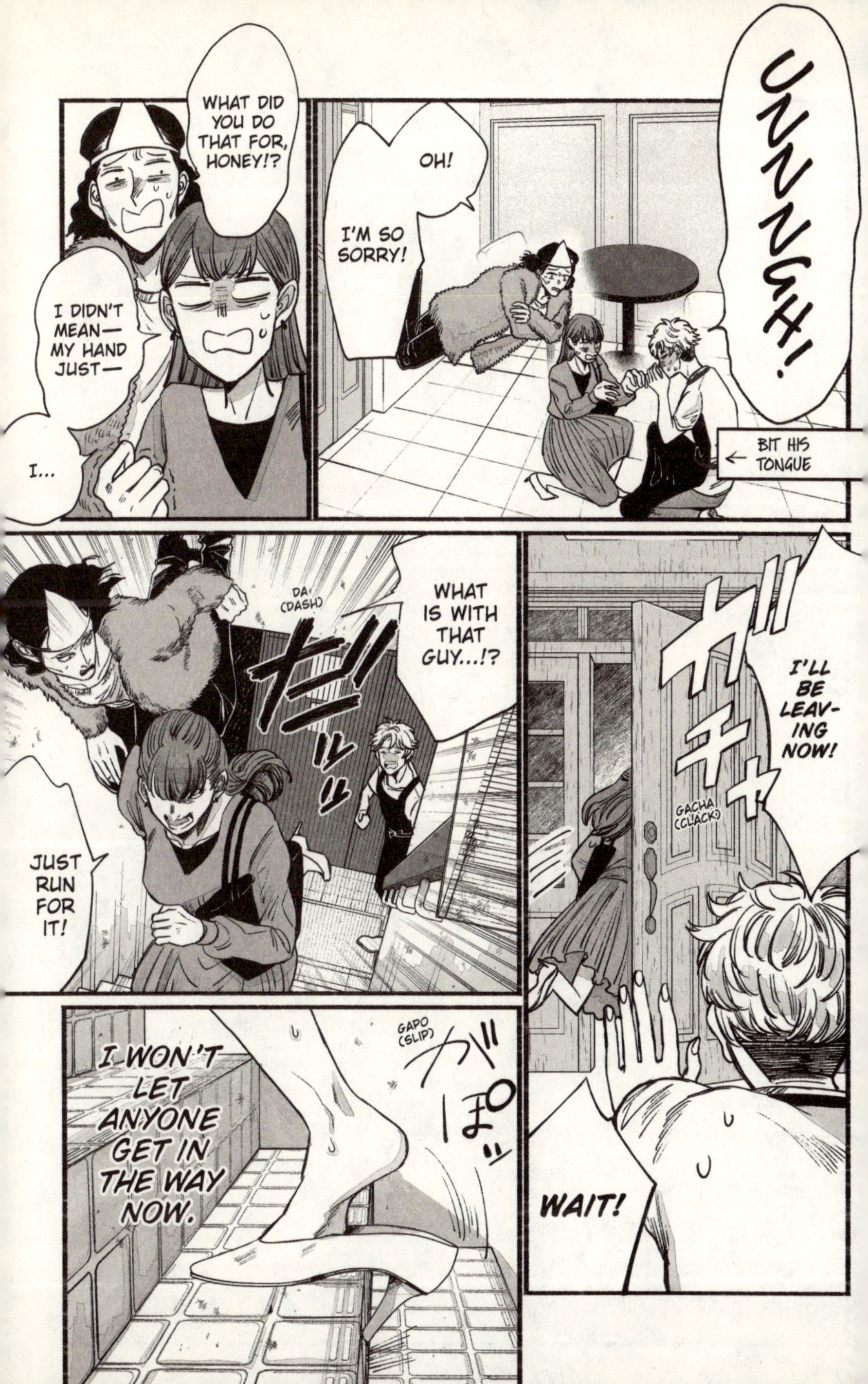
UNNNGH!
OH!
I'M SO SORRY!
BIT HIS TONGUE
WHAT DID YOU DO THAT FOR, HONEY!?
I DIDN'T MEAN— MY HAND JUST—
I...
I'LL BE LEAVING NOW!
ガチャ
GACHA (CLACK)
WAIT!
WHAT IS WITH THAT GUY...!?
ダッ
DA (DASH)
JUST RUN FOR IT!
がぽッ
GAPO (SLIP)
I WON'T LET ANYONE GET IN THE WAY NOW.

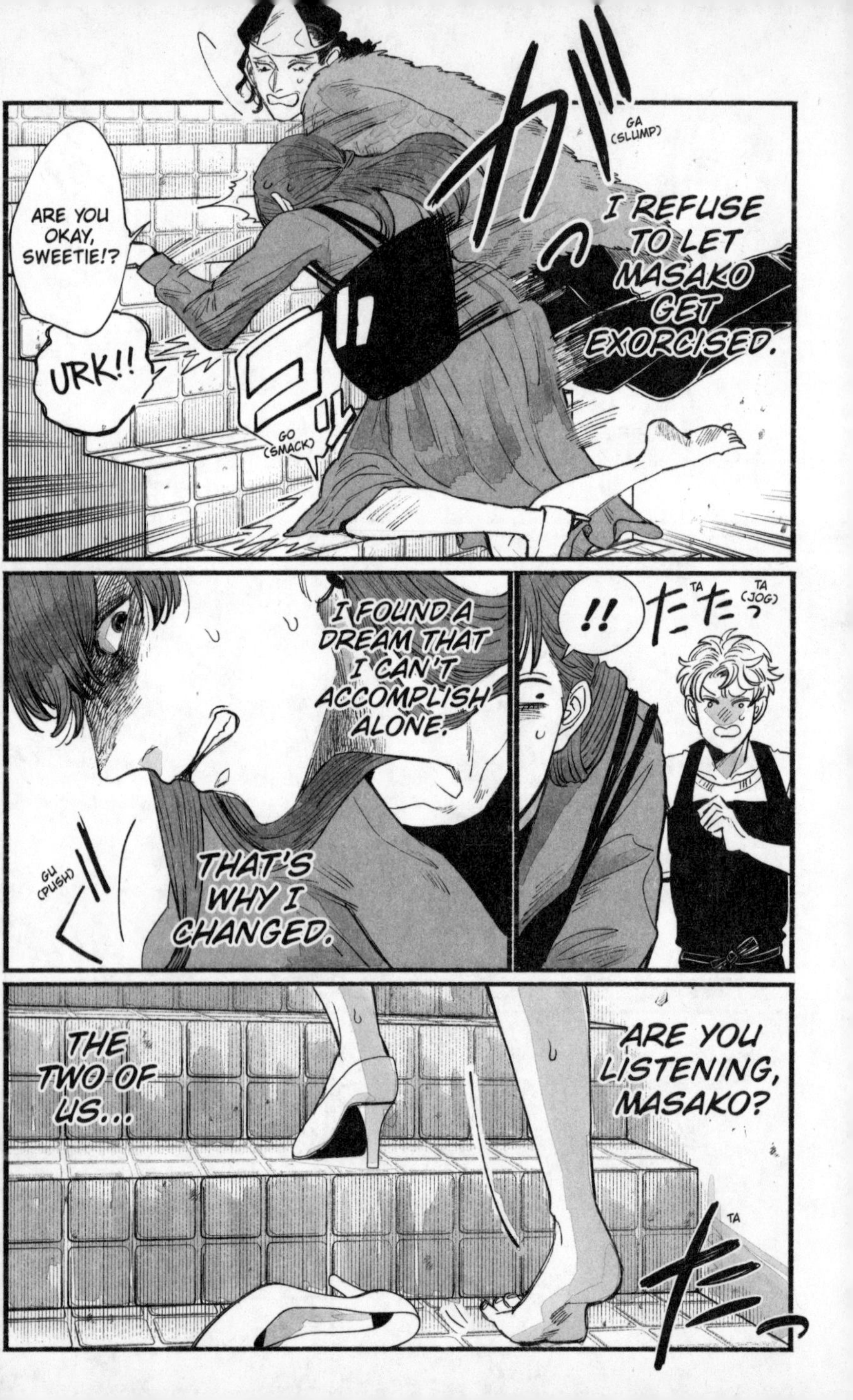
GA (SLUMP)
I REFUSE TO LET MASAKO GET EXORCISED.
ARE YOU OKAY, SWEETIE!?
URK!!
GO (SMACK)
TA TA (JOG)
!!
I FOUND A DREAM THAT I CAN'T ACCOMPLISH ALONE.
THAT'S WHY I CHANGED.
GU (PUSH)
ARE YOU LISTENING, MASAKO?
THE TWO OF US...
TA

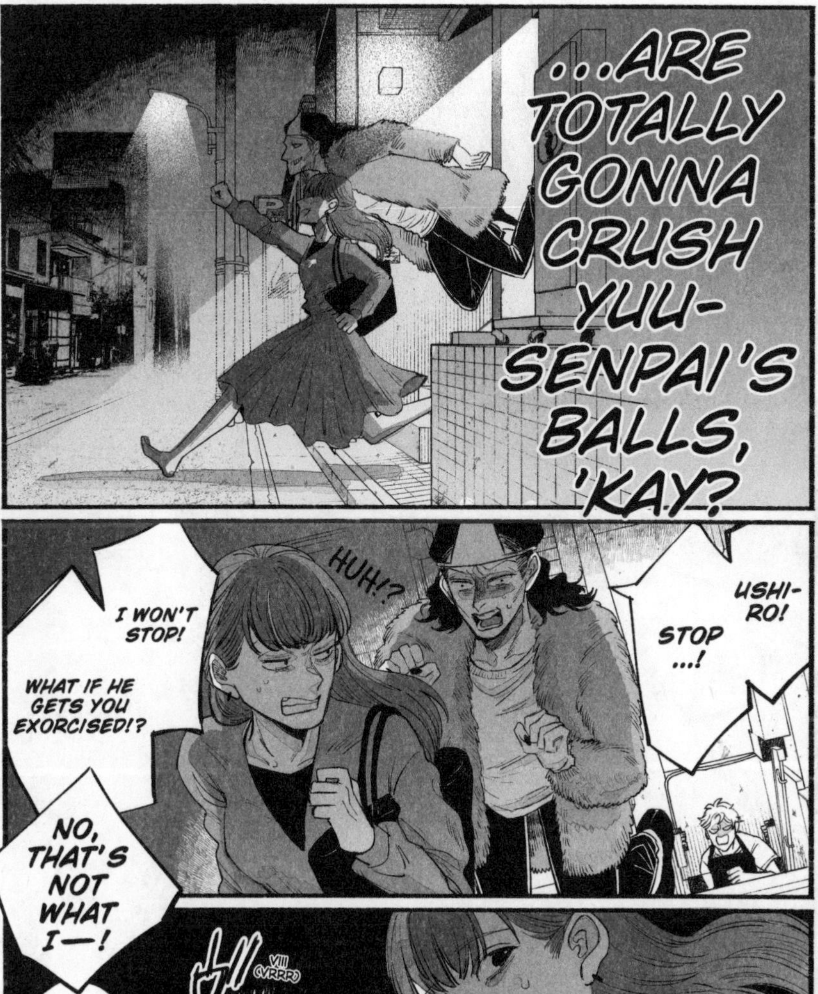
...ARE TOTALLY GONNA CRUSH YUU-SENPAI'S BALLS, 'KAY?
USHIRO!
STOP ...!
HUH!?
I WON'T STOP!
WHAT IF HE GETS YOU EXORCISED!?
NO, THAT'S NOT WHAT I—!
VIII (VRRR)
HUH ...?

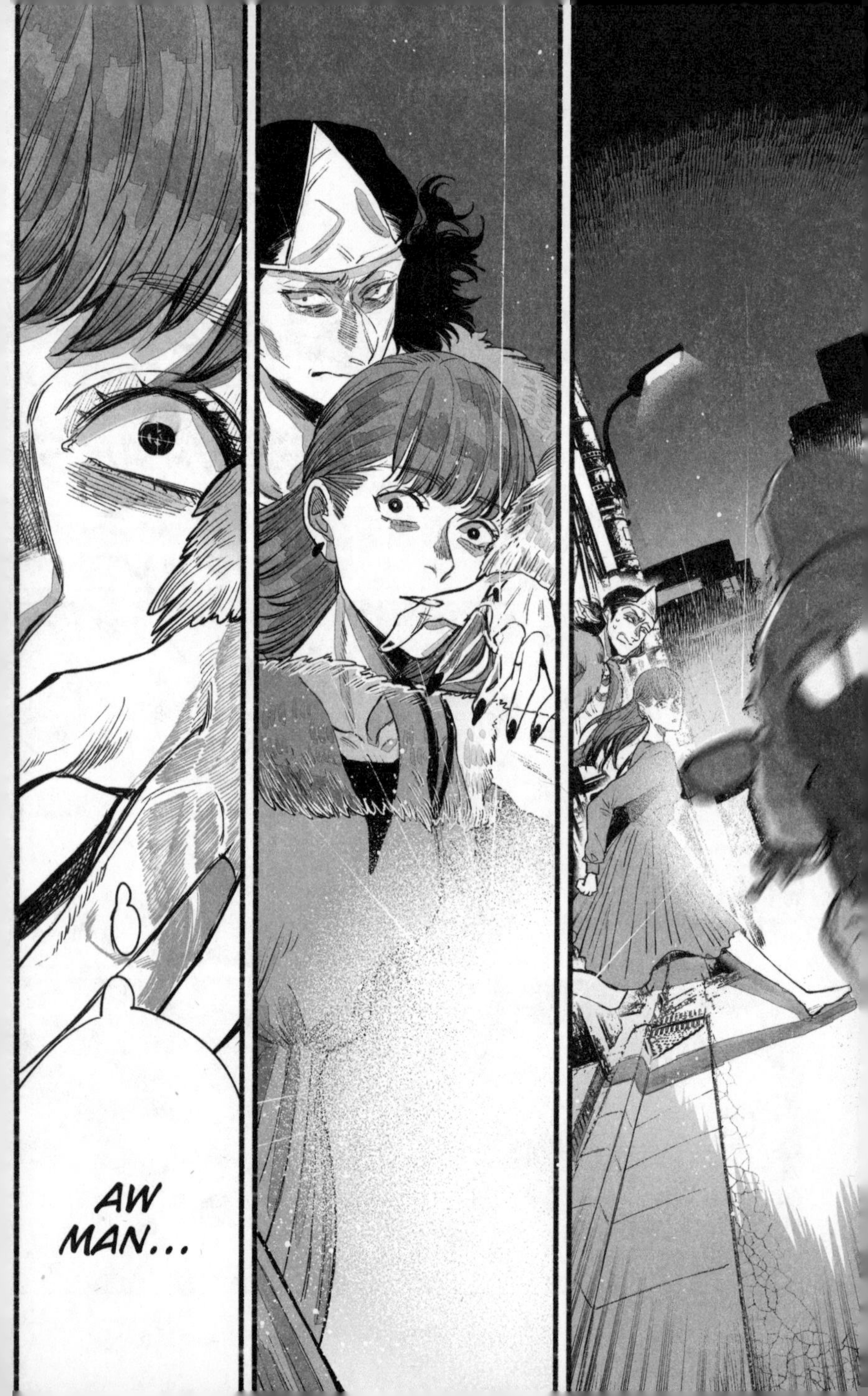
AW MAN...

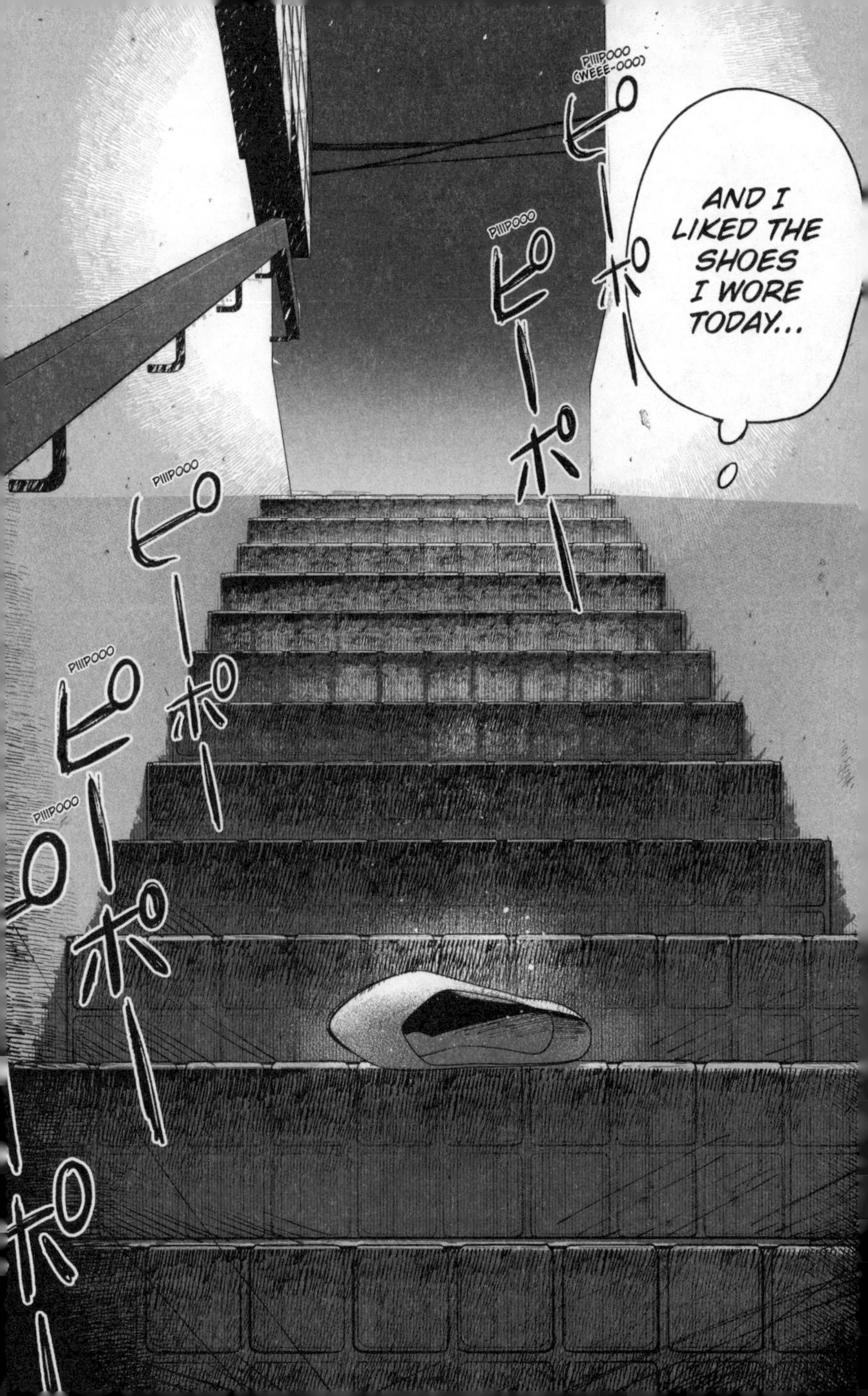

AND I LIKED THE SHOES I WORE TODAY...
PIIIPOOO (WEEE-OOO)
ピーポー
PIIIPOOO
ピーポー
PIIIPOOO
ピーポー
PIIIPOOO
ピーポー
PIIIPOOO
ピーポー

GOGOGOGO-GO-GHOST!

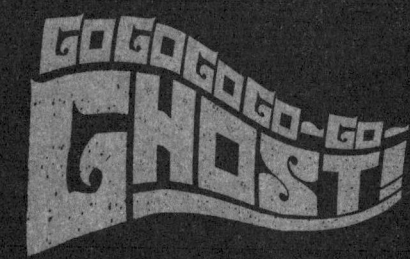

Chapter 7: Every Rose Has Its Thorn

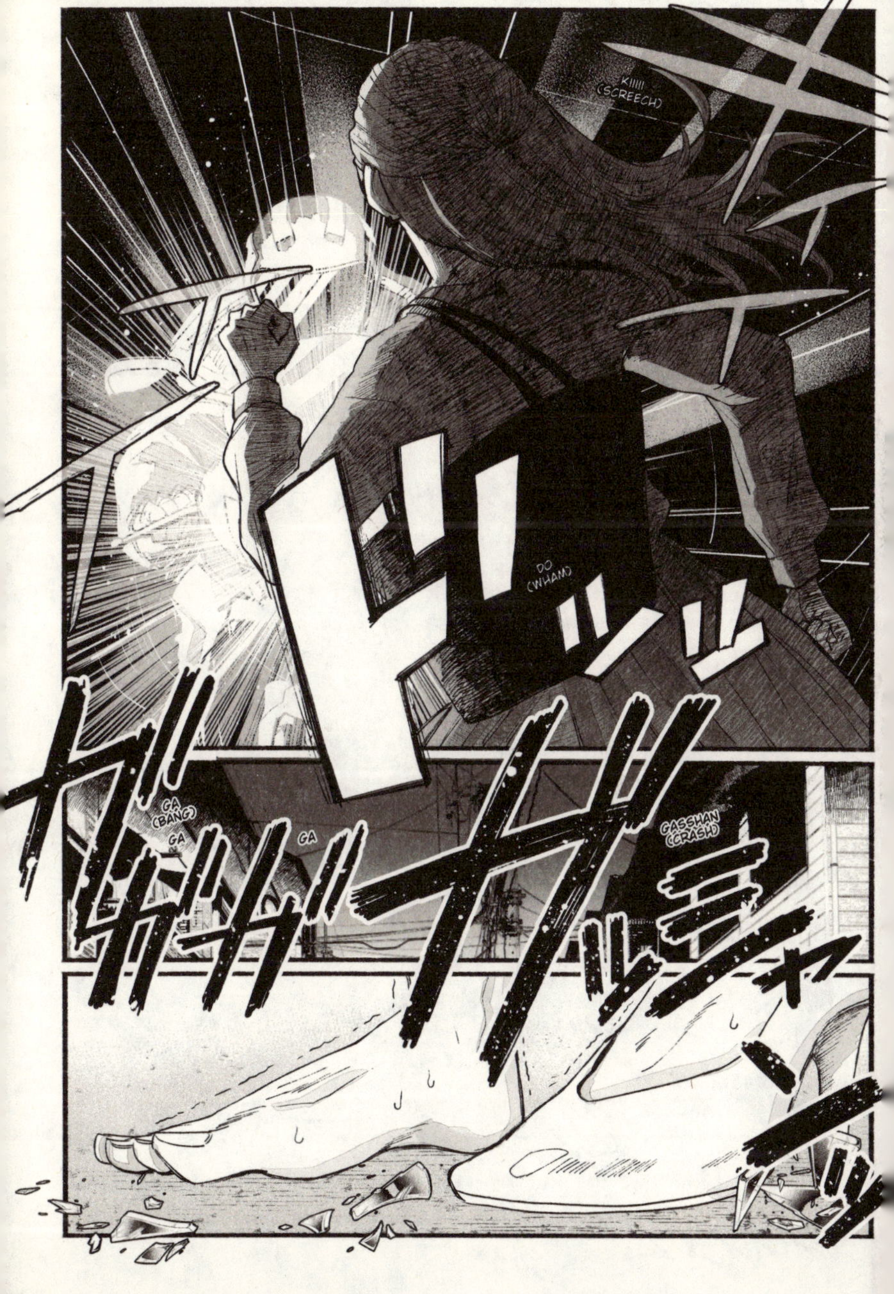
KIIII
(SCREECH)
DO
(WHAM)
GASSHAN
(CRASH)
GA
GA
(BANG)
GA

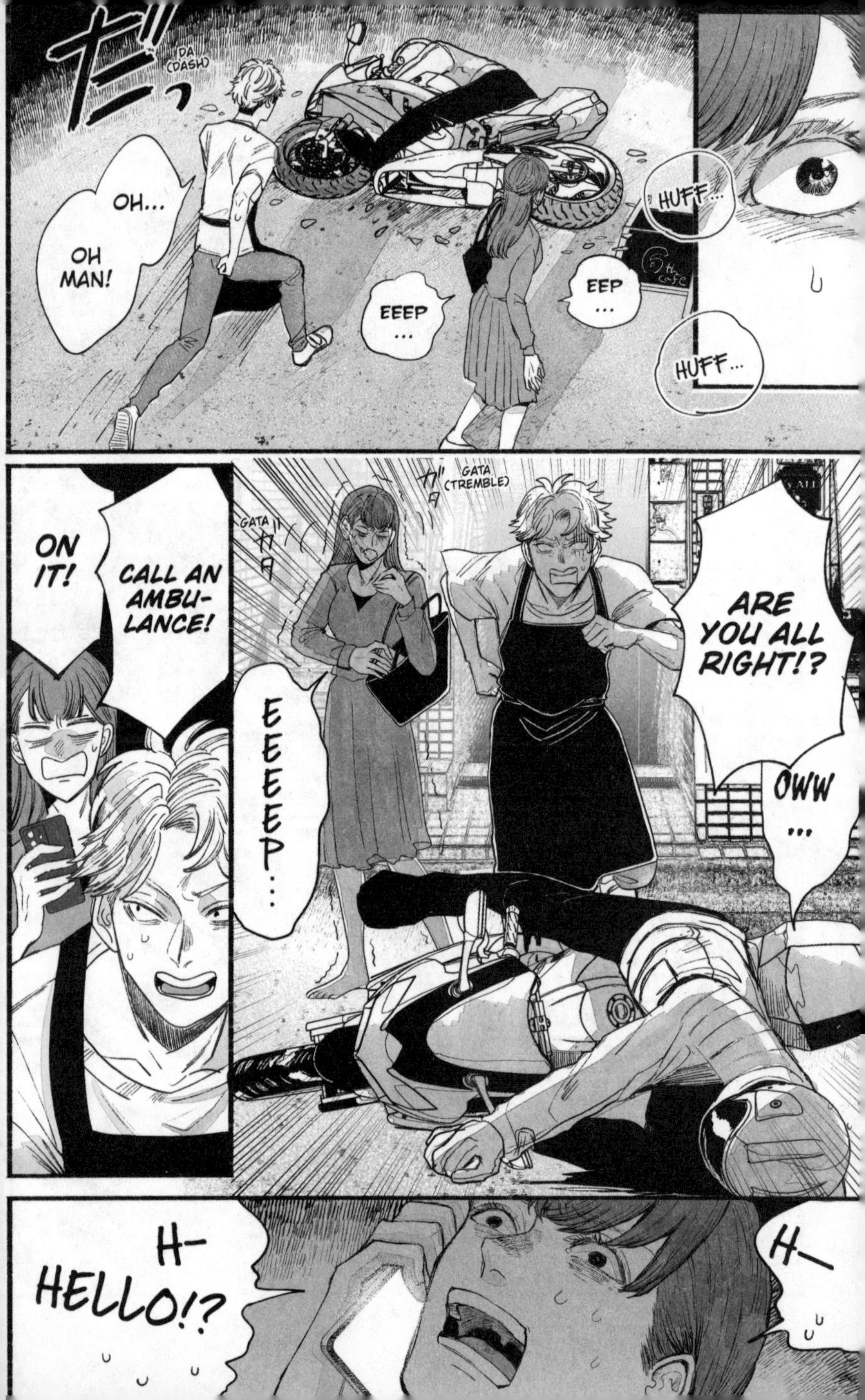
HUFF...
HUFF...
DA (DASH)
EEP...
EEEP...
OH...
OH MAN!
GATA (TREMBLE)
ARE YOU ALL RIGHT!?
OWW...
GATA
EEEEEP...
CALL AN AMBULANCE!
ON IT!
H—
H-HELLO!?

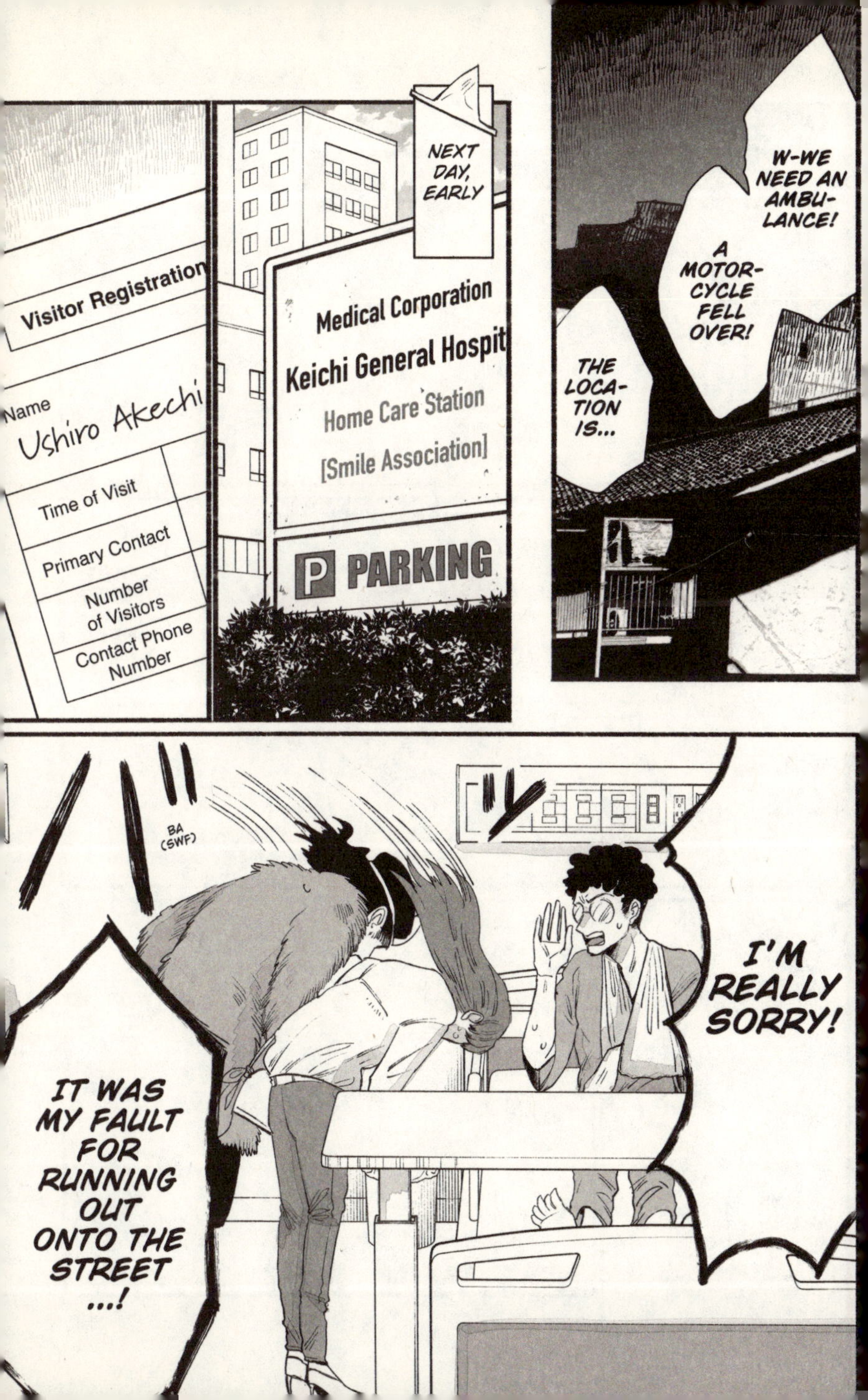
W-WE NEED AN AMBU-LANCE!
A MOTOR-CYCLE FELL OVER!
THE LOCA-TION IS...
NEXT DAY, EARLY
Medical Corporation
Keichi General Hospit
Home Care Station
[Smile Association]
PARKING
Visitor Registration
Name
Ushiro Akechi
Time of Visit
Primary Contact
Number of Visitors
Contact Phone Number
I'M REALLY SORRY!
BA (SWF)
IT WAS MY FAULT FOR RUNNING OUT ONTO THE STREET ...!

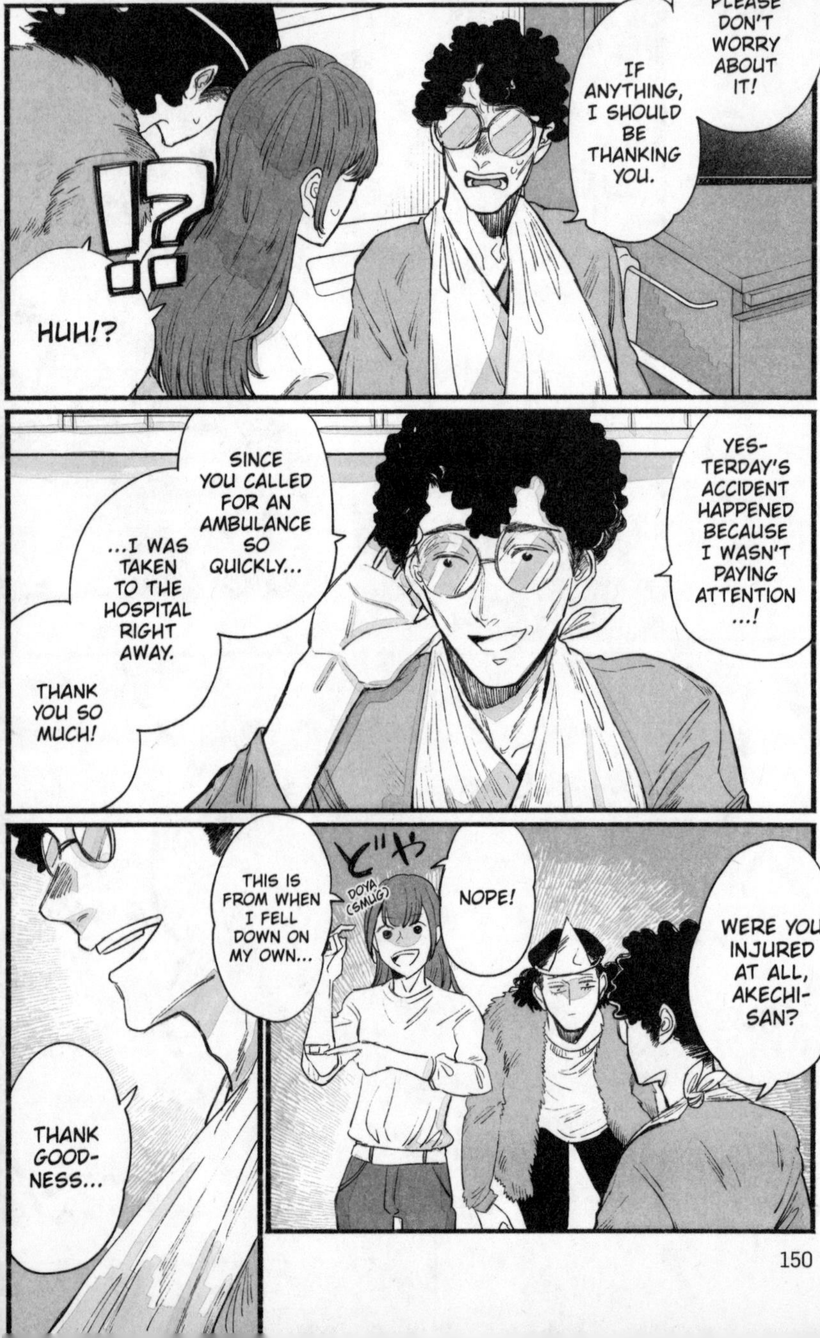
OH, NO! PLEASE DON'T WORRY ABOUT IT!
IF ANYTHING, I SHOULD BE THANKING YOU.
!?
HUH!?
YES-TERDAY'S ACCIDENT HAPPENED BECAUSE I WASN'T PAYING ATTENTION...!
SINCE YOU CALLED FOR AN AMBULANCE SO QUICKLY...
...I WAS TAKEN TO THE HOSPITAL RIGHT AWAY.
THANK YOU SO MUCH!
WERE YOU INJURED AT ALL, AKECHI-SAN?
NOPE!
どや
DOYA (SMUG)
THIS IS FROM WHEN I FELL DOWN ON MY OWN...
THANK GOOD-NESS...

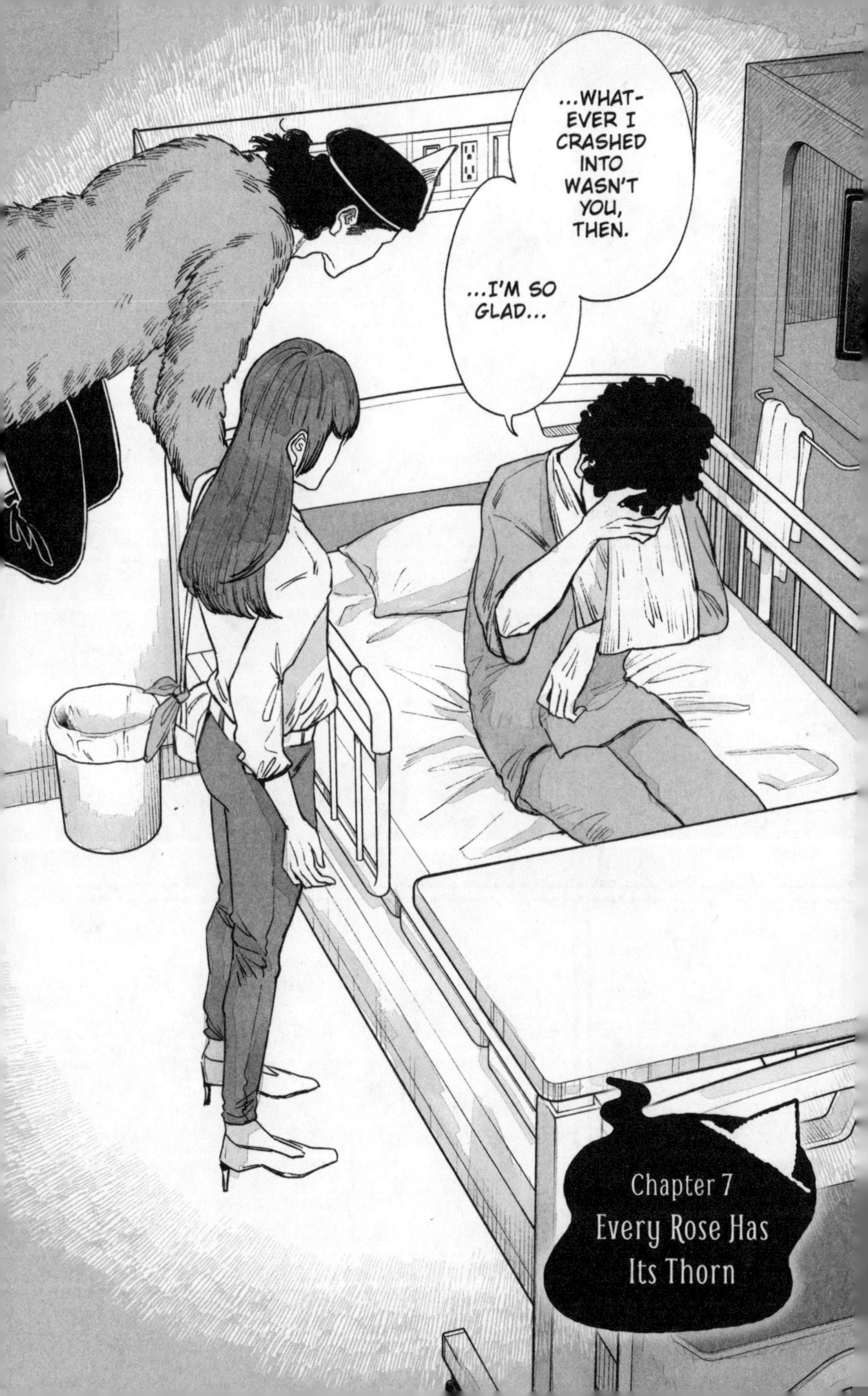
...WHAT-EVER I CRASHED INTO WASN'T YOU, THEN.
...I'M SO GLAD...
Chapter 7
Every Rose Has Its Thorn

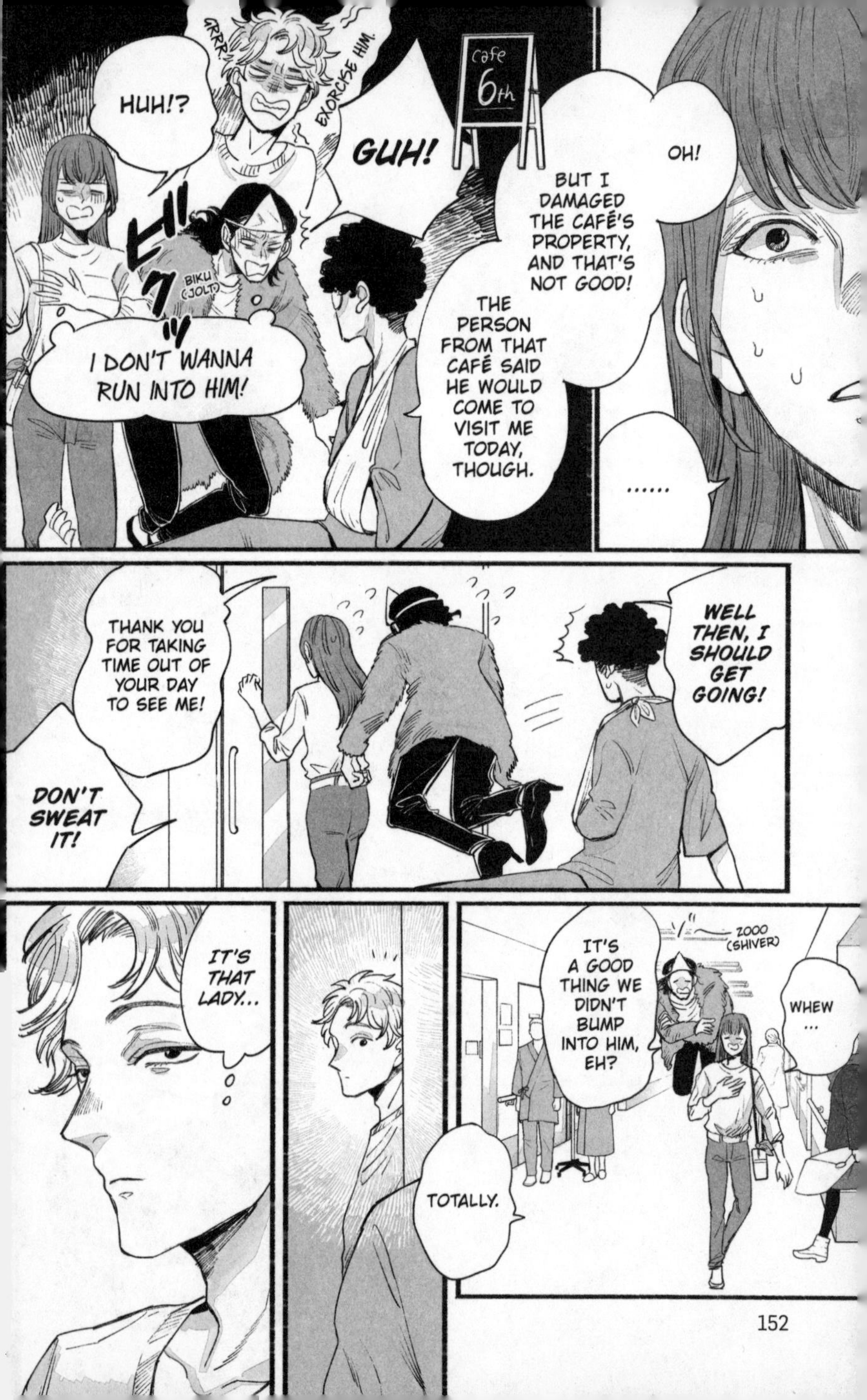
OH!
......
BUT I DAMAGED THE CAFÉ'S PROPERTY, AND THAT'S NOT GOOD!
THE PERSON FROM THAT CAFÉ SAID HE WOULD COME TO VISIT ME TODAY, THOUGH.
cafe 6th
GUH!
EXORCISE HIM.
GRRR
HUH!?
BIKU (JOLT)
I DON'T WANNA RUN INTO HIM!
WELL THEN, I SHOULD GET GOING!
THANK YOU FOR TAKING TIME OUT OF YOUR DAY TO SEE ME!
DON'T SWEAT IT!
WHEW ...
ZOOO (SHIVER)
IT'S A GOOD THING WE DIDN'T BUMP INTO HIM, EH?
TOTALLY.
IT'S THAT LADY...

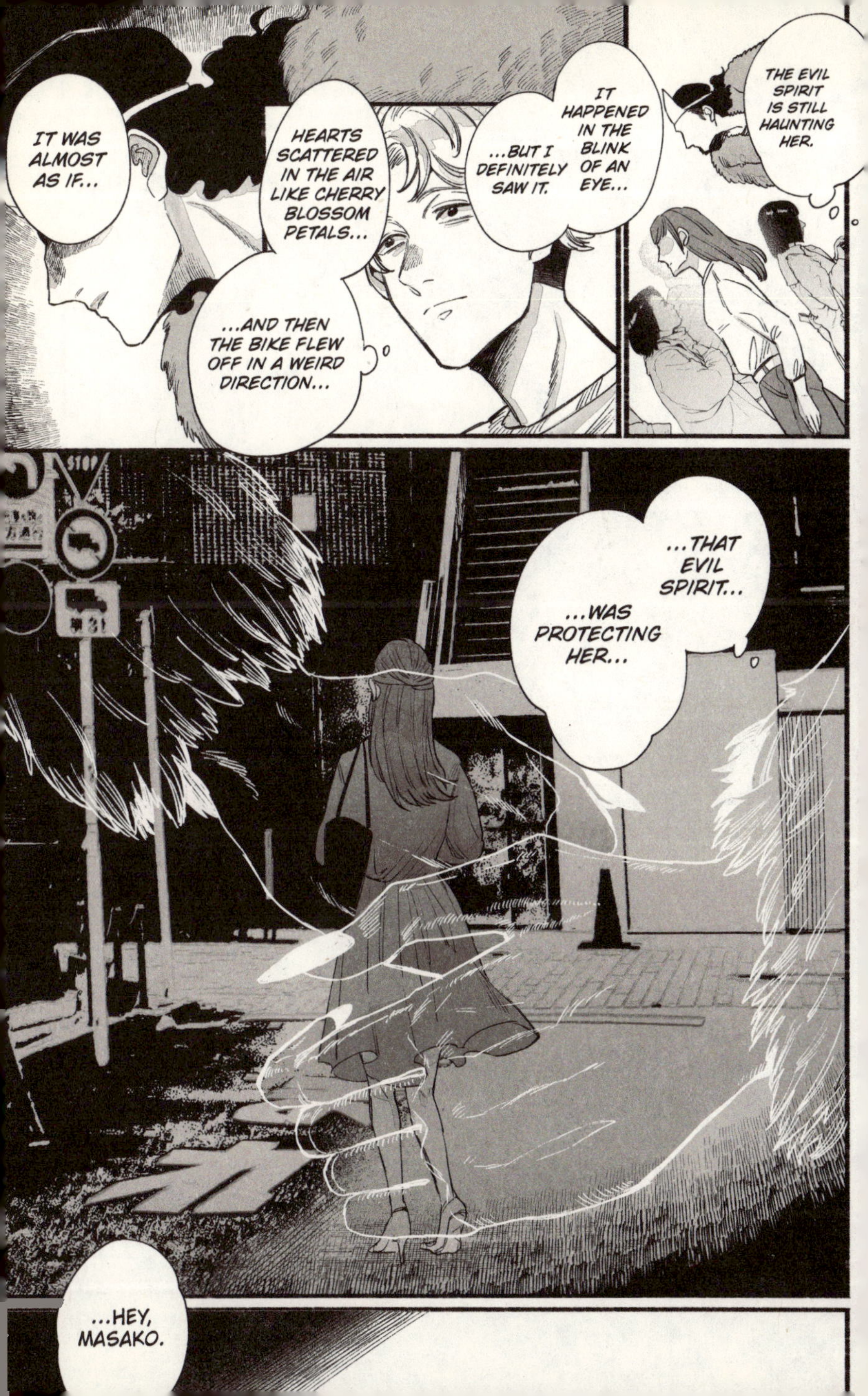

THE EVIL SPIRIT IS STILL HAUNTING HER.
IT HAPPENED IN THE BLINK OF AN EYE...
...BUT I DEFINITELY SAW IT.
IT WAS ALMOST AS IF...
HEARTS SCATTERED IN THE AIR LIKE CHERRY BLOSSOM PETALS...
...AND THEN THE BIKE FLEW OFF IN A WEIRD DIRECTION...
...THAT EVIL SPIRIT...
...WAS PROTECTING HER...
...HEY, MASAKO.

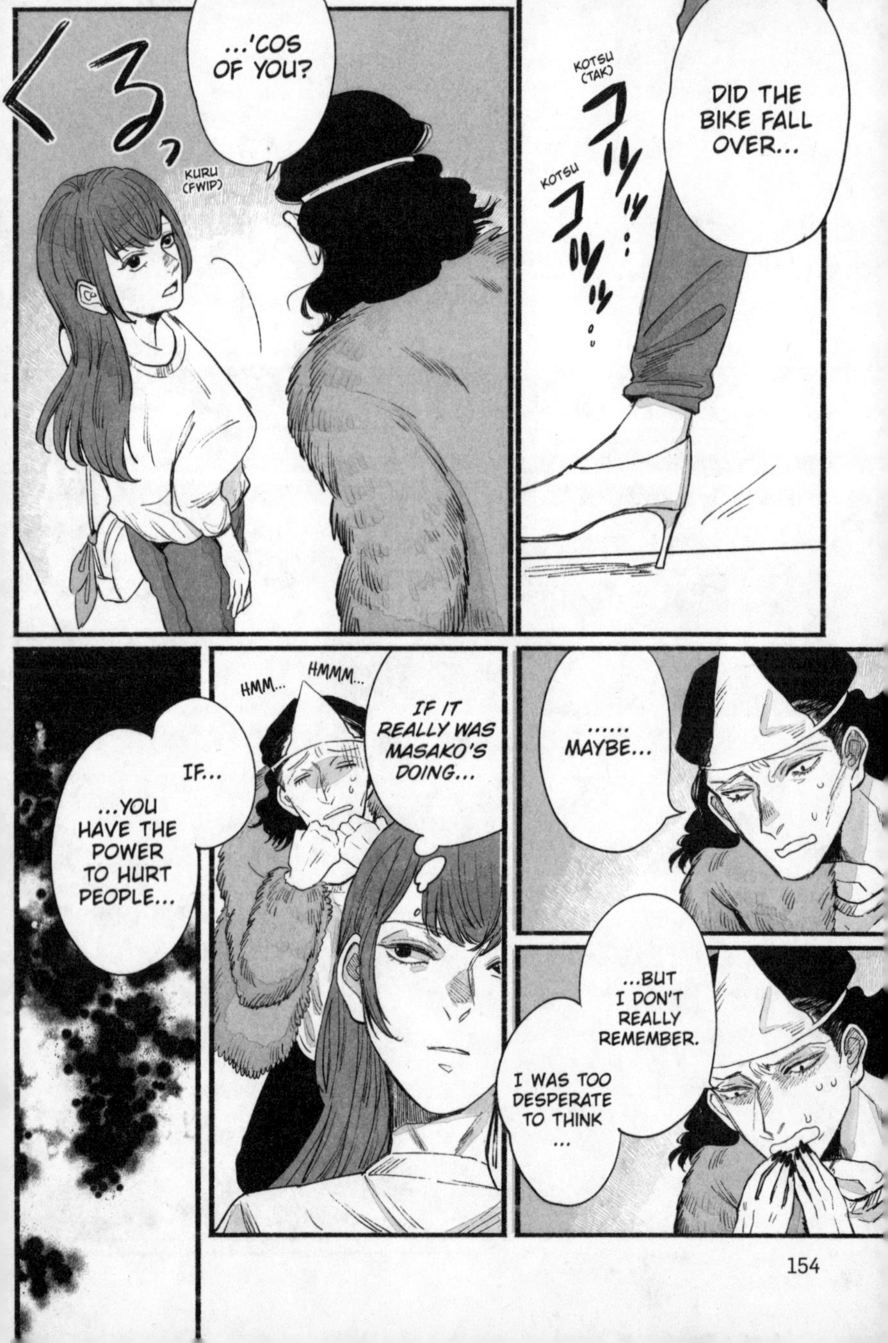
DID THE BIKE FALL OVER...
KOTSU (TAK)
KOTSU
...'COS OF YOU?
KURU (FWIP)
...... MAYBE...
...BUT I DON'T REALLY REMEMBER.
I WAS TOO DESPERATE TO THINK ...
HMMM...
HMM...
IF IT REALLY WAS MASAKO'S DOING...
IF...
...YOU HAVE THE POWER TO HURT PEOPLE...

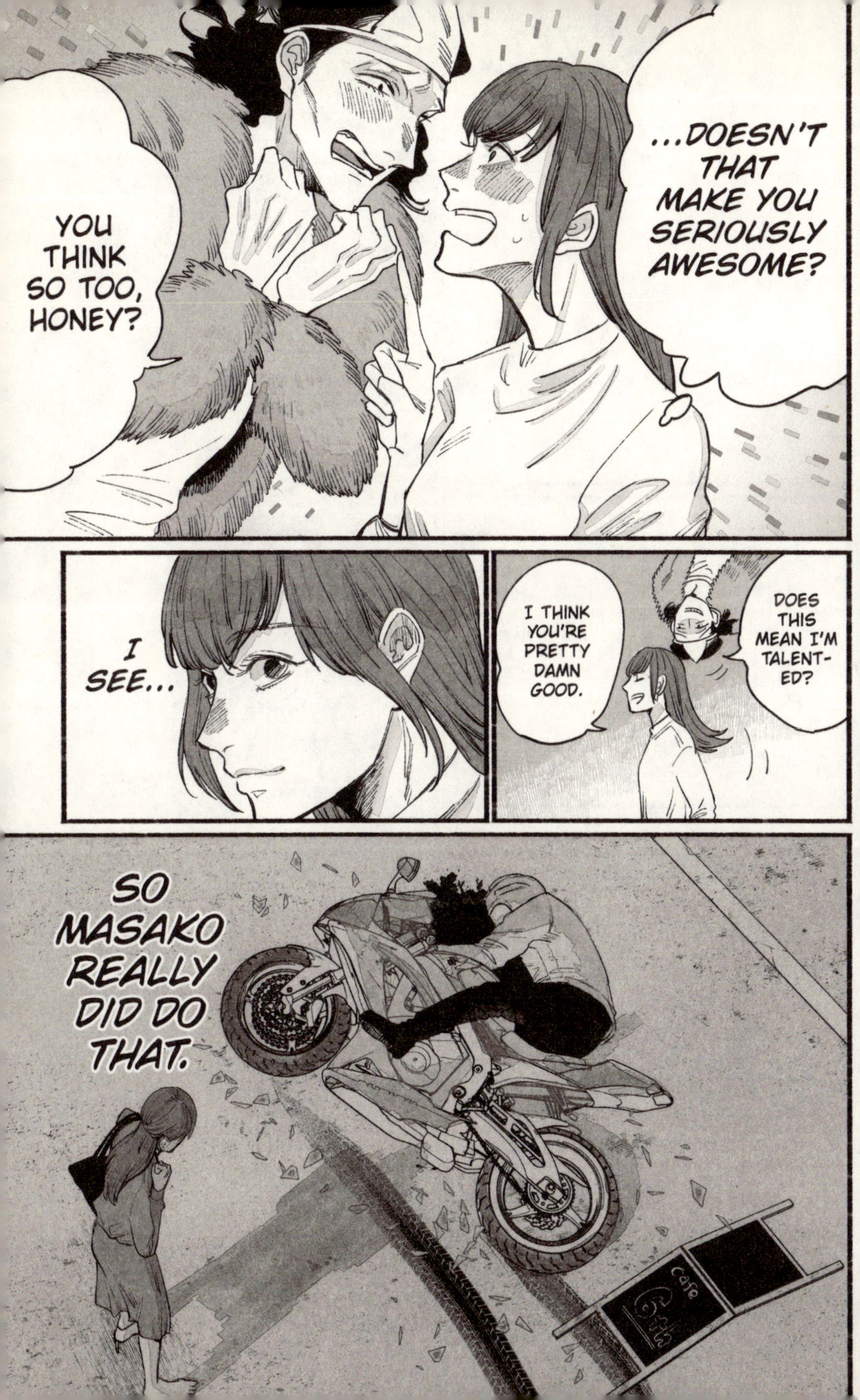
...DOESN'T THAT MAKE YOU SERIOUSLY AWESOME?
YOU THINK SO TOO, HONEY?
DOES THIS MEAN I'M TALENT-ED?
I THINK YOU'RE PRETTY DAMN GOOD.
I SEE...
SO MASAKO REALLY DID DO THAT.

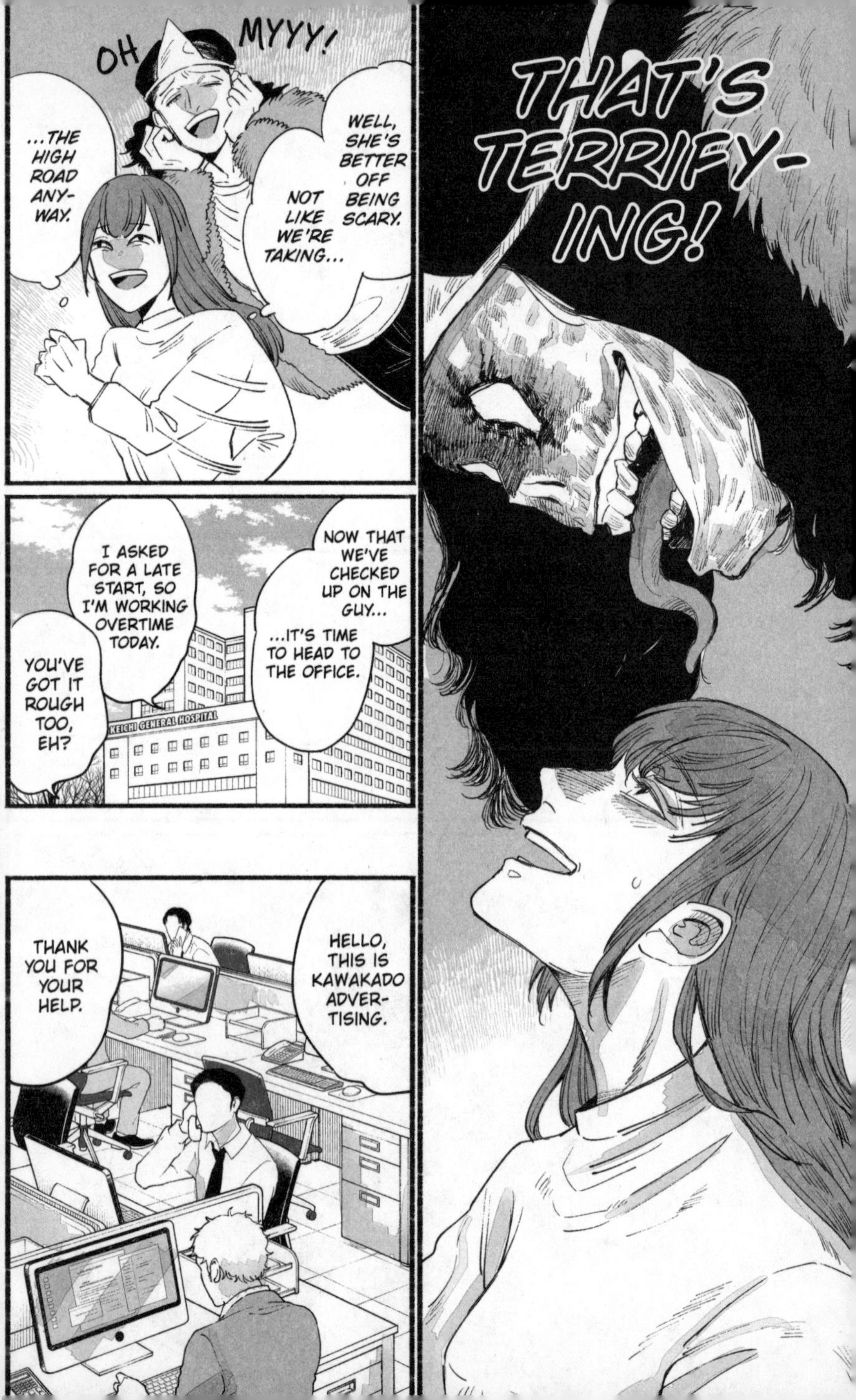
THAT'S TERRIFY-ING!
OH MYYY!
WELL, SHE'S BETTER OFF BEING SCARY.
NOT LIKE WE'RE TAKING...
...THE HIGH ROAD ANYWAY.
NOW THAT WE'VE CHECKED UP ON THE GUY...
...IT'S TIME TO HEAD TO THE OFFICE.
I ASKED FOR A LATE START, SO I'M WORKING OVERTIME TODAY.
YOU'VE GOT IT ROUGH TOO, EH?
KEICHI GENERAL HOSPITAL
HELLO, THIS IS KAWAKADO ADVERTISING.
THANK YOU FOR YOUR HELP.

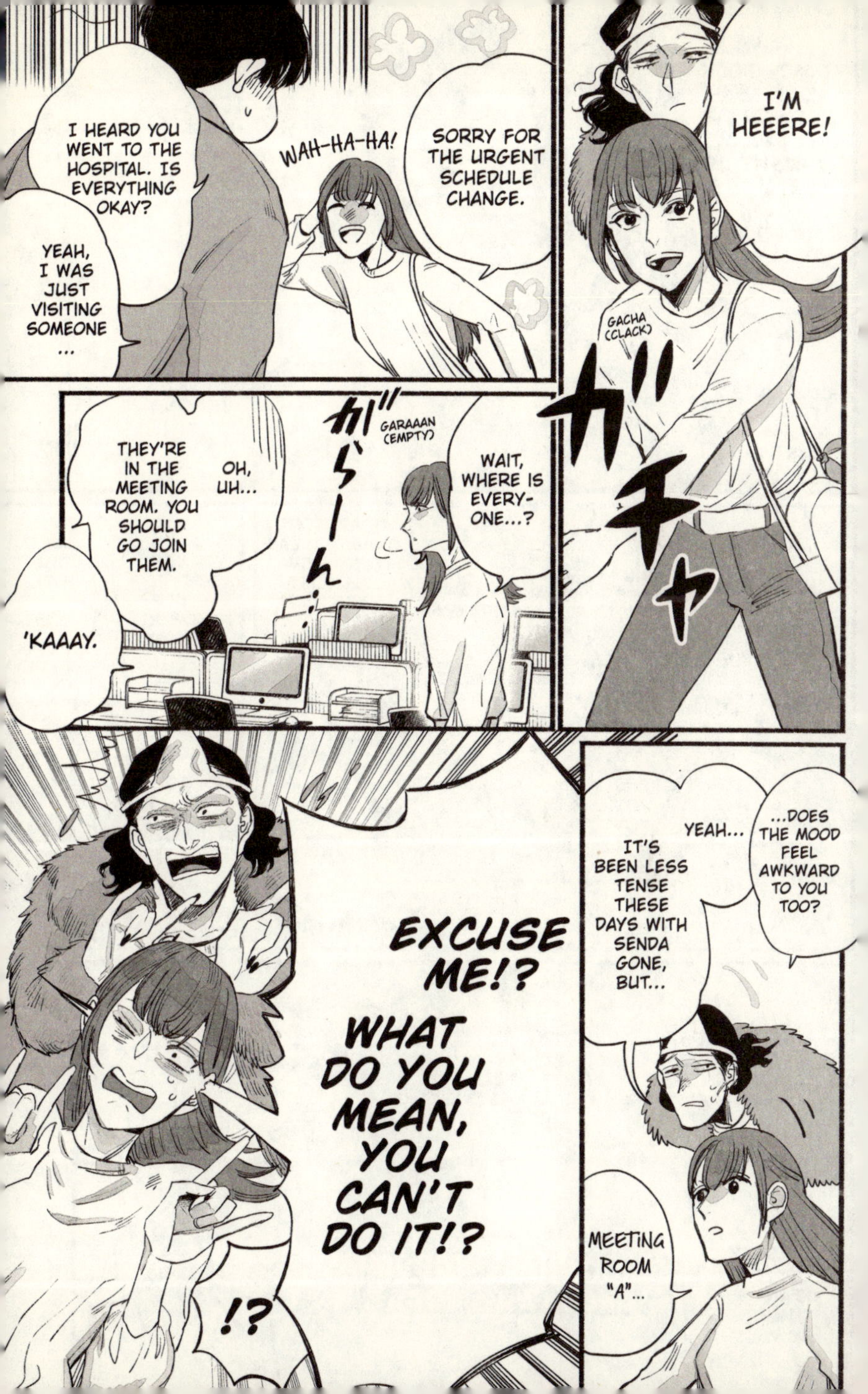
I'M HEEERE!
GACHA (CLACK)
ガチャ
SORRY FOR THE URGENT SCHEDULE CHANGE.
WAH-HA-HA!
I HEARD YOU WENT TO THE HOSPITAL. IS EVERYTHING OKAY?
YEAH, I WAS JUST VISITING SOMEONE ...
WAIT, WHERE IS EVERY-ONE...?
GARAAAN (EMPTY)
がら〜ん…
OH, UH...
THEY'RE IN THE MEETING ROOM. YOU SHOULD GO JOIN THEM.
'KAAAY.
...DOES THE MOOD FEEL AWKWARD TO YOU TOO?
YEAH...
IT'S BEEN LESS TENSE THESE DAYS WITH SENDA GONE, BUT...
MEETING ROOM "A"...
EXCUSE ME!?
WHAT DO YOU MEAN, YOU CAN'T DO IT!?
!?

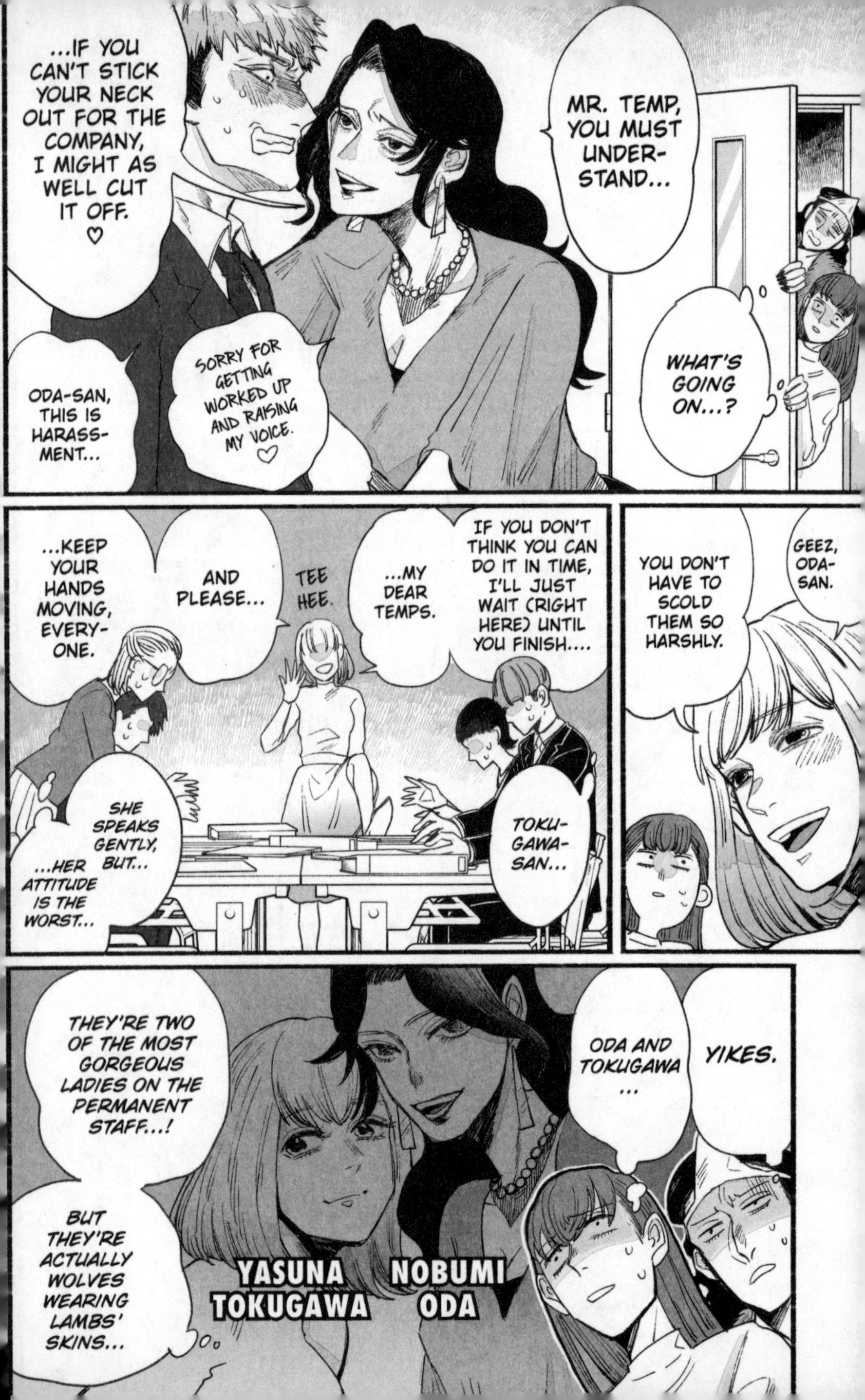
MR. TEMP, YOU MUST UNDERSTAND...
...IF YOU CAN'T STICK YOUR NECK OUT FOR THE COMPANY, I MIGHT AS WELL CUT IT OFF. ♡
SORRY FOR GETTING WORKED UP AND RAISING MY VOICE. ♡
ODA-SAN, THIS IS HARASSMENT...
WHAT'S GOING ON...?
GEEZ, ODA-SAN.
YOU DON'T HAVE TO SCOLD THEM SO HARSHLY.
IF YOU DON'T THINK YOU CAN DO IT IN TIME, I'LL JUST WAIT (RIGHT HERE) UNTIL YOU FINISH....
...MY DEAR TEMPS.
TEE HEE.
AND PLEASE...
...KEEP YOUR HANDS MOVING, EVERYONE.
TOKUGAWA-SAN...
SHE SPEAKS GENTLY, BUT...
...HER ATTITUDE IS THE WORST...
YIKES.
ODA AND TOKUGAWA ...
THEY'RE TWO OF THE MOST GORGEOUS LADIES ON THE PERMANENT STAFF...!
NOBUMI ODA
YASUNA TOKUGAWA
BUT THEY'RE ACTUALLY WOLVES WEARING LAMBS' SKINS...

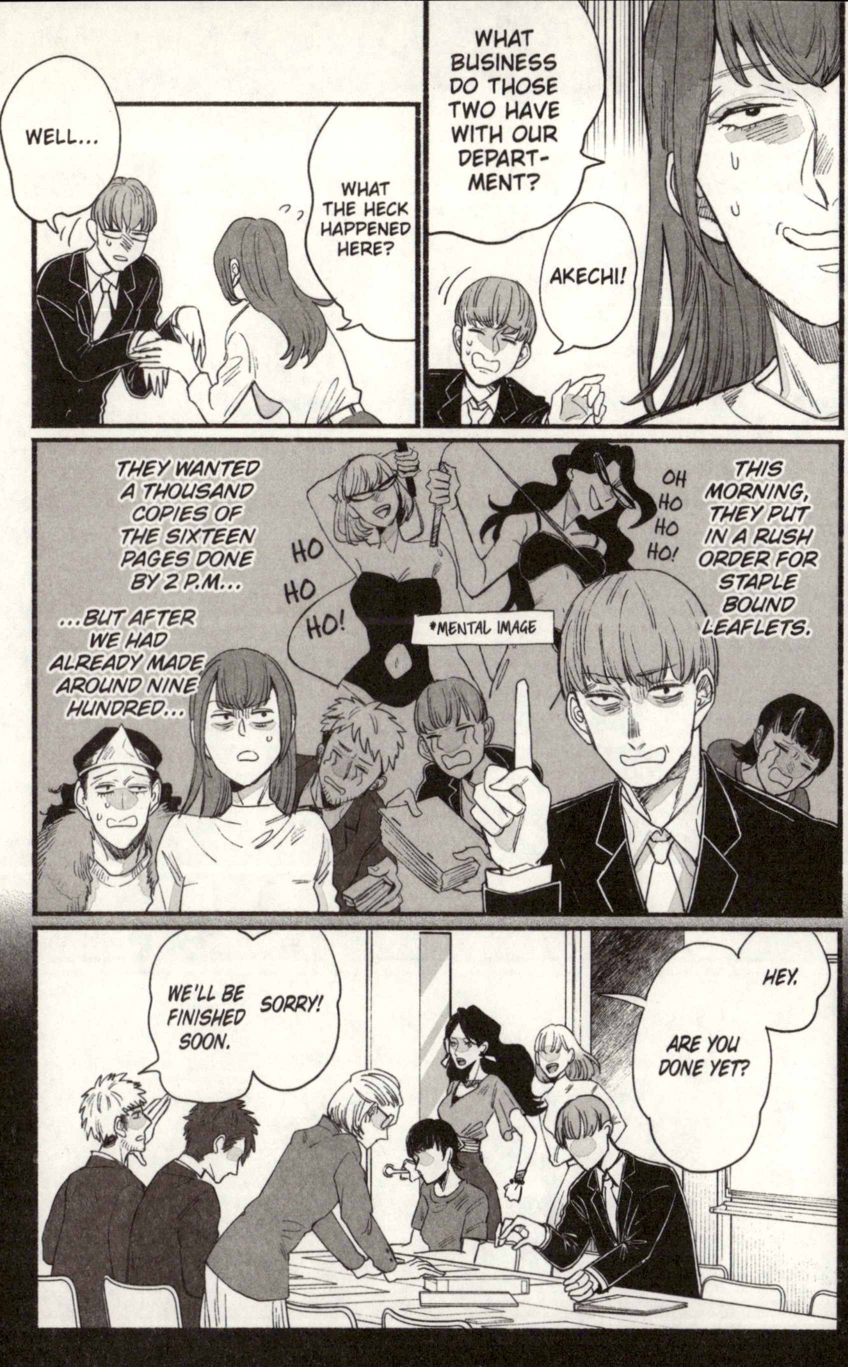
WHAT BUSINESS DO THOSE TWO HAVE WITH OUR DEPART-MENT?
AKECHI!
WHAT THE HECK HAPPENED HERE?
WELL...
THIS MORNING, THEY PUT IN A RUSH ORDER FOR STAPLE BOUND LEAFLETS.
OH HO HO HO!
THEY WANTED A THOUSAND COPIES OF THE SIXTEEN PAGES DONE BY 2 P.M...
HO HO HO!
*MENTAL IMAGE
...BUT AFTER WE HAD ALREADY MADE AROUND NINE HUNDRED...
HEY.
ARE YOU DONE YET?
SORRY!
WE'LL BE FINISHED SOON.

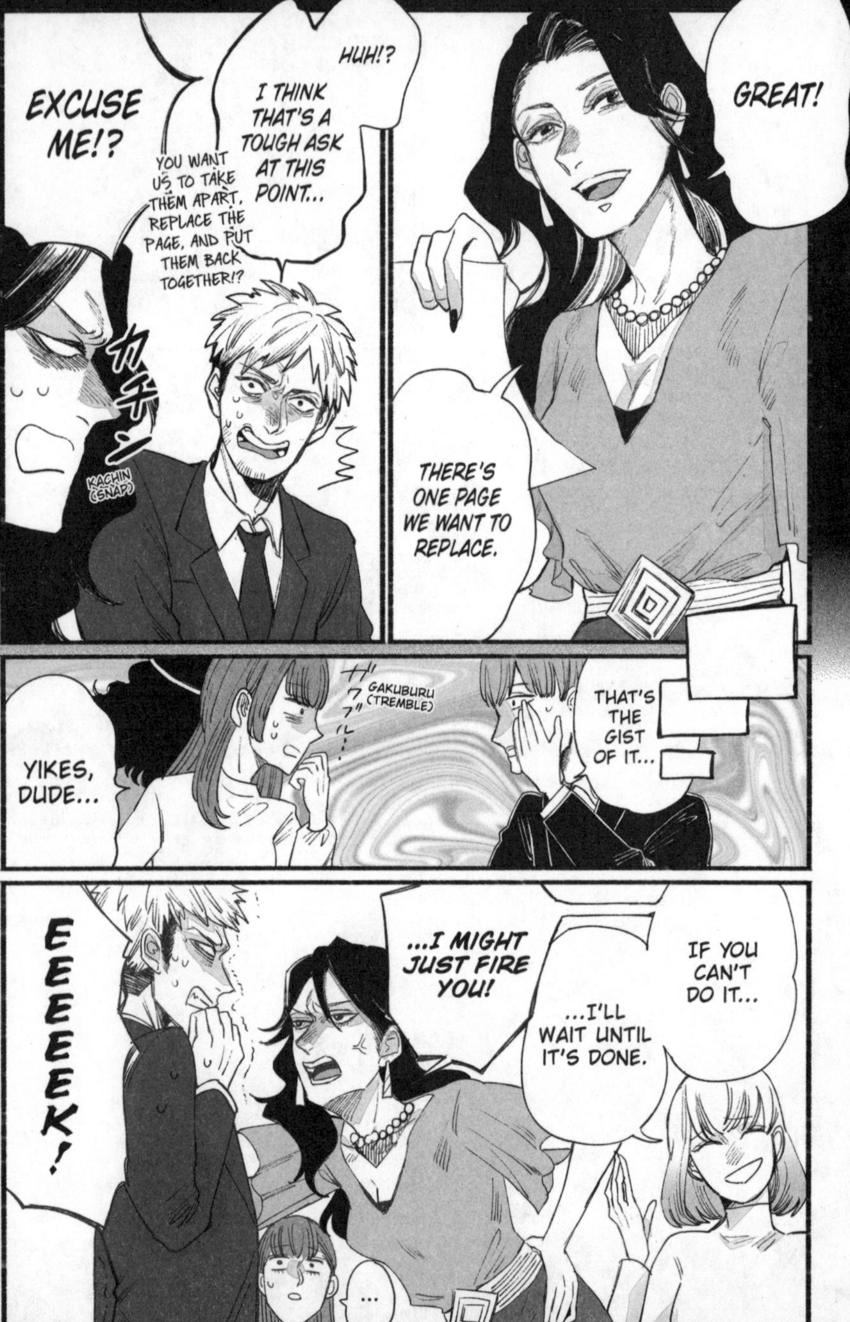
GREAT!
THERE'S ONE PAGE WE WANT TO REPLACE.
HUH!?
I THINK THAT'S A TOUGH ASK AT THIS POINT...
EXCUSE ME!?
YOU WANT US TO TAKE THEM APART, REPLACE THE PAGE, AND PUT THEM BACK TOGETHER!?
KACHIN (SNAP)
THAT'S THE GIST OF IT...
GAKUBURU (TREMBLE)
YIKES, DUDE...
IF YOU CAN'T DO IT...
...I'LL WAIT UNTIL IT'S DONE.
...I MIGHT JUST FIRE YOU!
EEEEEEK!
...

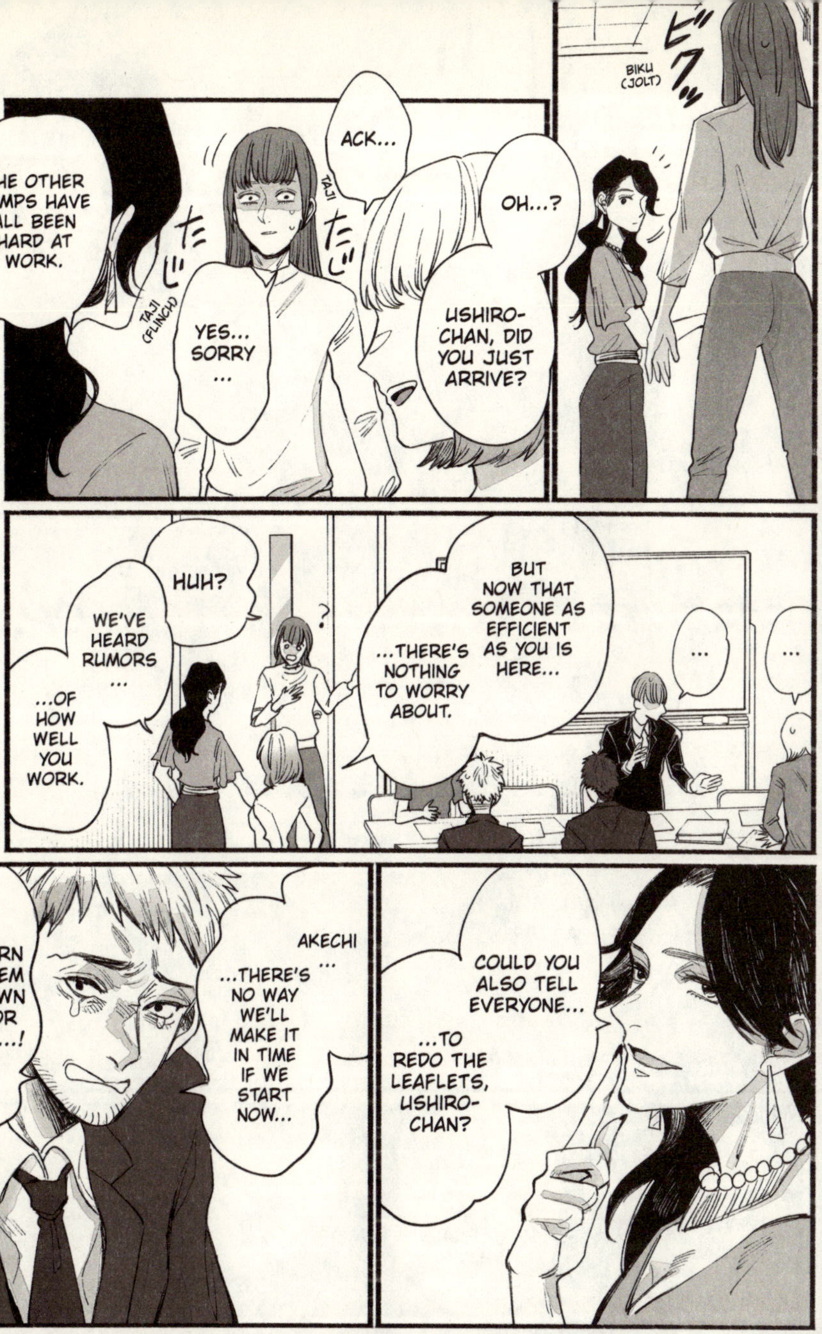
BIKU (JOLT)
OH...?
USHIRO-CHAN, DID YOU JUST ARRIVE?
ACK...
TAJI
THE OTHER TEMPS HAVE ALL BEEN HARD AT WORK.
YES... SORRY...
TAJI (FLINCH)
...
...
BUT NOW THAT SOMEONE AS EFFICIENT AS YOU IS HERE...
...THERE'S NOTHING TO WORRY ABOUT.
HUH?
?
WE'VE HEARD RUMORS...
...OF HOW WELL YOU WORK.
COULD YOU ALSO TELL EVERYONE...
...TO REDO THE LEAFLETS, USHIRO-CHAN?
AKECHI...
...THERE'S NO WAY WE'LL MAKE IT IN TIME IF WE START NOW...
TURN THEM DOWN FOR US...!

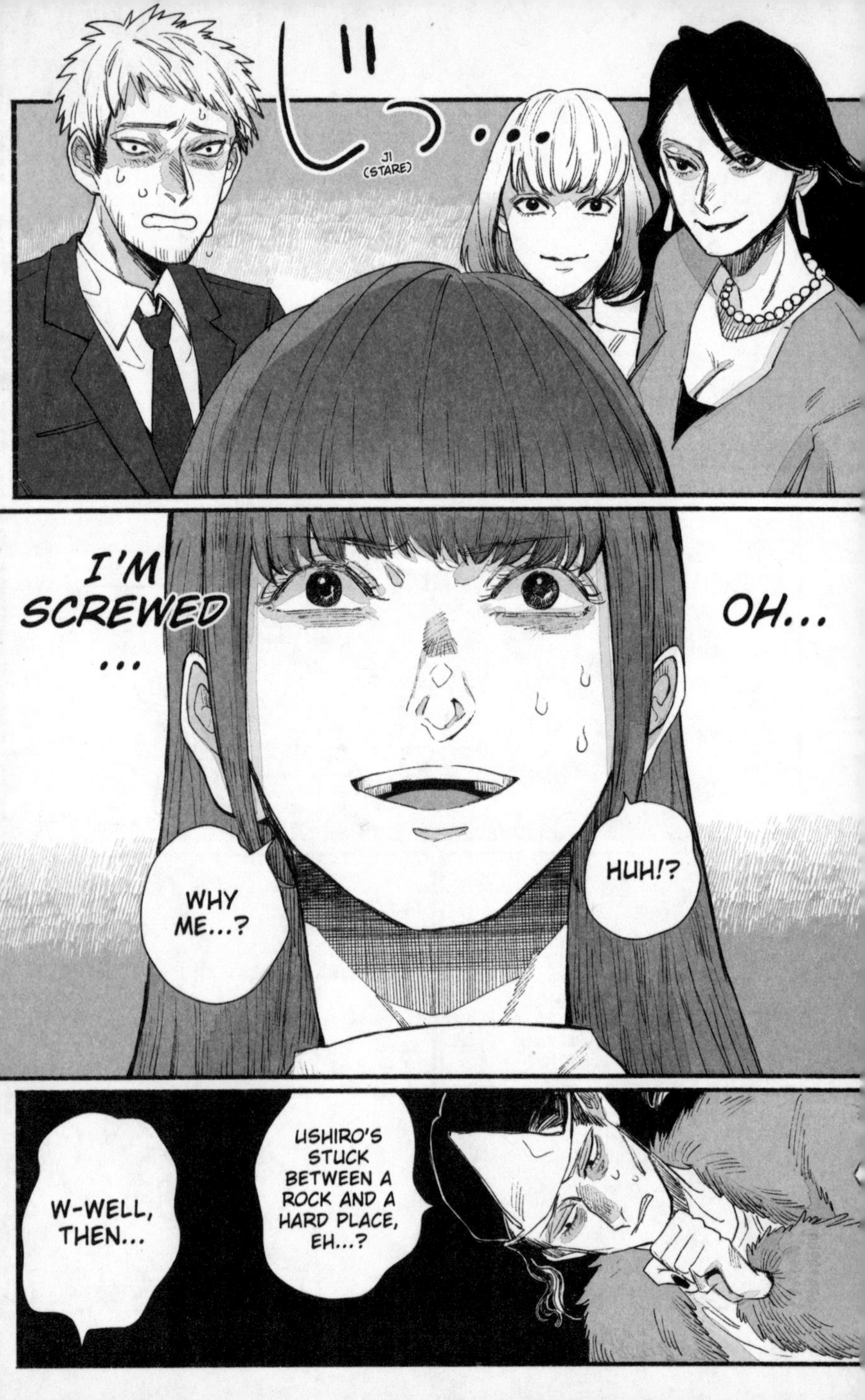
じっ…
JI (STARE)
OH...
I'M SCREWED...
HUH!?
WHY ME...?
USHIRO'S STUCK BETWEEN A ROCK AND A HARD PLACE, EH...?
W-WELL, THEN...

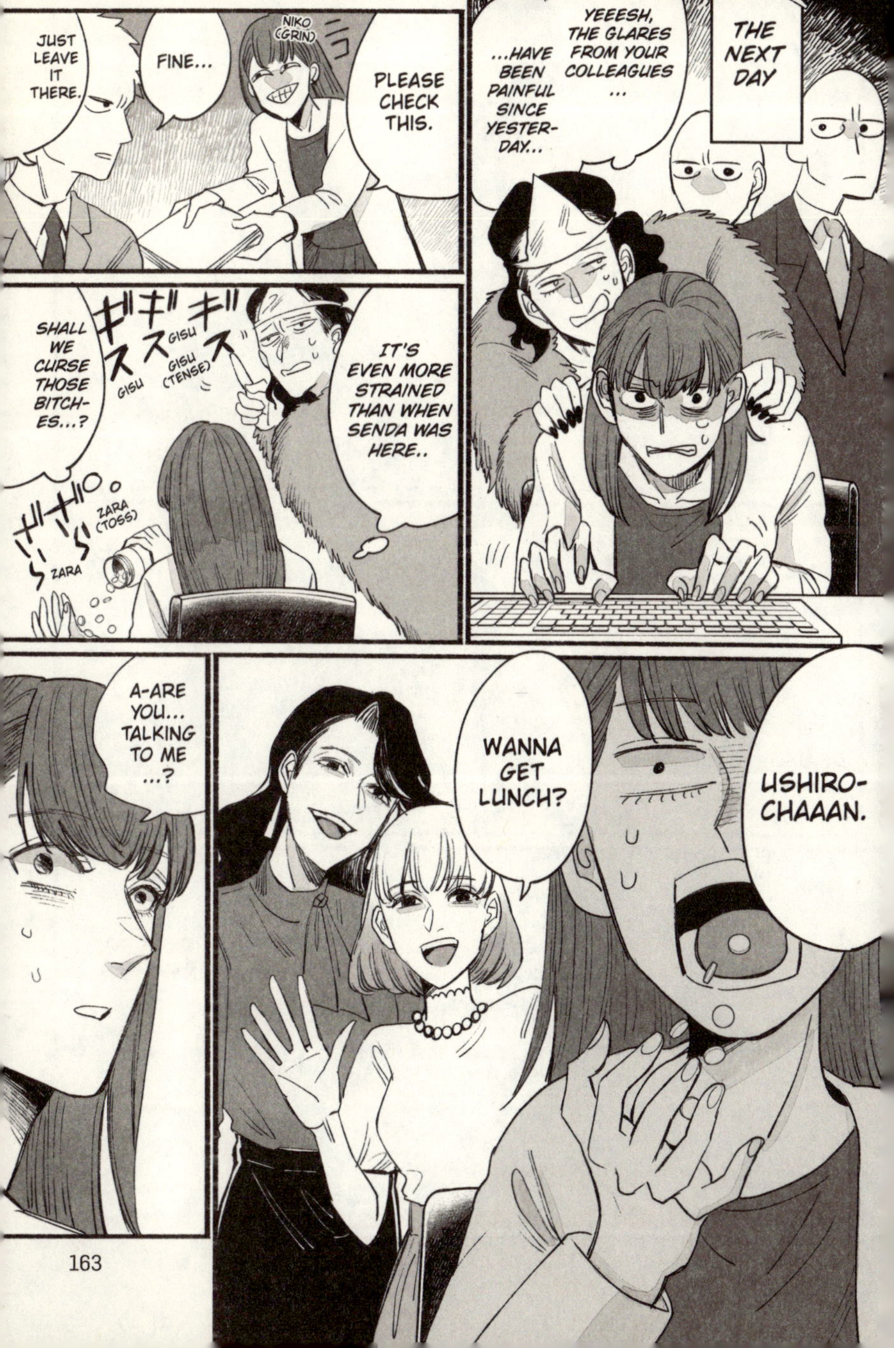

THE NEXT DAY
YEEESH, THE GLARES FROM YOUR COLLEAGUES ...
...HAVE BEEN PAINFUL SINCE YESTER-DAY...
PLEASE CHECK THIS.
NIKO (GRIN)
FINE...
JUST LEAVE IT THERE.
IT'S EVEN MORE STRAINED THAN WHEN SENDA WAS HERE..
GISU GISU (TENSE)
GISU
SHALL WE CURSE THOSE BITCHES...?
ZARA (TOSS)
ZARA
USHIRO-CHAAAN.
WANNA GET LUNCH?
A-ARE YOU... TALKING TO ME ...?

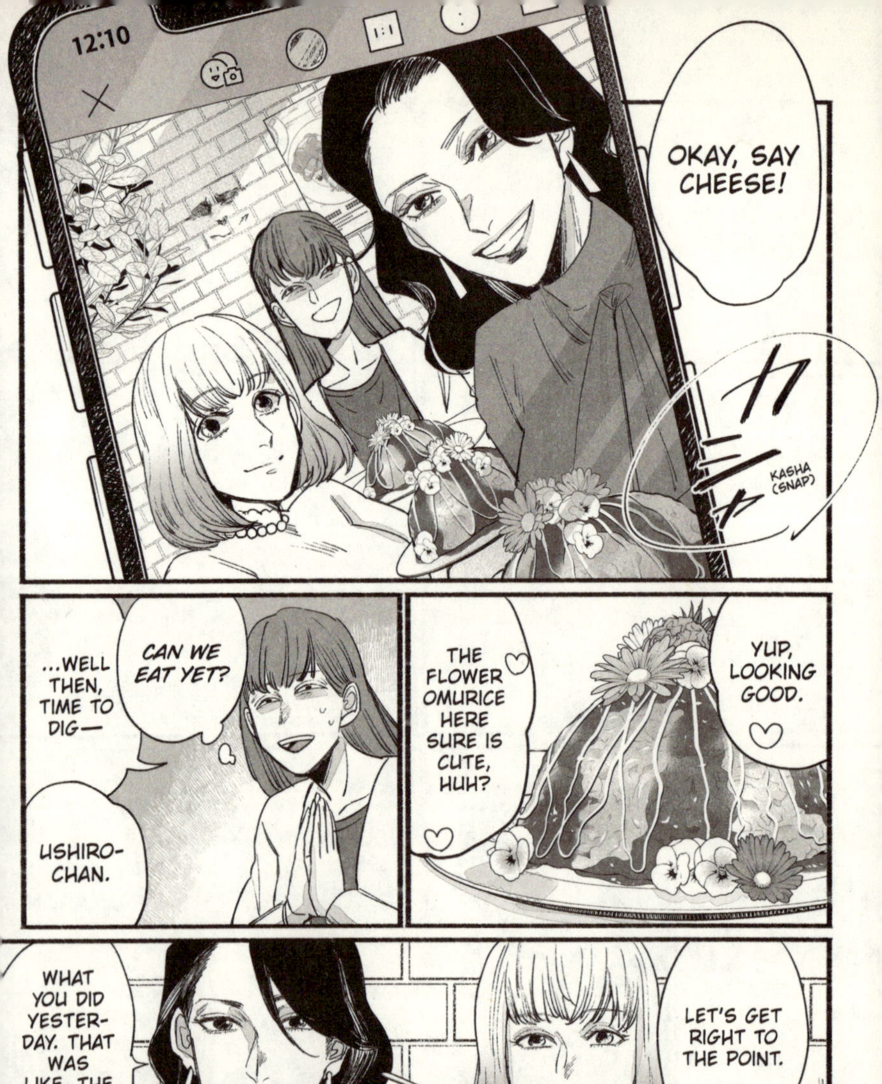
12:10
1:1
OKAY, SAY CHEESE!
カシャ
KASHA (SNAP)
YUP, LOOKING GOOD.
THE FLOWER OMURICE HERE SURE IS CUTE, HUH?
CAN WE EAT YET?
...WELL THEN, TIME TO DIG—
USHIRO-CHAN.
LET'S GET RIGHT TO THE POINT.
WHAT YOU DID YESTERDAY. THAT WAS LIKE, THE WORST.

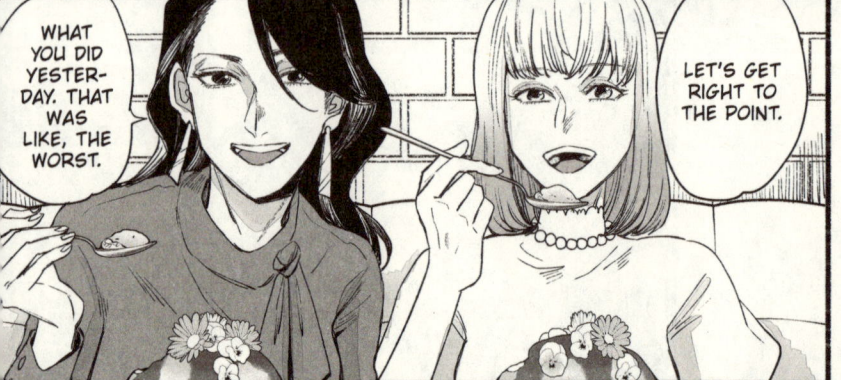

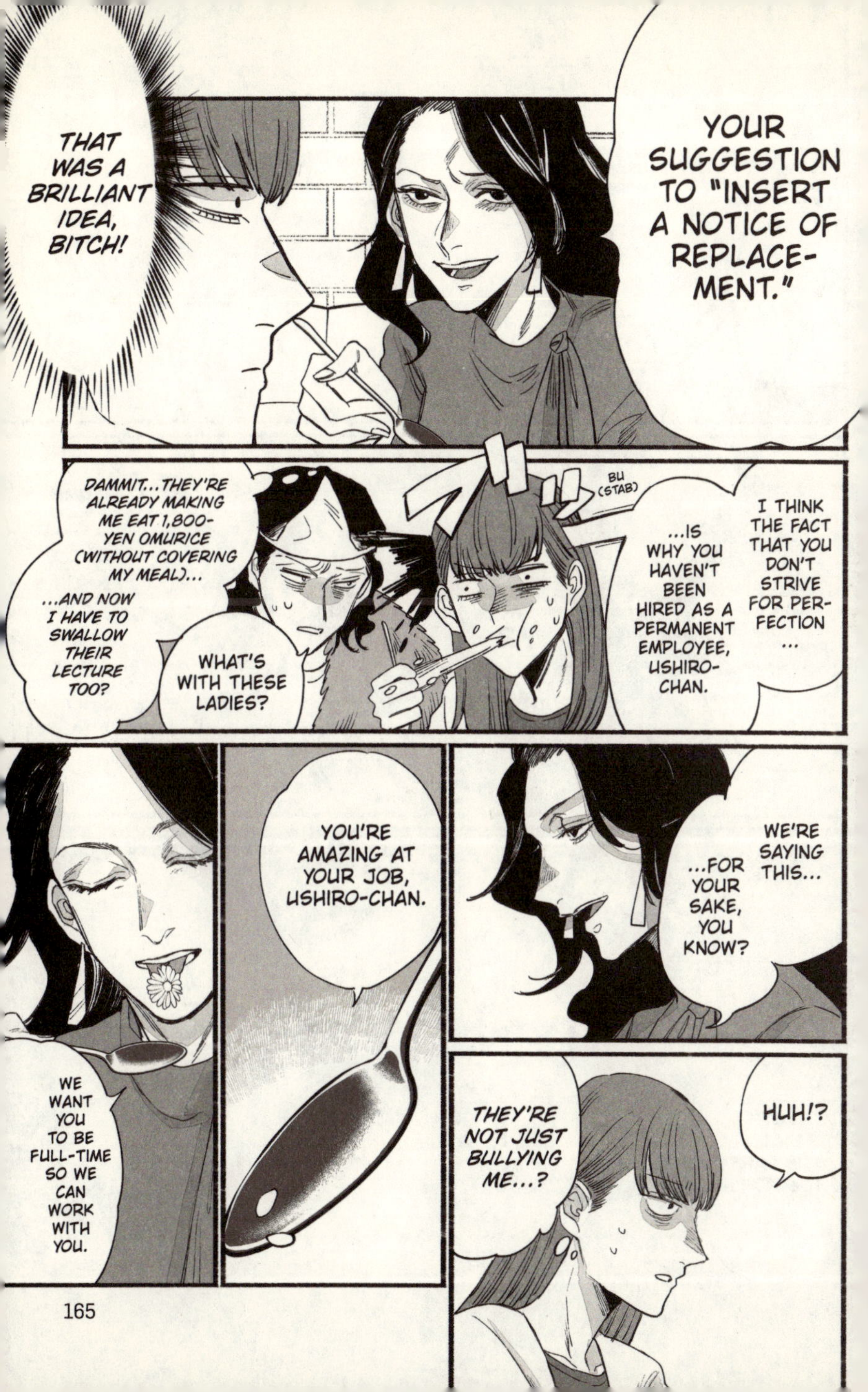
YOUR SUGGESTION TO "INSERT A NOTICE OF REPLACEMENT."
THAT WAS A BRILLIANT IDEA, BITCH!
I THINK THE FACT THAT YOU DON'T STRIVE FOR PERFECTION...
...IS WHY YOU HAVEN'T BEEN HIRED AS A PERMANENT EMPLOYEE, USHIRO-CHAN.
BU (STAB)
DAMMIT...THEY'RE ALREADY MAKING ME EAT 1,800-YEN OMURICE (WITHOUT COVERING MY MEAL)...
...AND NOW I HAVE TO SWALLOW THEIR LECTURE TOO?
WHAT'S WITH THESE LADIES?
WE'RE SAYING THIS...
...FOR YOUR SAKE, YOU KNOW?
HUH!?
THEY'RE NOT JUST BULLYING ME...?
YOU'RE AMAZING AT YOUR JOB, USHIRO-CHAN.
WE WANT YOU TO BE FULL-TIME SO WE CAN WORK WITH YOU.

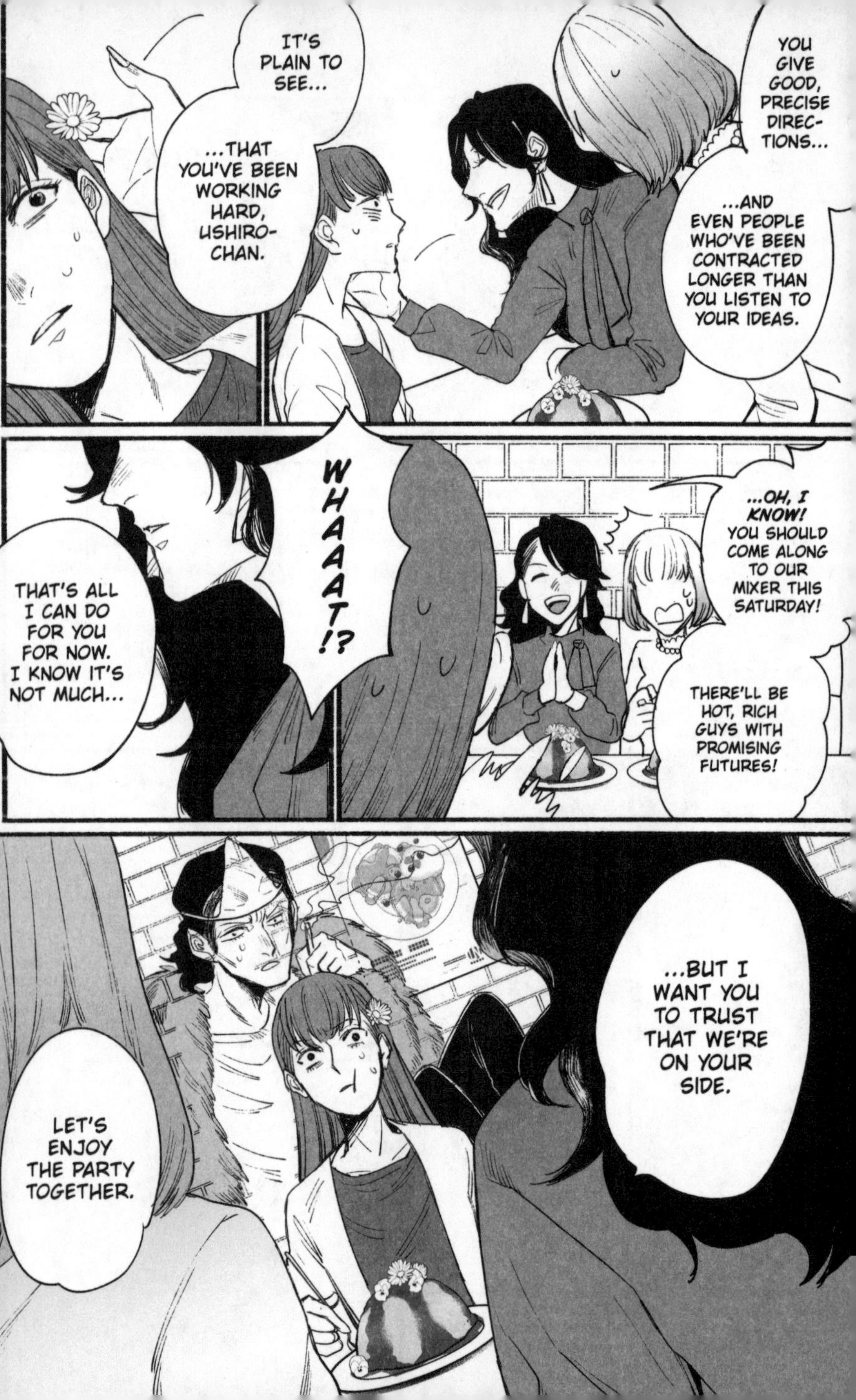
IT'S PLAIN TO SEE...
...THAT YOU'VE BEEN WORKING HARD, USHIRO-CHAN.
YOU GIVE GOOD, PRECISE DIREC-TIONS...
...AND EVEN PEOPLE WHO'VE BEEN CONTRACTED LONGER THAN YOU LISTEN TO YOUR IDEAS.
...OH, I KNOW! YOU SHOULD COME ALONG TO OUR MIXER THIS SATURDAY!
THERE'LL BE HOT, RICH GUYS WITH PROMISING FUTURES!
WHAAAAT!?
THAT'S ALL I CAN DO FOR YOU FOR NOW. I KNOW IT'S NOT MUCH...
...BUT I WANT YOU TO TRUST THAT WE'RE ON YOUR SIDE.
LET'S ENJOY THE PARTY TOGETHER.

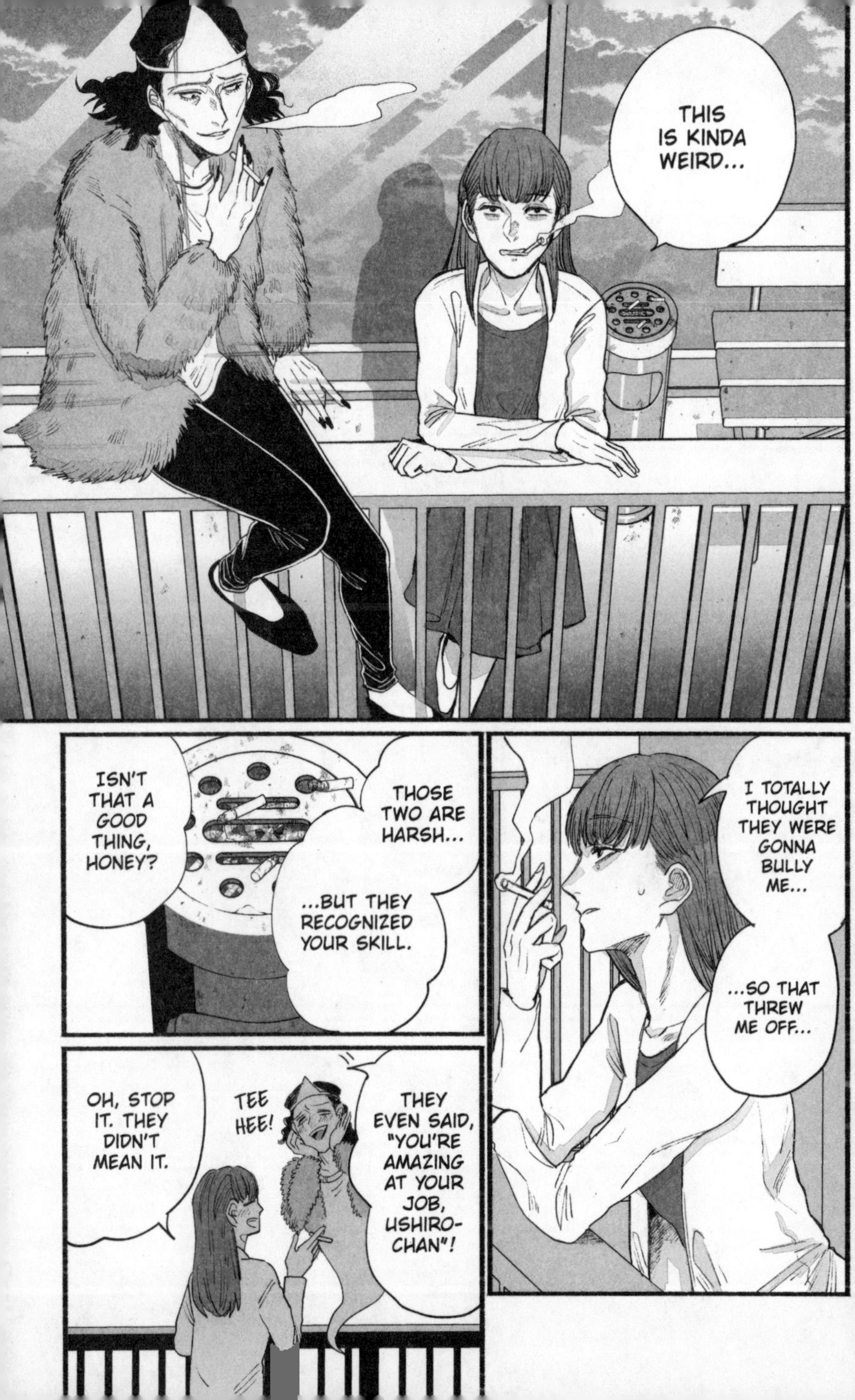
THIS IS KINDA WEIRD...
I TOTALLY THOUGHT THEY WERE GONNA BULLY ME...
...SO THAT THREW ME OFF...
THOSE TWO ARE HARSH...
...BUT THEY RECOGNIZED YOUR SKILL.
ISN'T THAT A GOOD THING, HONEY?
THEY EVEN SAID, "YOU'RE AMAZING AT YOUR JOB, USHIRO-CHAN"!
TEE HEE!
OH, STOP IT. THEY DIDN'T MEAN IT.

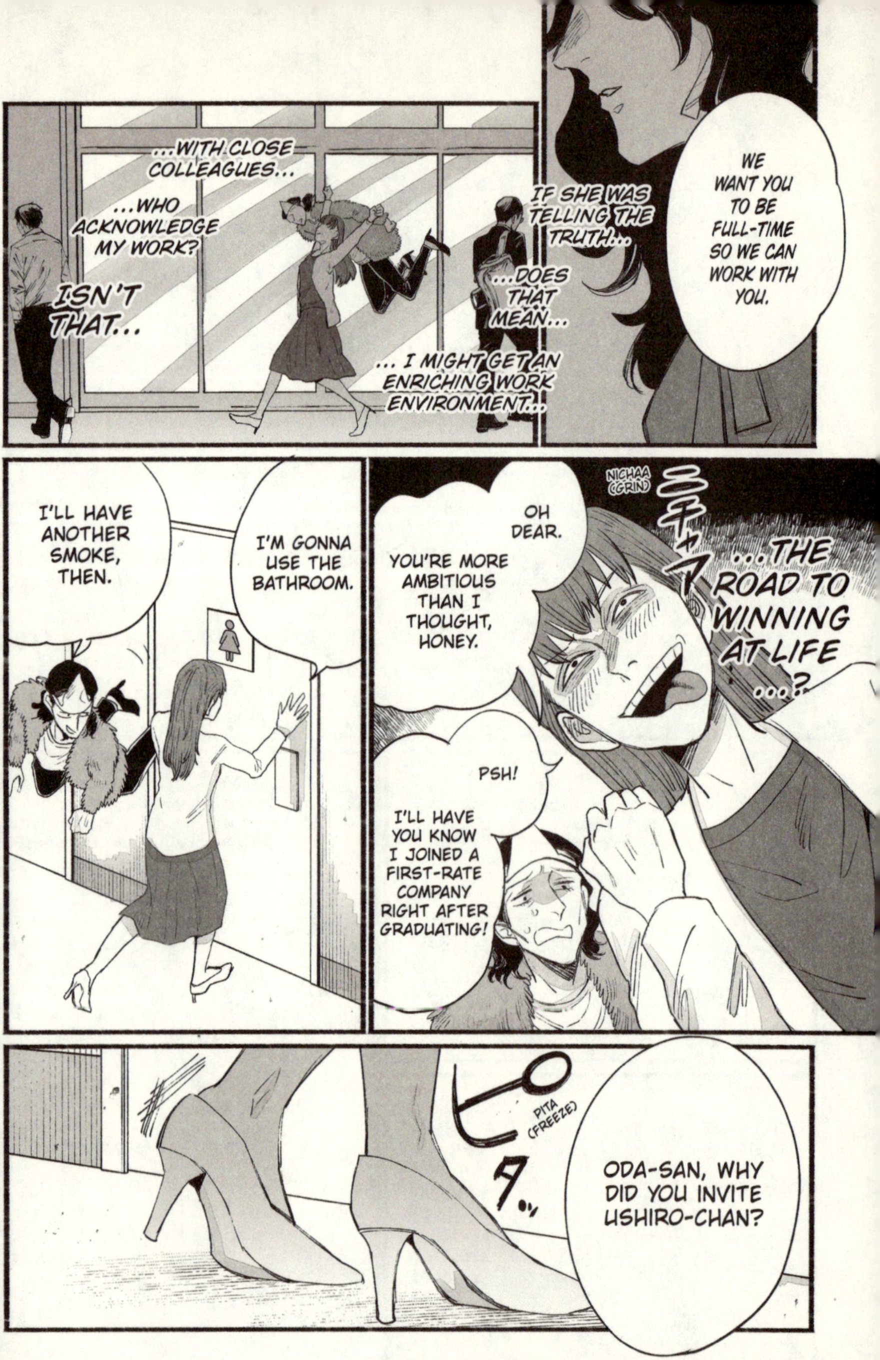
WE WANT YOU TO BE FULL-TIME SO WE CAN WORK WITH YOU.
IF SHE WAS TELLING THE TRUTH...
...DOES THAT MEAN...
...I MIGHT GET AN ENRICHING WORK ENVIRONMENT...
...WITH CLOSE COLLEAGUES...
...WHO ACKNOWLEDGE MY WORK?
ISN'T THAT...
NICHAA (GRIN)
...THE ROAD TO WINNING AT LIFE...?
OH DEAR.
YOU'RE MORE AMBITIOUS THAN I THOUGHT, HONEY.
PSH!
I'LL HAVE YOU KNOW I JOINED A FIRST-RATE COMPANY RIGHT AFTER GRADUATING!
I'M GONNA USE THE BATHROOM.
I'LL HAVE ANOTHER SMOKE, THEN.
ODA-SAN, WHY DID YOU INVITE USHIRO-CHAN?
PITA (FREEZE)

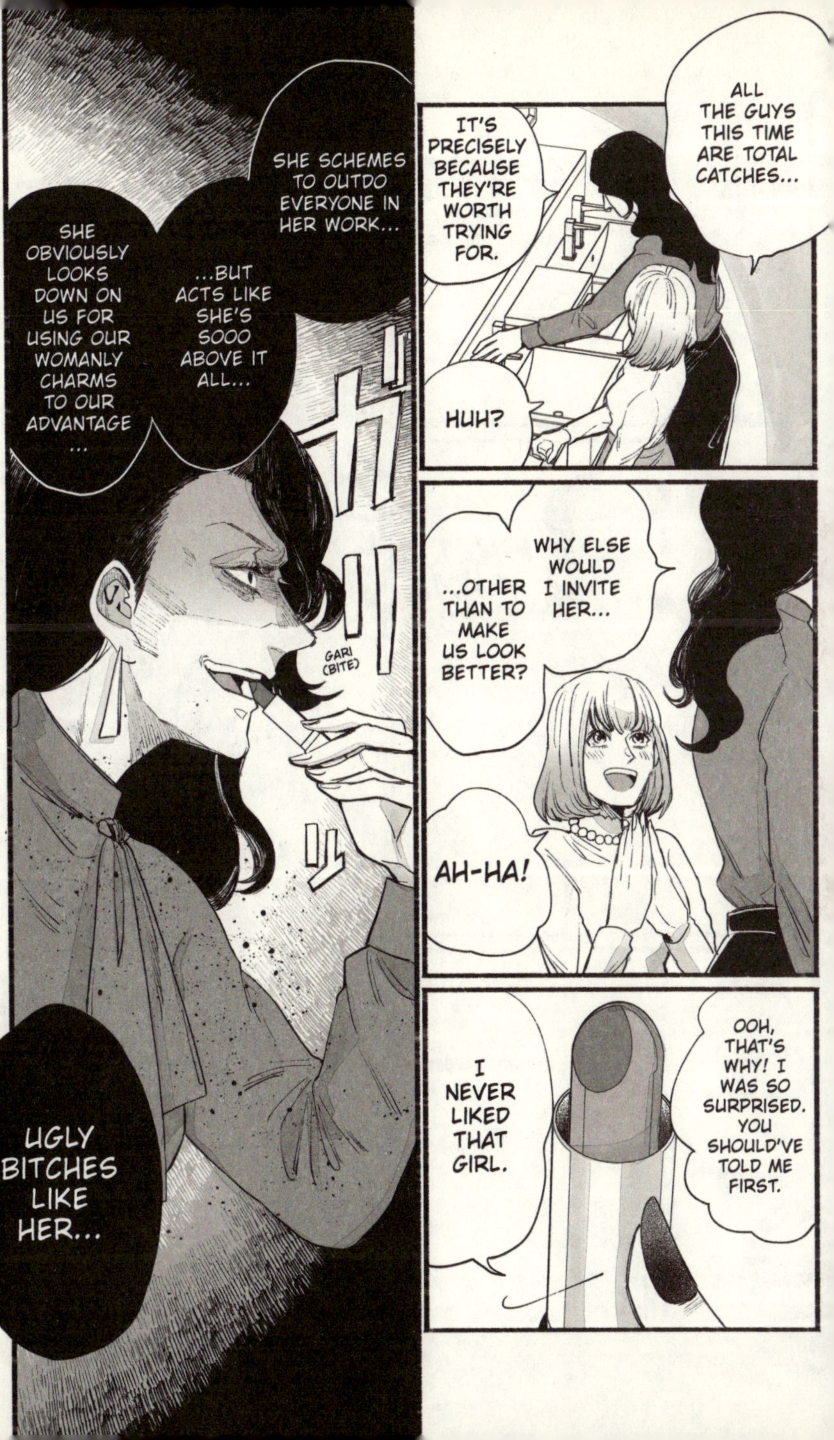
ALL THE GUYS THIS TIME ARE TOTAL CATCHES...
IT'S PRECISELY BECAUSE THEY'RE WORTH TRYING FOR.
HUH?
WHY ELSE WOULD I INVITE HER...
...OTHER THAN TO MAKE US LOOK BETTER?
AH-HA!
OOH, THAT'S WHY! I WAS SO SURPRISED. YOU SHOULD'VE TOLD ME FIRST.
I NEVER LIKED THAT GIRL.
SHE SCHEMES TO OUTDO EVERYONE IN HER WORK...
...BUT ACTS LIKE SHE'S SOOO ABOVE IT ALL...
SHE OBVIOUSLY LOOKS DOWN ON US FOR USING OUR WOMANLY CHARMS TO OUR ADVANTAGE...
GARI (BITE)
UGLY BITCHES LIKE HER...

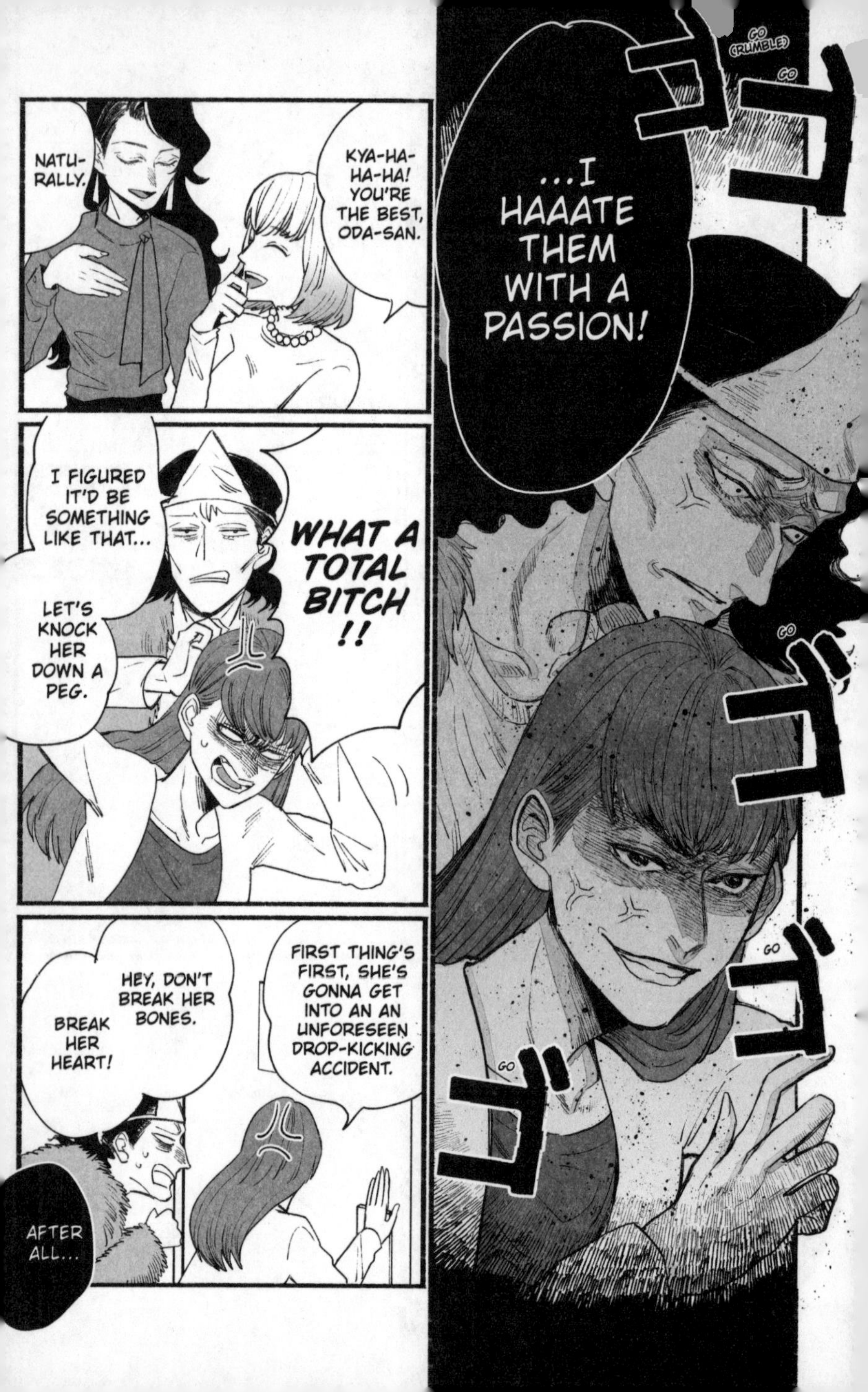
KYA-HA-HA-HA! YOU'RE THE BEST, ODA-SAN.
NATU-RALLY.
WHAT A TOTAL BITCH!!
I FIGURED IT'D BE SOMETHING LIKE THAT...
LET'S KNOCK HER DOWN A PEG.
FIRST THING'S FIRST, SHE'S GONNA GET INTO AN AN UNFORESEEN DROP-KICKING ACCIDENT.
HEY, DON'T BREAK HER BONES.
BREAK HER HEART!
AFTER ALL...
GO (RUMBLE)
GO
...I HAAATE THEM WITH A PASSION!
GO
GO
GO

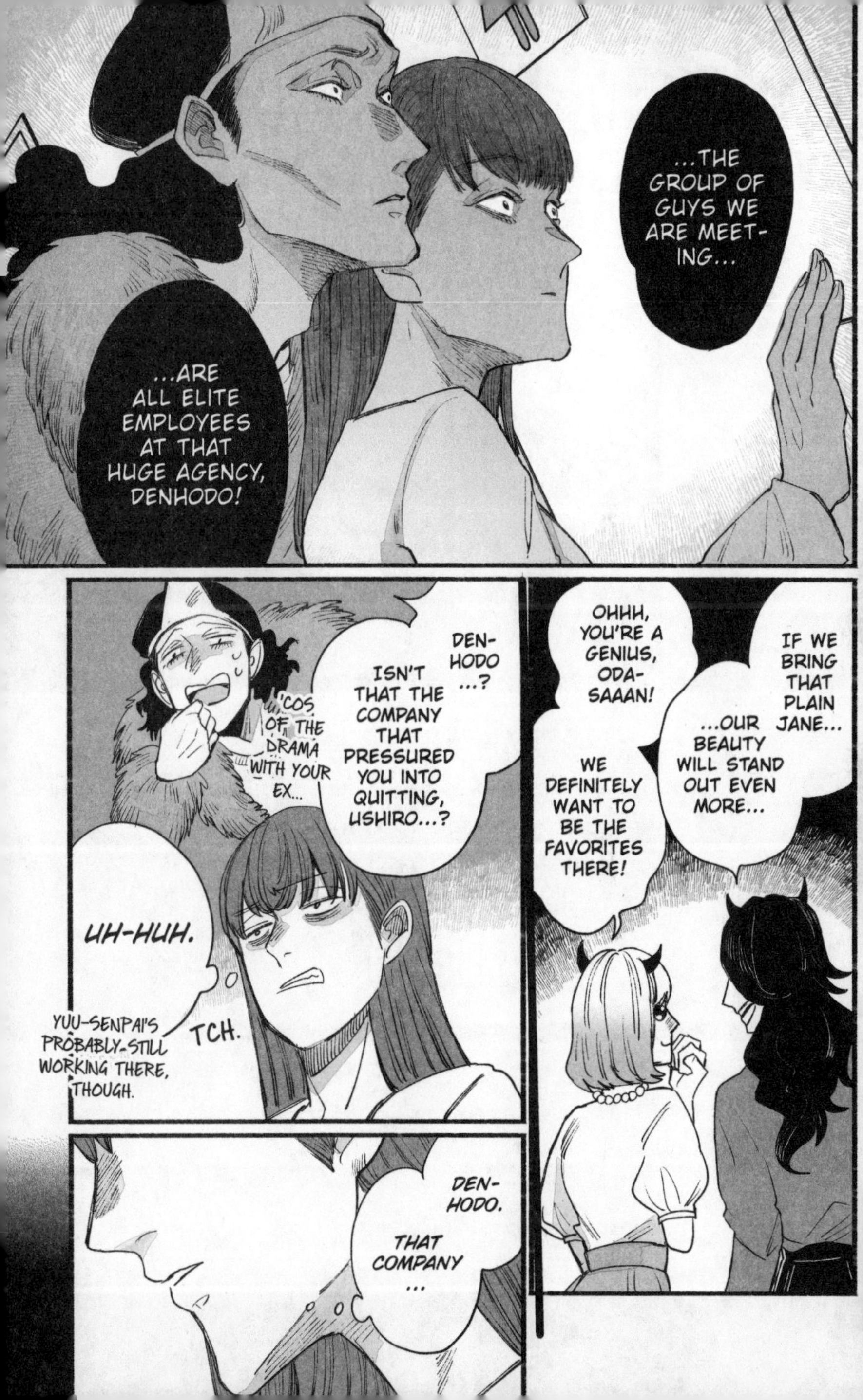
...THE GROUP OF GUYS WE ARE MEETING...
...ARE ALL ELITE EMPLOYEES AT THAT HUGE AGENCY, DENHODO!
IF WE BRING THAT PLAIN JANE...
...OUR BEAUTY WILL STAND OUT EVEN MORE...
OHHH, YOU'RE A GENIUS, ODA-SAAAN!
WE DEFINITELY WANT TO BE THE FAVORITES THERE!
DEN-HODO ...?
ISN'T THAT THE COMPANY THAT PRESSURED YOU INTO QUITTING, USHIRO...?
'COS OF THE DRAMA WITH YOUR EX...
UH-HUH.
TCH.
YUU-SENPAI'S PROBABLY STILL WORKING THERE, THOUGH.
DEN-HODO.
THAT COMPANY ...

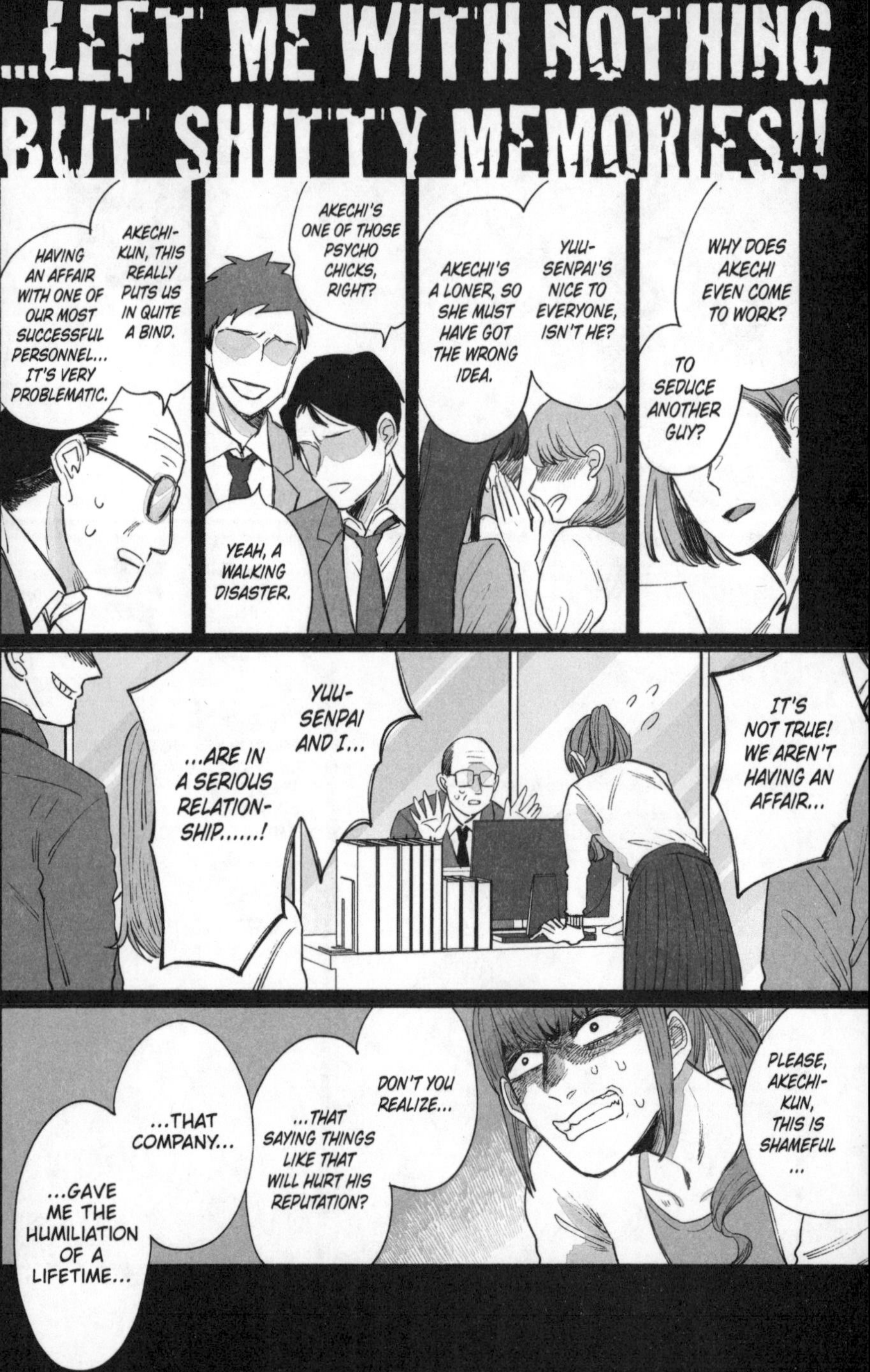
...LEFT ME WITH NOTHING BUT SHITTY MEMORIES!!
WHY DOES AKECHI EVEN COME TO WORK?
TO SEDUCE ANOTHER GUY?
YUU-SENPAI'S NICE TO EVERYONE, ISN'T HE?
AKECHI'S A LONER, SO SHE MUST HAVE GOT THE WRONG IDEA.
AKECHI'S ONE OF THOSE PSYCHO CHICKS, RIGHT?
YEAH, A WALKING DISASTER.
AKECHI-KUN, THIS REALLY PUTS US IN QUITE A BIND.
HAVING AN AFFAIR WITH ONE OF OUR MOST SUCCESSFUL PERSONNEL... IT'S VERY PROBLEMATIC.
IT'S NOT TRUE! WE AREN'T HAVING AN AFFAIR...
YUU-SENPAI AND I...
...ARE IN A SERIOUS RELATIONSHIP......!
PLEASE, AKECHI-KUN, THIS IS SHAMEFUL...
DON'T YOU REALIZE...
...THAT SAYING THINGS LIKE THAT WILL HURT HIS REPUTATION?
...THAT COMPANY...
...GAVE ME THE HUMILIATION OF A LIFETIME...

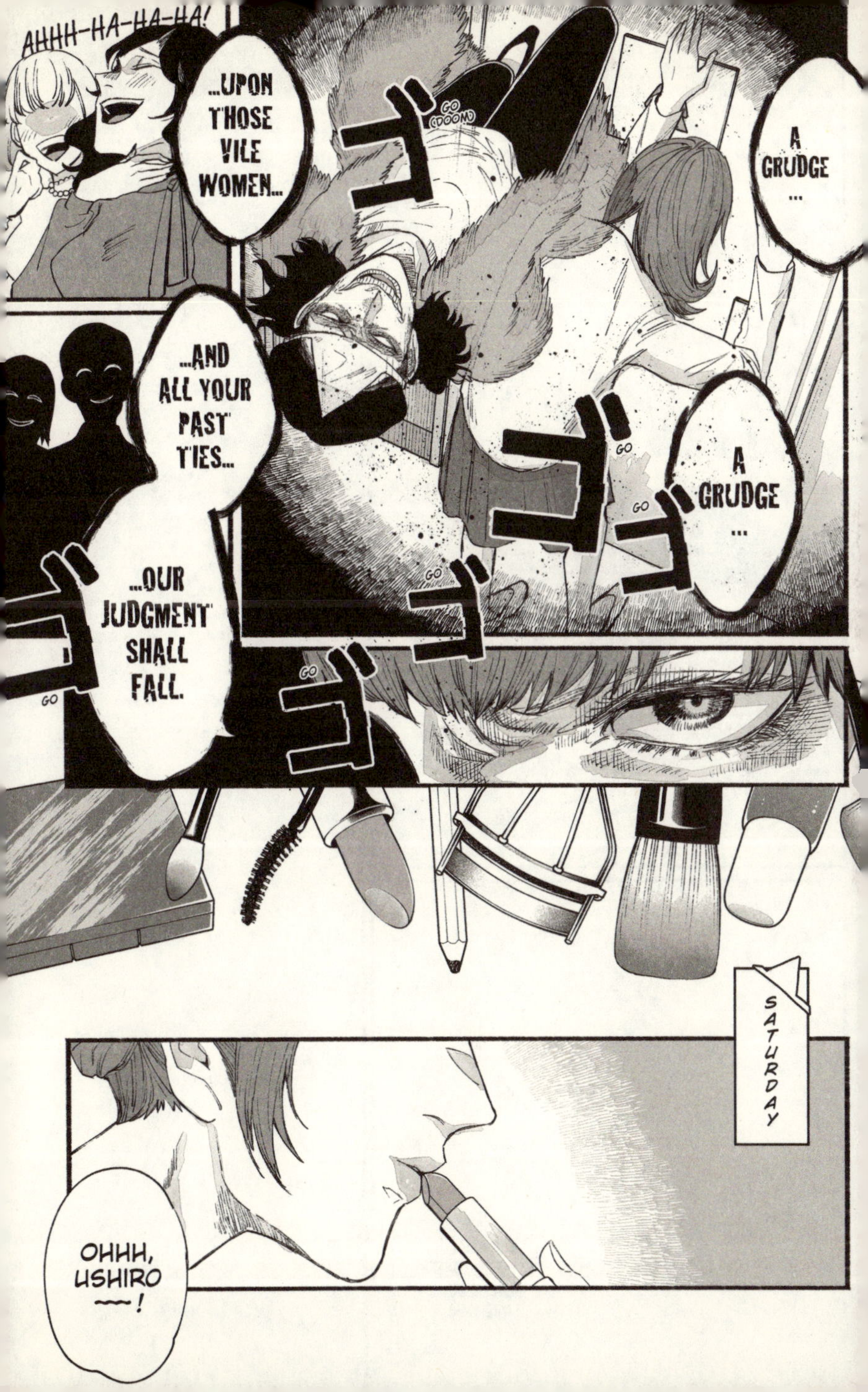
A GRUDGE...
GO (DOOM)
A GRUDGE...
GO
GO
GO
AHHH-HA-HA-HA!
...UPON THOSE VILE WOMEN...
...AND ALL YOUR PAST TIES...
...OUR JUDGMENT SHALL FALL.
GO
GO
SATURDAY
OHHH, USHIRO ~~~!

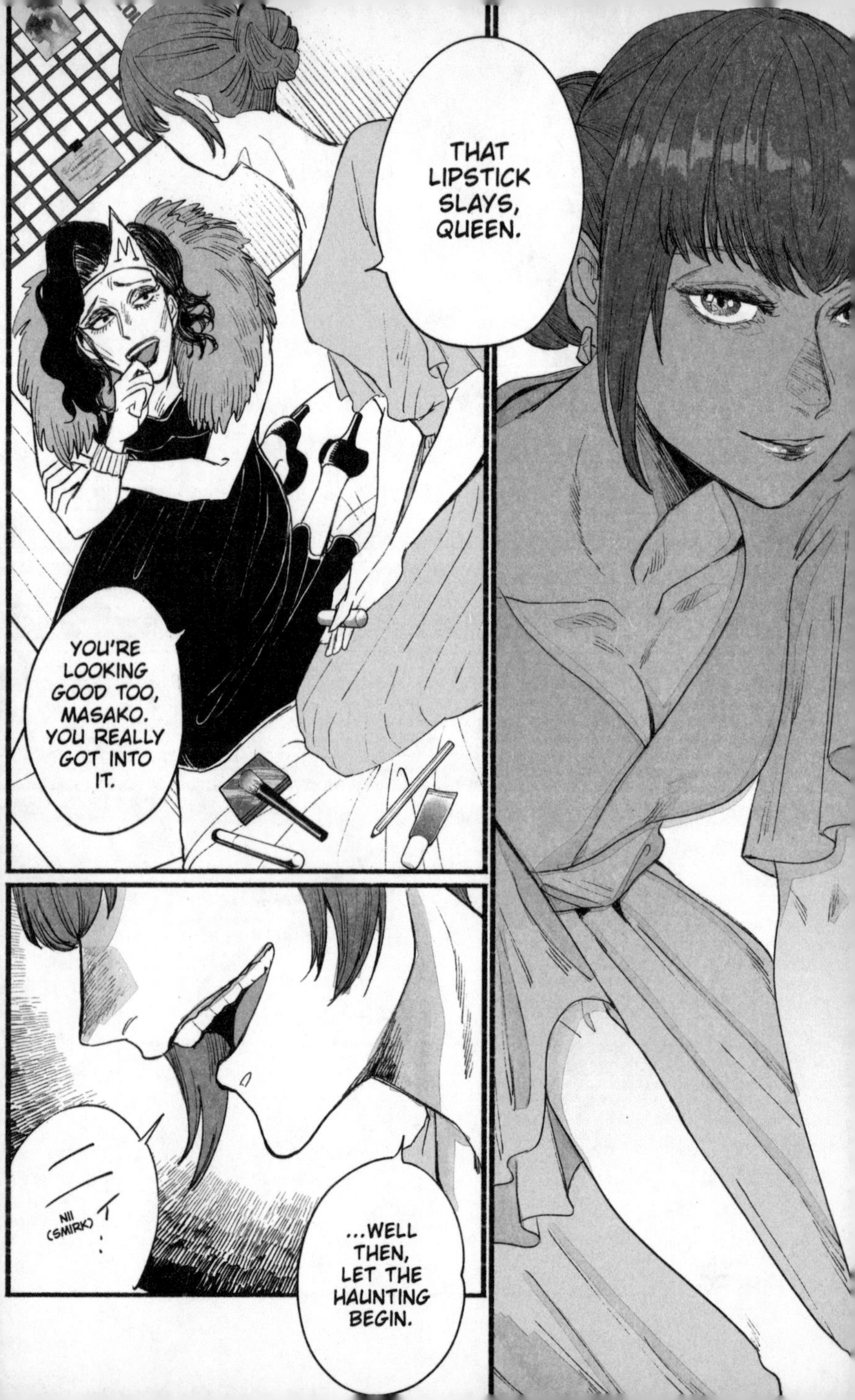
THAT LIPSTICK SLAYS, QUEEN.
YOU'RE LOOKING GOOD TOO, MASAKO. YOU REALLY GOT INTO IT.
...WELL THEN, LET THE HAUNTING BEGIN.
NII (SMIRK)

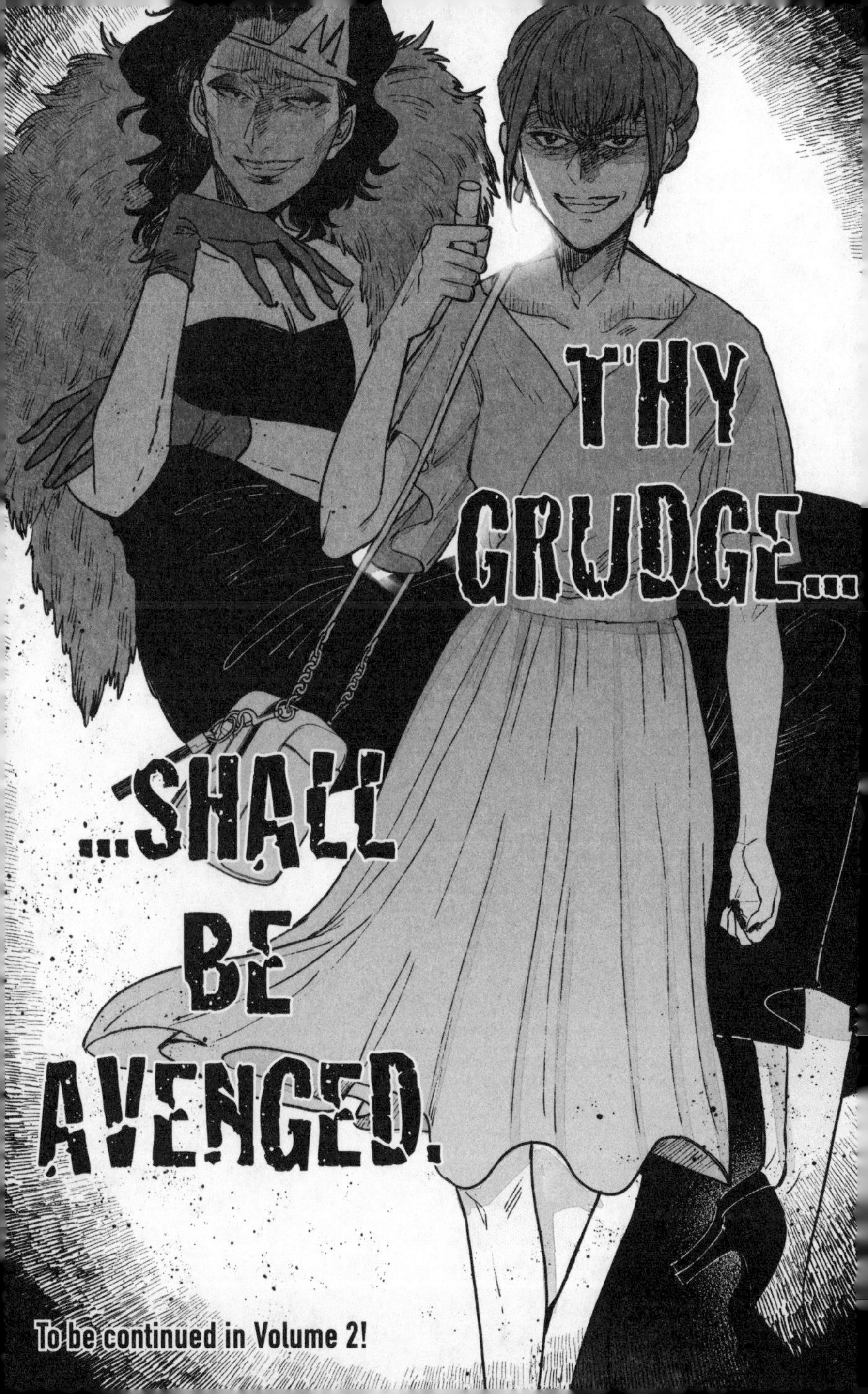

THY GRUDGE...
...SHALL BE AVENGED.

To be continued in Volume 2!

GOGOGOGO-GO-GHOST!

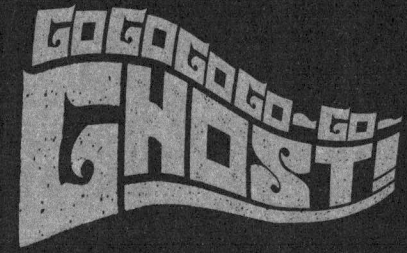

Bonus "Me and My Guardian Spirit" Miyako Hiruzuka

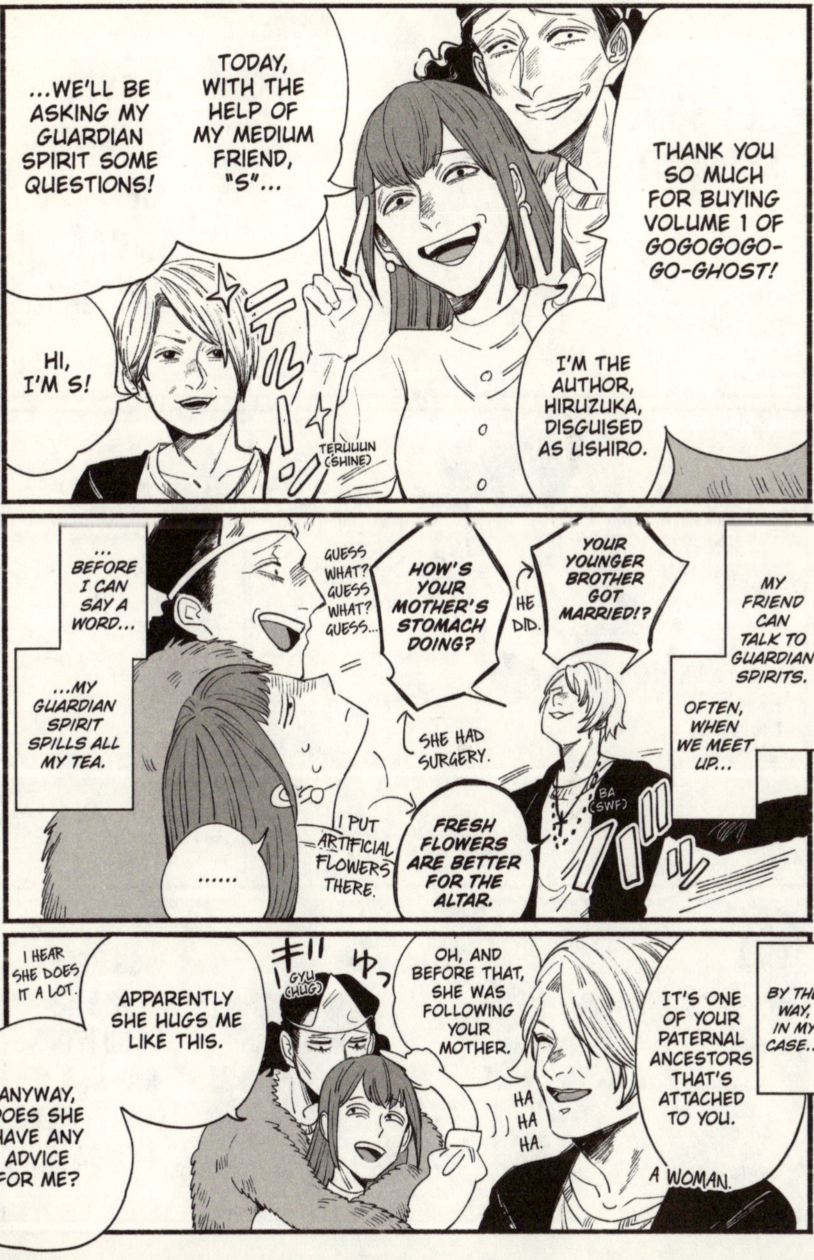
THANK YOU SO MUCH FOR BUYING VOLUME 1 OF GOGOGOGO-GO-GHOST!
I'M THE AUTHOR, HIRUZUKA, DISGUISED AS USHIRO.
TODAY, WITH THE HELP OF MY MEDIUM FRIEND, "S"...
...WE'LL BE ASKING MY GUARDIAN SPIRIT SOME QUESTIONS!
TERUUUN (SHINE)
HI, I'M S!
MY FRIEND CAN TALK TO GUARDIAN SPIRITS.
OFTEN, WHEN WE MEET UP...
YOUR YOUNGER BROTHER GOT MARRIED!?
HE DID.
HOW'S YOUR MOTHER'S STOMACH DOING?
GUESS WHAT? GUESS WHAT? GUESS...
SHE HAD SURGERY.
BA (SWF)
FRESH FLOWERS ARE BETTER FOR THE ALTAR.
I PUT ARTIFICIAL FLOWERS THERE.
...BEFORE I CAN SAY A WORD...
...MY GUARDIAN SPIRIT SPILLS ALL MY TEA.
......
BY THE WAY, IN MY CASE...
IT'S ONE OF YOUR PATERNAL ANCESTORS THAT'S ATTACHED TO YOU.
A WOMAN.
HA HA HA.
OH, AND BEFORE THAT, SHE WAS FOLLOWING YOUR MOTHER.
GYU (HUG)
APPARENTLY SHE HUGS ME LIKE THIS.
I HEAR SHE DOES IT A LOT.
ANYWAY, DOES SHE HAVE ANY ADVICE FOR ME?

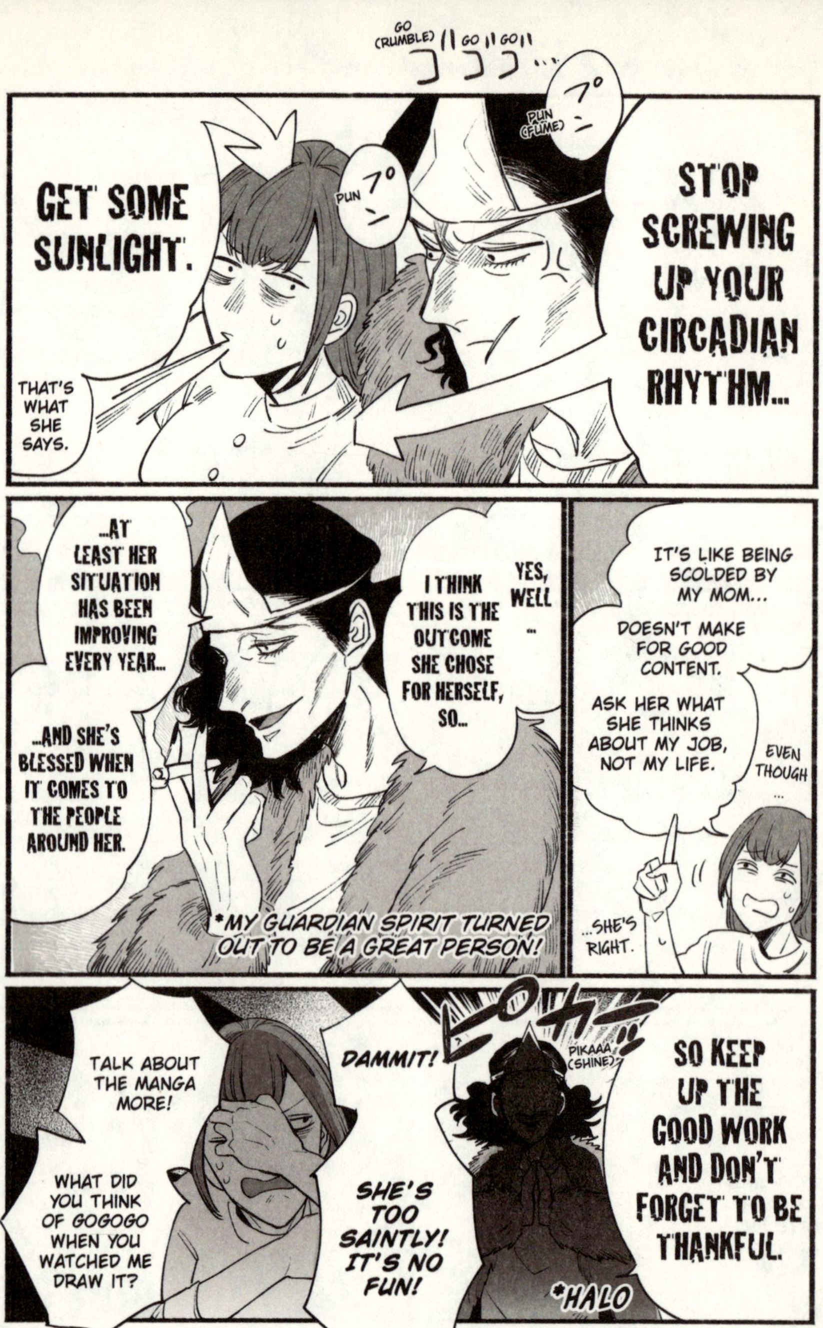
GO (RUMBLE) GO GO
PUN (FUME)
STOP SCREWING UP YOUR CIRCADIAN RHYTHM...
PUN
GET SOME SUNLIGHT.
THAT'S WHAT SHE SAYS.
IT'S LIKE BEING SCOLDED BY MY MOM...
DOESN'T MAKE FOR GOOD CONTENT.
ASK HER WHAT SHE THINKS ABOUT MY JOB, NOT MY LIFE.
EVEN THOUGH ...
...SHE'S RIGHT.
YES, WELL ...
I THINK THIS IS THE OUTCOME SHE CHOSE FOR HERSELF, SO...
...AT LEAST HER SITUATION HAS BEEN IMPROVING EVERY YEAR...
...AND SHE'S BLESSED WHEN IT COMES TO THE PEOPLE AROUND HER.
*MY GUARDIAN SPIRIT TURNED OUT TO BE A GREAT PERSON!
PIKAAA (SHINE)
SO KEEP UP THE GOOD WORK AND DON'T FORGET TO BE THANKFUL.
*HALO
DAMMIT!
SHE'S TOO SAINTLY! IT'S NO FUN!
TALK ABOUT THE MANGA MORE!
WHAT DID YOU THINK OF GOGOGO WHEN YOU WATCHED ME DRAW IT?

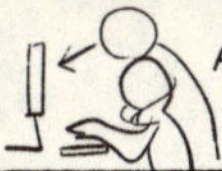
AT LEAST, I ASSUME SHE'D BE ABLE TO READ IT...

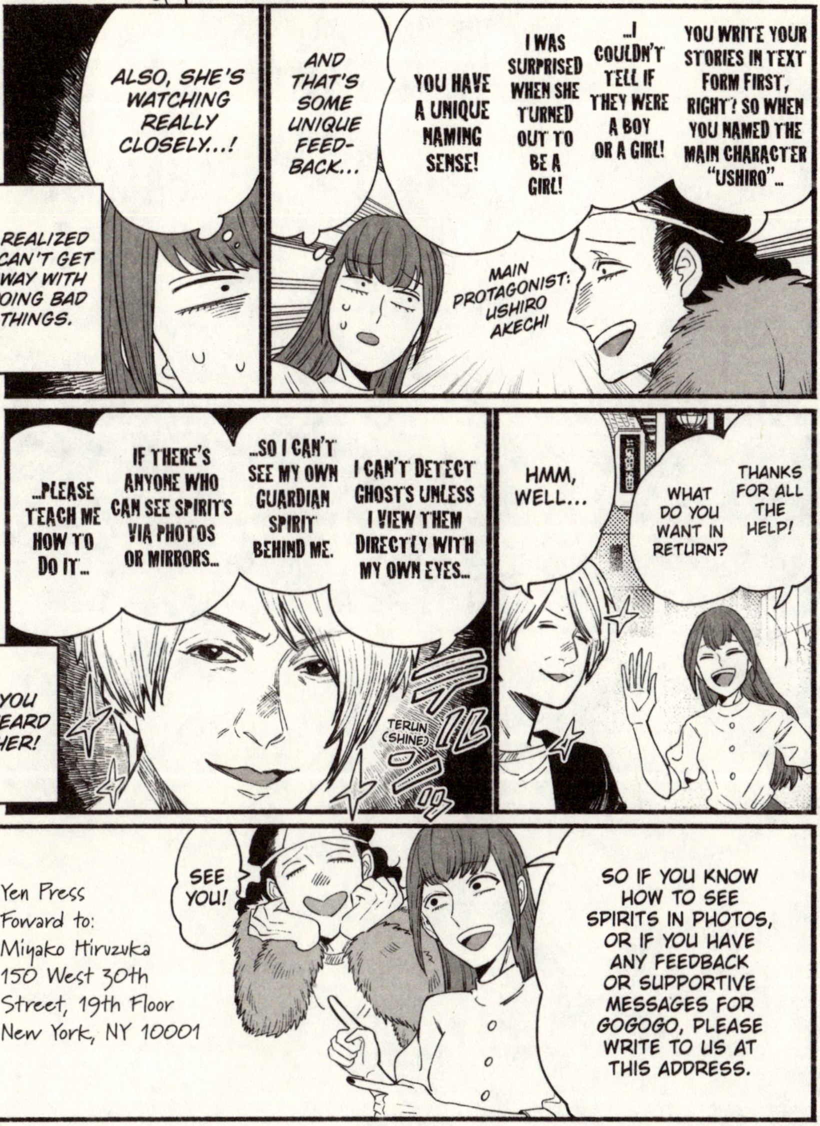
YOU WRITE YOUR STORIES IN TEXT FORM FIRST, RIGHT? SO WHEN YOU NAMED THE MAIN CHARACTER "USHIRO"...
...I COULDN'T TELL IF THEY WERE A BOY OR A GIRL!
I WAS SURPRISED WHEN SHE TURNED OUT TO BE A GIRL!
YOU HAVE A UNIQUE NAMING SENSE!
MAIN PROTAGONIST: USHIRO AKECHI
AND THAT'S SOME UNIQUE FEED-BACK...
ALSO, SHE'S WATCHING REALLY CLOSELY...!
I REALIZED I CAN'T GET AWAY WITH DOING BAD THINGS.
THANKS FOR ALL THE HELP!
WHAT DO YOU WANT IN RETURN?
HMM, WELL...
I CAN'T DETECT GHOSTS UNLESS I VIEW THEM DIRECTLY WITH MY OWN EYES...
...SO I CAN'T SEE MY OWN GUARDIAN SPIRIT BEHIND ME.
IF THERE'S ANYONE WHO CAN SEE SPIRITS VIA PHOTOS OR MIRRORS...
...PLEASE TEACH ME HOW TO DO IT...
TERUN (SHINE)
YOU HEARD HER!
SO IF YOU KNOW HOW TO SEE SPIRITS IN PHOTOS, OR IF YOU HAVE ANY FEEDBACK OR SUPPORTIVE MESSAGES FOR GOGOGO, PLEASE WRITE TO US AT THIS ADDRESS.
SEE YOU!
Yen Press
Foward to:
Miyako Hiruzuka
150 West 30th
Street, 19th Floor
New York, NY 10001

*This story is a work of fiction.

Special Thanks

Mahiro Uno-sama U-sama and H-sama from NARTI;S Editor O-sama

Ageo Wannyan Aozora Youchien-sama, Kuroe Hibiki-sensei, and you, the reader.

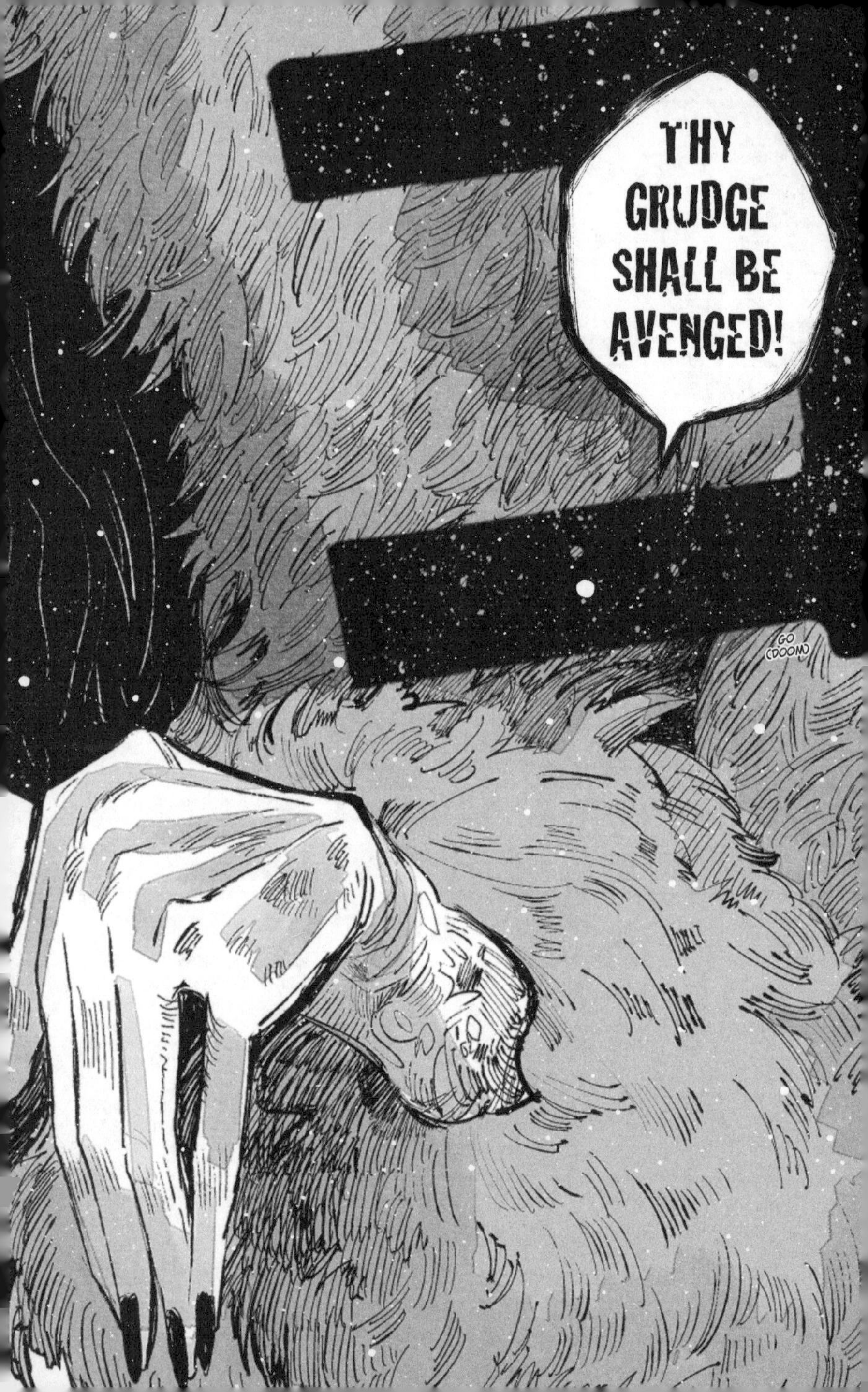
THY GRUDGE SHALL BE AVENGED!
GO (DOOM)

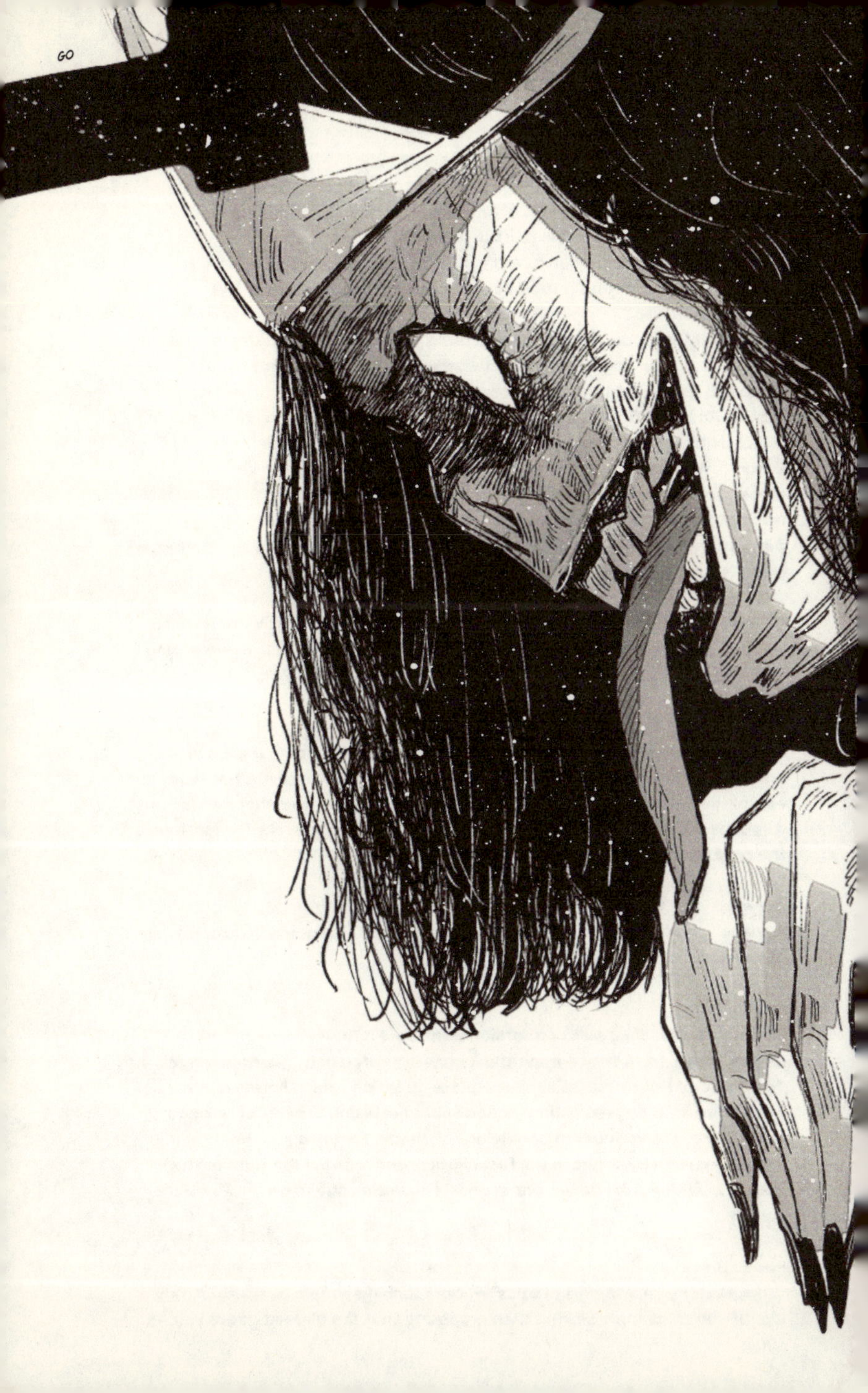
GO

Translation Notes

-san: The Japanese equivalent of Mr./Mrs./Miss. If a situation calls for politeness, this is the fail-safe honorific.

-kun: Used most often when referring to boys, this indicates affection or familiarity. Occasionally used by older men among their peers, but it may also be used by anyone referring to a person of lower standing.

-chan: An affectionate honorific indicating familiarity used mostly in reference to girls; also used in reference to cute persons or animals regardless of gender.

-sensei: A respectful term for teachers, artists, or high-level professionals.

-sama: An honorific which conveys great respect; may also indicate that the social status of the speaker is lower than that of the addressee.

-chama: An idiosyncratic honorific, mixing *-chan* and *-sama*; a kind of overly respectful baby talk.

No honorific: Indicates familiarity or closeness; if used without permission or reason, addressing someone in this manner would be interpreted as an insult or disrespectful.

Currency conversion: It was once a general rule of thumb that ¥100 is worth approximately one American dollar. In recent years, however, the purchasing power of the yen has gone down, with ¥100 being closer to 70¢.

Page 3
Ushiro: The given name Ushiro, which is not common in Japan, means or is homophonous with the Japanese word for "behind." Because it is not really an established name, it does not have a clear association with either gender, but it sounds quite similar to several common masculine names, like Ichirou, hence the confusion in the bonus comic.

Page 19
"Masao" and "Masako": Masao is a primarily masculine name in Japan, while Masako is a feminine name.

Page 26
Guardian spirit: *Shugorei*, or guardian spirits, are a fairly recent import to Japan, drawn from Western spiritualism and the idea of a "guardian angel." The particular characteristics of Japanese guardian spirits, however, have been influenced by preexisting ideas about ghosts and the role of ancestors, as well as by the various major religions of Japan. For instance, the triangular headpiece worn by Ushiro in the first chapter and Masako throughout the book is traditional for depictions of ghosts in Japan, due to an ancient burial custom.

Page 28
"That sketchy jar": "Spiritual sales"—approaching people by speculatively identifying some malaise, and then proposing that the blessed goods you

happen to be selling might help — is a common tactic to raise revenue and recruits for predatory religious organizations in Japan. One large organization with a substantial presence in Japan is well known for doing this with overpriced jars.

Page 33
Paying damages for an affair: Adultery is legal in Japan, but the individual whose spouse cheated on them has a right to sue their spouse's partner in the affair for damages. Such cases are considered especially difficult for the third party to win if there is any evidence that they hoped to induce a divorce.

Page 49
Kawakado: A spoof of Kadokawa, the company which publishes this manga in Japan. While Kadokawa is primarily a publisher serving the Japanese market, they are a rather large corporation with fingers in quite a few pies, including operating an advertising agency and various overseas businesses. In fact, Yen Press itself is co-owned by Kadokawa.

Page 114
Separate rooms for the bath and toilet: This layout is common in Japanese homes, even in Tokyo, where space comes at an extreme premium. Many Japanese people consider it essential that the toilet be situated in its own small room, separate from the cleaner facilities of the shower and bath.

Page 149
Nobumi Oda and Yasuna Tokugawa: These two women share surnames and similar given names with Oda Nobunaga and Tokugawa Ieyasu, who are both prominent figures in Japanese history. Oda Nobunaga is generally acclaimed as a unifier of Japan for putting an end to the *Sengoku* ("Warring States") period by force of arms in the late 16th century. His erstwhile vassal, Tokugawa Ieyasu, is likewise considered a unifier for putting in place a military government which lasted for more than 250 relatively peaceful years after Oda's death. Given that the position of head of state in that government became a hereditary possession of the Tokugawa family, Tokugawa Ieyasu can be seen to have rather shrewdly reaped the rewards of Oda Nobunaga's labors.

Page 164
Omurice: A dish consisting of a thin omelet enclosing a mound of fried rice, typically topped with ketchup. Flowers are not a common element, presumably being this restaurant's eye-catching and social media friendly specialty.

Page 149
Denhodo: A spoof combining two famous and extraordinarily lucrative Japanese advertising titans, Dentsu and Hakuhodo.

So I'm a Spider, So What?

MANGA VOL. 1-13
LIGHT NOVEL VOL. 1-16

AVAILABLE NOW!

I'M GONNA SURVIVE—JUST WATCH ME!

I was your average, everyday high school girl, but now I've been reborn in a magical world...as a spider?! How am I supposed to survive in this big, scary dungeon as one of the weakest monsters? I gotta figure out the rules to this QUICK, or I'll be kissing my short second life good-bye...

YOU CAN ALSO KEEP UP WITH THE MANGA SIMUL-PUB EVERY MONTH ONLINE!

KUMO DESUGA, NANIKA? © Asahiro Kakashi 2016 ©Okina Baba, Tsukasa Kiryu 2016 KADOKAWA CORPORATION

KUMO DESUGA, NANIKA? ©Okina Baba, Tsukasa Kiryu 2015 KADOKAWA CORPORATION

YenPress.com

Days on Fes

Kanade Sora had never been to a music festival before. But when her friend Otoha lures her along with a promise that her favorite band will be playing, she finds herself having more fun than she ever imagined. And if one small event was enough to hook her, what would a huge overnight event at a major venue be like? As Kanade dives into a whole new world of rocking out, will her life ever be the same?!

Volumes 1-5 Available Now!

Yen Press For more information, visit yenpress.com!

DAYS ON FES ©Kanato Oka 2019 / KADOKAWA CORPORATION

THE SAGA OF TANYA THE EVIL

Her name is Tanya Degurechaff and she is the Devil of the Rhine, one of the greatest soldiers the Empire has ever seen! But inside her mind lives a ruthless, calculating ex-salaryman who enjoyed a peaceful life in Japan until he woke up in a war-torn world. Reborn as a destitute orphaned girl with nothing to her name but memories of a previous life, Tanya will do whatever it takes to survive, even if she can find it only behind the barrel of a gun!

LIGHT NOVEL VOL. 1-12 AND MANGA VOL. 1-23 AVAILABLE NOW!

Carlo Zen 2013
Illustration: Shinobu Shinotsuki

Chika Tojo 2016 · Carlo Zen

The Detective Is Already Dead

When the story begins without its hero

Kimihiko Kimizuka has always been a magnet for trouble and intrigue. For as long as he can remember, he's been stumbling across murder scenes or receiving mysterious attache cases to transport. When he met Siesta, a brilliant detective fighting a secret war against an organization of pseudohumans, he couldn't resist the call to become her assistant and join her on an epic journey across the world.

...Until a year ago, that is. Now he's returned to a relatively normal and tepid life, knowing the adventure must be over. After all, the detective is already dead.

Volumes 1-8 available wherever books are sold!

YenPress.com

TANTEI HA MO, SHINDEIRU. Vol. 1
© nigozyu 2019
Illustration: Umibouzu
KADOKAWA CORPORATION

Miyako Hiruzuka

Translation: Minna Lin   Lettering: Alexis Eckerman

This book is a work of fiction. Names, characters, places, and incidents are the product of the author's imagination or are used fictitiously. Any resemblance to actual events, locales, or persons, living or dead, is coincidental.

GOGOGOGO-GO-GHOST Vol.1
©Miyako Hiruzuka 2022
First published in Japan in 2022 by KADOKAWA CORPORATION, Tokyo.
English translation rights arranged with KADOKAWA CORPORATION, Tokyo through TUTTLE-MORI AGENCY, INC., Tokyo.

English translation © 2024 by Yen Press, LLC

Yen Press, LLC supports the right to free expression and the value of copyright. The purpose of copyright is to encourage writers and artists to produce the creative works that enrich our culture.

The scanning, uploading, and distribution of this book without permission is a theft of the author's intellectual property. If you would like permission to use material from the book (other than for review purposes), please contact the publisher. Thank you for your support of the author's rights.

Yen Press
150 West 30th Street, 19th Floor
New York, NY 10001

Visit us at yenpress.com • facebook.com/yenpress • twitter.com/yenpress
yenpress.tumblr.com • instagram.com/yenpress

First Yen Press Edition: July 2024
Edited by Yen Press Editorial: Rory Nevins,
Danielle Niederkorn
Designed by Yen Press Design: Madelaine Norman

Yen Press is an imprint of Yen Press, LLC.

The Yen Press name and logo are trademarks of Yen Press, LLC.
The publisher is not responsible for websites (or their content) that are not owned by the publisher.

Library of Congress Control Number: 2024935187

ISBNs: 978-1-9753-8930-7 (paperback)
978-1-9753-8931-4 (ebook)

1 3 5 7 9 10 8 6 4 2

WOR

Printed in the United States of America